SEDUCING JANEY

A LIBERTY CROSSROADS ROMANCE

SHERRI HAYES

Seducing Janey

A Liberty Crossroads Romance

Sherri Hayes

Cover Design by Get Covers

ABOUT THIS BOOK

Can he convince her to give a relationship between them a chance?

Detective Janey Davis doesn't know what she'll find when her boss sends her two hours away to the small town of Liberty. It looks like something out of a magazine with its open fields and quaint buildings lining the street. Then she meets the man who's supposed to show her around and realizes the murder she's been sent to investigate isn't her biggest problem. It's falling for her new partner.

Kyle Reed has been a sheriff's deputy since returning from the Army ten years ago. He's determined to help Janey find out who murdered a man and dumped his body on the side of a country road. What he wasn't prepared for was the undeniable chemistry between them.

The more time they spend together, the attraction between them becomes impossible to resist. But will one night be enough, or can they find a way to make a relationship between them work when neither wants to give up the job they love?

CHAPTER 1

Janey Davis turned her head in the direction of Captain Lane's voice. He was motioning for her and her partner, Paul Daniels, to come into his office.

Paul stood and grabbed his jacket from the back of his chair. "Uh-oh. What did you do now?"

Rolling her eyes, Janey pushed away from her desk. At twenty-nine, she was one of the youngest detectives, and she'd worked hard to gain the others' respect. For the most part she had. Then she'd gone and lost her temper with a suspect about a month ago. The rate things were going, Paul was never going to let her live it down. "Marrying Megan has made you a comedian."

Her partner smirked, not even bothering to deny it.

"Besides," Janey said as they made their way across the room, "who's to say you're not the one that's going to be in the hot seat? He wants to see you, too, remember?"

Paul chuckled, but didn't comment.

When they strolled into Captain Lane's office, he pointed to the chairs in front of his desk. She lowered herself onto the pleather cushion that had seen better days and waited to see what had caused the deep crease in her boss's brow.

"I got a call from the Warren County sheriff. Last night they discovered the body of a man who'd been tased and then beaten to death with some kind of metal pipe or bat."

That got her attention. Before she could speak up, Paul did. "You think it's connected to our case?"

Her boss stood and paced behind his desk several times before stopping to fix them both with a look that said he meant business. "I think it's a possibility. So does Sheriff Jenkins, which is why I want you to head up there and check it out. If it's the same perp, we need to know."

Paul shifted in his seat. She knew what was going through his mind. It was Friday afternoon and this weekend was his parents' fortieth wedding anniversary. They were having a big party in Cincinnati to celebrate. He, Megan, and his daughter, Chloe, were supposed to hit the road as soon as he got home from work.

Captain Lane noticed Paul's reaction. "Something wrong, Daniels?"

"No, sir. I just had plans with my family this weekend. It's my parents' anniversary." He hesitated and then pulled his shoulders back. "But if it's the same person, we need to find that out. I'll call my mom. I'm sure she'll understand."

Janey was sure she wouldn't. She'd met Marilyn Daniels on several occasions. The woman was a great mother, very understanding from what Janey had observed, but she wouldn't be happy if her oldest son wasn't there for such an important event. "How about I go and check things out? It may be nothing, right? And I'm sure the captain wouldn't want you to miss your parents' anniversary party if it's just a coincidence. Right, Captain?"

Paul and Captain Lane both stared at her for several moments before the captain cleared his throat. "I suppose that would work."

"Great." Janey jumped up before anyone else could get a word in edgewise. "Do you have all the information I'll need?"

Captain Lane handed her a piece of paper. "Ask for Deputy Kyle Reed. He's expecting you."

She took the paper and went to leave.

"Oh, and Davis?"

"Yes, Captain?"

"Remember you're in their jurisdiction. Sheriff Jenkins's father was a good friend of mine, which is why he called me." Captain Lane narrowed his eyes a little in warning. "Got it?"

Janey grinned. "Of course. I'll be the model of professionalism."

Captain Lane shook his head. "Fine. Now get out of here, both of you. And Daniels?"

"Yes?" Paul asked.

"Enjoy your weekend."

"Thank you, sir." Paul followed Janey back to their desks before saying anything. "You didn't have to do that, you know. My mom would have understood."

"She so wouldn't have." He looked as if he were about to argue, but she didn't give him a chance. "Doesn't matter now anyway. I'm going up north to check out the body and the crime scene and you're going to Cincinnati to spend the weekend with your family."

After a moment, Paul sighed. "Thank you. I owe you one."

Janey chuckled and retrieved her purse from the drawer. "You owe me way more than one, but who's counting?"

After stopping by her apartment to pack a bag, Janey headed two hours north to the small town of Liberty where the Warren County Sheriff's Office was located. She could have gone first thing in the morning, but she'd never been good at waiting. It was one of her many quirks that drove her partner crazy sometimes.

The drive through the country was refreshing. It wasn't often she made it out of Indianapolis these days—she had no reason to. Her life was there. Her job was there.

It was after eight by the time she pulled up in front of the large stone building that housed the Warren County Sheriff's Office. She had no idea if Deputy Reed would still be around or not, but at the very least she figured she'd introduce herself and see if they could recommend a place to stay. That was one of the downsides to small towns. They rarely had hotel chains.

Several people looked her way as she walked inside, their gazes following her every movement. It was a good thing she wasn't overly self-conscious.

A young man who looked barely out of high school stepped forward as she approached the glass. He wore a uniform, so she had to assume he was old enough to be a deputy at least. "Good evening, ma'am. Can I help you?"

Janey showed her badge. "I'm Detective Janey Davis from the Indianapolis PD."

She opened her mouth to say more, but the young deputy interrupted her. "You're here about the murder, right?" He didn't wait for her to answer before picking up the phone and dialing. "The detective from Indy's here. Uh-huh. Okay. Will do." The deputy hung up the phone, walked around the desk, and opened the door to allow her back into the station area. "Can I get you some water or coffee, Detective?"

"No, thank you," Janey said, remaining where she was. "If Deputy Reed has already gone home, I can come back in the morning—"

"That won't be necessary," a deep voice said from behind her.

Janey spun around to face the newcomer, surprised at how he'd been able to sneak up on her. He looked to be in his mid-thirties and had sandy blond hair in need of a trim. He was also tall with broad shoulders that pulled at the worn T-shirt he was wearing. At five foot six inches, Janey was used to most men towering over her, but standing next to this man she felt smaller than usual. He had to be at least six two. "Hello."

The man stepped forward and extended his hand to her. She took it automatically.

"My apologies. When you weren't here by eight I decided to head home," he said.

It took a second or two for her brain to catch up, but eventually she registered what he'd said. "I take it you're Deputy Reed?"

He grinned and she felt her chest clench a little in response. "I am."

Janey tried to ignore her body's reaction and pulled her hand out of his firm grip. "I didn't mean to drag you back in after you'd gone home for the evening."

"It's not a problem. I was still in the parking lot when Deputy Sims called. Are you Detective Daniels or Detective Davis?"

She realized then she hadn't introduced herself. "Davis. Detective Janey Davis."

Deputy Reed smiled wider if that were possible, and Janey felt all the moisture leave her mouth.

He held her gaze for a long moment and then glanced around as if searching for something. "Is your partner with you?"

"No. It's just me." She swallowed. "Detective Daniels had a family obligation this weekend."

"So you came alone?"

"Yes." Was it her or did he act as if he liked that her partner wasn't there? She tried not to examine it too closely. "Look, if you're already done for the night we can touch base in the morning. I was just anxious to get up here and take a look at things while they're fresh. If you can point me in the direction of the nearest motel . . ."

He shrugged, letting her know it wasn't a big deal. "I'm used to getting called out at all hours. It's part of being a deputy in a rural county."

When he took a step toward her, Janey felt her internal temperature rise. What the hell was wrong with her? "Still—"

"It's no trouble. Really." A woman came through the front doors and waved to Deputy Reed as she walked past. He nodded in her direction, and then returned his attention to Janey. "It's too late to head out to the crime scene, but the body is downstairs if you'd like to take a look."

"Yes. Please." Her palms were sweating and her heart was beating at a faster-than-normal pace. She needed to get it together. Hopefully looking over the body would settle her hormones.

Deputy Reed strolled over to a door on her left and opened it. "Once we're finished, I'll take you to this little place I know where you can bunk for the night."

Not trusting her voice, Janey nodded and followed him through the door. They walked down a single flight of stairs that opened up into a long hallway. It was empty, but considering the late hour, she had to imagine that most of the staff had gone home.

Halfway down the hall, Deputy Reed stopped and gave two sharp raps on a gray door.

"Come in if you dare," said a voice on the other side.

Deputy Reed chuckled before pushing the door open and going inside.

The first thing Janey noticed upon entering the room was the color. There was color everywhere—a stark contrast to the gunmetal gray of the hallway. It was also unlike any other morgue she'd ever seen.

A woman around Janey's age pushed a pair of magnifying glasses onto her forehead and looked up from the body she was examining. Her gaze went directly to Deputy Reed. "I thought you'd gone home for the night." The way she grinned at him made Janey wonder if there wasn't something going on between the two of them.

He closed the door and moved closer to the woman. "I did, but duty calls, so I'm back."

That was when the woman seemed to notice Janey. She looked at Deputy Reed and raised an eyebrow in question.

"Dr. Mackenzie Mallory, I'd like you to meet Detective Janey Davis from the Indianapolis PD. She's here about our John Doe."

Dr. Mallory removed her gloves and offered her hand to Janey. "Welcome. And you can call me Mac. Everyone around here does."

The doctor's warm smile immediately put Janey at ease. "Thank you. And please call me Janey."

* * *

Kyle had been on patrol at dawn when the call had come in about an unconscious man lying in a ditch along the side of a country road. When he'd arrived on scene, it didn't take him long to realize this wasn't someone who'd gotten drunk and passed out trying to walk home. It was a dead body.

He'd called it in to dispatch and then promptly dialed his boss. Noah was one of his best friends. They'd both grown up around Liberty and he'd want to know about a possible murder in his jurisdiction. In a rural county like Warren it was rare for someone to die of anything other than natural causes or an automobile accident. Most of what they dealt with involved DUIs, domestic violence calls, and some vandalism from bored teenagers.

It had taken several hours for Mac and her assistant, Brandon, to gather all the evidence and load the body into the van. Kyle had stayed on scene along with another deputy while Mac and Brandon did their thing to make sure none of the locals decided to stop and take a closer look.

By the time Kyle had strolled back into the station hours later, he'd planned to check in with Mac then head home to crash. His plans had been waylaid when Noah spotted him in the hall. He'd been pulled into Noah's office and told that two homicide detectives from Indianapolis would be coming to take a look at the body and the crime scene.

He wasn't given a whole lot of information other than the John Doe he'd found earlier that morning might be linked to another homicide case in Indianapolis. And the icing on the cake? Noah informed Kyle that he was to be the two detectives' tour guide. He was to make sure they were shown around and had access to everything they needed.

At first, Kyle wasn't thrilled with his new assignment, but things were looking up. The pretty blond detective standing beside him talking to Mac was a benefit he hadn't been expecting. She was of average height, probably around five five or five six, and had long dark eyelashes that framed her gray eyes.

He let his gaze linger over her curves as she spoke to Mac about the John Doe. Janey Davis had long legs that led up to a nice round ass.

"Kyle's the one who found him," Mac said, pulling him out of his daydream.

Janey Davis looked at him as if waiting for something. Of course, he hadn't been paying attention. His mind had been on other things. "Sorry. I must have missed the question."

Mac rolled her eyes. "Janey was asking how the body was found."

"A call came in through dispatch about someone passed out along the side of the road. When I went to check it out, I found our John Doe here."

"Did you notice any footprints at the scene?" Janey asked.

Kyle shook his head. "It's been pretty dry around here lately. Aside from the body itself, everything else appeared to be undisturbed. Not even the corn a few feet away had any damage. No signs of a struggle."

"So the body was most likely dumped there."

"That would be my guess," Kyle said, agreeing with her assessment.

Mac pointed to marks on the victim's arms. "Given the guy's size, I would have expected him to put up more of a fight if he'd seen his attacker coming, but I haven't been able to find any defensive wounds. There was some dirt under his nails. I sent a sample off to a lab that specializes in soil samples."

Janey nodded and leaned in to take a closer look at the bruise the Taser left on John Doe's abdomen. "Might be able to help us narrow down where he was killed."

They spent a few more minutes looking over the body before saying good night to Mac and going upstairs. It was almost dark by the time he escorted Janey out to the parking lot. She halted beside a silver SUV, which seemed to suit her.

"You mentioned knowing somewhere I could crash for the night?" she asked after unlocking her vehicle.

"I did." He smiled, hoping it had the effect on her he wanted it to. "It's a little outside of town. You can follow me there."

She opened her door, not looking him. "That isn't necessary. I'm sure I can find it if you give me directions."

"I have no doubt about that, but considering I'm going to be dumping you on my sister's doorstep, I figure I owe her a bit of an explanation." Janey's eyes went wide as she met his gaze. He couldn't help but laugh. "It's not as horrible as it sounds. Ava runs a bed and breakfast, and I happen to know she has a free room."

"I don't want to cause trouble between you and your sister."

"You won't. Besides, the closest motel is over a half hour away and I wouldn't recommend it."

He waited for several moments while she weighed her options. "All right. If you're sure she won't mind."

Kyle stifled a chuckle. He was sure his sister *would* mind, but she'd get over it. "I'll pull my truck around."

The drive to his sister's place didn't take long. Ava only lived about ten minutes outside Liberty. His sister must have heard them pull up because by the time they exited their vehicles she was standing on her front porch. "I didn't expect to see you tonight."

"Can't I just drop by and see my little sister?" Kyle asked, bounding up the stairs. He pulled her into a hug and kissed her on the cheek.

She batted him away. "Of course you can, but you usually don't. At least, not at this time of night. Shouldn't you be at home getting ready for your shift?"

"Normally, yes, but plans change." He nodded at Janey who was walking toward them, a backpack slung over one shoulder. "Ava, I'd like for you to meet Detective Janey Davis. She's here consulting on a case and needs a place to stay for a night or two."

His sister raised an eyebrow. "And you figured you'd bring her to me."

"Of course."

Ava shook her head then looked at Janey. "It's not that I mind having you. It's just that I wish my brother would've given me a heads-up."

"If it's a problem, I'm sure I can find somewhere else," Janey said.

"Not without driving a ways. Besides, I do have room."

She motioned Janey to follow her inside, and Kyle trailed after them. He knew he should leave and let Janey get settled, but he didn't want to. Not yet.

Ava led them down the short hallway to the kitchen. "Are you hungry? I'm sure I can dig something up for you."

"Thank you, but I ate a sandwich on the drive up."

His sister nodded. "Make yourself at home. Kyle knows where everything is if you need something and don't see it. I'm going to run upstairs and get a room ready for you."

Janey placed her purse and backpack on the large farm table that took up almost half his sister's kitchen. "I don't want you to go to any trouble."

Ava ignored her protest. "I'll be right back."

When they were alone, Kyle went to the cabinet and began making tea. He'd rather have coffee, but considering it was after nine and he actually needed to sleep tonight he figured tea would be the better option.

Once the kettle was on the stove, he returned his attention to Janey. She hadn't moved from her position beside the table. "You can sit down, you know."

She met his gaze and then looked at the table as if she were seeing it for the first time. "I'm debating whether or not I should go."

"If you go now, my sister will be insulted."

"And whose fault would that be? You never should have brought me here." Her eyes lit up with her annoyance.

Kyle leaned against the counter and crossed his arms over his chest. He would have loved to move closer, but something told him he might regret it. "Would you rather have spent the night at my house?"

She straightened her shoulders and jutted out her chin. "That's not what I meant, and you know it."

"That's not a no." He was enjoying pushing her buttons.

Janey snorted. "Are you always this arrogant?"

He chuckled. "Only when I have a beautiful woman standing in front of me."

It took her a moment to respond. "I'm here to do a job, Deputy Reed."

"So am I." He paused and lowered his voice a little. "And it's Kyle. We are going to be working together, after all."

She swallowed, her gaze never wavering.

He stared back at her, wondering what she saw there. She was a detective. It was her job to look beyond the surface.

They stood unmoving and locked in each other's gaze until Kyle heard his sister at the top of the stairs. He turned, breaking the connection, and removed the kettle from the burner. "Do you take milk or sugar in your tea?"

"Sugar." Her voice sounded a little strained, which made him grin. Having her around was going to be fun.

Janey had set her alarm for six the next morning. She wanted to get up and moving before things in the house got too hectic. The night before she'd run into another couple who were staying at the bed and breakfast with their two young children. While she liked kids well enough, she knew what breakfast could be like when there were children involved and she wanted to avoid that. More than anything, she needed to stay focused on why she was there and not get distracted.

She finished getting dressed and headed downstairs to see if there was something quick she could grab to eat or if Ava could recommend a local restaurant. When she rounded the corner, Janey did a double take. Ava stood at the counter rolling out dough while her brother, Deputy Kyle Reed, stood next to her holding a little boy who didn't look to be more than two. Unlike the night before, Deputy Reed was wearing his uniform.

A few seconds passed before he noticed her standing there. "Good morning, Detective."

Ava looked over her shoulder. "I'm making cinnamon rolls but they won't be ready for another hour. I could make you something else if you don't want to wait."

"Thank you, but if you could point me in the direction of some coffee I'll be good," Janey said. She'd worry about food later.

"It's by the sink. Kyle started it about fifteen minutes ago, so it should be ready. And there are mugs in that cabinet." She motioned toward the one to the right of the sink, directly above the coffee maker.

"Thanks." Janey took her time selecting a mug, pouring her coffee, and adding the sugar. It was something she could have easily done in less than a minute, but she needed the distraction. A good night's sleep hadn't lessened her reaction to Deputy Reed . . . Kyle. If anything, it was worse.

When she turned back around, coffee in hand, he was no longer standing at the counter with his sister. He'd moved to the large wooden table, the boy on his lap, playing with sugar packets. They were lining them up to form a train. She felt her heart clench again.

"Are you sure I can't make you something? Surely you need more than coffee before you and Kyle head out." Ava's voice was almost like an electric shock to her system.

Before she could answer, Kyle did. "We'll grab something in town. Noah wants to meet Detective Davis before she and I head out to Butler Road."

"Noah?" Janey asked.

Kyle grinned up at her, and she felt her heart rate pick up. "Sheriff Jenkins. He called this morning and asked if I could bring you by. He wants to meet you."

"Oh. Well, I guess that makes sense. I am in his jurisdiction, after all." Janey took another sip of her coffee and placed it down on the counter next to the sink. "We should probably get going, then."

He shook his head. "There's no rush. Finish your coffee. Besides, Noah's probably at the diner having breakfast right now. If we go to the station this early, we'll just be hanging around waiting."

Janey picked her coffee back up and rested against the counter as she watched Kyle and the little boy push the packets of sugar around and make little choo-choo sounds. He looked up at her a couple of times, but for the most part he focused on the child on his lap. It was a complete contradiction to how he'd been the night before when they'd been alone.

Ava kissed the top of the little boy's head before walking to the sink to wash her hands. Janey stepped to the side to give her room. "He comes over in the mornings when he can to watch Cole for me so I can cook. I don't ask him to. He just does it."

"That's what family's for, right?" Not that Janey would know. The only family she had were the people she worked with—Paul in particular. He, his wife, Megan, and daughter, Chloe, had sort of adopted her.

"It wasn't always like this. Kyle's ten years older than me. But after my husband was killed . . ." Ava paused. She cleared her throat and reached for a towel to dry her hands. "Sorry. I didn't mean to—"

"There's no need to apologize."

Ava met Janey's gaze, a look of sad resignation in her eyes. "He was killed in the line of duty. A sixteen-year-old kid who'd robbed a liquor store."

"I'm sorry."

"Thank you." Ava took a deep breath. "It's been almost two years. Cole was just a baby. Which is why I decided to move back home." She looked over at her brother and her son. "There's no way I could have done it on my own, and luckily I didn't have to."

Janey was glad Ava had a strong support system, but hearing how great her brother had been wasn't helping Janey's attraction to him.

"Let me pop these in the oven," Ava said, "and then I'll make us all some eggs and toast."

"Really, that isn't necessary. I'm . . ."

The look Ava gave Janey had the words dying in her throat. Apparently she'd be having breakfast this morning whether she liked it or not.

A half hour later, belly full of not only eggs and toast but bacon and fresh fruit, Janey and Kyle made their way into town. All along the main street there were little shops. Most of their signs still read closed, but she could see people moving around inside, getting ready to open.

"Is this your first time in Liberty?" Kyle asked as they turned down the street that led to the station.

Janey nodded. "I don't get out of Indy very often."

"That's too bad."

She raised an eyebrow in question as he pulled into the parking lot and found a spot. "Why's that? I happen to like Indianapolis."

"Because you're missing out. Sure, the big city has a lot to offer, but so do places like Liberty."

"Like?"

"Like . . . I bet you all don't have hog roasts in the big city."

Janey laughed. "Hog roasts? We do eat pork in Indianapolis, you know."

He smiled and turned to face her. His knee grazed her leg when he changed positions, reminding her how tall he was. "Eating pork in a restaurant isn't the same thing at all."

"Really? And how is it different?" Her heart was pounding in her chest and it had nothing to do with their conversation.

Kyle rested his arm on the back of the seat and leaned in. "You'd have to see for yourself."

"And how would I do that?" She knew it was the wrong question to ask the moment the words slipped from her lips.

"Ethan's family is having a roast tonight. Come with me and I'll show you."

"I don't know if that's a good idea." Janey knew she wasn't misinterpreting the signals Kyle was sending out. She'd promised her captain she'd be the model of professionalism. Somehow, she didn't think going on what would essentially amount to a date with one of Sheriff Jenkins's deputies would qualify.

"I think it's a great idea. And besides, most of the town will be there." One side of his mouth turned up in a smirk. "You'd be perfectly safe."

"I can take care of myself. Maybe it's you who should be worried about your safety."

His smile grew. "I think I'll take my chances."

He swiftly got out of the vehicle, leaving her sitting there wondering what had just happened. She had no idea what she'd agreed to. Well, not exactly agreed to, but she sure hadn't said no. Maybe the country air was getting to her.

Kyle was still grinning when she joined him in front of the building.

"You can wipe that smile off your face. I didn't agree to go with you."

Instead of responding to her comment, he asked, "Ready to meet Sheriff Jenkins?"

Janey narrowed her eyes a little but nodded.

The station was busier than it had been the night before. It still wasn't anything like where she worked, but there were several people moving about. One woman had on a headset. Janey figured she had to be their dispatcher.

"Noah's office is this way," Kyle said.

"After you." That smile of his got bigger again. Janey could only imagine what was going through his head at that moment. "You call your boss by his first name? Is that a small-town thing?"

"Maybe. But in this case, it's that we've known each other most of our lives. His brother and I played football together in school."

"So you're friends."

It wasn't really a question, but he answered anyway. "Yep."

Not much chance the sheriff would help keep Kyle from crossing professional boundaries, then. If anything, they'd probably be giving each other pats on the back.

Kyle walked to the far side of the room. He stopped in front of a big door with the word SHERIFF embossed on the glass. "I think you'll like Noah. He's a lot like me."

Great.

* * *

Kyle knocked twice before entering Noah's office. The room had wall-to-wall bookshelves which Kyle had always found a little confining, but Noah seemed to like it. He said it gave him places to put things. The only contrast to all the wood was a single window at the back. It wasn't enough, in Kyle's opinion.

"Perfect timing," Noah said.

"I figured you'd just be getting in." Kyle motioned toward Janey. "Noah, I'd like for you to meet Detective Janey Davis."

Noah stood and extended his hand to her. "It's a pleasure to meet you, Detective Davis. Your captain speaks highly of you and your partner."

"Thank you. I appreciate you allowing me to come take a look at things. We've run into a dead end on our case back home. If this is related, it could provide the lead we need to locate the suspect."

"We don't get many murders around here, so when Kyle discovered the body I did a little research. That's how I found out about your victim in Indianapolis. The similarities were too close for me to pass them off as coincidence without doing some more investigation." Noah sat down and leaned back in his chair. "I trust Kyle is taking good care of you . . . showing you around?"

Janey glanced over at Kyle and then turned her attention back to Noah. For a moment, he wondered if she'd object to him being her liaison. "Yes. He is. We stopped by the morgue last night to have a look at your John Doe. There was a similar bruise on the body. Not exactly like the one on our victim in Indy, but close enough," she said.

"Murdering someone can be unpredictable."

"Exactly. From what I've seen so far, I'm not willing to say they're not related." Again, she glanced over at Kyle then back to Noah. "I'm looking forward to visiting the crime scene."

"Well, I won't keep you. Just let me or Kyle know if there is anything you need." Noah looked down at some papers on his desk before glancing up again. "Do you mind giving me a minute with Deputy Reed? There are some things I need to go over with him."

"Of course." Janey exited the room, and the door closed with a click behind her.

As soon as they were alone, Noah leaned forward, clasping his hands on his desk in front of him. "I heard you dropped her off at your sister's last night."

"Ava had an open room. It made more sense than having her drive to a motel out by the highway."

He nodded in understanding. "And Ava was okay with it?"

Kyle wondered if there was more to Noah's question than there seemed. Why would he care if Ava was upset? "She wasn't thrilled I didn't give her a heads-up, but you know my sister. She doesn't turn anyone away if she can help it."

"No, she doesn't. Which is why you shouldn't take advantage of her good nature." This wasn't the lecture Kyle had been anticipating.

He debated voicing what was going through his head. If something was going on between his sister and Noah, Kyle wasn't sure he wanted to know about it. Noah was two years older than Kyle, which meant he was almost twelve years older than Ava. "I'll make it up to her. I always do."

Noah nodded again and picked up his phone. "Let me know if you two find anything. If this looks like the same person killed both these men, we need to know. I don't want a murderer running around Warren County."

"I'll call you."

Kyle found Janey standing a few feet from Noah's office, talking to Hayden, one of their dispatchers. Or maybe *talking* wasn't the most accurate term. Listening to Hayden ramble on was more like it.

When Hayden saw Kyle her eyes glazed over a little. He knew she had a bit of a crush on him, but as far as he was concerned she was off limits. She'd turned eighteen last summer and applied for the dispatcher's job. He liked her well enough, but she still had a lot of growing up to do. Kyle was thirty-five years old. He was interested in women who knew what they wanted out of life, not ones who'd barely graduated high school and were only beginning to figure out their path.

"Morning, Hayden."

She blushed. "Good morning, Kyle."

"Are we ready?" Janey asked.

"Yep. I need to grab the report, and then we can be on our way."

Hayden's eyes widened and she shifted her weight forward some.

"You're going to the crime scene, right? The guy Kyle found is big news around here, but you probably see stuff like this all the time in the city."

Janey met his gaze for a brief moment, and a type of silent communication passed between them. He went to retrieve the file while she responded to Hayden's question. "Yes, we see quite a few murders, unfortunately."

"What's it like?" he heard Hayden ask. "I've never seen a dead body before." She paused. "Well, except at a funeral, but it has to be different, right?"

He didn't give Janey time to answer. "Got it. We should probably get going."

"It was nice meeting you, Hayden."

"Sure. Maybe I'll see you tonight at the hog roast," Hayden called as they left.

Once they were outside, he heard Janey chuckle.

"Sorry about that. Hayden's lived here all her life and she's a little starstruck about the big city."

"I could tell," Janey said as they reached his county-issued SUV. It was what they would be taking to the scene. "Crazy thing is, I remember when that was me."

Kyle stopped and stared at her. "Which part?"

Janey climbed into the passenger seat without answering.

He waited until they were on their way and tried a different approach. "Somehow I can't see you being like Hayden."

A smile pulled at the corners of Janey's mouth. He hadn't fooled her. She knew exactly what he was doing. "You'd be surprised."

"Hmm. Now you have me curious."

"Curiosity killed the cat, you know."

It was his turn to laugh. "You're a hard nut to crack, Janey Davis."

She didn't say any more until he'd pulled up behind another deputy's SUV. Noah had posted someone overnight to be sure nothing was messed with. He was taking it personally that a murder had happened on his turf.

They both got out and walked over to where Ethan stood leaning against the hood of his vehicle. He straightened when he realized Kyle wasn't alone. "Morning, ma'am."

"Janey Davis, I'd like you to meet Deputy Ethan Price. Ethan, this is Detective Davis from the Indianapolis PD," Kyle said.

Ethan removed his hat and gave a little bow. "It's a pleasure to meet you, Detective."

"Thank you." Janey seemed pleased with Ethan's southern manners. For some reason that irritated him.

"Anything new overnight?" Kyle asked.

Ethan shrugged and resituated his hat on his head. "A few cars slowed down to get a better look, but no one stopped."

"Where did you find the body exactly?" Janey asked, not wasting any time.

"Over here." He took her to the spot in the ditch where John Doe had been lying. "His leg was extended out toward the road, which is most likely what drew someone's attention and prompted them to call it in."

She nodded and knelt down. "Mac said the guy had been dead for at least twelve hours before you found the body."

It didn't feel right to stand over her, so he bent down, balancing his weight on the balls of his feet. "That doesn't narrow it down much."

"No. But it does tell us that whoever dumped the body is most likely familiar with the area."

"Why do you say that?" he asked.

Janey met his gaze and stood. He followed suit.

She turned in a circle, taking in their surroundings. "How far is the highway from here?"

"At least twenty minutes. And that's if you're not entirely paying attention to speed limits."

"This isn't exactly a well-traveled road, correct?"

No, it wasn't. It was one of those back-country roads that didn't even have a center line painted on it. There was no need since ninety-nine percent of the people who used it were local. "You think whoever it was had to know where they were going."

"I'd almost guarantee it. This is too remote to be random. If it were off a main road, I could see it being a convenience thing, but not here."

Before he could formulate another question, Janey was striding away from him. She halted a foot or so from the edge of the cornfield, looked to both sides, and then turned to her right and began walking. He jogged to catch up. "What are you looking for?"

"I'm not sure."

Kyle remained silent, letting her do whatever it was she was doing. After fifty paces, she spun around and headed back in the opposite direction. They were about thirty feet on the other side of the crime scene when she stopped.

"What is it?" he asked.

She reached into her pocket and pulled out a pair of gloves. After slipping them on, she pushed a few of the cornstalks out of the way.

A second later, a huge grin spread across her face. She looked up at him. "We may be in luck."

He moved to see what she'd found. There, a few feet inside the cornfield, was a pile of empty beer bottles. "I doubt it's related. Probably a bunch of high school kids."

"Exactly." She released the cornstalks and faced him. "And if they come here often, which from the looks of it they do, then they may have been here the other night." She paused. "We may have witnesses."

CHAPTER 3

Janey worked with Ethan to take pictures of the area and put the beer bottles in plastic evidence bags while Kyle called Sheriff Jenkins. There had to be at least twenty bottles that appeared to have been recently discarded. It was wishful thinking that the kids had been around when the body was dumped, but at the moment it was the best lead they had.

She'd dropped another glass bottle into a clear plastic bag when her phone began to vibrate. She held her bag out to Ethan. "Can you take this?"

"Yes, ma'am."

His formal reply had her grinning. She removed her gloves and dug her phone out of her pocket. Paul's name flashed across the screen. "Miss me already, huh?"

Paul laughed. "Something like that. Have you found anything?"

"Well, I'm standing in a cornfield surrounded by empty beer bottles. Does that count?"

He was quiet for a long moment. "Okay, I'll bite. Why are you standing in a cornfield surrounded by empty beer bottles?"

"They're about thirty feet from where Kyle found the body,

probably left by some teenagers. I'm hoping we can get an ID off the prints and that one of them saw something."

"Kyle?" he asked, and she could hear the wheels turning in his head.

"Deputy Reed."

"I see."

Janey made her way out of the cornfield and walked another ten feet or so away from the vehicles to get a little privacy. "It's a small town. Things are laid back here. You know how it is."

"If you say so." She knew he didn't believe her.

"Aren't you supposed to be celebrating your parents' anniversary today?" she asked, trying to change the subject.

"We're heading over to the reception hall in about half an hour. Ma wants to look over everything and make sure the caterers didn't screw something up. She's not used to other people doing the cooking."

"I'm sure it'll be fine." Janey looked across the two-lane road at the wide expanse of soybeans that went all the way back to a row of trees about a mile away. Then her gaze fell on Kyle. He was still on the phone, nodding at whatever was being said. She couldn't read the expression on his face. He looked somewhere between frustrated and resigned.

"Janey? Did you hear me?" Paul asked.

She averted her eyes from the distracting deputy. "Sorry. I was thinking about the case. I don't know if this is the same person or not. I mean why dump one victim behind a dumpster in an alley and the next in the middle of nowhere two hours away?"

Paul didn't respond right away. "Maybe they knew it would be another jurisdiction and were hoping no one connected the dots."

"Maybe."

"You don't think so?" he asked. Paul had taught her to trust her instincts.

"I don't know. Something feels off. The change in location bothers me. Why here?"

"He or she is familiar with the area?"

"I thought about that," Janey said. "It's possible. Especially given how far it is from the main road."

She heard a muffled voice in the background and then the sound of Paul sucking in a lungful of air. "Janey, I need to go. I'll call you later."

"No, he won't," Megan said in the background.

Janey chuckled. "I'll see you on Monday." She slipped the phone back into her pocket and went to see what, if anything, the sheriff had to say about what they'd found.

Kyle and Ethan were loading the bagged evidence into the back of Ethan's SUV when she approached the vehicles. "Everything all right?" Kyle asked.

"Yep." She ignored the question in his eyes.

Ethan closed the back and locked it. "I think that's everything. I'll get it back to the station so they can start pulling the prints." Without waiting for a response, he walked to the driver's side of his vehicle and opened the door. "Hope to see you at the hog roast tonight, Detective Davis." He climbed inside the SUV and was off before she had a chance to answer him.

Janey couldn't help but laugh. In less than four hours she'd been asked if she was going to this pig roast—hog roast—whatever they wanted to call it, by three different people. What was so special about cooking a pig that had everyone in this little town so fixated on it as if it were some huge, not-to-be-missed event?

She felt Kyle come up behind her, and her amusement swiftly turned to something else entirely. "We should stop by the diner and grab some lunch."

"I'm not hungry." Her words came out as not much more than a whisper.

He stepped closer and her body went on alert. Not from fear, but from anticipation. "Neither am I, but it's a good place to ask around to see if anyone knows who might have been in that field the night before last."

"All right." She took a deep breath and turned to face him, trying to shake off the torrent of emotions swirling around inside her. "Let's go."

She managed to take two steps before he put his hand on her arm to stop her. Sure, she could have pulled away, but the feeling of his warm hand on her bare skin had her temperature rising.

Kyle came up behind her again, but this time he stood close enough that his chest was touching her back. He leaned in so his mouth hovered right above her ear. "Don't run away from me, Janey."

"I'm not."

"Aren't you?" He didn't move an inch.

"We have a job to do. I'm trying to catch a killer." Again, she could have easily walked away—his grip wasn't all that tight—but she didn't. Something was keeping her rooted to the spot.

"Don't try and change the subject." He skimmed the palms of his hands down her arms, leaving tingles in their wake. "We have plenty of time to get to the diner, and the fingerprints will take a while. This is about you and me."

She swallowed. "There is no you and me."

Her words hung in the air for a long moment before he spoke. "Come with me tonight. Let me show you a good time."

"And then what?" She had no idea what prompted her to ask or even what kind of a response she was hoping to get.

"And if, after that, you don't want anything to do with me, I'll back off."

They stood there for what felt like forever, not moving. She closed her eyes in an attempt to get her bearings. What would it hurt to go on a date with him? Chances were good that after this weekend she'd never see him again. His life was here in Liberty. Hers was two hours south in Indianapolis.

Janey turned around to face him. They were standing so close she had to tilt her head back in order to look him in the eye. "One date."

He smiled. "That's all I'm asking."

She held his gaze, searching for any deception. She didn't find any. "Deal."

"You won't regret it. I promise."

"I'll hold you to that."

He snorted, which broke some of the tension. "I'm sure you will. Now, let's see if anyone at the diner knows anything."

As they drove into town, Kyle gave her what he called the nickel tour. He pointed out the local hardware store, the library, and some of the little shops they passed.

"Have you lived here all your life?"

Kyle nodded. "I own the house where Ava and I grew up. It's about a half mile from here."

"You never wanted to leave? See what the outside world had to offer?" Janey asked.

"I spent four years in the Army. That was enough for me."

He turned down a side street and pulled into a parking lot. There were a few other vehicles, but if not for them she wouldn't have pegged it for a parking lot at all. There were no signs—no lines dividing the places for cars. It was just an empty piece of pavement.

She climbed out of the SUV and followed Kyle down a walkway that ran between two buildings. It led to the main street they'd been on moments before. He made a right and pulled open a door, motioning that she should go inside.

"This is it?" she asked, looking for a sign.

"This is it." He pointed toward a little sign in the window that she'd missed. The sign looked like it had seen better days. It was faded, but the words *Liberty Diner* were still there.

Janey figured it must be one of those hole-in-the-wall places that only the locals knew about. Hopefully the food was decent and she wouldn't get sick from it.

* * *

Kyle waited for Janey to enter the diner and then followed her inside. At the sound of the bell over the doorway, Claire Lawrence, the owner, looked up to see who the new arrivals were. She grinned when she saw them. "Find a seat wherever. I'll be with you in a minute."

He and Janey made their way to an open booth and sat down

across from each other. Kyle did a quick scan of the area and noticed Janey doing the same. It was almost noon and the lunch rush would be flooding in soon. The other waitress, Kennedy, was behind the counter, stocking the pies.

Claire came over to their table and handed them both a menu even though he didn't need one. "I didn't expect to see you in today, Kyle."

"Plans changed," he said.

"I heard you were the one to find that man yesterday. It's terrible to think of something like that happening so close to home." Claire turned her attention to Janey. "You must be the detective from Indy."

"Word travels fast."

Claire shrugged. "It's a small town and this is big news."

"Not much happens around here, huh?" Janey asked.

"Not like this." Claire visibly shuddered. "They can keep the crime in the big cities. I like it here in our quiet little town."

Kyle figured this was as good a time as any to question Claire and see if she'd heard anything that might help them. "The major crimes anyway. We still have plenty to keep us busy, including bored teenagers that like to get into mischief."

Claire nodded. "That's true. Just last week some kids spray-painted the high school parking lot."

"At least it was spray paint and not something worse," Janey said.

"That's true. I hadn't thought of it that way."

Kyle laid his menu on the table. "You haven't heard of any kids partying in some of the cornfields, have you? I'm looking into some complaints we've received."

"Sorry, I haven't. But if I do, I'll let you know."

"Thanks, Claire. I'd appreciate it," he said.

"Do you two need a few minutes, or do you know what you want?"

Kyle glanced at Janey, but she was still looking over the menu. "I think we might need a few minutes."

"I'll go grab you some waters and be back." Claire scurried away to greet another table. Things were going to start getting hectic, but that was what he wanted. Sometimes observing people was the best way to the next lead.

"How busy does this place get during lunch?" Janey asked, her focus still on her menu.

"There are only a few places to eat in town, so most of the locals come here at least a couple of days a week."

Janey nodded. "Do *you* come here a lot?"

"Probably more than I should, but I'm not a great cook and I try not to take advantage of my sister any more than necessary."

"So that's a yes, then." Janey met his gaze and there was a spark of amusement in her eyes.

He grinned back at her.

"Here you go," Claire said, placing a glass of water in front of each of them. "Do you still need some more time?"

Kyle let Janey answer since he'd known what he wanted the moment he sat down. "I'll have the roast chicken, please."

Claire jotted it down on her pad. "Anything to drink besides the water?"

"No. I'm good. Thanks."

"And you?" Claire asked, looking to Kyle.

"I'll take my usual."

Janey quirked her eyebrow up at his answer.

Claire made another note. "Burger and fries it is."

Once they were alone again, or as alone as they were going to be in a public place like the diner, Kyle relaxed back in his seat and focused on Janey. "I told you a little about me, so I think it's only fair you share, too. Have you always lived in Indianapolis?"

"No," she said after taking a long drink of her water. "I moved there after I graduated high school."

"And where were you before that?" he asked, curious.

She hesitated, which he found interesting. Why wouldn't she want him to know where she grew up? "Outside of Fort Wayne."

"Fort Wayne is a decent-sized town."

"It is."

He sat forward, placing his forearms on the table. "Why does my asking about where you grew up make you uncomfortable?"

"It doesn't." At his skeptical look, she clarified. "I just don't like to talk about it, that's all."

For a moment he thought about pushing the issue. It was in his nature to get to the truth, but Janey wasn't a suspect. He was going to have to be patient. "All right."

"Thank you." She averted her gaze and took another look around the room. "There's a restaurant not far from Paul and Megan's house that's a little like this."

"Paul Daniels, your partner?" If she didn't want to talk about the past, he'd take information about her present.

Janey nodded but offered nothing more on the subject. "So what's your plan? Are we going to talk to all these people before we leave?"

"Nope."

"No?"

He shook his head. "I told Claire I was looking for information. She knows who the farmers in the area are. She'll make sure to mention something about it to each of them and see if she gets any hits. If she does, she'll let me know."

"You're counting on her gossip?"

"Not exactly," he said. "Claire overhears a lot of things she doesn't share, but she's in a unique position to help us out from time to time. That's why Noah comes here every morning. If she's gotten wind of anything, she can let him know discreetly. She's been a great source of information since she moved to town."

"She didn't grow up here?"

"No. She moved to Liberty about four years ago after her divorce. I'm not sure what all happened, but she got a large settlement out of it and she used it to buy the diner."

Janey tucked a loose strand of hair behind her ear. "Sounds like there's a story there."

"I'm sure there is, but I don't like to pry."

She released one hard laugh. "You could have fooled me."

Kyle smiled and leaned forward again. "I'm not interested in Claire. You, on the other hand . . ."

Janey sobered. "Why me?"

"Why not you?"

Claire arrived with their food, silencing any response Janey might have made. They spent the next several minutes eating and listening to what was going on around them. Most of the chatter was about the weather. It hadn't rained in over a week and the farmers were beginning to worry about their crops.

No one mentioned the dead body that was found the previous day, which Kyle found a bit odd. The only reason he could come up with was that they were unsure of Janey. Everyone else in the diner was local. She was an outsider.

They were finishing up when Claire came by with a slice of pie for each of them and the check. "Gerald said Fred Mitchel mentioned that he ran off some kids from one of his fields a week or so ago. You just never know about kids these days."

He nodded and thanked her for the information. "No, you don't."

To her credit, Janey waited until they were back in his SUV before commenting on what Claire had said. "I'm impressed. That's quite a system you all have worked out."

Kyle grinned as he put the key in the ignition and started the engine. "Let's go pay a visit to Mr. Mitchel and see if he got a look at any of the kids he ran off."

Mitchel's farm was a good twenty minutes from town in the opposite direction from where he'd found John Doe's body. That didn't mean anything, though. Most sixteen-year-olds in the county had a driver's license, since not having one severely limited one's mobility. There was no public transportation in Warren County.

Janey stared out the window as he drove. She appeared to be deep in thought about something.

"Penny for your thoughts?" he asked.

She turned her head to look at him then went back to watching the fields. "I was thinking about the case. My case. In Indianapolis. He was found behind a dumpster in an alley. It's a heavily trafficked area, and yet no one saw anything."

"Were you able to identify the victim?"

"Yes. Travis Merrick. He was a construction worker. Clean record.

Nothing out of the ordinary that would explain how he would wind up dead in an alley behind a dumpster. His wife said he'd called to say he was running late after work, but then he never came home."

Kyle realized then why she kept looking at the fields. "Why would whoever it is change the dump site so drastically if it was the same person that killed both guys?"

Janey nodded.

"Do you think it's a copycat, then?"

"Too early to say, but I'm not ruling it out."

Kyle slowed as Mitchel's farm came into view. He was hoping the aging farmer had some information for them. Not only could it provide them with a lead that would catch the killer, but it also meant Janey would have an excuse to stay a little longer.

He turned onto the dirt driveway and followed it to the old farmhouse. Two golden retrievers ran out to greet them, barking and wagging their tails. A few seconds later, the screen door at the side of the house opened and out stepped Fred Mitchel.

"He doesn't look pleased to see us," Janey said, noting the scowl on the old farmer's face.

"Don't take it personally. He's not a fan of visitors in general, which is probably why he complained about the kids being in his field."

"Do you want me to wait here, then?" Janey asked. "If he's not fond of visitors, I doubt my presence will help loosen his tongue."

"Nah. It'll be fine. Fred's more bark than he is bite." Kyle turned off the engine and placed his hat on his head. "Let's go see if we can get Mr. Mitchel to vent to us about those crazy kids."

CHAPTER 4

Janey wasn't so sure about Kyle's assessment of Fred Mitchel. As they crossed the lawn, the irritation on his face didn't lessen. He wasn't happy to see them.

"Afternoon, Fred," Kyle said when they reached the edge of the porch. "I was hoping we could talk to you about the kids you ran off a couple of weeks ago."

Fred Mitchel's gaze shifted from Kyle to her, then he turned his head and spat over the porch rail. "Who's she?"

"This is Detective Davis. She's visiting from Indianapolis." Kyle didn't seem bothered by Fred Mitchel's attitude.

The farmer looked her up and down. "She here about the body you found?"

Janey stayed quiet, letting Kyle decide how much to share. "Among other things."

"Humph." Mitchel took a step forward. "And what does that have to do with me and the kids I chased off my property?"

Kyle shrugged. "Probably nothing."

"And yet you're here harassing me." Mitchel huffed again and crossed his arms over his chest. "Well, on with it. What do you want to know? I've got work to do."

"Where were the kids when you discovered them?"

"Cornfield." Short and to the point.

"How many were there?" Kyle asked.

"Don't know. Maybe ten. Fifteen." Mitchel shrugged. "Was gettin' dark."

Kyle nodded. "Did you happen to recognize any of them?"

"No." Disappointment settled in Janey's gut. Unless they got a hit on those fingerprints, they'd struck a dead end again.

"Thank you for your time, Fred. We'll let you get back to work." Kyle headed toward his SUV and she followed.

"That was a waste," she said once they were inside the vehicle.

He nodded. "It was worth a shot."

"Now what?"

"Now . . ." The look Kyle gave her had her heart rate picking up. "I drop you off at my sister's so you can rest up for our date tonight."

Janey bit the inside of her cheek. She had no idea if going to this shindig with him was a good idea or not, but if she was being honest with herself, she had to admit she wanted to go. It had been a while since a guy had piqued her interest the way Kyle did. "I was talking about the case."

"We cross our fingers and hope the lab gets a hit on one of those fingerprints."

It was close to three by the time he dropped her off at Ava's with a promise to be back to pick her up around six. Ava was in the living room folding laundry. She glanced behind Janey expectantly, and then frowned. "Kyle isn't coming in?"

"He'll be back later." Janey wasn't sure how much he'd want his sister to know, but figured she'd find out eventually. "Apparently there's some sort of pig roast tonight."

A sly smile crossed Ava's face as she took a towel from the basket.

"What?"

"Nothing." When Janey continued to wait, Ava sighed. "It's just been a while since Kyle showed any real interest in anyone. It's good to see. I want him to find someone. Settle down. He deserves to be happy."

Curiosity nagged her, but she wasn't sure she wanted to know. Kyle lived here in Liberty. Her life was in Indianapolis. Granted, it wasn't a huge distance, but it was far enough.

Realizing how absurd her train of thought was, Janey excused herself and went to grab a shower. She told herself nothing was going to happen tonight, but even she didn't believe it. Besides, it was better to be prepared. If nothing happened, it wouldn't hurt to make sure everything was shaved and neatly trimmed.

It was as she was standing at the end of her bed in nothing but a towel that Janey realized she had a problem. The only clothes she'd brought with her were khaki pants and shirts—her work attire. Somehow she didn't think that would help her to fit in at what sounded more like a community barbecue.

Janey threw on some clean clothes and headed back downstairs. Ava was roughly the same size. Hopefully, she wouldn't mind letting her borrow something. Janey didn't think she had time to make it to the nearest mall and back before Kyle returned to pick her up.

"Ava?" Janey called out when she didn't find her in the living room or the kitchen, the only two rooms she'd been in on the first floor.

"In here."

Janey followed Ava's voice to what had to be the master bedroom.

"Hey. Come in," Ava said, setting aside the book she was reading.

"I didn't mean to bother you in your personal space."

Ava waved her comment away. "It's fine. I was just enjoying some peace and quiet while I can. What did you need?"

For a moment Janey reconsidered. It didn't feel right asking Ava, Kyle's sister or not, if she could borrow an outfit. She didn't even know the woman. "Nothing. Never mind."

"Janey, just spit it out."

"I was wondering if maybe you had something I could wear tonight. All I brought with me were work clothes. I wasn't planning on going out."

Before she'd even finished her sentence, Ava was up and moving toward her closet. "I'm sure I have a dress that would fit you. Let me see . . ." She rooted around in her closet, pushing hangers to one side until she found what she was looking for. "What do you think?"

The dress was navy blue with a white belt at the waist. It was simple but cute. "As long as it fits, I think it will work."

Ava held it out to her. "Go try it on. You can use my bathroom if you want. And if it doesn't work, we can find something else."

"Thanks, Ava. I really appreciate this."

Janey hurried into the bathroom and stripped out of the clothes she'd put on a few minutes earlier. Since the dress had wider straps, she was still able to wear her bra, which was a good thing. She wasn't exactly small on top. It was a little loose around the middle, but the belt took care of that. Otherwise, it was a pretty good fit. On the downside, there was no way she'd be able to carry her gun. Considering her options, it was a sacrifice she was going to have to make.

"What do you think?" Janey asked when she stepped out of the bathroom. She did a little twirl and loved how the skirt flared up slightly.

Ava moved in for a closer look. "Wow. I think it looks much better on you than me."

"Thanks, but I doubt that." Kyle's sister had one of those hourglass figures, and a dress like this would only highlight that.

A sad smile crossed Ava's face, and Janey wondered if the other woman was thinking about her late husband. "I'm glad it fits. Now you can go out and have a good time tonight."

The way she said it gave Janey the impression that Ava wouldn't be attending. "Aren't you going? Your brother said most of the people in the area would be there."

"Oh, they will be. The Price family does this every year. It's a big deal around here."

"But you're not going." It wasn't a question.

Ava shook her head. "I have lots to do here. Besides, I need to get Cole to bed by eight or he'll be cranky all day tomorrow."

Janey chose to keep her mouth shut. She didn't know Ava well enough. "Well, I should probably go upstairs and finish getting ready."

"Let me know if you need anything else." Ava smiled and lifted Cole from his playpen. "I'm going to go make this little guy some dinner."

It didn't take Janey long to finish getting ready. She was a minimalist when it came to makeup. A little bit of eye shadow, some mascara, and a touch of lip gloss. That was it. Anything more had her feeling as if she had goop slathered all over her face.

With five minutes to spare, she descended the stairs, but Kyle was already standing near the front door waiting for her. He wore a pair of faded jeans and a burgundy shirt with the top two buttons undone. She had the urge to run her hand down the front of his chest and slowly release each button.

His gaze moved down her body, and then back up to her face as she walked toward him. "You look amazing."

"Thanks," Janey said, trying to ignore the butterflies tumbling around in her stomach. "I borrowed the dress from your sister."

He offered her a hand. "We should get going. They'll be pulling the hog out of the pit soon. I don't want you to miss it."

Janey had no idea what the big deal was, but she was willing to give him the benefit of the doubt. "Let me just say goodbye to Ava."

The words had barely left her mouth when Kyle's sister poked her head out of the kitchen. "You two have a good time. I won't wait up." She winked.

Heat rushed to Janey's cheeks. Of course Kyle noticed. "We'll see you later, sis."

Ava waved as they walked out the door, Kyle's hand resting on Janey's lower back.

"That wasn't awkward at all," Janey mumbled.

"You want to talk about awkward? Try walking in on your little sister going at it with her husband on the couch." He shuddered as he pulled open the passenger door of his truck for her.

Janey giggled and brushed past him to climb inside the cab. "Got an eyeful, did you?"

"Oh yeah. There is no amount of brain bleach that'll get rid of that memory."

* * *

The best part of the Prices' annual hog roast was that the family farm had plenty of space for everyone. A large farmhouse sat in the center of the property, surrounded by more than one thousand acres of farmland. There were four barns, and all of them served a purpose. Tonight one had been converted into a dance hall of sorts.

Kyle parked his truck along the long driveway, hopped out, and went to help Janey. He hadn't even thought about her not having something to wear when he'd asked her to come with him tonight. Then again, he wouldn't have cared if she'd stayed in what she'd worn earlier.

They had to walk a ways to reach the roasting pit where everyone was gathered. It was situated on the back side of the barn to keep the smoke away from the other festivities.

"What's everyone waiting for?" Janey asked as they approached the crowd.

"You'll see."

A few minutes later, Ethan, his brother Evan, and their father emerged from one of the other barns, all three of them with shovels. They made a beeline for the mound of fresh dirt covering the pit and began digging. After a few minutes three other men stepped up and took turns removing the dirt. This back and forth went on until they reached the sheet metal underneath. Ethan and Evan pried the metal back while their father, wearing heavy gloves, pulled out burlap sacks.

"Are those the pigs?" Janey asked in a low whisper.

Kyle nodded. "Best pork you've ever tasted. Trust me."

"It doesn't look all that appetizing at the moment."

A few of the guys stayed behind to cover the pit up again so no one accidently fell in, while everyone else moved into the barn. Kyle guided Janey over to a long table set up with drinks. "What would you like? They've got everything from water and Kool-Aid for the kids to beer."

Janey glanced around, looking slightly uncomfortable. "I think I'll just stick to water."

"Two waters," Kyle told Elena, Ethan and Evan's sister, who was manning the table.

She opened a cooler to her left, dug two bottles of water from the ice, and placed them on the table.

He picked up the drinks. "Thanks, Elena."

"Enjoy your evening."

Kyle handed Janey one of the waters and guided her over to a less crowded area of the barn. It would take ten minutes or so for the meat to be ready, and the band was still getting set up. For the moment, there wasn't much to do besides wait. Wait and try to get to know his date a little more.

"How long have you been a detective?" he asked. Work seemed to be a safer subject with her than her past.

She sat down on a nearby chair, and he lowered himself into the seat next to her. "Almost six years. I worked patrol for a couple of years before that."

"Why did you decide to change?"

"I always wanted to be a detective. That was always the goal. So at the first opportunity, I took the test." The look on her face told him all he needed to know. Janey loved her job. He knew the feeling. Being a deputy made him feel connected to the community. He didn't want to be anywhere else.

"I know what you mean. As soon as I got my discharge papers from the Army, I applied to the sheriff's department."

"Did you ever think about working in a bigger city?"

Kyle tried not to read more into her question than there really was. "Not really. Ava was still in school and I wanted to be here for her last years of high school." He took a drink of his water. "I think I can do more good here. People . . . they care about each other. Even Fred Mitchel, who acts like everyone and everything annoys him. I've seen him pitch in and help a neighbor whose crop was about to go bad because he couldn't get it in fast enough."

Janey rolled her bottle of water between her fingers. "That's hard to imagine."

"People can surprise you."

She met his gaze and whispered, "Yes, they can."

Kyle had an undeniable urge to kiss her in that moment. The only thing that stopped him was where they were. Not that he had any problem kissing Janey in public; more that he wanted a little privacy the first time it happened.

He stood, needing to move. "Why don't we see if the food's ready? I'm starving."

There was already a line at the food table. Several people stopped to introduce themselves to Janey. Most already knew who she was.

With their plates piled high, Kyle and Janey headed outside to one of the picnic tables. He should have known they wouldn't be alone for long. Within minutes of sitting down, Avery Richards and Mac joined them, both with full plates of their own.

"Mind if we join you?" Avery asked after she'd already begun sitting down.

Kyle figured he should probably make introductions. "Janey, this is Avery Richards. She's the town pharmacist."

"Nice to meet you," Janey said.

Mac picked up her fork and stabbed a chunk of pork. It was almost violent, which made Kyle think something was up. "Bad day?" he asked.

"Just disappointing, that's all." He knew she had to be talking about their John Doe. Unfortunately, with Avery at the table, they couldn't talk in detail.

"It'll work itself out. It always does," Janey said. Her optimism surprised him. She'd been the frustrated one earlier when they had come away from Fred Mitchel's without a name.

He took a chance and placed his free hand on her leg. She tensed for a moment and then relaxed. Her reaction gave him confidence that he wasn't misreading things. Janey felt the same pull he did.

Avery began asking Janey about life in Indianapolis. He was only half paying attention since most of what they were saying had to do with stores and restaurants. His focus was on the feel of Janey's soft skin under his fingers. He gradually pushed the hem of her skirt out of his way, giving her time to stop him, but she didn't.

There was a break in the conversation when Mac and Avery turned to watch two of the Johnson boys try to see how many pieces of watermelon they could shove down their throats in sixty seconds. Janey took the opportunity to lean over and whisper in his ear. "You're making it very hard to concentrate."

He inched his fingers up a little higher on her thigh. "Do you want me to stop?"

She hesitated, and for a moment he thought she was going to say yes. He nearly jumped out of his seat when he felt her nails scratch along the inside seam of his jeans. If she kept it up, he wasn't going to be able to leave the table for a while.

Kyle placed his hand over hers, stopping her movement. "Would you like to dance?"

A small crease formed in Janey's forehead.

"Don't tell me you don't like to dance," he said, linking their fingers.

"It's not that. I just figured . . ."

There was a hint of insecurity in her tone, which threw him for a minute. Janey didn't strike him as the insecure type.

He glanced over to see that Mac and Avery were still otherwise occupied before leaning in closer to Janey. "If we leave now, everyone is going to assume we're going back to my place."

Her gaze searched his. "And that's not what you want."

Kyle chuckled. "Oh, it's definitely what I want." He brought her fingers up to his lips and placed a soft kiss on her knuckles.

"Then . . ."

"This is a small town. Like it or not, people gossip."

She broke eye contact, looked over his shoulder, and then met his gaze again. "I get it."

Her tone of voice told him she didn't. "There are going to be people who will speculate no matter what, but we don't need to add fuel to the fire. I'd rather keep them guessing. They don't need to know what's going on in my personal life."

Janey took a deep breath and got up from the table. "Didn't you mention something about a dance?"

In less than a minute she'd gone from flirty to hurt, and he had no idea why. Didn't she understand how small towns worked? He had every intention of taking her home with him tonight if she was willing, but the rest of Warren County didn't need to know that.

He picked up their empty plates and tossed them in a nearby trash can then led her back into the barn where the makeshift dance floor was set up. Several couples were already dancing, so he pulled her against him and started to move with the music. She followed his lead, swaying her hips to the music, but he could tell something wasn't quite right. He wanted the playfulness of five minutes ago back.

"Are you going to tell me what I did wrong?"

She blinked. "You didn't do anything wrong. I'm just being overly sensitive, that's all."

"I'm just trying to protect you."

Janey smiled. "I know. Thank you for that." She scratched her nails along the back of his neck right below his hairline, and the sensation went straight to his groin. "How long do we have to stay before it's safe to leave?"

It was his turn to blink. "You still want to?"

She tilted her hips forward, brushing the part of him that was already sitting up to take notice. "Does that answer your question?"

CHAPTER 5

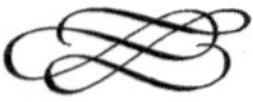

Janey was irritated with herself. Here she was with a man she really liked, and she was being stupid. Logically she knew he was telling the truth. She'd grown up in a neighborhood that wasn't all that different from Liberty. If she and Kyle ran out of here pawing at each other, it would be all anyone wanted to talk about.

Granted, she was most likely on her way back to Indianapolis soon unless new information turned up, but that didn't mean she'd never return. If there was a connection between the two cases, she might have to come back. There was no sense making the investigation harder because she couldn't keep her hormones under control . . . or her insecurities.

They ended up dancing for another hour. Some of the families with younger children began to filter out as the sun sank lower in the sky, leaving an older crowd inside the barn. The teenagers gathered outside near the fire pit and she was tempted to go out and talk to them—see if any of them would admit to being in the cornfield—but she let it go. Even if some or all of them were there that night, they would likely close ranks.

"You ready to go?" Kyle asked, pulling her from her thoughts. Another song had ended and the band was taking a break.

Butterflies filled her stomach again and she nodded.

Kyle was careful to keep a respectable distance as they made their way out of the barn and down the driveway. A few people waved goodbye as they passed, wishing them a good night. Once they were both settled inside his truck, he reached for her hand. "Do you want me to drop you off at Ava's or would you rather go back to my place?"

She knew what he was asking, and she appreciated it. All too often guys assumed that a date meant she'd be putting out. More than once she'd had to set them straight. But tonight she wanted to be with Kyle. As crazy as it sounded, she wanted time alone with him when all the barriers of professionalism and propriety were gone. "I'd love to see your place."

That hung in the air for a moment before he put the vehicle in gear and headed toward town. The air in the cab was thick with tension as they drove past fields full of crops not quite ready to harvest. Kyle rubbed his thumb along the inside of her wrist as the sun continued to set. She closed her eyes, letting the sensations take over.

Janey felt his gaze on her and turned to look at him. Concern marred his features. She smiled, letting him know she hadn't changed her mind.

A few minutes later, he pulled up to an old Victorian-style house. She couldn't see much detail since it was now almost completely dark, but she thought it had brown or black shutters on the windows.

"This is it," he said, then got out and came around to get her door. "Thanks."

Once her feet were on the ground, Kyle crowded closer, pressing her back against the edge of the seat. There was heat in his eyes—heat Janey desperately wanted to tap. She slid her palms up his chest and cupped the back of his neck with her right hand.

That was all he needed. He grabbed hold of her hips with so much force it took her breath away. Then his lips were covering hers and the thought of breathing went out the window altogether.

Kyle molded her body to his as much as their clothing would allow and wasted no time darting his tongue between her parted lips. He ran his hands up the length of her back and then down over her ass. She wanted his hands everywhere.

He was breathing hard when he finally broke the kiss. "I've wanted to do that all day."

Before she could respond, he kissed her again.

"Janey?" he asked, not bothering to remove his mouth from hers this time.

"Yes?" It was hard to talk or even think at that moment.

"I want to take you inside." He peppered kisses along her jaw and down her neck. "Tear off all your clothes." She felt his hand slide up the back of her thigh. He paused right below her backside for a moment before tracing the edge of her panties. "And then, once I have you naked, I want to learn every inch of you."

She sucked in a breath, hoping her next words came out as confident as she hoped. "What are you waiting for?"

Janey expected him to rush them into the house, but he didn't. He covered her mouth with his again and lifted her back onto the seat, this time positioning himself between her legs. Even then he still wasn't close enough for her liking.

"We need to go inside. Too many clothes," she said between kisses.

Kyle's chest vibrated, but he didn't stop kissing her. He'd said he wanted to get her naked, and given they were both law enforcement, she doubted he'd risk getting down and dirty in his driveway. She wrapped her legs around his waist, needing more friction, hoping he'd get the message. If he didn't get it soon, she was going to spell it out for him.

Then she felt his thumb glide up and down the front of her panties. A moan erupted from her throat and she didn't even try to stop it. Luckily, there was some distance between Kyle and his neighbors. Although she wasn't sure at that moment if she would have cared even if someone did happen to overhear them.

She dug her fingers into his shoulders and neck as he continued to touch her. Their mouths were fused together, tongues exploring and tasting. She felt as if she were going to catch on fire from the inside out if she didn't come soon.

"Kyle?"

"Hmm." He cupped the back of her head with his free hand and met her gaze. "Do you want me to keep touching you, Janey?"

She lifted her hips. "If you stop now, I'll never forgive you."

He laughed and gave her a hard kiss. The pleasure between her legs went up another notch as he increased the pressure of his thumb exactly where she needed it.

Janey tilted her hips up to meet every downward motion of his hand, driving her toward her orgasm. She was close. So close.

And then she was soaring. Her breath caught in her throat and her entire body shook. Kyle took her in his arms and held on tight, letting her ride out her climax.

She rested her forehead on his shoulder as she caught her breath. "That was unexpected."

"You've never had an orgasm before?" His tone was full of shocked disbelief.

She gave him a gentle shove, which did nothing to move his solid form. "That's not what I meant, and you know it."

Kyle angled her chin up and brushed his lips against hers. Unable to resist, she pulled his mouth closer and took what she wanted.

Seconds later they were moving. He placed her feet on the ground, moved her away from the truck, and slammed the door. She giggled as he guided her along the side of the house, and then proceeded to fumble with his keys trying to get inside.

They'd barely made it over the threshold before he was on her again. He pushed her back against the wall and hiked her dress up around her waist. She couldn't keep track of his hands. They were constantly moving, touching her everywhere.

"We need to get you out of this dress," he mumbled as he placed open-mouthed kisses on her collarbone.

She couldn't remember the last time she was this turned on. "You have on more clothing than I do."

To her surprise, he stepped back and removed his shirt. A light brown sprinkling of hair covered his torso. And beneath that were the muscles she'd only gotten hints of before.

Unable to resist, Janey placed both hands on his chest, letting the fine hairs tickle her palms, being careful to avoid the top of his gun where it peeked out of his waistband. She looked up, meeting his gaze. "Not bad, Deputy Reed."

He closed the distance between them again, tangling his fingers in her hair with one hand while he removed his gun and holster with the other, tucking them into a nearby drawer. "I promise it only gets better from here."

"Rather confident, aren't you?"

"Uh-huh." With that he crushed his mouth over hers and went to work proving his point. Their clothing fell to the floor—first her dress, then his pants. He reached behind her to unhook her bra. Once she felt it give, Janey shrugged out of it, wanting to feel his bare chest against hers.

But as soon as her bra was out of the way, Kyle cupped her ass and lifted her feet off the ground. The move happened so fast she let out a squeal of surprise and grasped at his shoulders to stabilize herself.

"Sorry," he whispered against her lips as he helped her wrap her legs around his waist.

Janey ran her fingers through his hair as he headed toward the stairs, presumably taking her to his bedroom. "No complaints here. Just maybe give me a little warning next time."

He chuckled. "I'll keep that in mind."

Kyle hadn't planned on getting Janey off in his driveway, but when she'd responded to his kiss the way she had, he'd needed to touch her . . . and keep touching her. Hearing her moan and gasp at what he was doing had been addicting and he hadn't wanted to stop.

He still didn't want to stop. She clung to him as he climbed the stairs to his bedroom. It would have been easier to have her walk, but he hadn't wanted to release her even for that short amount of time. She'd be leaving soon enough. Going back to her home, her life, in Indianapolis. He wasn't sure how he felt about that.

All thoughts of anything but the gorgeous woman he held in his arms left his brain when she leaned down and scraped her teeth along his neck. His erection throbbed and he almost tripped over his own feet. He landed a firm swat to her backside. "Behave."

She did it again and then laughed. "Nope."

He picked up his pace, which only amused her more.

As soon as Kyle reached the bedroom, he walked over to the bed and dumped her on top of the sheets. "I'm going to make you pay for that, woman."

Janey scooted back on the bed and propped herself up on her elbows, not seeming the least bit worried about his threat. She lifted her leg and rubbed the ball of her foot along the part of him that was trying to burst through his boxer briefs. If he wasn't careful, he was going to embarrass himself.

Taking hold of her ankle, he placed her foot flat on the bed and climbed on top of her. "You like playing with fire, don't you?"

"I don't know what you mean," she said, a look of feigned innocence on her face.

In response, he took one of her nipples into his mouth and sucked hard. Janey let out a shriek followed by a sound that told him it wasn't going to take much to get her there a second time. She arched her back and held his head to her chest. He was more than happy to oblige her silent request. Sucking on Janey Davis's breasts was something he could do for hours. He alternated sucking and licking, even taking a page out of her book and scraping his teeth along the sensitive flesh. Once her left nipple was nice and hard, he turned his attention on the other one.

Janey brought her feet up to the waistband of his boxer briefs and tried to push them down his hips, but they were giving her trouble. She growled in frustration.

"Getting a little impatient?"

"Yes." She huffed. "I want these off."

He released her breast, placed a soft kiss on her lips, and leaned back on his heels. "Your wish is my command."

She snorted. "I highly doubt that."

Kyle smirked down at her while he worked his underwear the rest of the way off. He dropped them onto the floor beside the bed and retook his position between her legs. This time, though, he brought his face level with hers. He brushed the back of his fingers along the side of her face. "You might be surprised."

The atmosphere around them shifted. All playfulness dissipated.

Needing to prove his point, Kyle rolled over, lying next to her on the bed. "I'm all yours."

She turned her head to meet his gaze as if trying to gauge if he was serious or not. After a long moment, she pushed her panties down her legs and kicked them off the end of the bed. "Condom?"

He grinned and nodded toward the stand next to his bed. "In the top drawer."

Janey crawled over him, her derriere conveniently up in the air less than a foot above his face. He took advantage of the situation and gave her a playful bite on her right butt cheek. She collapsed over his lap, laughing.

All laughter ceased when he slipped two fingers between her legs. She gasped and fisted the sheets. "Lower."

He did as she requested. It wasn't hard to know he'd found the right spot. Janey pushed herself back against his fingers. "Is this what you were wanting me to do?"

That seemed to bring her out of her fog. She scrambled to sit up.

"Not exactly." She held up a single foil square and ripped it open. When she began to roll it down his length, he had to press his hands into the mattress to keep from reaching for her. However, the moment she was finished, he pulled her down on top of him, flipped them over, and used his weight to press her into the mattress.

Janey grinned up at him. "That didn't last long."

"Next time." He tangled his fingers in her hair and kissed her with everything he had. She met him stroke for stroke and hooked her knee around his hip, urging him closer.

Propping himself up on one elbow, he reached between them and lined himself up. Kyle held Janey's gaze as he pushed inside. As he began to move, she met each one of his thrusts with one of her own. She was there with him in the moment, taking what she needed.

He kept up a steady rhythm, enjoying the friction and the way her breasts bounced each time he surged forward. Janey looked down, watching their bodies as they came together. It was incredibly erotic. And it was making it difficult to keep his climax at bay.

She scraped her nails along his scalp, sending shots of electricity down his spine. He closed his eyes, trying to concentrate on anything other than how good she felt. Then she snaked her hand between them. The moment he registered what she was doing, he almost came right then and there.

"Janey," he said through gritted teeth.

"I know."

If he'd been ten years younger, he might not have been able to hold on, but by some miracle he managed. Her breath came faster, harder, and her hand moved at an almost fevered pace, driving her toward her goal.

A gasp escaped her lips a moment before he felt her muscles tighten around him. She dug her nails into his neck so hard they probably broke the skin. It flipped a switch in him. Kyle let himself go and allowed all the sensations he'd been keeping in check overtake him. He felt the energy surging and leaned forward to capture her lips as he thrust one last time.

They lay there, him still inside her, as their breathing slowed. He felt her fingers graze over the spot on his neck where her nails had dug into his skin. "I didn't mean to mark you with my nails like that."

He snorted and kissed the tip of her nose. "I'll take the exchange any day."

"Still, we should probably clean it. I don't want it to get infec—"

His kiss effectively silenced her. Janey kissed him back, but he could tell she was still concerned. "I'll let you look at it in a little while, okay? But I just finished making love to a beautiful woman, who I still happen to have in my arms, and I'd like to focus on that right now."

Kyle thought she was going to argue with him, but she didn't.

Maybe he wasn't the only one who didn't want to break the connection quite yet.

He didn't want to move, but eventually he had to. After rolling off her, he removed the condom and threw it in the trash can beside his bed. He'd had every intention of pulling her into his arms again, but when he turned back around, Janey was sitting up. The look on her face had him worried. "What's wrong?"

She shot him a weak smile. "I was just wondering what your sister's going to say when I come home tonight."

"I hadn't planned on you going back to my sister's tonight." He scooted closer, circled his arm around her middle, and tugged her back down until she was lying beside him again.

"I thought you didn't want people in town to know."

He shrugged. "It would be easier if they didn't, but I'm not going to sneak you off in the middle of the night just to be sure my neighbors don't figure out I brought a woman home with me. Besides, my sister doesn't count."

Janey frowned, which wasn't what he wanted. He wanted her smiling again, laughing.

"If you go back to my sister's tonight, who's going to make sure the marks you gave me aren't getting infected? Hayden?" he asked.

It worked. Janey rolled her eyes at him. "Fine. I'll stay. But I'm letting you handle your sister. I'm not going near that one. If she asks, I'm going to tell her she has to talk to you. Got it?"

Kyle grinned. "Yes, ma'am."

They lay there for a while, her head resting on his chest. It was peaceful, something he hadn't felt in a while, especially not with a woman. It made him want to hold on to that feeling for as long as possible.

"Janey?" he asked, making sure she hadn't fallen asleep.

"Yeah?"

"When do you have to head back to Indy?"

She moved so she could see his face. "I have to be at work at eight o'clock Monday morning, so I was planning to head back in the morning unless something came up."

He combed his fingers through her hair and tried to keep his voice even. He didn't want her to feel any pressure. "Push your plans back a few hours and spend the day with me tomorrow."

CHAPTER 6

IT WASN'T Janey's alarm that woke her on Sunday morning. Kyle gently roused her from sleep with barely-there kisses followed by what she was beginning to think were magical fingers. He brought her to yet another orgasm thanks to those talented digits before reaching for another condom.

After her fourth climax in less than twelve hours, she lay there trying to catch her breath while Kyle cleaned up in the bathroom. Janey wished she'd thought to bring her bag with her last night or had Kyle swing by his sister's house to pick it up. All she had to wear were the clothes she'd worn the night before, and the thought of putting her dirty panties back on wasn't appealing.

Janey was still lying on the bed when Kyle strolled out of the bathroom with nothing but a towel wrapped around his waist. She could still see drops of water clinging to his chest and had the urge to lick each and every one of them.

"If you keep looking at me like that, we're not going to make it out of the bedroom today." His husky voice had the muscles in her belly clenching in remembrance.

"You're the one who decided to walk out of the bathroom in nothing but a towel," she said, getting up.

He raised one eyebrow. "Would you rather have me walk out naked? That can still be arranged."

She held his gaze as she left the bed and passed by him on her way to the bathroom. "I'm sure it could be, but since someone got me all dirty last night, I'm in need of a shower."

"Want some company?" he asked, placing a hand on her hip to stop her.

As tempting as that was, Janey needed a few minutes to herself. She shook her head. "Maybe you could go downstairs and get my clothes instead."

His eyes darkened and he pulled her against him. He gazed down the length of her body, and then placed a lingering kiss on her lips. "Enjoy your shower."

By the time she opened her eyes, he'd stepped out into the hall. She tried to clear the cobwebs out of her head. It amazed her how he could do that to her so easily.

Janey headed into the bathroom to start her shower. He'd laid a couple of towels on the counter for her, which she thought was rather sweet. She tried not to take it for anything other than what it was. Given she'd never been in his house before, she wouldn't have had a clue where the towels were and she would have felt weird rummaging through his closets trying to find some.

Then she noticed the toothbrush lying next to the towels. It was brand new—still in the package. Her heart rate sped a little and she felt warmth bloom in her chest.

"It's nothing, Janey," she mumbled to herself. "He just has good manners. That's all."

After turning the water on, she tested it to make sure it was the right temperature and stepped into the tub. From what she'd seen of Kyle's house, which admittedly wasn't much, it was old but well taken care of. She wondered how long it had been in his family.

There was shampoo and conditioner along the back edge of the bathtub. When she opened the body wash, a sigh left her before she could stop it. Janey knew every time she smelled that scent she would think of Kyle.

The mirror over the sink was steamed up by the time she pulled back the shower curtain. She stepped out onto the fluffy bath mat and reached for one of the towels. Realization that she didn't even have a brush for her hair had her going over her options. She thought she might have a ponytail holder in her purse. It wouldn't be pretty, but she'd have to make it work until she could get her things.

Kyle was sitting on the end of the bed waiting for her when she walked out. Her blue dress—the one she'd borrowed from his sister—was draped over his lap. He held it out to her and she took it. "Thanks."

"Your bra and panties are on top of the dresser. I figured you'd want the bra. I wasn't sure about the panties." His smirk said it all.

Janey wasn't one to go around without panties on, especially in a dress, but this might have to be an exception to the rule. She recalled them being rather damp when she'd stripped them off the night before. Just thinking about putting them back on was making her feel dirty again. "I need to get my things from Ava's anyway. I'm sure she'll want to get the room ready for someone else."

"So is that a no on the panties?" he asked with a light in his eyes.

She had the yearning to push him back on the bed and wipe that smug grin off his face, but she didn't. "As long as we go there first, I think I'll survive."

"I might be willing to test that assumption."

Reaching for her bra, Janey dropped the towel and began getting dressed . . . or at least as dressed as she could be without panties or clean clothes. She knew she needed a diversion or they were going to end up right back where they started the day—in his bed. "I thought you wanted us to spend the day together."

"Oh, we would be." There was no mistaking his meaning.

She shot him an incredulous look. "Outside of your bedroom."

Kyle chuckled and stood, slapping his hands on his thighs. "In that case, I'm going to go see what I can throw together in the kitchen."

He paused for a moment at the door, taking a long look at her once more. She saw the conflict in his eyes, but after several long moments he turned on his heel and disappeared into the hallway.

A deep sense of feminine pleasure filled her. Her body wasn't perfect. What woman's was? But when Kyle looked at her she felt like the most beautiful woman in the world. It was clear he liked what he saw.

It only took a few minutes to put her bra on and slip into her dress. Pulling her hair up into a ponytail took a little longer. Every time she thought she'd gotten all her hair gathered together and twisted the band in place, a section wasn't lying flat so she had to take it out and start again. After the fifth try, she gave up. She figured she'd fix it once they got to Ava's and her things.

On her way downstairs, Janey paid more attention to her surroundings than she had going up the night before. There were six doors on the top floor. She assumed at least one of the other doors was a bathroom, which meant the house likely had five bedrooms. It was a lot bigger than she'd thought it was.

When she reached the bottom of the stairs, a muffled curse pointed her in the direction of the kitchen. She followed the sound and found Kyle frantically waving his hand in the air. "Did you burn yourself?"

"I hate cooking. Did I mention that?" He removed two pieces of bread from the toaster and threw them onto a nearby plate with more force than necessary.

"I'm not sure making toast qualifies as cooking."

He narrowed his eyes at her.

Janey laughed and sashayed over to stand in front of him. It had been a while since she'd had this much fun with a guy. She picked up the hand he'd been shaking when she'd entered the room. "Would you like me to kiss it and make it better?"

His eyes darkened. "No. But I'm sure I can find something else you can kiss and that would definitely make me feel better."

She went up on her tiptoes and gave him a quick peck on the cheek. "There. Did that make it better?"

Without warning, Kyle picked her up and set her on top of the counter next to him. One of the plates went crashing into the sink. He ignored it and set about getting the type of kiss he'd wanted—one that was far from the innocent peck she'd given him.

He held her exactly where he wanted her, much like he had outside the night before. She couldn't have moved far even if she'd wanted to. Not that she did.

Her head was spinning when he pulled back, his chest heaving with his labored breaths. He retrieved the plate from the sink, placed two pieces of toast on it, and set it on the table. Then he put another two pieces of bread in the toaster. Aside from his breathing, one would never have known he'd just kissed the living daylights out of her.

Janey hopped off the counter and straightened her dress, making sure everything was covered. "Do you have any coffee?"

"I'll get it," he said.

"That's okay—"

He cut her off with another kiss and slowly walked her backward until her knees hit the chair.

She sighed and sat down at the table. "Fine."

* * *

Stopping at his sister's went about as well as could be expected. Ava was all smiles until Janey was out of sight. "Is this a one-time thing, or do you plan to see her again?"

Kyle leaned against the back of the couch, his stance casual. "I don't know. We haven't discussed it."

His sister snorted then mumbled something under her breath that sounded a lot like *"Men,"* and then headed into the kitchen, Cole on her hip. She was gone all of two seconds before she marched back into the room. He'd known she wouldn't let it go. "Why haven't you discussed it?"

Luckily, he was saved from answering by the sound of Janey's footsteps on the stairs. He pushed away from the couch and went to meet her. "Got everything?"

"Yep," Janey said, and then looked at Ava. "Thank you so much for letting me stay here. I appreciate it. How much do I owe you for the room?"

"Anytime. And don't worry about it. I'm sure Kyle will figure out some way to make it up to me."

He reached for Janey's suitcase. "We should get going."

She gave it up without a fight, which surprised him. "Thanks."

"Call me later," his sister called as they walked out the door.

Kyle put Janey's suitcase in the trunk of her SUV and held her door open for her. Over breakfast they'd decided she'd drive her vehicle back to his place and leave it there while they were gone. He insisted it would be better that way since his place was closer to town and the road she'd need to take back to Indianapolis.

"You going to tell me where it is we're going?" she asked after she'd parked her vehicle in his driveway and climbed into the cab of his truck.

He'd considered his options carefully. They only had a few hours, so they couldn't go too far. "Have you ever been horseback riding?"

It took her a moment. "Yes."

"Good."

Silence filled the cab.

"Is that a problem?" Kyle asked.

"No. Just . . . unexpected, I guess."

He glanced over at her and winked. "I'll take that as a compliment."

It took them almost a half hour to reach their destination and another twenty minutes to get their horses saddled and ready to go. She hoisted herself onto her horse, showing she did know what she was doing, and pointed it toward the trail.

The forest closed in around them, sheltering them. It was what he loved about coming here.

Janey tightened her grip on the reins as the trail sloped downward. "Do you do this often?"

"Every now and then." He let that hang in the air for a while before adding, "Sometimes it's nice to get out here by myself. Gives me the opportunity to think." There was no one but the two of them for as far as the eye could see. They were completely surrounded by nature. It was perfect as far as he was concerned.

"I've never been here before. It's nice." She paused. "Quiet."

Kyle grinned. "A lot different from the city."

"Yes," she agreed.

The trail they were on gradually led down to the river. He'd taken it many times over the years, first as a boy and then as an adult. Kyle picked up his pace a little, pulling ahead when the ground beneath them leveled out some.

Janey was right behind him. She was comfortable on a horse, more so than he'd expected. It made him even more curious about her.

When he reached the water's edge, Kyle loosened his hold on his mount's reins, allowing him to drink. He reached into his saddlebag, removed the bag of trail mix they'd been given, and sat back in his saddle. The river was fairly calm here, but he could hear more rapidly moving water not far downstream.

Coming up beside him, Janey followed his lead, allowing her horse to drink. He offered her some of his snack and she lifted herself in her saddle to grab a handful. "Thanks."

They sat there for several minutes watching the water go by and listening to the sounds around them. As much as he loved coming up here by himself, he found that having Janey with him made it better rather than taking something away.

His sister's question this morning popped into his mind. He hadn't answered her, but even then he'd known. Yes, he wanted to see Janey again. But was that what Janey wanted? He had no idea.

Uncertainty gripped him. He'd dated his fair share of women in his thirty-five years, but for some reason asking Janey if she wanted to make this more than a one-night stand, or weekend fling or whatever, had him sweating.

The situation struck him as amusing. Or maybe ironic was a better word. He was a police officer. Over the years he'd had to talk down more than one out-of-control drunk or jealous husband. This should have been cake.

But it wasn't.

"Want to share what's so funny?" Janey asked when she noticed the goofy grin on his face.

Kyle reached for her hand and was pleased when she laced their fingers together. "I've been thinking."

She waited for him to continue.

"I'd like to see you again."

The seconds ticked by as they sat there, the sounds around them suddenly seeming louder than they had a few moments before. It was one of those times when he really wished he had the ability to read her mind. "I thought . . ."

"What did you think?" he asked, curious.

When she didn't move away from him, he took that as a good sign. She looked down at their linked hands. "I wasn't thinking it was going to be anything more than last night. And today."

"Is that all you want?" He held his breath waiting for her answer.

"I live two hours away."

Kyle dropped her hand and shifted in his saddle so he could touch her face. He tilted her chin up until she was looking at him. "That doesn't answer my question, Detective."

She smiled at his use of her title. "I know, but I'm trying to think rationally."

"Does that mean you do want to see me again?"

Janey removed his hand from her face but didn't release it. "I've tried the long-distance thing before and it doesn't work."

He opened his mouth to argue, but she cut him off.

"We both have unsolved cases. Cases that might very well be connected. I don't want it to be awkward if we have to work together again."

"You're worried we couldn't work together professionally if things didn't work out between us?"

"Aren't you?" she asked.

One of his best friends was his boss and they'd figured it out. Even if he and Janey couldn't, Kyle thought it was worth the risk. "No. I'm not. I like you, Janey."

"I like you, too."

All his anxiety fell away. Janey wanted this, too. She was just scared. He didn't quite understand her fear, but he wouldn't dismiss it either. "What are you so afraid of?"

Instead of answering his question, she asked one of her own. "What about the women around here? Claire, for example."

"Claire isn't my type." He squeezed her hand and grinned. "And you didn't answer the question."

Janey sighed and looked toward the river. "I don't want to get attached and then you decide it isn't worth it."

Kyle knew in that moment that she was speaking from experience. "What if I get attached and you decide I'm not worth it?" He rubbed his thumb along the inside of her wrist. Her pulse was beating rapidly under her skin. "You know as well as I do that there are no guarantees in life."

She held his gaze for a long moment before rising up and pressing her mouth to his. It was completely unexpected, but not unwelcome. Kyle cupped the back of her head and held her to him for as long as possible, enjoying the feel of her lips.

"You make it very hard to say no to you," she whispered, lowering herself back into the saddle.

Kyle smiled and traced the outline of her lips with his index finger. "Then say yes."

She held his hand in place against her cheek. "Just promise me something, okay?"

"I'd promise you just about anything if you agree to see me again."

"Somehow I doubt that." She grinned and lowered their hands to rest on her leg. "Promise me that if you change your mind, you'll tell me."

Another puzzle piece fell into place. "I promise."

She looked down for several minutes, seeming fascinated with their hands. When she met his gaze once more there was determination and something else that had him wishing for more room in his pants. He was mentally doing the calculations of how quickly they could get to the stables, return the horses, and make it back to his house when Janey picked up her reins and began moving away.

"Wha—"

She had a serious look on her face, but the heat was still there. "I think I might have forgotten something at your place."

"Really?" he asked, catching on to her line of thinking.

Janey nodded and turned her horse in the direction of the trail. "Yeah. I think we should head back. I wouldn't want to leave it behind."

"We wouldn't want that, now, would we?"

"Certainly not."

CHAPTER 7

Eight hours later, Janey let herself into her apartment, kicked off her shoes, and carried her suitcase into the bedroom. As she removed each item and tossed it into the hamper, she couldn't help but smile. Nearly every article of clothing she'd brought with her now had a memory of Kyle associated with it.

"You really shouldn't get yourself too attached, Janey," she said to herself. She'd learned the hard lesson years ago that most people didn't stick around for long.

But try as she might, the happy feeling she got whenever she thought of him wouldn't go away. Especially not after their goodbye. He'd walked her out to her vehicle, placed her suitcase in the back seat, and put his arms around her waist, his left hand cupping her ass.

Then he'd kissed her. It wasn't the passion-filled kiss they'd shared earlier, but one that left her wanting more. His lips and tongue had teased her to the point where she wanted to say "screw it" and drag him back into the house. But right as she was about to do exactly that, he'd released her. The smug grin on his face had told her he'd known exactly what he was doing.

Once she'd been able to think again, she'd promised to text him when she got home, and climbed in her vehicle. He'd leaned in to give her one more brush of his lips across hers before she drove away.

The entire scene occupied her thoughts the entire way home.

Without overthinking it, Janey picked up her phone and sent Kyle a quick text.

Janey: I'm home.

It didn't take long for the reply to come through.

Kyle: I'm sitting on the side of the highway with a thermos full of coffee. It's going to be a long night. Someone kept me from getting much sleep last night. 🌚

She didn't even hesitate.

Janey: Who kept who up last night?

Kyle: What can I say? Having you in my bed was just too tempting.

She sat down on the edge of the bed and typed her response.

Janey: Sorry I was such a temptation for you.

Kyle: I'm not.

She bit the inside of her cheek and type her response.

Janey: Neither am I.

He didn't respond right away and she began to wonder if she'd been too forward. She tried not to psych herself out too much, though. He was working, and more than likely he'd tagged a speeder or gotten sent on a call. Still, the insecure part of her kept whispering in her ear that she shouldn't have said that. She should have played coy or hard to get or whatever. Then again, that ship had already sailed. There wasn't much more of her for him to get that he hadn't already gotten.

Janey set her phone down on the bed and finished putting her things away. By the time she threw a load of laundry into the washer and tucked her suitcase into the closet, she'd almost given up hope of hearing from him again that night. It was getting late and she had to be up early the next morning. Her captain would want to be briefed on what had happened over the weekend.

She'd just closed her eyes when her phone dinged, alerting her to a new message.

Kyle: Still awake?

Janey: Maybe.

Kyle: LOL. Does that mean you're already in bed?

Janey: Yes.

She paused for a brief second before she continued typing.

Janey: I have this nice big bed all to myself.

Kyle: *groans* You're killing me.

A bubble of laughter erupted from deep in her chest.

Janey: I think you'll survive.

Kyle: Maybe not. I still have eight hours left on my shift. Sitting here thinking of you lying in that bed. Naked.

Janey: Who says I'm naked? Maybe I'm a flannel pajamas type of girl.

Kyle: Hmm. That just means I can imagine getting you out of them.

The visual image that created in her mind made her nipples harden. It was crazy how easily he could get a reaction from her body with only a few words. Then again, she could vividly remember how he could make good on those words of his. She had whisker burn on her inner thighs from earlier.

She was still off in fantasy land when her phone dinged once more.

Kyle: I'll let you get to sleep. I'll call you tomorrow night before my shift. Sweet dreams.

He knew exactly where her mind had gone. It should bother her that he could read her so well, but it didn't. Of course, that might have something to do with the fact that all she could think about was buying a pair of flannel pajamas so he could peel them off her one button at a time.

Knowing she needed to get to sleep and he had work to do, she typed her response.

Janey: Good night. Stay safe.

Returning her phone to the nightstand, she leaned back into her pillow and sighed. She had no idea if this long-distance relationship with Kyle would work. The last time she'd tried such a relationship it had ended with her heart being broken after she'd found out her boyfriend of two years had been cheating on her. According to him, no man could go more than a week without sex.

At the time, Janey had believed him and blamed herself. After all, it hadn't been the first time she hadn't been good enough to hold onto someone she cared about. Then she'd met her partner, Paul. His wife had been killed by a drunk driver, leaving him to raise their young daughter by himself. He'd dedicated his entire life to taking care of his daughter. Although he didn't talk about it, she knew he hadn't slept around with random women after his wife died and he hadn't dated either. There had been no one serious in his life until he met Megan.

He was the best man Janey knew and it had given her hope. Hope that there was a decent guy out there for her. She had no idea if Kyle was that guy, but as scary as it was, she was willing to give him a chance. If she'd learned anything from watching Paul and Megan's relationship unfold, it was that sometimes you had to follow your heart.

Janey closed her eyes, ready to drift off to sleep, when her phone rang. She snatched it up and glanced at the caller ID. Paul.

"Hey. I didn't expect to hear from you tonight."

She heard a lot of movement in the background. "Are you back in town?"

"Yeah. I got back about two hours ago."

"Good. We got a case."

She sat up, threw the covers off her, and made a beeline for her closet. Her thoughts immediately went to the case she'd been working on all weekend. Or at least part of the weekend. "The same MO?"

"No. This one looks like a robbery gone bad from the initial reports, but there were at least a dozen witnesses."

Janey knew what that meant. Each one of the witnesses would have to be interviewed. "Give me the address and I'll meet you there as soon as I throw on some clothes."

It took her twenty minutes to dress and make her way to the crime scene. She parked her vehicle two blocks away from all the flashing lights and went to find her partner.

One of the patrol officers gave her a curt nod as she ducked under the crime scene tape. He'd asked her out once not long after she'd made detective, but she hadn't wanted to mix work with pleasure. It was a good thing she'd turned him down, too, since a few weeks later he'd ended up meeting his wife. They now had two little ones with a third on the way.

She shook her head. It was strange how life worked sometimes.

Paul was standing next to the coroner with a notepad in his hand. He looked up as she approached. "Sorry to drag you out as soon as you got back in town, but it will go a lot faster with two of us."

"You said there were a dozen witnesses?"

He tilted his head toward a group of people who were being guarded by two patrol officers. "At least. Those are the people who stuck around. Given the area, though, I'd guess there are more. Tomorrow morning we'll probably have to come back and go door to door."

"Sounds like fun." Janey pulled out her notepad and pen. "I guess I should get started."

It was four in the morning by the time they finished interviewing their last witness, a young mother who'd recently moved into the area and was now questioning whether or not it was a good neighborhood in which to raise her family. Janey was exhausted. Between all the exercise she'd got and the two-hour drive back to Indianapolis, she'd been ready to get some much-needed sleep. As it was, she could barely keep her eyes open and she still had to go back to the station and file her report.

"You got everything?" Paul asked.

"Yeah." She could feel the bags forming under her eyes, but sleep was going to have to wait. They'd divided and conquered, which meant they needed to compile all their notes and look for similarities. Going through witness statements was a lot like trying to put together a puzzle that had a lot of wrong or irrelevant pieces mixed in.

"Why don't we head over to the truck stop? I need some food before we head to the station."

As soon as he mentioned food, her stomach growled. "Food sounds great."

Paul opened the door to his car and climbed behind the wheel. "I'll meet you there."

Fifteen minutes later they were sitting in a corner booth, cradling mugs of coffee. The diner at the truck stop wasn't fancy, but it was open twenty-four hours a day, which came in handy when they had to pull an all-nighter.

"What ended up happening with the beer bottles?"

She took a sip of her coffee. "Unless they found something after I left, nothing so far. Apparently, it's not uncommon for the local teens to party in the cornfields. Even if we track down whoever the beer belonged to, it doesn't mean they were there Thursday night."

"Any other leads?"

Janey shook her head. "Not really. We don't have the full autopsy report yet. Maybe that will turn up something."

"I'm not getting my hopes up. If it is the same person who's behind this, they didn't leave much the first time around."

"If it is the first time," Janey said.

Paul raised his eyebrows as he peeked up at her from over his coffee cup. "You think there are more victims?"

"I don't know, but it seems too clean for a first timer. This person either has had practice or knowledge of forensics." No DNA on the first body. The only visible marks were from a Taser and the blunt force trauma of the fatal blow. These didn't feel like rash killings to her. These were planned out. Or, at least, that's what it seemed to her.

He nodded. "I was thinking the same thing over the weekend. It's too clean. If it were a heat-of-the-moment type killing then it would be sloppier."

Their waitress, a young woman who didn't look to be much past eighteen, strolled up to their table with their food. Paul's plate was piled high with eggs, bacon, and home fries. Janey had gone for something a bit healthier. "Can I get you two anything else? More coffee?"

"Yes, please," Janey said, knowing they'd both need more caffeine.

Paul picked up his fork and dug in before their waitress had left the table.

"What would Megan say if she saw you eating that?" Paul had his yearly physical last month and his blood pressure was slightly elevated. Nothing major, but his doctor recommended that he eat more fruits and vegetables and less meat and potatoes. Since then, Paul's wife had completely revamped their diet, sending him to work with a packed lunch full of things like carrot sticks and hummus.

"I eat the rabbit food most of the time, but I've been up all night and I need my protein."

Janey chuckled. "I'll remember to mention that the next time I see her."

"You wouldn't."

She just shrugged. No, she wouldn't, but he didn't need to know that.

They finished eating their breakfast but neither seemed to be in any hurry to leave. They had a pile of paperwork waiting for them at the station, let alone the debriefing about her trip to Liberty. It was going to be a very long day.

* * *

Kyle parked his patrol vehicle and headed into the station. It had been a slow night for the most part. He'd tagged Brad Napper, owner of the local hardware store, going seventy in a fifty-five. Brad was well known for having a lead foot. Especially on the country roads where there wasn't a lot of traffic.

The rest of his shift had been quiet. He'd made his rounds, checked on the local businesses to make sure they were locked up tight, and patrolled some of the lesser-used roads for any signs of suspicious activity, but nothing looked out of place. The most excitement he got was when he was driving past the diner, saw some movement, and then a second later realized it was a raccoon raiding their dumpster.

All that non-activity had given Kyle a lot of time to think about the weekend he'd spent with Janey. Every time he closed his eyes he could see her laid out on his bed, her blond hair fanned across his pillow as she smiled up at him. Those lips of hers begged him to kiss them. It was as if he were addicted to the taste of her mouth. Crazy, but he couldn't deny it. He'd spent hours kissing Janey as they'd lain in his bed Sunday afternoon, and he couldn't wait for a repeat performance.

There was only one problem with his fantasy. She lived two hours away.

Granted, two hours wasn't the other side of the world. He could drive down and back in one day if he wanted to, but given both their jobs, it wasn't something they could do on a whim. Being a deputy meant he had a fairly set schedule. Yes, he could get called out for something special or pick up extra shifts from time to time, but it wasn't the same for Janey. She was a detective, which meant she was almost always on call.

Mac waved to him as he climbed the stairs, hurrying to catch up. "Morning."

"You're here early," he said, opening the door and motioning for her to go first.

"I was hoping to go over the body one last time before it's released to the family. They're supposed to be in to sign the release forms at noon."

"Do you really think you missed something?" Knowing Mac, that was unlikely.

She heaved a sigh. "No. But considering I haven't found much, I'm holding out for a miracle, I guess."

"Still no hits on the fingerprints or DNA, I take it?"

"The fingerprints were a bust and the DNA won't be back for at least a week." She sounded frustrated, which he could completely understand. There was a murderer on the loose—maybe a serial killer if their John Doe turned out to be related to Janey's victim in Indianapolis. No evidence meant no suspect.

"Hopefully we'll get lucky and get a hit on the DNA, then."

"Maybe. But I'm not holding my breath. I did get some material from under John Doe's nails, but it looked like dirt to me." She hugged the binder she'd been holding to her chest and worried the bottom of her lip with her teeth.

"What is it?" he asked, not liking her hesitation.

"There's just something about this case. I don't like it."

"You and me both. Janey and I searched the area where the body was dumped but didn't find anything new that would point us in the direction of the killer. I was really hoping we'd get a hit on the fingerprints. At least we could talk to the kids and find out if they saw anything. Right now there are too many unanswered questions."

She nodded, and then did a complete one-eighty. "Speaking of Detective Davis, I heard she spent the night at your house after the hog roast."

That was one thing about small towns. It was really hard to keep a secret. "I didn't think you were one to listen to gossip."

"It's not gossip if it's true. Besides, I drove by your house on the way into town on Sunday and saw her vehicle parked outside. It doesn't take a rocket scientist to put two and two together."

There was no reason to deny it, especially not to Mac. He liked Janey, and if he had his way, it wouldn't be the last time she spent the night at his house. "Yeah. She spent the night."

Mac glanced down and then over to the door that led to the stairwell before looking at him. "Are you going to see her again? Unofficially, I mean."

Kyle always knew Mac had a bit of a crush on him, but she'd never pushed the issue. They'd known each other since they were kids, and to be honest he'd never seen her as more than a friend. Growing up, she'd been a tomboy, right there beside him and the other guys climbing trees and playing with bugs. Even though he'd seen her growing up into a beautiful and incredibly smart woman, he'd never really thought of dating her. He could laugh and joke with Mac for hours, but that was all it had ever been for him. "Yes."

"I thought maybe you might. When she was here"—he saw her swallow and she averted her eyes again—"you two had chemistry."

He knew he needed to be honest, even if it hurt. "I like her."

Mac nodded. "I like her, too. She'll be good for you, I think."

"Mac—"

"I should get going. Twelve o'clock will be here before I know it."

She crossed the room and reached for the door handle. "I'll catch up with you later."

Before he could respond, she'd opened the door and disappeared. He could hear her footsteps as she descended the stairs to the basement.

Kyle debated going after her but decided against it. What would he say to her, in any case? He'd never lied to her. He'd never given her false hope. None of which made him feel any better.

Taking a deep breath, he signaled to the desk attendant to buzz him in. He'd give Mac a little time. For now, he had a report to finish and some sleep to catch up on.

CHAPTER 8

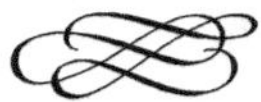

JANEY DOWNED what had to be her tenth cup of coffee. It was the only thing keeping her going. After breakfast, she and Paul had driven to the station to begin typing up their reports. Halfway through they'd gotten a tip for one of their other cases, so as soon as they'd finished filing their report they had to head out. She was close to thirty-four hours with no sleep, and she was feeling it. If not for the coffee, she'd have been conked out on her desk. All she wanted was her bed. Instead, her eyes glazed over from staring at the passing buildings as Paul drove them to the station after chasing another dead end.

"You still awake over there, Davis?" Paul asked.

"Yeah. It's just been a long couple of days, that's all. My bed is calling my name."

"I'm with you there."

When they got back, Janey planned to get in her vehicle, swing by a drive-through on the way home because there was no way she had the energy to make dinner for herself, and then go home and crash. She was having daydreams of her nice comfy bed when Paul's phone rang. He answered it and put it on speaker since he was driving. "Daniels."

"I missed you this morning."

He glanced at Janey before clearing his throat. "Um, I'm driving so I have you on speaker. Janey's with me."

"Hi, Janey."

Janey chuckled. "Hello, Megan. Sorry I kept him out all night."

"Are you guys on your way home?" Megan asked.

Paul made a right and moved into the left lane. "Turning in to the station parking lot now."

"Any idea when you'll be home?"

He parked the car and shot Janey a look. Paperwork was the last thing either of them wanted to do, but it was part of the job. "We probably have about a half hour of paperwork to do and then I can head out."

"Good. That will give me time to finish the ribs and bake the mac and cheese," Megan said. "Janey, you should come, too. I'm making plenty."

It was tempting. She loved ribs.

"Come on. You've got to eat. Besides, Chloe would love to see you."

Megan wasn't going to make this easy. And apparently, neither was Paul. "She's right. You do have to eat."

Janey rolled her eyes at her partner. "All right."

"Yay. I'll see you in a bit." Megan paused. "And Paul?"

"Yes?"

"Don't take too long." Megan's flirty goodbye to her husband had him swiftly grabbing for the phone.

Sure enough, a second later his phone dinged, letting him know he had a text message. Janey didn't see it, but whatever it was had her partner sweating under the collar. Knowing Megan, it was probably a picture of her wearing very little.

Janey opened the door and stepped out. When she noticed he wasn't doing the same, she poked her head back into the vehicle. "You coming, Daniels?"

He looked up at her, then back down at his phone before reaching for the door handle. "Yeah."

Shaking her head, she walked inside, knowing he was right behind her.

Less than forty minutes later, she was pulling into Paul and Megan's driveway. Paul climbed out of his vehicle ahead of her, and she followed him up the driveway to the side of the house.

Their home was in a small subdivision with lots of other young families. It was the exact opposite of the condo where Janey lived. Then again, she didn't have kids. Or even a dog. So there was no need for a yard.

Plus, there were definite perks to living in a condo. One of those was the close proximity to nightlife. Janey loved to dance, and she frequented a couple of clubs that were within walking distance of her home. That wasn't something one would find in the suburbs.

It wasn't something you'd find in a small town like Liberty either.

Before going inside, Janey checked her phone. Kyle said he'd call her tonight, but she had no idea when. And that little voice inside her head kept telling her not to get her hopes up.

She tucked her phone into her pocket and went inside. Either he'd call or he wouldn't. She would have to deal with it either way. There was no point in stressing about it.

"Janey!" Chloe saw her before she'd stepped over the threshold. The little girl hopped off her chair and ran toward Janey at full speed.

Bending down, she embraced the little girl.

"I haven't seen you in soooo long," Chloe said as she continued to hug her.

Janey laughed. "It's only been two weeks."

Chloe removed her arms from around Janey's neck and reached for her hand. She led her to the table and resumed her seat before handing Janey a piece of paper. "I started the first grade."

The paper had the letter *D* at the top and the rest was lines. Chloe had begun making her uppercase D's to match the example. She was already halfway done filling the page.

Janey pretended to examine the paper, nodded, and handed it back to Chloe. "Do you like your teacher?"

"Yes! Mrs. Simon is really nice." Chloe leaned in as if she were going to confide something to Janey. "Daddy and Mommy are in the other room."

Pressing her lips together to keep from spoiling what Chloe felt was a serious moment, Janey asked, "What do you suppose they're doing in there?"

"Kissing," she whispered.

"You think so?"

Chloe nodded. "I think Daddy likes kissing Mommy. He does it *a lot*."

Luckily, she was saved from answering when the couple in question strolled back into the room. Megan's hair looked slightly out of place and her shirt wasn't quite sitting right. Paul, on the other hand, had a rather smug look on his face.

"Everything is pretty much ready. We just need to finish the ribs off on the grill and carry the rest of the food outside."

Two hours later, she was sitting in Paul and Megan's backyard, belly full, and with no desire to move. Paul was helping Chloe build a sandcastle in her sandbox while Janey and Megan watched on from the sidelines.

"How was your trip to . . . where was it again?" Megan asked.

"Liberty. It's a small town about two hours north of here." Janey contemplated whether to say anything about Kyle to Megan. Although Megan was younger than her by several years, she was the only close girlfriend Janey had. The downside was that if she told Megan, Megan would tell Paul. For that reason, she decided to keep it to herself. At least for the time being.

"I've never heard of it. What's it like?"

"It was nice," Janey said. "Small, but quaint." Trying to think of things she could say without giving too much away or revealing things about the case, she added, "I went to a hog roast."

"A what?" The look on Megan's face was priceless.

"They roast a pig in the ground all day, and then dig it out and serve it at a big party in the evening. They had a band, dancing, and a bonfire."

"Sounds . . . interesting."

Janey shrugged. "It was fun."

Megan looked doubtful.

"Hey," Paul said, coming up to them and wiping the sand from his hands. "I'm going to take Chloe inside so we can finish her homework and get her ready for bed."

Janey stood. "I should probably go."

"You don't have to," Megan said.

"I know, but I should head home before I'm too tired to drive. It's been a very long day."

She said her goodbyes and made her way home. With every mile she drove, her exhaustion began to catch up with her. By the time she reached her front door, Janey felt as if she had weights on her eyelids. All she wanted to do was fall into her bed and sleep for the next twelve hours.

* * *

Janey had no idea how long she'd been asleep, but something was making a noise and it wouldn't stop. She groaned and forced her eyes open.

To her surprise, it was light out and the insistent noise was coming from her phone.

Forcing her feet to the floor, she went to get her phone from the dresser. The incoming call was from Paul. "What's up?"

"Did I wake you up, Davis?"

She rubbed the sleep from her eyes and stretched. "Yeah. I guess I forgot to set my alarm."

He released a loud sigh. "You realize you were supposed to be at work over an hour ago, right?"

Glancing at the clock confirmed what he'd told her. It was after nine in the morning. She was an hour late for her shift. "Shit. I'll be there as soon as I can shower and change."

It had been a while since Janey had gotten ready in such a mad dash. Even still, it was pushing ten by the time she ran into the station.

"About time, Davis," her captain said as she rushed by him on her way to her desk. He didn't look amused.

"Morning, Captain."

She slid into her seat at her desk across from Paul. He raised his eyebrows in question. "You sure you're okay?"

"I'm fine. I was just exhausted. I thought I'd set my alarm before I nodded off, but I guess not. Knowing my luck, it'll go off at six tonight."

He gave her a long look and then nodded. "You ready to get started, then?"

The bulk of their day was spent on paperwork and searching through records. They went over their cold cases to see if anything new jumped out at them. Most of the time it didn't, but sometimes they got lucky, like today when there'd been a break in a case they'd been working on for well over a year.

Janey was climbing into Paul's car when it hit her that she hadn't heard from Kyle. Or, at least, she didn't think she had. Truth be told, she hadn't looked at her phone other than to take Paul's abrupt wake-up call.

Sure enough, a check of her phone showed that she had a missed call from last night. Based on the time stamp, Kyle had probably called her right before his shift.

Paul was still talking to the store clerk, so she sent a quick text.

Janey: Sorry I missed your call. I fell asleep early last night. Call you later?

A response came about a minute later, right as Paul was getting into the vehicle.

Kyle: I'll be waiting.

The corners of her mouth lifted in a tiny smile.

"Something you want to share, Davis?" It was only then she

realized Paul hadn't started the car. Instead, he was looking at her, waiting.

She put the phone away and reached for her seat belt. "Nope. Just checking to see if I had any messages, that's all."

Paul looked doubtful but didn't push it. Starting the engine, he maneuvered them into traffic.

Luckily, there were no new cases sitting on their desks when they returned to the station, so they were able to write up their report on the lead they'd pursued and call it a day. She was eager to get home, not only because she had plans to call Kyle but because she wanted some downtime. It felt as if she'd been going nonstop since she got back to Indianapolis. A nice bubble bath and a glass of wine sounded close to perfect.

* * *

Kyle had just woken up when he got the text from Janey. He'd been getting a little worried when she hadn't answered his call last night, but he figured she might be at a crime scene or something. Then she hadn't messaged him back either. He knew they were still feeling things out and that it would take time, especially with their schedules, but it had made him nervous. He cared about Janey more than he probably should given they'd known each other for a few days. That didn't change the fact that his heart rate increased every time her name popped up on his caller ID.

Removing his French bread pizza from the microwave, he checked the clock for what had to be the twentieth time in less than an hour, and then carried his dinner to the table. It was crazy how nervous he was waiting for her to call. Janey wasn't his first girlfriend. Hell, he'd been in a war zone and hadn't been this anxious.

His pizza almost slipped from his fingers when his phone rang. He didn't even bother to look to see who it was before answering. "Hello."

"Hi," Janey said.

He leaned back in his chair, his pizza forgotten. "You called."

"I told you I would, didn't I?" Her voice filtered through the line, easing the tension that had been building.

"You did."

The line was quiet for a long moment before Janey spoke. "Sorry about last night. After we talked Sunday evening, I got called out to a major crime scene. We were there all night, and then I worked straight through the day. By the time I got home, I was drained. I didn't even hear the phone ring when you called."

"Sounds exhausting."

She released a half laugh/half snort type sound that had him grinning. "It really was."

"I'm sure it didn't help that I'd kept you up for most of the previous night either."

Janey released a soft sigh, one that had him needing to adjust himself. "Yes, you did."

"I didn't hear any complaints at the time." He loved flirting with her.

Instead of stroking his ego, she gave him sass. "Confident, aren't you?"

"Very."

"You might have to work on that cockiness, Deputy Reed."

"You were quite fond of that part of my anatomy, if I recall."

He could almost see her rolling her eyes at him through the phone. "I said cockiness. Not cock."

Kyle laughed. "Is there a difference?"

"I'm beginning to wonder."

He didn't think he could grin any wider if he tried. "How was your day?"

"Boring. Yours?"

"About the same. I did run into Mac this morning at the station. She wanted me to tell you hi."

There was a long silence on the other end of the phone.

"Janey? Everything okay? You didn't fall asleep on me again, did you?"

She chuckled. "No. I'm still here."

"Okay. So why did you get quiet on me?"

"Mac likes you." Then she hurried to add, "Not just as a friend."

He released a loud breath. "I know."

"And . . ."

If this wasn't such a serious conversation, Kyle would be amused by the way she was trying to get him to tell her his feelings for Mac. "And I don't feel the same way."

"You live in the same town. You work together. You're friends. A relationship between you two would be easy."

"Who are you trying to convince?" He sat up and began picking the pepperoni off his pizza. "It's you I want, Janey. Not Mac."

She didn't say anything.

"Is this about the long-distance thing again?"

"It's only been two days and we're already having trouble."

He raised an eyebrow. "This is trouble?"

"You know what I mean."

"No. I don't think I do."

Janey exhaled. "Right now things are new and it doesn't bother you that I missed your call, but eventually you're going to get tired of it. Eventually, you're going to decide it's not worth it."

A few things clicked into place in his head. He might not be a detective, but as a police officer he'd learned to read people pretty well. She wasn't talking in the hypothetical here. She was speaking from experience. "Who was he?"

"What?"

He didn't beat around the bush. "Who was the guy who broke your heart?"

It took her a while to answer, so long in fact that he didn't think she was going to. "His name was Ted." She hesitated. "It was a long time ago."

Apparently, it wasn't long enough if she was still letting it affect her relationships. "What happened?"

"It's not important."

"Janey?"

"Yes?" When they were teasing each other, she was all confidence. At the moment, she sounded anything but.

"I want to understand why you're so hesitant about us giving this a shot, and I can't do that if I don't know what happened between you and Ted to make you feel this way."

Again there was a long pause. It took everything in him to sit there and wait her out. "I was seventeen. He was nineteen. We started dating when I was a freshman and he was a junior. Everything was great until he went off to college in Ohio."

He could already see where this was going, but he kept his thoughts to himself.

"At first, things were the same as they always were. We talked on the phone almost every day, and he'd come home on breaks. Then things started to change. He still came home, but we didn't do all that much talking when he was there. All we really did was fool around."

She stopped talking.

He waited, but after several minutes he grew concerned. "You all right?"

"Yeah." He thought he heard a sniffle, but he couldn't be sure. "Then the summer between my junior and senior year, things changed."

He was trying not to push, but he also wanted to understand. "What happened?"

"A lot of things." It came out in a whisper, but in a firmer voice she went on. "When he went back to school in the fall, he was distant. I didn't hear from him for two weeks. Then one Saturday night he called me to say he couldn't do it anymore, that this long-distance thing was too much for him to try and balance with school and everything."

A long silence filled the air and he got the distinct impression that she was leaving something out, but he didn't want to push. As she'd mentioned before, their relationship was new. Trust was something that came with time, and he was willing to earn hers.

"I found out a few weeks later that he had a girlfriend at college and that they'd been dating for several months." Janey released a heavy sigh. "It took me a long time to move on. I almost failed the first quarter of my senior year. I probably would have flunked out entirely if not for my grandmother. She sat me down after seeing my grades and told me I needed to get my act together and not let what happened destroy my future."

He was at a loss for words. "She sounds like a smart lady."

"She was." The love for her grandmother came through the phone. "I miss her."

"I'm sorry." Kyle wished he could be there to hold her. He didn't like having these types of conversations over the phone.

"Like I said, it was a long time ago."

She might be trying to brush it off, but he knew better. "He was an ass."

That got a weak chuckle out of her. "Yes. Yes, he was."

CHAPTER 9

JANEY COULDN'T BELIEVE she'd told him all that. Or that she'd almost told him about her daughter. She never talked about that. Paul knew about Ted, but she'd never told him about the baby. It wasn't something she liked to relive, and yet tonight it had been on the tip of her tongue.

Reaching for the glass of wine she'd brought into the bathroom with her, she took a long drink. "Sorry. I didn't mean to dump all that on you."

"That's what boyfriends are for, right?"

The sides of her mouth tilted up in a smile. "Is that what you are? My boyfriend?"

"I guess that's up to you, now isn't it?" The teasing lilt was back.

When she didn't answer, he cleared his throat and got all serious. "Janey Davis, will you be my girlfriend?"

She shook her head and giggled. "You're insane."

"Maybe." He waited until her laughter died down. "You didn't answer the question, though."

Leaning her head back against the cool porcelain of her tub, she closed her eyes. It was crazy . . . insane. They hadn't known each other for that long. They didn't even live in the same town. Agreeing to be his girlfriend made no logical sense, and yet her instinct was to say yes. "Don't you want to date other people?"

His answer was simple and direct. "No."

She took another sip of her wine, hesitating before giving her response. Not because she didn't want to be his girlfriend, but because she knew what it would mean. At least, to her. "Okay."

"Okay?"

"Yes. Okay. I'll be your girlfriend."

"Good." She could picture him on the other end smiling from ear to ear. "When can I see you again?"

Janey sat up, sloshing the water and sending some over the side of the tub. "Um. I don't know."

"I have next weekend off. What if I come down to visit?"

"Come here?" She wasn't sure why, but she'd always thought she'd be the one traveling to see him all the time.

"Why not?" He paused. "Unless you don't want me to come to your place."

"No. It's not that." She hurried to clarify. "I just didn't think you'd want to come to Indy."

"I'm down that way at least a few times a year. Now I have a reason to go more often."

Her belly did a little flip when his voice dipped low. It was as if he were right there beside her, whispering it in her ear instead of two hours away.

"I'm on call Saturday night, but we could do something during the day." She was already mentally going through a list of the other detectives to see if maybe she could trade with someone. Paul would do it if she asked, but then she'd have to tell him why she needed to switch.

"I'll have to hope everyone behaves themselves Saturday night so you don't get called out, then."

The water was beginning to cool, so she drained the rest of her wine and placed the empty glass on the floor. "Can you hold on for a minute?"

"Sure. Everything all right?"

"Yeah. I just need to get out of the bathtub and dry off, and I can't do that holding the phone."

He gasped. "You were naked the whole time and you didn't tell me?"

Janey rolled her eyes. "Yes. Naked. Wet. And covered in bubbles. Hold on."

Right as she pulled the phone away from her ear, he groaned. She couldn't help but chuckle. Men. They were so predictable.

She took her time drying off and putting lotion all over her body. As her hands skimmed over her skin, she imagined what it would be like having him in her space. Her condo was much smaller than his family home, but it was big enough for her.

After wrapping a towel around herself, she picked up the phone again, and strolled into her bedroom. "Miss me?"

"You're killing me."

She chuckled. "Nah. I think you'll survive."

"Doubtful. My cock is about ready to bust out of my pants thinking about you wet and naked. I don't know if I can wait till next weekend."

His voice dropped low again, causing her body to warm. It remembered every detail of their time together. "It'll be a very long two weeks."

"Ten days."

Her mouth was suddenly dry. Ten days until they saw each other again. Ten days until he was in her bed.

It was her turn to clear her throat. She needed to change the subject. Pronto. "What time does your shift start?"

There was a long silence, and then she heard him sigh. "I should probably head out. I want to check on a few things before I start on patrol tonight."

"Everything all right?" Liberty was a small town, but that didn't mean it was crime free.

"Yeah, it's fine. Ava wanted me to swing by and check on her chickens. She thinks a fox or a raccoon has been sniffing around, and she wants to make sure they can't get in the coop. I told her I'd stop by before my shift."

Janey opened her top drawer and selected a pair of dark blue panties. Tossing her towel in the hamper, she cradled the phone against her shoulder and shimmied her clean underwear up her legs. "Such a good brother."

He laughed. "I'll call you tomorrow. Sweet dreams."

"Good night."

She was smiling by the time he disconnected.

After throwing on one of her favorite old T-shirts, Janey made herself some herbal tea and climbed into bed. She wasn't on call tonight, so unless there was a break in one of their cases, she had the evening to herself.

There was absolutely nothing on television, so she popped in a movie. By the time the credits rolled, she was barely able to keep her eyes open.

She stopped the movie and was about to turn the television off when something on the news caught her eye.

"The body of a man was discovered today in the alley behind me," a reporter was saying. "Police say it's too early to speculate on the cause of death, but that the man appeared to have been hit over the head with a blunt object and that a Taser may have been used to subdue him."

Without even thinking about it, Janey reached for her phone.

A few seconds later, Paul answered, his voice groggy. "Hello?"

"There's been another one."

It took him a second to answer. "Another what?"

"Blunt force trauma to the head and a Taser used. This one was on the eastern side of the city. It was on the news. They found the body today in an alley."

"Guess we know what we'll be doing tomorrow."

"Yeah."

Paul sighed. "Get some sleep. It's probably going to be a long day tomorrow."

She knew he was right. "I'll see you in the morning. Good night."

"Good night."

Janey looked down at her phone and bit her bottom lip. Kyle would be on patrol. She shouldn't bother him. But if it were her, she'd want to know. Especially since it could be tied to the case in Liberty. She thought it was a stretch that there'd be two bodies with similar markings, but three? That wasn't a coincidence.

Janey: They found another body. Taser. Blunt force trauma.

His response came back almost immediately.

Kyle: Where?

Janey: East side of the city.

Kyle: Male?

Janey: Yes.

Kyle: Can't be random.

Janey: I don't think so either.

Kyle: I'll let Noah know in the morning.

She knew she needed to let him go. Not only did he need to focus on work, but she needed to get some sleep. Paul was right. Tomorrow would be a long day. Given there were now three victims, the higher-ups would no doubt want to be involved. There was going to be red tape up the wazoo. Just what they didn't need.

Janey: If we find out anything else, I'll let you know.

Kyle: Thanks.

She was about to put her phone down when it pinged again to let her know she had another message. It was a picture of Kyle in his uniform, sitting in his patrol car.

Kyle: Wishing you sexy dreams.

He knew just what to say to get her mind off the case and onto something a lot more pleasant.

Plugging her phone in beside her bed, Janey snuggled under the covers. She let her thoughts drift to Kyle. He'd be there in ten days. With her. In her home. In her bed.

She rolled over and spread her fingers over the empty space beside her. Running the tips of her fingers up and down the cool sheets, she imagined him there—his large body next to hers. The feel of his arms, his legs, his chest. Then he'd look at her with those blue eyes of his and that confident smile on his face and her heart would skip a beat.

Sighing, Janey retracted her hand and turned over on her back. It was going to be a long ten days.

* * *

Kyle strolled into the diner the next morning, removed his cap, and quickly located Noah. His friend had his nose in the morning paper.

"I'll be with you in a minute," Claire said as she carried three plates to a nearby table.

"That's okay. I'm here to see Noah."

She set the plates down on the table in front of her. "I'll be by with some coffee, then."

Nodding, he made his way down the aisle to where Noah was sitting.

His friend folded the paper he'd been reading and set it aside. "Wasn't expecting you this morning. Did you tick your sister off or something?"

Kyle sat down, and before he could get a word out, Claire was there with the coffee. "Your usual?" she asked him.

"Yes, please."

With that she was gone, leaving the two men alone.

"Ja—" He caught himself. "Detective Davis contacted me last night. Apparently there's been another victim."

"Same MO?" Noah asked.

"Looks that way. Detective Davis and her partner are going to check it out today. She said she'd let me know once they had more information."

Noah frowned. He glanced around. The diner was full of locals—the same as it usually was at this time of day. Luckily for them and their current conversation, none of them were close. "I don't like the idea that there may have been a serial killer in our town." He paused. "Or heaven forbid, is still here."

"I know. If this third victim turns out to be connected to the others . . ."

His friend took a sip of his coffee. An outside observer would think the two of them were talking about nothing more serious than the weather. "I want you to stay on top of this."

Kyle blinked. "You don't want to call in a detective from the state patrol?"

"No." Noah met his gaze with hard determination. "I know we don't have a full-time detective right now and that you've only been filling in when needed, but at the moment you know more about this case than anyone else here." Without so much as a pause, he added, "Plus, you're nailing the pretty detective from the city."

Almost choking on his coffee, Kyle forced the liquid down his throat.

"Can't say I blame you. She's easy on the eyes."

"Thanks. I think."

Noah chuckled. "Did you really think I wouldn't find out? Hell, I'm pretty sure half the town knows she spent the night at your house."

"Guess we weren't as stealthy as we thought."

"Yes, well, I'm not sure I'd call making out in your driveway stealthy."

"Who—"

"Your neighbor, Mr. Thompson, called me. He wanted to make sure I knew just what kind of officers I had working for me." Noah's amusement was clear. He was grinning from ear to ear like the Cheshire cat.

Kyle grunted. "I should have known."

"Yes, you should have. You grew up around here. You know how it works in a small town."

Claire walked up to the table, two plates in her hands, and placed them in front of Kyle and Noah.

"Thanks," they both said.

"Can I get you anything else at the moment?"

They both looked at each other, and Noah answered her with a smile. "I think we're good."

"Holler if you need anything," she said, already backing away.

They ate in silence for a few minutes, each one too focused on their food for conversation. Kennedy refilled their coffee and gave Noah a wink before heading back behind the counter.

"I think she likes you," Kyle said to Noah.

His friend shot him a confused look. "She flirts with everyone."

It was true. Kennedy did flirt with most of the male diners, but that wasn't the point. "You should ask her out."

"Why would I do that?"

"She's single. You're single."

"So?"

"Don't you like her?" Kyle had no idea why he was pushing so hard. Okay, he did. While he loved Noah like a brother, he wasn't sure how he felt about Noah and Ava. Not that there was a Noah and Ava.

Noah polished off the rest of his eggs and bacon before responding. "I like her just fine, but that doesn't mean I'm going to date her." He pushed his plate aside and reached for his coffee. "Why don't you ask her?"

"Can't."

He raised an eyebrow in question. "Seeing the pretty detective again?"

Kyle raised his coffee cup to his lips and grinned. "Next weekend. I'm driving down to Indy."

"Good. You can find out what's going on with the case."

"That isn't exactly my motivation for going," Kyle said.

"I'm sure you can find some time in between your bouts of sex to acquire a bit of information." Noah finished his coffee. "I meant what I said. I want you to stay on this. I don't like the idea of a killer running around in my town."

Kyle didn't either. He gave his friend a curt nod.

After saying goodbye to Noah, Kyle drove to Ava's. He was a little later than usual, but his sister knew not to count on him showing up at a specific time. Given his job, the end of his shift didn't always line up with what it said on a clock.

"Anybody home?"

Ava was at the stove. She turned to look at him. "I was starting to think you weren't coming this morning."

"Sorry. I had to swing by the diner and talk to Noah." He pulled out the chair next to Cole's and ruffled his nephew's hair as he sat down.

"Something happen last night when you were out on patrol?" She finished stirring whatever was in the pot and removed it from the stove.

"No." He hesitated, knowing as soon as he brought up Janey's name his sister would latch on like a dog with a bone. "Janey contacted me last night with an update on the case, and I needed to fill him in."

Seeming to forget completely about why he and Janey were thrown together in the first place, she focused instead on the fact that she'd made contact with him. "How is Janey?"

"Fine." That, of course, was an understatement of epic proportions. Janey was way beyond fine.

His sister busied herself pouring what looked to be pie filling into several containers. She liked to make big batches when she could get the ingredients on sale at the local farmers' market and freeze it so she could use it later. "Hopefully they aren't keeping her too busy in the city."

Kyle knew what she was doing. His little sister was fishing to see if he and Janey were still seeing each other. "Considering they found another victim last night that looks to be connected to the case she's been working on and the man I found out by Sherman's place . . ."

"Oh no!" His sister's shoulders dropped and sadness for this stranger she'd never met filled her face.

Cole took that moment to drop a grape. It rolled across the floor and landed a few feet away from Ava. She reached down to pick it up without missing a beat.

"It's the same person, do you think?" she asked as she walked over to wash the grape before placing it once again in front of Cole.

"We don't know." They didn't, but his sister was smart. She knew, the same as they all did, that the probability was high.

Ava wiped her hands off and sat down across from him. She

picked up a piece of cereal and rolled it along the tips of her fingers for several moments before meeting his gaze. "You'll be careful, won't you?"

He opened his mouth to speak, but she cut him off.

"I know what you're going to say. You don't know yet why these men are being targeted. But that's all the more reason for you to be careful. I already lost my parents and a husband. I don't know if I could take it if I lost you, too."

Kyle covered her hand with his. He and Ava hadn't always been close, but since they'd both moved back to Liberty they'd gotten to know each other as adults. She was still his little sister and he was still the big brother—that wasn't ever going to change, but she was right. They were each other's only family. They were all each other had. "I'll be careful. I promise."

Ava stood and walked around next to him. She leaned down and hugged him. "I love you."

He wrapped his arms around her waist and returned the hug. "Love you, too."

They broke apart when Cole squealed. He apparently wanted in on the affection.

Kyle reached over, plucked him out of his booster seat, and stood him on his lap. "I think someone's jealous," Kyle said to Ava.

She smiled and ran a hand over her son's head and down his back. "Family hug?"

He stood, resting Cole on his hip, and brought Ava in for another hug. Cole let out a joyous giggle as Kyle and Ava both circled their arms around him.

This was why he'd moved back to Liberty.

CHAPTER 10

THE CAPTAIN WAS WAITING for them when Janey and Paul arrived at the station. He ushered them both into his office and closed the door. The look on his face was grim, and she braced herself.

"I spent an hour last night on the phone with the commissioner. He's not happy; nor am I."

Janey and Paul shot each other a look.

Their captain didn't seem to notice or didn't care. He crossed his arms in front of him. "I'm assuming you've both heard they found another dead body yesterday?"

"Yes, sir," Paul said. "Janey saw it on the news last night and called me. We figured we'd take a ride out to the crime scene today and drop by the coroner's office."

Captain Lane looked straight at her. "Where are you at with this case? Have you found anything new? Did they turn up any DNA or fingerprints in Liberty?"

"Mac—" She stopped and started again. "Their coroner, Dr. Mallory, found something under the victim's nails and sent it off to the lab. To my knowledge, they're still waiting on the results."

Paul chimed in. "We've been going through the evidence again, but there isn't much there. Whoever it is doing this is really good at cleaning up the evidence."

"Well, you need to find something. The commissioner already had a reporter call him yesterday asking if the cases were related. All bets will be off if they find out about the third victim in Liberty. We'll have a shitstorm on our hands, and I don't need to tell you what that means."

"No, sir," they both said in unison.

"Good." Captain Lane waved his hand, dismissing them. "Now get out of my office and find some evidence."

Janey and Paul hurried out of the captain's office, grabbed the file they needed, and headed out. The captain was right. They needed to find a lead somewhere and fast. If not, the press was going to descend and that was never a good thing.

The drive to the east side of town was slow. There was an accident, and as they were in an unmarked car and it wasn't an emergency, there wasn't much they could do except wait it out like everyone else.

It was almost ten by the time they pulled up to the crime scene. There was still yellow tape blocking the alley, and a patrol officer was standing guard. They both flashed their badges and he nodded for them to pass.

Janey had a sense of déjà vu. The alley was flanked by brick walls. It was roughly two car lengths wide, but some of that space was filled by three dumpsters that were positioned randomly along the right side of the alley.

As they approached the second dumpster, they could see the chalk outline of the body. Paul turned three hundred and sixty degrees, taking in their surroundings from the vantage point of their victim. "Off the beaten path and unlikely to be seen from the main road."

"Same as the other one," she said, agreeing with his assessment. She walked around to the side of the dumpster. "I don't see any signs of a struggle and minimal blood splatter."

Paul was scanning the area. He was looking for anything that might be a clue, the same as she was. They'd worked together long enough to trust the other's process. It was one of the advantages of working with the same partner for so long.

She knelt down to get a different perspective. It wasn't an overly sanitary place. Janey was still trying to come up with a way the attacker was convincing their victims to follow them down an alley.

Of course, the obvious answer was sex, which meant the suspect they were most likely looking for was a woman. The only potential problem with that theory was that none of the victims had been so hard up for cash they couldn't afford a decent hotel. It could be a prostitute, but that theory didn't feel right. They had to be missing something.

Janey was about to stand up when something caught her eye. "Daniels."

He turned to face her, lifting one eyebrow in question.

She pointed to what had caught her eye under the dumpster. It looked like a ring, but it was too far away for her to be sure.

"I'll get a blanket from the car," Paul said.

Since it was still an active crime scene, they didn't want to contaminate any potential evidence. Especially now.

Paul returned a few minutes later with a blanket and camera. He took a picture of the dumpster, then spread out the blanket and lowered himself down onto it so he could reach underneath.

Before he disturbed anything, he took several more pictures. With a pencil, he picked up the item. She was ready with an evidence bag when he held it up.

"You were right. It's a ring."

She examined it through the plastic. "Looks like a class ring."

"I don't recognize the school, though, so maybe a high school?" he asked, thinking out loud.

"Probably. And definitely a woman's ring." As excited as she was with this find, Janey tried to rein it in. The ring could have been there for weeks or months.

"Might not have anything to do with the murder, but at the very least maybe we can find its owner and return it to her. Do our good deed for the day."

Janey nodded, sealed the evidence bag, and tucked it into her pocket.

They took another look around, making sure they didn't miss anything else, and then headed for the coroner's office.

When they arrived, the coroner was not in a pleasant mood. "I'll tell you the same thing I told the other detectives. I don't have anything for you yet and won't for several more days."

"All we need are the basics. Do you have a cause of death?" Paul asked.

"Blunt force trauma to the skull. A first-year med student could have told you that."

"And there was evidence a Taser was used?" Janey prompted.

"Yes. The poor guy probably never saw the blow to the head coming."

Paul nodded at the body lying on the exam table. "Any idea what was used to hit him over the head?"

"Appears to have been made of metal. My best guess? A bat, most likely, given the shape of the wound. Once I get the lab results back, I should be able to tell you more."

Janey took a step closer to the body. "Anything else that you noticed? Were you able to pull any skin from under the nails?"

The coroner huffed. "No. And if you'll excuse me, I do have work to do."

"Of course," Paul said, nodding that Janey should follow him out. "We'll look forward to reading your report."

Janey waited until they were out in the hall to speak. "Someone woke up on the wrong side of the bed this morning."

"I'm sure the brass are breathing down his neck as much as they are ours." Paul checked his phone and returned it to his pocket. "Let's get that ring over to the lab so they can swab it for prints and DNA. It's a long shot, but right now it's the best lead we have."

Things went much smoother at the lab. Amy, one of the lab techs, had the ring logged and back to them in less than thirty minutes. Unfortunately, there were no usable fingerprints. "I'll give you a call once we have the DNA results."

"Much appreciated."

Amy grinned up at Paul, a dreamy look in her eyes. "Anytime, detective."

Janey had no doubt that Amy would be the one calling Paul personally with the results. No wonder they'd gotten such friendly service. "I thought maybe women would stop flirting with you so much once you had a ring on your finger."

They'd left the building and were almost to his car. He stopped and looked at her with confusion.

She tilted her head down and raised her eyebrows. "Please don't tell me you didn't notice."

He continued walking. "She was just being friendly."

Janey snorted. "Sure. You keep telling yourself that. Wanna bet Amy will make sure to call you directly with the lab results?"

"I'm the lead detective on the case. It would make sense for her to call me."

"Uh-huh."

They reached the vehicle and Janey climbed in.

Paul got behind the wheel and started the engine. He glanced over at Janey. "Should I have done something differently? Megan has always said I'm oblivious to stuff like that."

Chuckling, Janey put on her seat belt. "You can't help how charming you are, Daniels. Besides, sometimes it comes in handy. And if it means Amy will get the results to us that much faster, then I'm not going to complain too much."

* * *

The first thing Kyle did when he woke up was check his phone. He'd been secretly hoping there'd be a message from Janey. It didn't matter if it was about the case or just a quick hi.

He shook his head and threw the covers off his naked body before heading into the bathroom. After taking care of business, he jumped in the shower, shaved, and got dressed in a pair of jeans and a T-shirt.

He didn't have to be at the station for a few hours and he wanted to get in some target practice.

Grabbing his range bag, several boxes of ammo, and his service pistol, he locked up his house and drove to the range. He waved to a couple of guys he knew on his way in. Living in such a small town, it was almost impossible to leave one's house and not run into someone you knew.

Kyle blew through two hundred rounds of ammo before calling it quits for the day. He packed up his things and was headed out when he ran into an old buddy of his from the Army. "Austin? Is that you?"

"Hey, man." His old friend smiled and embraced him in a firm hug. "How've you been?"

"Good. You?"

"Can't complain. Wouldn't matter if I did anyway."

Kyle stepped back and took a good look at Austin. He had a few gray hairs around his temples, but other than that he hadn't changed much since the last time Kyle saw him. "What are you doing in Liberty?"

"I needed to get out of the city, so I took a job as a park ranger. I figure communing with nature has to be better than people screaming about how unfair their life is because someone took their parking space."

They'd served two tours together and they'd seen a lot of shit. After Kyle's second tour, he got out of the Army and came home. For several reasons. One was that he'd seen what being in a war zone had done to guys who'd been deployed over and over again. He didn't want to end up like that. "So you're here permanently?"

Austin shrugged. "We'll see how it goes. For now I'm renting a cabin not too far from here."

"Well, if you ever want to get a beer sometime, give me a call." Kyle took out one of his cards, scribbled his cell number on the back, and handed it to Austin.

"You ended up in law enforcement, huh? Couldn't get enough of the insanity?" Austin asked, nodding toward the insignia on Kyle's range bag.

"Something like that." Kyle's gaze fell on the clock that hung above the counter. "Look, I need to run. Give me a call and we'll get that beer."

"Will do." He slipped Kyle's card in his bag. "It was good to see you."

"You, too." Kyle walked toward the door but stopped a few feet from the exit. "Don't be a stranger."

Austin held up his arm in acknowledgement, and then disappeared behind the door that led to the shooting lanes.

Once outside, Kyle made a beeline for his car, threw his range bag behind the seat, and drove home. He needed to get changed, eat, and call his girlfriend.

Recalling their conversation the night before brought a smile to his face. He knew he'd thrown her off guard, but that had been his intention.

Kyle pulled into his driveaway fifteen minutes later. He had enough time to change and pop the leftovers Ava had sent home with him in the microwave before calling Janey. He snatched his range bag from behind the seat and jogged inside.

It took him less than five minutes to put on his uniform and attach his sidearm. With one last check to make sure he wasn't forgetting anything, he grabbed his cell and headed downstairs. He was already dialing Janey's number as he was putting his dinner in the microwave.

She picked up on the second ring. "Hey, handsome."

"Please tell me you're taking another bath tonight." His imagination hadn't stopped creating vivid imagines of her naked, wet, and covered in bubbles, as she'd so eloquently put it.

Janey's laugh was deep and sultry. "Not tonight. Tonight I was thinking of doing some yoga."

Thoughts of her ass in the air had him shifting to make more room in his pants. A common occurrence around Janey. "Tease."

"I promise to make it up to you when you get here."

The microwave dinged. He removed his food and carried it to the table. "I don't know. Between last night and tonight . . . and then no doubt all the teasing between now and when I get there . . ." He blew out a loud breath. "That's a lot to make up for."

"You'll just have to trust me."

He paused, pretending to think about it, and let out a defeated sigh. "All right."

"You're crazy," she said, chuckling.

"You know it." Kyle stabbed a piece of meat with his fork. "So how was your day?"

"Long. I walked in the door about five minutes before you called."

He looked at the clock. "Did you get stuck at a crime scene?"

"No. Daniels and I were going through all the evidence again trying to find some connection between our victims."

"Any luck?" He didn't want to make this all about work, but if he didn't ask, Noah would be up his ass.

"Not so far. The body they found yesterday has all the same markings as the other two. We're going on the assumption they're connected for now."

"Anything I can do to help?" he asked. It wasn't as if he didn't have connections.

"Not at the moment. We're still waiting on lab results and combing through paperwork." She paused. "We did find a ring at the crime scene today. No idea if it's connected to our killer, though. People throw lots of things in alleys."

"I know. You should see some of the things I find in the alleys here."

"Come across a lot of strange things in that small town of yours, do you?" The conversation turned more lighthearted after that, which was what he'd wanted. He was calling his girlfriend, not Detective Davis.

They talked until he reluctantly had to go or risk being late for the start of his shift. "I'll call you tomorrow night around the same time?"

"I look forward to it."

Kyle disconnected the call and took his dishes to the sink. After a swift rinse, he loaded everything into the dishwasher, swiped his keys from where he'd left them on the counter, and dashed out the door.

Given how late it was, the parking lot only had about ten cars in it and he recognized all of them. He climbed out of his vehicle and jogged up the stairs. Halfway up, he ran into Ethan heading in the opposite direction. He looked to be in a hurry. "Heading out?"

"Some of the cows got loose and Dad needs some help getting them rounded up. I'll have my radio with me if you need anything."

"Let's hope for a quiet night, then."

Ethan nodded and raced down the stairs toward his vehicle. He pulled out of the parking lot as Kyle reached for the door to go inside.

One of the nice things about working the night shift was that things were quieter at the station. Sure, there was still activity—a police station never completely stopped—but there was next to no civilian traffic this time of day. Everyone there worked for the department or the county.

Hayden waved as he passed by dispatch on the way to his desk. He waved back, and he could have sworn he saw her blush.

"There you are." Kyle looked up at the sound of Noah's voice.

"Hey," Kyle said. "What are you doing here so late?"

"Waiting on you."

Noah motioned for Kyle to come into his office, so he changed direction and headed in to talk to his boss.

"Close the door."

Kyle did as instructed.

"Did you find out anything more about the victim they found yesterday in Indianapolis?"

That's what this was about? Kyle lowered himself into a chair. "It looks to be the same as the others. Janey said they found a ring at the scene, but they don't know if it's connected yet."

"A ring? What kind of ring?"

Kyle shook his head. "I don't know. They're still looking into it."

Noah frowned. "You didn't ask?"

"No." He leaned forward and met his friend's gaze. "If you want me to find out information from her in an official capacity, that's fine, but if so, I need to do it on official time—hers and mine. Our conversation was off hours and I didn't want to make it seem like an interrogation."

They stared at each other for a long moment, before Noah sighed. "You're right. I don't like it, but you're right. Tomorrow I'll file the paperwork to get official copies of all the files on the other two murder victims. Maybe if you and I put our heads together, we can come up with a link between the victims. I don't doubt that Detective Davis and her partner are good at their jobs, but they don't know Liberty the way we do."

They sat for a minute not speaking before Noah dismissed him.

"Is it all right with you if I let Janey know you'll be making the request? I don't want her to think we're trying to step on their toes."

"Go ahead." Noah leaned back in his chair and folded his arms across his chest. "I wouldn't want to be responsible for causing problems in your relationship."

Kyle resisted the urge to roll his eyes. "Thanks. I appreciate it."

"Sure." His friend stood and reached for his keys. "Be safe out there tonight."

"Always am." Kyle opened the door and strode out into the main part of the station. After a brief stop at his desk to check his messages, he made his way out to his patrol vehicle to start his shift. Nothing like a talk with the boss to get the evening off on the right foot.

CHAPTER 11

EVERY EVENING KYLE would call Janey around six o'clock. She'd begun to anticipate it. So much so that Paul was beginning to get suspicious.

It all came to a head two days before Kyle was scheduled to come visit. Paul and Janey had been called to a hit and run. The victim was a teenager who'd been walking home from school. The young woman hadn't survived. It was heartbreaking seeing her lying there on the side of the road—even for someone who'd seen her fair share of dead bodies. It always hit hard when a child was involved.

Her phone rang as they were taking statements from witnesses. Janey had known who it was right away, so she didn't bother to look at the caller ID. She sent it straight to voice mail and went on with her interview.

Her partner noticed.

They were leaving the scene when he confronted her. "Something going on I should know about?"

She swallowed, nervous. "Like?"

"You've been acting . . . strange lately."

"In what way?" She should have known he'd catch on sooner or later. It wasn't as if she typically walked around all melancholy, but even she noticed a difference in her demeanor. Paul had worked with her for going on six years. He was bound to figure it out sooner or later.

He furrowed his forehead, deep in thought. "You seem"—he paused and glanced in her direction before turning his attention back to the road—"overly cheerful lately."

"Do I?" She looked out the window, hoping he'd let it go.

She should have known better. "Who called you when we were talking to that witness?"

"I forwarded it to voice mail."

"Yes." He drew out the word. "And you didn't bother to look to see who it was first. That tells me that you already knew who it was . . . that you were expecting the call."

Janey considered her options. She could lie to him. It was a personal matter, so it wasn't as if he needed to know who she was talking to and why.

Even thinking that had her feeling guilty. Especially after how she'd encouraged him to explore things with Megan. So she decide to be honest, albeit vague. "It was Officer Reed. I've been giving him updates on the case."

While that was true, it wasn't as if that was all they'd talked about during their nightly conversations. In fact, it'd only come up once or twice. More often than not, their talks steered clear of work-related topics.

Paul twisted his mouth to one side. "I didn't know you were still in contact with him. I guess that makes sense considering one of the victims was found in their jurisdiction."

She didn't comment.

They drove for several minutes before he broke the silence again. "Why is Officer Reed your contact, though? Don't they have a detective up there that should be handling the investigation?"

Janey was beginning to understand how he'd felt when she kept asking him how things were going with Megan. "I don't know. I wasn't introduced to a detective while I was there."

"So you were with Officer Reed the entire time?"

She saw the trap clear as day, but she had no idea how to avoid it. "Most of the time. Yes."

Again, Paul grew quiet. He didn't say anything until they reached the station. "When are you seeing him again?"

Not if, but when. "Umm."

He cut the engine and removed the keys from the ignition. "I knew something was going on after I caught you humming at your desk the other day. That, and you've done your best for the last week to leave exactly at five. I'm usually the one anxious to get home these days."

The gig was up. It wasn't as if she were trying to hide her relationship with Kyle. Not really, anyway. "He's driving down on Friday afternoon."

Paul nodded. "Staying for the weekend?"

"Till Sunday. He has to work Sunday night."

Her partner opened his door and got out. She followed suit.

They walked side by side across the parking lot to the station entrance. Right as they were about to go inside, Paul spoke up. "You two should come by on Sunday. I'll fire up the grill."

"I don't—"

He raised his eyebrows in question.

"I'll think about it."

Paul chuckled. "Don't feel so good when the shoe is on the other foot, now does it?"

He walked inside, leaving her standing there with her mouth hanging open.

It was after eight o'clock before she strolled into her condo. Kyle had left a message earlier saying he was sorry he'd missed her and that he'd talk to her soon. So far things had been great between them. The distance, while frustrating, didn't seem to trouble him. Instead, he'd said he couldn't wait to see her again.

It was a far cry from her previous experience.

Janey moved around her kitchen, gathering items to make a quick stir fry for dinner. It was late and she was starving.

As her food cooked, she picked up her phone and sent Kyle a quick text.

Janey: Sorry I missed your call tonight. We were at a crime scene.

A few seconds later came his reply.

Kyle: I figured you might be. Are you just now getting home?

Janey: Got home a few minutes ago. I'm making dinner. I was starving.

Kyle: What are you having?

Janey: Stir fry. I'm too tired to make anything else.

Kyle: Sounds more appetizing than my dinner. Hot dogs.

Janey filled her plate with the stir fry she'd made and retrieved a fork from the drawer. She was too hungry to bother carrying it over to the table.

Janey: Ava didn't send you home with leftovers today?

Kyle: She took Cole to visit his grandparents. She'll be back Thursday.

Janey knew Kyle and Ava's parents were deceased, so she had to assume he was talking about Ava's late husband's parents.

Janey: Where do they live?

Kyle: Kentucky. It's about a four-hour drive from here.

That had to be a long drive with such a young child.

Janey: So you're fending for yourself until she gets back?

Kyle: Something like that. I'll grab something at the diner in the morning, and then I have some frozen pizzas I can warm up. I'll survive.

She chuckled.

Janey: I'm sure you will.

Kyle: I've got to go. I'll call you tomorrow. Sweet dreams, baby. I miss you.

Janey grinned. And before she could second-guess herself, she typed her response.

Janey: I miss you, too.

She finished eating and cleaned up the small mess she'd made in the kitchen. It wasn't much—she'd kept her meal simple—but it still took almost fifteen minutes to put everything back in its place and load the dishwasher.

Satisfied her kitchen was in order, she switched off the lights and headed for the living room to see if there was anything on television. It was still early, but she didn't feel like going out. In fact, she hadn't been out clubbing since she got back from Liberty. Carla had asked Friday afternoon if she'd wanted to go out for drinks, but Janey had turned her down in favor of going home and waiting for Kyle's call. It was very unlike her.

Janey glanced at her phone, and then at the television. She was becoming a hermit. It wasn't healthy. Besides, she doubted Kyle was rearranging his life so he could talk to her. He had his sister and his friends. She'd just have to figure it out.

Balance. That's what she needed. She couldn't get completely swept up in Kyle and forget her friends.

Her hand was inches from the phone when she remembered how Paul had realized she was seeing someone. Carla was the type of person who easily picked up on subtle changes in people's behavior. It's what made her a good police officer.

While Paul might tease her about her new relationship, he would drop it if she asked him to. Carla? Not so much. Her friend was a diehard romantic. She was always trying to set Janey up with guys they ran into in the bar, pushing them together, hoping sparks would fly. Most of the time, however, Janey was looking for a way to get the guys to leave.

Carla's heart was in the right place, but she tended to go toward guys who liked to party. Janey loved to dance, but that was pretty much where it ended. She was too old for binge drinking and body shots.

Sighing, she settled back on the couch and flipped through the channels until she found something decent to watch. She'd call Carla tomorrow.

* * *

Kyle's Thursday night shift felt as if it was moving at a snail's pace. Other than tagging a speeder about ten miles outside town, it had been a quiet night. He'd had a lot of time to think about his upcoming weekend with Janey. While he'd enjoyed their phone calls and texts over the last two weeks, he couldn't wait to see her again.

He needed to get home and get some sleep, but first he had to swing by Ava's. She'd sent him a text the day before to let him know she and Cole were home, and he'd told her he'd see her in the morning.

It was a little after eight when he pulled up to Ava's bed and breakfast. The house seemed quiet, but then again Ava hadn't scheduled any guests since she knew she'd be out of town. He took the steps two at a time and let himself in, not bothering to knock.

"Anybody home?"

"In the bedroom," she called back.

He found Ava curled up in bed, Cole tucked beside her, watching the morning news.

This wasn't like her. He couldn't remember the last time his sister was still in bed at eight o'clock in the morning. She was an early riser. Always had been. "Are you feeling okay, sis?"

"I'm fine." When he gave her a skeptical look, she added, "I just thought I'd take the morning off, that's all."

If he didn't know her well enough, he probably would have let it go. He did know her, though. "Did something happen at Andy's parents'?"

Ava pressed her lips together and avoided his gaze.

Kyle crossed the room and took a seat on the end of the bed. "What happened?"

She shook her head. "It's nothing really."

He waited.

"Molly just said she thinks I work too much. That I'm not spending enough time with Cole because I'm too focused on the B&B."

"Does she not expect you to work so you can provide for you and Cole?" Kyle didn't understand where this was coming from. Granted, he'd only met Molly and her husband, Jacob, a few times, but they seemed to be practical people. Surely they understood that, being a single mom, Ava had to work, and the bed and breakfast allowed her to work from home.

Again, she hesitated. "I don't think it's the work, exactly. I don't think she likes the fact that Cole is exposed to so many strangers."

"I see."

"I explained to her that I make sure he's never alone with them, but ..."

"But what?" he prompted when she didn't continue.

"She implied that one of these days I'd have my back turned and something would happen to him." Ava met her brother's gaze, a pleading look in her eye. "Do you think that's true? Am I putting Cole at risk by running the B&B?"

"No, I don't." He took her hand in his and squeezed. "You're a great mom and you're careful about who you let stay here. Molly is overreacting. Maybe she's missing her son and doesn't like the fact that you and Cole live so far away."

"I told her they should come visit," Ava said.

"That's a good idea."

"I thought so. But she said Jake's too busy with work."

Kyle didn't like the way Molly had been trying to guilt trip his sister. "Their loss, then." He scooted closer and made sure she was looking at him. "Anything I can do to help?"

She gave him a tiny smile. "Want to help me make some cinnamon rolls?"

"Sure," he said, standing. "And then I need to talk to you about this weekend."

Ava lifted Cole from her lap and got out of bed. "What's this weekend?"

It was his turn to feel guilty, especially knowing how her visit with her in-laws had gone. "I'm off this weekend, so I was going to drive down to Indy."

The smile on his sister's face got bigger. "You're spending the weekend with Janey."

It wasn't really a question, but he answered it anyway. "Yes." Then he hurried to add, "But if you need me to stay here—"

"Don't be ridiculous. I'll survive. It's not the first time I've met with their disapproval, and I doubt it'll be the last." She picked up Cole and brushed past Kyle on her way to the kitchen. "You just have to promise me one thing."

"What's that?" he asked.

"I want you to ask her if she'll come for Labor Day weekend. You can say I invited her if that makes it easier."

He opened his mouth to respond, but she cut him off and reached into the cabinet for her rolling pin.

"I know what you're going to say. You don't know if she has to work, yada, yada, yada." She waved the rolling pin around in time with her last three words.

"You know me so well."

It was as if he hadn't said a word. "She won't be working the entire weekend, surely, which means she can come here for a day or two. Right?"

Ava finally came up for air as she placed the rolling pin down on the counter and pulled out her mixing bowl.

"I don't know."

She gave him a look that said she didn't like that answer.

"I'll ask, okay? That's all I can do. Happy?"

"Yes." She continued moving around the kitchen, Cole still on her hip.

He reached for his nephew, and the little boy came to him willingly. "Why are you so eager for her to come for Labor Day weekend?"

"I just want to get to know her better, is all. It's been a while since I've seen you this interested in a woman and, well, we really didn't have much chance to talk when she was here the last time."

"She stayed in your house." From his perspective, Janey and Ava had spent plenty of time getting to know each other already. Wasn't there some unspoken girlfriend bond or something that happened when borrowing each other's clothes?

"We had two real conversations. Two. And even then I don't know all that much about her. Where's she from? What's her family like? Does she have any siblings?"

"She's from Fort Wayne. I believe all her family is dead. And no, she doesn't have any siblings."

"Okay, smart ass."

He shrugged. "You asked."

Ava began putting ingredients into the bowl. "I like her, okay. I think she'd be good for you. But I know that long-distance relationships aren't sustainable forever. Eventually, one of you is going to have to move. I want her to feel . . . welcome."

"In other words, you're trying to bribe her into moving to Liberty."

"Joke all you want, big brother, but it's scary moving to a new town, even if you're doing it for love. I want her to know she has a friend. Friends. Here."

He thought about that for a moment and realized she was right. While he liked Indianapolis well enough, it wasn't home. He was a small-town guy. Not to mention, his sister was here. "Thank you."

She stopped what she was doing and gave him a questioning look.

"For wanting to make Janey feel comfortable here."

It was Ava's turn to shrug. "Like I said, I like her."

Kyle set Cole down on the floor and handed him a toy from the basket Ava kept in the corner. Then he walked over and gave his sister a hug from behind. "Thanks, sis."

She bumped him with her hip, and he stepped back. "You're welcome. Now grab me the eggs from the refrigerator."

For the next hour he helped her make the cinnamon rolls. Well, she made them for the most part while he kept Cole entertained. He hadn't spent much time around children since Ava was little, but he loved spending time with his nephew. He'd seen a lot of horrific things when he was overseas and even some pretty terrible ones as a deputy. There were a lot of good people in the world, but he saw a good number of them at their worst. It was amazing the joy he felt when Cole would look up at him with those big eyes of his and give him a toothy smile.

"So when are you leaving?" she asked as she slid a batch in the oven, interrupting his thoughts.

"I'll go home and catch a few hours' sleep, and then I'll head out this afternoon." He didn't need more than a few since he planned to be spending the night in Janey's bed.

Ava nodded. "You don't want to fall asleep behind the wheel."

"That wasn't quite my concern, but sure, let's go with that."

She rolled her eyes at him again. "You're such a guy."

He laughed. "Thank you?"

"You know what I mean. All you think about is sex."

"That's not true. I think about other things. Food, for example. How long until those rolls are done?"

"Ten minutes. Think you can last that long?" She finished dividing and wrapping the remaining dough and put it in the freezer.

He sighed. "It'll be hard, but I suppose I'll manage."

"Good for you. Now, why don't you wash the dishes for me while I get dressed?"

Kyle stood to attention and saluted his sister. "Yes, ma'am."

She lifted Cole from the floor and shook her head. As she was leaving the room, he could have sworn he heard her mumble "smart ass" under her breath.

CHAPTER 12

KYLE LEFT his house around two in the afternoon and headed south toward Indianapolis. The drive was fairly uneventful until he was about ten minutes outside the city. Traffic slowed until it was inching along. He tried to be patient, and normally it wouldn't have bothered him, but he was anxious to get to his destination. Janey's condo was not far from downtown and he wanted to be there when she got home from work.

After almost a half hour of stop and go, traffic began to move a little. It was still slow going, given it was close to five o'clock on a Friday evening, but at least he wasn't hitting the brakes every two seconds.

His heart rate picked up when he saw the sign saying Janey's exit was one mile ahead. He was almost there. According to the GPS, he'd arrive at his destination in seven minutes.

Once he was off the highway, he weaved through several residential streets, making note of his surroundings. It was a cop thing. He was getting a lay of the land, so to speak. In this case, it would also help him know Janey better. This was where she lived and worked.

"You've arrived," his GPS announced.

He followed the instructions Janey had given him and located the parking garage to her building. It was smaller than what he'd imagined. When she'd said she lived in a condo building, for some reason he pictured a high-rise with twenty-plus floors, but in reality it was no taller than any other building in the area and consisted of only five floors.

Parking his car wasn't difficult. Visitor spaces were clearly marked. He removed his bag from the back seat and went in search of her unit.

Janey had given him her pass code so he didn't have to wait in the garage for her to get home. He used it to get inside the building and then to her floor. They appeared to have a decent amount of security, which he could appreciate. It made him feel better knowing her building was secure and not just anyone could show up at her door unannounced.

While she'd given him her code to get to her condo, she had no way of giving him a key to get in, so he parked himself outside her door and waited.

At five thirty-seven, the elevator dinged, drawing his attention. The doors opened and Janey strode into the hallway. She spotted him immediately, and a radiant smile spread across her face.

"You made it."

Kyle pushed himself up off the floor and stood. "Did you think I wouldn't?"

"Some people have trouble finding the parking garage," she said. "I was expecting a phone call saying you were lost."

When she was within a few feet of him, he opened his arms, inviting her closer.

She walked into his embrace, and he wrapped his arms around her, letting her soft warmth seep into him. It felt wonderful to hold her again. Even better than it had felt the first time he'd stepped foot on American soil after his first deployment. Having her in his arms felt right.

Before he could wax sentimental, Janey pulled back. "Come inside."

She removed her key from her pocket and unlocked the door.

The inside of her condo had an industrial flair to it. There was exposed duct work along the ceiling and the same brick surrounding the windows as was on the outside of the building.

"What do you think?" she asked.

He thought he might have detected a hint of nervousness in her question—like she wanted him to like it but wasn't sure if he would or not. It was quite different from his home, but he hadn't expected it to be exactly the same. Even with the industrial elements, it had a certain amount of charm. "I like it. Did this used to be a factory or something?" He knew a lot of old manufacturing buildings were repurposed into housing.

"A shoe factory." Janey made her way into the kitchen. "Hungry?"

"I could eat."

Janey nodded. "I wasn't sure what you'd like, so I thought we could order in. There are several restaurants that will deliver." He'd thought her nerves were regarding what he thought of her condo, but she still sounded anxious. Or maybe *jittery* was a better word.

He walked over, took hold of her hands, and turned her to face him. "I'm not a picky eater. Whatever you want is fine."

She gave him a shaky smile and reached for a stack of what he assumed were takeout menus. "Okay. How about Italian? There's a little place—"

Kyle cut off her words with a kiss.

She froze for a second and then melted into him exactly as he'd hoped she would. Her arms circled his neck and she pulled his body closer to hers.

"That's better," he mumbled against her lips.

"Hmm," was her only response before she fused their mouths together again.

Before long he had her pressed up against the counter and her hands were dangerously close to the erection straining in his jeans to get out. "I thought you were hungry."

"I am." She kissed his jaw and down his neck.

He chuckled as he tilted his head to the side to give her better access. "I meant for food."

She popped the button on his jeans, relieving some of the pressure. A moment later he felt her hand dip inside and palm his cock.

What was he saying again?

Taking her face in his hands, he crashed his lips over hers and plunged his tongue inside her mouth. Janey moaned and flexed her fingers around his erection.

"Bedroom."

She ignored him, pushing his jeans down his hips and dropping to her knees. Her face was level with his very hard cock, and the only thing covering it was the thin layer of his underwear.

Leaning in, she gave his cock a very wet kiss, soaking the fabric. When she sat back on her heels again, she took hold of either side of his boxer briefs and yanked them down. His erection bobbed eagerly in her face.

Janey placed her hand at the base of his cock and guided him to her mouth. All he could do was hold on. She'd done this to him once before, but he couldn't remember it feeling this good. Then again, maybe it was just the fact that it was happening here and now, and the feel of her mouth was all that mattered. The world could blow up around them and he'd be oblivious.

As good as it felt, though, he didn't want to come like that. Call him crazy, but he wanted to be inside her. He'd driven for two hours to see her again, to feel her, and that's exactly what he wanted to do.

Lifting her from the floor, Kyle set her back on her feet. "Either you tell me where your bedroom is, or I'm going to take you right here on your kitchen counter."

She licked her lips, sending his pulse racing. Did the thought of them having sex on her kitchen counter turn her on?

Going up on her tiptoes, she gave him a hard kiss. She took his hand and led him out of the kitchen and through the living room.

Kyle barely noticed Janey's bedroom because the moment they stepped over the threshold she began stripping. First came her shirt, then her bra, then she was removing her pants. "Are you waiting for an engraved invitation, Deputy?"

He smirked and finished removing what was left of his clothes.

Janey sauntered toward him, her hips swaying, calling to him. He pulled her flush against him, their naked bodies aligning perfectly.

Wasting no time, he picked her up, wrapping her legs around his waist, and carried her to the bed. Her mattress gave way as he lowered them both down on it, fitting her beneath him, cradling himself between her legs. She felt just as good as he remembered.

Now that he had his hands on her, he didn't want to stop touching. His fingers explored her body, moving top to bottom and back up again.

Janey seemed to be doing the same, relearning, remembering what he felt like. He bucked his hips when she cupped his ass, her fingertips skimming along his cheeks. He wanted to be inside her, but he didn't want to rush either.

"It feels like it's been longer than two weeks," he said as he kissed down her neck on his way to her breasts.

She gasped as he took one of her nipples into his mouth. "It does."

As he licked and sucked, enjoying the feel and taste of her, Janey laced her fingers through his hair, holding him to her chest. Her breasts were perfect. They weren't huge, but they fit nicely in his mouth and hands with a little to spare. Not to mention how sensitive they were. Every time he scraped his teeth against her nipple a little moan escaped her throat. It had his cock ready to burst solely from the sound of her pleasure.

One of her hands left his head, and he heard a drawer opening.

He released her nipple and glanced up, although he had a pretty good idea of what she was doing.

Janey shoved a condom in his face. "I want you inside me. Now."

Kyle chuckled and took the condom from her. He leaned back on his heels and ripped the package open. "Impatient tonight?"

"You're not?"

He rolled the condom down his length and lowered himself on top of her again. "I was trying to go slow. Savor the moment."

She circled her legs around his waist, digging her heels into his ass, urging him forward. "Later."

* * *

Thirty minutes later, Janey had her head tucked into the crook of Kyle's shoulder, listening to his heartbeat. He had his arm around her, running his fingers through her hair. It was strangely hypnotic. Or maybe it was the postorgasmic endorphins.

She must have hummed or something because he asked, "Happy?"

"Very." Janey glanced up at him. "You?"

He smiled down at her. "I have a beautiful woman lying naked in my arms. What's not to be happy about?"

"So that's all it takes?" she asked, teasing. "A naked woman?"

Shifting his weight, he brought them face to face. He leaned closer, bringing their lips a breath apart. "Not quite."

Janey's heart was racing. It was like this every time with him. "I forgot *beautiful*, right?"

He nodded and gave her a soft kiss. "Right."

The sound of his stomach growling caused them both to chuckle.

"I should probably order us some food." Janey inched her way out of bed and went to find a long T-shirt.

"Not bad." Kyle propped himself up on one arm. "But I think I still prefer you naked."

She ignored his comment. "Italian still good or did you want something else?"

"Italian's fine. I think I'm gonna need the carbs."

He gave her that sexy smile of his, and it did something to her insides. "I'll get the menu."

It took almost an hour for their food to be delivered. Janey had returned to the bed and they'd spent the time talking. He told her about Ava's visit with her in-laws. Janey had never had in-laws before, but she'd heard horror stories from some of her coworkers.

They sat in her bed, surrounded by takeout containers full of spaghetti and meatballs, lasagna, and fettuccini alfredo. It had been a long time since Janey had eaten in her bed, but neither one had seemed anxious to leave.

"What's Ava going to do?" Janey asked once they started to eat.

"Nothing." He stabbed one of the meatballs and added it to his plate. "Or at least, she's not going to change what she's doing now. Ava screens all the families before she books them. Molly and Jacob are overreacting. It's happened a lot since Andy died."

"I'm sorry. That has to be horrible for Ava."

He paused for a long moment. "My sister wanted me to invite you to Liberty for Labor Day weekend. I promised her I'd ask."

"Okay." Janey was caught off guard a little at the invitation. She knew she'd be visiting Liberty again, especially if she and Kyle continued their relationship, but she hadn't planned on it being so soon.

"Okay, you'll come, or okay, you'll think about it?" Kyle asked as he twirled some pasta onto his fork.

"I'd have to check my work schedule." That anxious feeling returned and settled in the pit of her stomach. She didn't understand it, though. Everyone in Liberty had been friendly. But maybe that was the point. She felt comfortable there, and on some level that frightened her. She still didn't know if this thing between her and Kyle was going to last.

"I'll have to work, at least to help out during the parade, but you could hang out with Ava. She says she wants to get to know you better."

"Why?" Janey regretted the question the moment it left her mouth.

"She likes you. Besides," he said, giving her a wink, "you are dating her brother."

She froze with the fork halfway to her mouth. Things with her and Kyle felt like they were getting serious fast, and she wasn't sure how she felt about that.

"Hey, what's wrong?" He must have noticed she'd stopped eating.

"Nothing." When he gave her a look that said he wasn't buying it, she clarified. "I was just thinking that it feels like this thing between us is moving really fast. I mean we've only known each other for a few weeks."

"Is that a bad thing?"

Janey took a moment to think about it. Was it a bad thing? She liked him. A lot. Things between them, despite the distance, had been really good. In some ways, she felt closer to him already than she ever had to any of the other guys she'd dated. Even Ted, and she'd dated him for three years.

She decided to be honest. "I don't know."

"If it helps, it's a little scary for me, too."

"Really?" She was surprised by his admission. He didn't seem to have an issue with the pace of their relationship.

"I think about you all the time. You're the last thing I think about before I fall asleep and usually the first thought I have when I wake up. Not to mention the fact that most nights you star in my dreams as well."

She lowered her head as she felt heat rush to her cheeks.

Kyle lifted her chin so she would look at him again. "I've never felt this way about a woman, Janey, and yes, that scares me a little."

"Thanks."

He brushed his thumb along her lower lip and grinned. "Anytime."

They finished eating and put the leftovers away in the refrigerator. Once everything was cleaned up, it was still early, so they decided to get dressed and go for a walk. It was tempting to spend his entire visit in bed, but she didn't want their time together to be all about sex. She'd been there and done that before. She liked him. Really liked him. And despite her trepidation regarding the long-distance thing, she was going to give this thing between them an honest try.

"Got your keys?" he asked as they headed out the door.

"Keys, gun, phone. I'm all set."

He held open the door and motioned for her to go first.

It was a nice evening. It was warm, but there was a gentle breeze. Several people were out walking their dogs. She waved to a jogger they passed as they rounded the corner.

"A friend of yours?"

"Not really," Janey said. "We've passed each other jogging a few times. I don't think we've ever said more than 'hi' or 'good morning.'"

"You don't get that kind of anonymity in Liberty. Everybody knows everybody, or at least they know their mom or their cousin or . . . you get the idea."

Janey steered him into a little shop that sold the best cupcakes. "Isn't that weird? Everyone knowing everyone's business?"

"Sometimes," he said. "But you get used to it. Besides, when push comes to shove, the community pulls together, and I like that."

While she could see the appeal, Janey couldn't imagine that happening in a city as big as Indianapolis. Or even Fort Wayne, for that matter.

Before she could stop it, the question slipped out of her mouth. "Do you ever think about living somewhere else?"

They were standing in the bakery, looking at the menu, but he stopped and turned to face her. The look on his face was serious. "I traveled a lot in my early twenties. I've seen a lot of places, but nowhere but Liberty has ever felt like home."

"Oh." Well, she guessed she got her answer.

"But," he added, "I've also learned that home has a lot more to do with people than it does with a place."

The way he was staring at her had all the moisture leaving her mouth. "We should . . . probably order."

He held her gaze for a moment longer, nodded, and turned his attention to the menu again.

They ended up getting a chocolate cupcake and a red velvet cupcake. Finding a table by the window, they split the treats in half and each took a piece.

"These are really good." He downed his half of the chocolate cupcake in two bites.

"I know," Janey said. "I eat way more of them than I should. Every time I pass by this place, I can't resist stopping in."

She was still working on her first half when he finished his red velvet cupcake. "Going to finish that?"

Janey pulled her cupcakes closer when he pretended to snatch them from her plate. "These are mine. If you want more, go order yourself more."

He chuckled but didn't make any move to get up and order another.

They sat watching the people pass by as she finished her cupcakes. "Have you ever thought about getting a dog?"

She polished off her last bite and began gathering up her trash.

He did the same.

"Not really. My schedule is too crazy." She waited for him to dispose of his trash as well before they headed back out onto the street.

"Makes sense." They began walking back toward her condo. "I've thought about getting a dog, and then I talk myself out of it. Like you said, crazy schedules and dogs don't mix. While mine might not be as crazy as yours, I work long hours and sometimes pick up shifts during the day."

"You could get a cat." He shot her an 'are you kidding me?' look, which made her giggle. "I'm serious. I've thought about getting one myself, but the timing never felt right. Cats are a lot more independent than dogs, you know."

"I've heard."

"You don't like cats?" she asked, picking up on his mood.

"I've never had a cat. But I've heard stories."

"We had a pair of cats when I was growing up. They weren't so bad. One of them loved to lie in your lap. She'd curl up into a ball and fall asleep."

They were approaching the front of her condo when someone called her name. She looked up to find Paul striding toward them. Her heart sank. If he was here, there must have been a break in one of their cases, which meant she wasn't going to be spending the rest of her evening snuggled up to the man next to her. Instead, she'd most likely be combing through files and evidence.

Janey plastered on a fake smile and braced herself for a long night.

CHAPTER 13

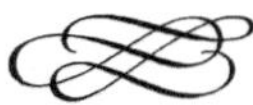

A MAN APPROACHED THEM. He was tall, around six foot, with dark brown hair. If Kyle had to guess, he was in his mid to late thirties.

Janey stiffened beside him, and he immediately went on alert. Was this an ex? He'd called her by name, so the man knew her.

"I called your cell, but you didn't answer," the man said.

"I left my phone upstairs."

The new arrival turned his attention to Kyle. He gave him a once-over and offered his hand. "You must be the new man in Janey's life."

Kyle shook the man's hand, trying to remain neutral, but it was proving to be difficult. "I am. And you are?"

It was Janey who spoke. "Kyle, this is my partner, Paul Daniels. Paul, this is Kyle Reed."

Now that he knew who the man was, he relaxed a little. Paul's face said he was here on business, which Kyle figured explained Janey's reaction. "I've heard a lot about you."

Paul glanced in Janey's direction, and then back to Kyle. "I can't say the same. She's been rather tight-lipped about you." He looked at Janey again. "Megan wants to talk to you about that, by the way."

Janey grimaced. Again, he had no idea who Megan was. He vaguely recalled her mentioning someone by that name before, but he couldn't recall who she was. A friend, he assumed. Maybe Paul's girlfriend or wife?

"Anyway, I don't want to take up your entire evening, but the lab called with the results on that ring, and I didn't want to wait until Monday to go over them with you."

The three of them made their way upstairs to Janey's condo. She unlocked the door and they all filed inside. "Did you want something to drink? I've got iced tea, lemonade, or I can make some coffee."

"I'm good, thanks," Paul said, making himself at home on her sofa. He removed a file folder from his jacket and laid out its contents on the coffee table.

Janey took the seat across from him.

"They found small traces of the victim's blood on the inside of the ring. Based on where we found it, I say there's a good chance it belonged to the killer."

"Have we gotten any hits yet on the ring itself?"

"No. It's taking a while to run down possible school matches when all we have is LBHS."

"Liberty-Bass High School." They both stared at him. "It's the local school district. It goes about ten miles south of Liberty all the way to Bass."

"I guess it's a good thing you're here," Paul said. "We could have spent another few weeks trying to figure that out."

"Do you have a picture of the ring?" Kyle asked.

Paul picked up one of the papers and handed it to him. "Looks like one of our class rings. Would have been someone in Ava's class, too. I wonder if she'd recognize it."

"Ava?" Paul asked.

"Kyle's sister."

Paul returned the picture to the file. "Do you think she'd be willing to take a look?"

"Sure. Let me see if I can get her on a video chat."

It took a few minutes to get everything arranged. Kyle called her first, knowing she'd be furious with him if he initiated a video call with her and expected her to converse not only with him but with

Janey and a man she'd never met. It wouldn't matter if the man was a detective and they were calling about a police matter.

"Of course, I'll help if I can. Do you have the ring?" Ava asked.

"We have a picture of the ring. The actual ring is locked up in evidence." Janey held the picture up to the phone so Ava could see it.

His sister concentrated hard on the picture. "It definitely looks like one of our class rings. I don't know who it belonged to, though." She paused. "You might want to contact Kelly's. They're the ones we all bought our class rings from. They should have a list of everyone who purchased a class ring and what all the specifications were for them. At the very least, it would narrow down your search."

"Thanks, Ava," Kyle said, turning the phone back around so he could see his sister.

"Anytime." She lowered her voice a little, but not enough considering he was only a few feet away from Janey and Paul. "How's your weekend with Janey going so far?"

Kyle rushed out of the room to get some privacy, but he didn't miss the smirk on Janey's partner's face.

Once he was alone in Janey's bedroom with the door closed, he addressed his sister. "The weekend was going fine. Better than fine, really, until her partner showed up with new evidence in the case."

"Are you pouting?" His sister was finding amusement in his plight.

"I'm not pouting. I understand the importance of looking at the new evidence as soon as it's available."

"But . . ."

"You know what? I'm not talking to you about this. You're my baby sister. You're not even supposed to know about sex."

Ava laughed. "You do remember I have a son, right? Cole. Your nephew?"

"I prefer to think about that as a onetime deal."

His sister snorted. "Do I need to remind you of the time you walked in on me and Andy?"

Kyle really needed to move the conversation away from sex—his sex life and Ava's—something he really didn't want to think about. "Are you feeling better?"

"I'm fine. Or I will be. You're right. I can't let her get to me. I'm a good mom. I know that. It's just easy to forget that when I'm there listening to her tell me all the things she thinks I'm doing wrong."

"Isn't that kind of what mothers-in-law are supposed to do?"

She cracked a smile. "Yeah."

"If you need me, call me. I'm only two hours away."

Ava dismissed his offer. "Don't worry about me. You have fun with Janey. I'll make sure not to disturb you. I wouldn't want to interrupt your sexy times."

With that, she waved to the camera and disconnected the call.

Kyle shook his head and returned to the living room. Paul appeared to be leaving. "I'll make some calls in the morning and see if I can get a printout of all the class rings purchased through Kelly's for that year. Being the weekend, I'm not holding out much hope we'll have anything before Monday."

"Probably not." Janey's gaze drifted to Kyle. There was a look in her eye he'd seen before, and it had him itching for them to be alone.

Paul walked over to the door, folder in hand. "I'll see you two Sunday, then. Megan's anxious to meet you," he said to Kyle.

"Sunday?"

Janey glanced at him, a nervous expression on her face. "Sorry. I hadn't had a chance to tell you yet. We've been invited over for a cookout at Paul and Megan's house on Sunday."

Not exactly what he'd expected to be doing right before he headed home, but these were Janey's friends. There were worse ways to spend an afternoon. "I guess we'll see you Sunday, then."

Once Paul was gone, Janey locked up. She kept her back to him for an extended period of time, took a deep breath, and turned to face him. "Sorry I didn't tell you about the cookout. I meant to earlier, but we got a little sidetracked."

Kyle pulled her into his arms and gave her a kiss. "Yes, we did."

She circled her arms around his neck, resting her elbows on his shoulders. "So you're not upset?"

"Why would I be upset?" He rubbed his thumb back and forth

along the small of her back. It was so nice being able to touch her like this.

"I know you came down to spend the weekend with me. You probably figured it'd be just the two of us."

He chuckled. "I wasn't expecting for us to be locked away in your condo all weekend. I figured we'd have to come up for air sooner or later."

Janey smacked his shoulder. "You know what I mean. I didn't want you to feel like you had to hang out with my friends. Megan can be a little pushy."

"You have met my sister, right? Or did you forget that she wanted me to invite you to spend Labor Day weekend in Liberty?" He didn't bother to mention he and Ava's phone conversation. His sister could be a royal pain in the ass when she wanted something.

"So you're okay spending your last few hours here on Sunday over at Paul and Megan's?" She still seemed a bit unsure.

"Positive."

She bit the inside of her lip, appearing to be deep in thought. Then she looked up at him. "Thank you."

"Why are you thanking me? It's not a big deal. We'll have other weekends together."

"That's not what I mean." She paused. "Well, not exactly anyway. I'm not used to guys being so . . . accommodating."

"That's me," he said, lifting her feet off the ground and bringing their faces level. Her lips were right there, calling to him. "Accommodating."

She took the hint and closed the distance between them. Her mouth covered his and she wrapped her legs around his waist, bringing her center in line with his groin. "Very accommodating."

* * *

Janey loved kissing him. His lips and tongue were so sure against hers. He knew what he wanted and he wasn't afraid to go after it.

Kyle palmed her ass, holding her body in place. His fingers

massaged the flesh of her cheeks, sending her arousal up a notch. The man knew how to kiss . . . and other things.

Kyle backed them up against the door, using it for support so he could free one of his hands to release the snap on her shorts. Once they were unsnapped, the zipper pulled apart and he slipped his fingers inside her waistband. It didn't take him long to find what he was looking for.

She moaned, grinding herself against his hand.

"Feel good?"

"Yes," she said. "Don't. Stop."

He released her mouth and kissed a line from her jaw to her ear. "Yes, ma'am."

Janey didn't even care that she was being bossy. She was so close and all she cared about in that moment was her impending orgasm.

"Come for me, baby."

He scraped his teeth along her neck, and that was all it took. She gasped as her orgasm rippled through her.

"You okay?" he asked a few moments later. She was still trying to catch her breath.

"That was . . ." Words really couldn't describe it. "Wow."

"Glad you enjoyed it."

She lifted her head from where she'd been resting it on his shoulder. They were still up against the door. And he was still very aroused. The evidence was right there against the inside of her thigh. "Did you want to take this into the bedroom?"

Kyle shook his head.

"No?"

"No." She'd seen that look in his eyes before. Several times. "I have this fantasy of taking you up against a door, and I figure this is the perfect time to make that a reality."

"You want to have sex against my door?" She'd never done that before, but the more she thought about it, the more she wanted to try it.

"Think your neighbors will mind?"

At that moment, she didn't much care what the neighbors thought. If they had a problem with it, she'd deal with it later.

Janey reached for the hem of her shirt and began working it up her torso.

Kyle laughed and used his free hand—the one that had brought her only a few moments ago to a powerful orgasm—to help her get the shirt over her head.

"Now you," she said, going for his T-shirt.

It took a little maneuvering, but soon it joined hers on the floor.

She reached behind her to unclip her bra, but before she could get it undone, Kyle had his mouth covering her nipple. She tried to concentrate, but all she could think about was him sucking on her breast.

"Having trouble?" he asked. "Need some help?"

"I can't concentrate with you doing that."

He looked up at her, a twinkle in his eye. He knew exactly what he was doing. "Would you like me to stop?"

"No."

A deep rumble came from his chest as he redoubled the assault on her nipple.

It took her several attempts, but eventually she felt the clasp of her bra come loose.

Kyle didn't miss a beat. He took hold of the middle of her bra, pulled it down, and tossed it somewhere behind him. Then he went right back to what he'd been doing before. Only this time there was no fabric between him and the object of his attention.

Tilting her head back against the door, Janey let the sensations roll over her. The way he would alternate between licking and nibbling on her sensitive flesh had her squirming against hm. She didn't want him to stop, but she needed more at the same time.

"Kyle?"

"Yes?" he asked as he worried her nipple between his teeth.

"I need you inside me." She tugged at his hair, trying to get his attention. "Now."

"Well, since you asked so nicely." He gave her a hard kiss and lifted her higher, making sure to hold above the waistband of her shorts. "Get rid of your shorts, Janey."

Reaching down, she pushed her shorts down her legs. Before she could get them past her knees, though, he latched onto her nipple again and sucked. Hard.

Janey gasped. "Kyle."

"Can't help it. You taste too good."

She grunted as she kicked the last of her clothes onto the floor. As soon as she was free, she returned her legs around his torso and dragged his mouth away from her breast, making him look at her. "Your turn."

His smile had her heart skipping a beat and her pulse racing. He held her gaze as he reached into his back pocket, removed his wallet, and extracted a condom. "Hold this for me."

She took the condom from him, and he went to work removing his jeans. Once they were on the floor, he kicked them out of the way and plucked the condom from her fingers. He swiftly rolled it down his erection and lowered her into position, lining himself up with her entrance. "Ready for me?"

"More than ready." She'd been ready the moment he'd pushed her up against the door.

He eased inside her, taking his time and driving her crazy. Janey used the little bit of leverage she had to try and make him go faster.

It didn't work. If anything, he went slower.

"More. I need more."

"You need more?" he asked.

"Yes. You're going too slow."

Without any warning, he plunged the rest of the way inside. Her muscles flexed around the intrusion, welcoming him. She covered his lips with hers and sighed. "Much, much better."

His chest vibrated with his amusement as he began to move. Every time he thrust inside, a zing of pleasure radiated from her sex throughout her body.

They moved and kissed and touched, letting their bodies communicate in the most primitive way. She didn't have to think about anything except him . . . them. Everything outside them in that moment disappeared, and all she could do was feel.

She slowly felt her climax building. It was as if she were climbing a mountain, waiting to tumble over the other side. She dug her nails into his shoulders, feeling it getting closer and closer.

As if he knew she was almost there, he adjusted his hand so his thumb was directly over her clit. She bucked her hips and moaned into his mouth.

"That's it, baby. Come for me. Let me feel you."

He increased the pressure on her clit, and she couldn't hold it back any longer. Her world exploded. She had to bite into the side of his neck to keep from screaming out.

Kyle let her ride out her orgasm, continuing to move inside her. When she lifted her head, he had a smug look on his face. "Ready?"

He didn't give her a chance to respond before picking up his pace. Where before it had been all about going slow and feeling every inch of him as he filled her, this was hard and fast and unrelenting. He pounded into her over and over again, her back slapping against the door.

It was rough. It was primal. And her body loved it. She could already feel another orgasm building.

His lips captured hers in an almost brutal kiss and he plunged his tongue inside her mouth. She met him thrust for thrust, needing to be closer. It was unlike anything she'd ever experienced before during sex.

One of his hands cupped her breast, massaging it. His touch was surprisingly gentle, a direct contrast to how he was pounding into her. It sent her head spinning and her body craving more.

She needed . . .

Kyle seemed to sense exactly what she needed. He shifted them so that with every thrust of his hips, he was brushing against her clit.

Her eyes rolled back in her head as her entire body caught fire. She felt the skin on his back give under her nails. She felt as if she were falling and she was desperately trying to find something to hold onto.

This time her climax snuck up on her. Her entire body began to shake and then it shattered.

She heard Kyle grunt and let out a loud gush of air before collapsing against her.

"You okay?" he asked, his voice barely above a whisper.

Janey nodded, unable to speak. She was all right. At least, she thought she was. Then again, she still felt as if she were floating.

"Think you can walk?"

She took several deep breaths before speaking. "Don't know."

He chuckled and leaned back so he could look at her. "I'll take that as a compliment."

"You really should."

Kyle set her on her feet, making sure to keep hold of her until he was sure she wasn't going to fall.

"I need to go clean up."

She nodded. "I'll meet you in the bedroom."

He cupped the side of her face and gave her a long, lingering kiss before heading for the bathroom.

Janey leaned back against the door and sighed. She was never going to be able to look at her front door again and not think of what they'd just done.

Gathering up their clothes, she carried them into the bedroom. She threw her clothes into the hamper, laid his on a chair, and climbed into bed to wait for him.

CHAPTER 14

THEY LAY in bed Saturday evening, Janey with her head on his shoulder. They'd made love several times since waking up that morning, but it didn't feel rushed. They were just enjoying their time together. It was one of the most relaxing weekends he'd had in a long while. Maybe ever.

Janey had gotten a call from another detective about an hour before, but luckily she didn't have to leave. Aside from the brief interruption the night before, the odds had definitely been working in their favor.

In between bouts of sex, they talked. He'd shared with her a little of his time in the Army, and she'd told him more about her grandmother. She sounded like an amazing woman. He would have loved to have met her.

What Janey had been vaguer about was how she'd ended up with her grandmother. He was trying not to pry, to let her share what she was comfortable with, but he had to admit he was curious. Then again, he was curious about everything that had to do with the woman in his arms.

"How old were you when you started living with your grandmother?"

Janey ran the tip of her finger down the inside of his arm. "Four."

Younger than he'd thought. Kyle couldn't imagine how confusing that must have been for her at that age. At any age, really. Hell, it was confusing to him.

He was trying to figure out how to ask what happened to her mother, when she went on.

"My mom threw my clothes and a couple of toys in a bag one morning and took me to Grandma's. I thought we were going to visit, but then my mother left. She didn't come back."

He was starting to understand Janey's issues with abandonment. First her mother, then Ted. And Kyle still didn't know what had happened to her father. She'd never mentioned him. "Ever?"

Janey shrugged. "She showed up one night when I was ten. It was late and I was already in bed. Someone knocked on the door, and I remember hearing Grandpa arguing with someone. I sneaked downstairs to see who it was." She paused and he waited. "I'm sorry. You don't want to hear this."

Kyle rolled them onto their sides so they could face each other. "I do. I want to learn everything there is to know about you, Janey."

"Why?" She seemed genuinely confused why he wanted to know about her family.

"Why not?" He brushed the hair away from her face and looked deep into her eyes. "You're my girlfriend and I care about you."

She searched his face, no doubt trying to determine if he really meant it. "My mom is a drug addict. Or she was. I haven't seen her since she showed up that night when I was ten. I don't even know if she's still alive."

There was a blank look on her face, almost as if she were bracing herself for his reaction. Kyle had to wonder if there was a story there as well. He let it go, however. "Did you ever think of using your resources to try and find her?"

"I seriously thought about it a couple of years ago. Paul said he'd help me if I wanted him to, but . . ."

"But?"

Janey flipped onto her back, looking up at the ceiling. "I thought over all the different scenarios and decided that maybe it was best if I didn't know." She turned her head to look at him. "What if I found her and she's clean, living a great life, yet never attempted to contact me? Or what if she's still strung out on cocaine or meth or heroin?" Sighing, she refocused on the ceiling again. "No, it's better not knowing, I think."

Reaching for her, Kyle tucked her against his side once more. She came willingly, snuggling into him. "I understand. Sometimes not knowing is better."

She nodded against his chest. "Not everyone understands. Carla thinks I'm crazy for not wanting to know."

Kyle hadn't met Carla yet, but Janey had mentioned her several times. He knew they were friends and that they went out to clubs together, but he didn't get the impression that they hung out beyond that.

Clearing his throat, he dove into territory that he usually avoided at all costs. She'd shared something deeply personal with him and he felt the need to do the same. "When my parents died, I was the one who found them."

Janey reared back to look at him. "You said they died in a car accident."

He nodded. "I was six months out of the police academy. It was late and I got a call on the radio that there'd been an accident out on Collins Road." Kyle felt the emotions of that night bubbling to the surface. He did his best to breathe. "They were already dead when I found them. There was nothing I could do."

She wrapped her arms around him and buried her face in his neck. He held tight, soaking in her warmth. Given her job, he didn't have to tell her the graphic nature of what he'd seen. She could no doubt picture it. He wished he could unsee his parents lying there in their car, blood caked on their faces, but he couldn't. Until the day he died, he'd remember.

"We're quite a pair, aren't we?" she mumbled against his neck.

Kyle kissed the top of her head, breathing in the scent of her shampoo. It was oddly comforting. "I'll be paired with you anytime."

She brushed her lips along his neck, sending a chill down his spine. He shivered and she noticed. "Cold?"

"Not at all." He trailed his fingers down the length of her spine then flattened out his palm to cup her ass. Her skin was so soft, so feminine.

He moved his hand lower, lifting her leg so it wrapped around his waist. She was still so wet from their last round of sex. He dipped his hand between her legs, touching her heat.

Janey gasped and pushed against his fingers as he slipped them inside her. She reached up, pulling his mouth down to hers. Their tongues mingled as he moved his fingers in and out.

Kyle was about to reach for another condom when her phone rang.

She whimpered. "I have to get that."

Reluctantly, he removed his fingers and let her go. He was as hard as a rock, and seeing her roll over to get her phone, her bare ass facing him, wasn't helping his predicament.

"Sure. I'll be right there," he heard her say before disconnecting the call.

Janey turned to face him, but he already knew what she was going to say.

"You have to go to a crime scene."

She sat up and crawled out of bed, leaving the sheet behind. "It sounds like a domestic dispute gone bad. Hopefully I won't be gone too long."

He put his feet on the floor and began gathering his clothes.

Janey finished dressing, making sure to grab her gun and her badge. "The remote is on the coffee table if you want to watch some TV. Or I have some books you could read if you like mysteries. There's also—"

"Go. I'll be fine. I'm sure I can find something to keep myself busy for a few hours."

She closed the distance between them, rose onto her tiptoes, and placed a long lingering kiss on his lips.

His erection was still protesting the fact that it wasn't going to be getting what it wanted anytime soon. He took hold of her hips and pulled her against him, letting her feel every hard inch of him through his jeans. "Hurry back."

Her breathing was labored when she stepped away. She was flushed and her eyes were still dilated with arousal. He was glad he wasn't the only one who was fighting the urge to forget the outside world and go back to bed.

She took a deep breath. "I'll leave a key on the kitchen counter. In case you need to go out while I'm gone."

He shoved his hands in his pockets and nodded.

Turning on her heel, she took two steps out of the room, and then ran back in to give him another hard kiss on the lips. "I'll be back as soon as I can."

She raced out of the room, and a few seconds later he heard the front door open and close.

Kyle ran a frustrated hand over his face and head. He knew how this worked. He had at least two hours to kill before Janey would be back.

Heading into the living room, he found the remote and made himself comfortable on her couch. Hopefully there was at least something decent on he could watch while he waited. Otherwise it was going to be a very long two hours.

Janey didn't get home until after midnight. What she'd hoped would be an open-and-shut case had turned out to be more complicated. A man had shot his estranged wife and child in their family home. Then he'd turned the gun on himself.

The complication was that not only did the wife have a restraining order against her husband but the man was a felon, which meant he hadn't gotten the firearm legally. That caused a lot of red tape and got the ATF involved. Not exactly the way she'd hoped her night would play out.

Kyle was waiting in the living room, surfing through channels, when she'd walked in the door. He'd taken one look at her, turned off the television, and carried her to the bedroom.

She was feeling better the next morning, more like herself. Getting called out to a crime scene that involved a child was always emotional, but it was even worse when it was a family. Janey would never understand how a father—or mother, for that matter—could kill their own child.

"Feeling better?" He nuzzled his nose against her neck.

"Yeah."

He pulled her against him, her back to his front. "Want to talk about it?"

Last night things had been too raw. She could still see the bodies lying there. It wasn't an easy image to forget.

"She had a restraining order and the husband was a convicted felon. Armed robbery."

"Black market?" His voice was calm and even. Exactly what she needed.

Janey shook her head. "I don't think so. The firearm was purchased legally five days ago."

"So you're thinking straw purchase."

"Yeah." At least there would be someone to hold responsible. Still, it didn't seem quite enough. They should be made to walk though that crime scene as she had and understand what their actions had caused.

Kyle sighed. "We don't see that kind of stuff that often in Liberty. Everyone knows everyone else and their business. It can be a pain sometimes, but it does tend to keep people honest. It's hard to hide anything when you have nosy neighbors."

She could see the benefits of that. Although, it wasn't as if the family had been isolated. They'd lived in a neighborhood, too. The closest house was only about thirty feet away. The neighbors were the ones who'd heard the gunshots and called it in. "I can't get the image of that little girl out of my head. The neighbors said she was supposed to start kindergarten in a couple of weeks."

He held her tighter and she leaned into him. It had been a long time since she'd felt she could lean on anyone. "Anything I can do to help?"

Janey turned in his arms, facing him. "No. But thank you." She glanced at the clock and back to him. "We should probably get up and start getting ready. Paul wanted us there at one, and it's already after eleven."

"Maybe we should save some time and take a shower together."

He raised and lowered both eyebrows several times, causing Janey to laugh. "Somehow I don't think that would speed things up at all."

"Maybe not, but it would certainly be more fun."

She scraped her teeth over her bottom lip as she thought about having him in the shower with her. Maybe what she needed was to get her mind off the crime scene and onto something a lot more pleasant. The idea definitely had appeal.

Before she could change her mind, Janey hurried out of bed and began making her way toward the shower. At the doorway, she stopped, turned, and gave him her most flirtatious look. "Do you promise to wash my back?"

A slow smile spread across his face as he scrambled out of bed.

Two hundred pounds of naked man barreled toward her. He picked her up, fireman style, giving her the perfect view of his ass.

She sunk her teeth into his backside, and he landed a swat to her rear. "Behave."

Janey giggled. "Or what?"

"Or I might have to wash more than just your back."

"Promises, promises."

* * *

Somehow, they made it to Paul and Megan's with a few minutes to spare. They used all the hot water in her shower before finally taking their activities back to the bed. Janey had been able to forget about the crime scene and focus on Kyle for over an hour.

Chloe was the first to see them. Janey was starting to think the little girl had a sixth sense or something. Even if Chloe was upstairs in her room, she'd race down the stairs within seconds of Janey walking through the door. It was uncanny.

"Who's this?" Chloe asked, looking up at Kyle.

Kyle knelt down and offered Chloe his hand. "I'm Kyle. And you must be Chloe."

She shook his hand and nodded. "Are you Janey's boyfriend?"

He grinned. "Yes, I am."

Chloe gave him a good once-over. "What's your job?"

"I'm a police officer." He didn't seem to have an issue answering Chloe's questions.

"Like Daddy and Janey?"

Paul cleared his throat and stepped forward. He extended his hand to Kyle.

Kyle stood and took it.

Looking down at his daughter, Paul explained. "Janey and I investigate crimes after they've happened. Kyle here tries to prevent the crime from happening so Janey and I don't have to deal with it."

It was a very simplistic way of explaining the differences between their jobs, but as it turned out, it made sense to a six-year-old.

Megan approached with a huge smile on her face. "Hi, I'm Megan. Paul's wife."

"Nice to meet you," Kyle said. "And thank you for inviting me."

They moved into the backyard and Paul fired up the grill. "I heard you got called out last night," he said to Janey.

Most of the time she and Paul worked together, but that wasn't always the case, especially on the weekends. Given her partner had been a detective for more than ten years, he got most of his weekends off. She, however, was still paying her dues. "Yeah. Domestic dispute."

Paul nodded. They'd both been called out to their fair share of domestic issues, both as detectives and even more so as patrol officers. She didn't need to tell him how bad the scene had been. He would know.

Not wanting to talk about last night anymore, she steered the conversation toward something more productive. "Did you make any progress on the ring?"

"I spoke to the manager at Kelly's. She's going to send over a list of all the rings purchased that year. Hopefully we'll be able to find a match."

"If you need any help, let me know. We'll assist you in any way we can," Kyle said.

Paul placed the meat Megan had brought out onto the grill. "We might take you up on that. If the person is somehow connected to Liberty, you'll know the territory a lot better than we do."

"The high school is small. My graduating class had sixty-seven students. I think Ava's had seventy-something. If who you're looking for is female, that will cut your list of suspects in half."

"Does your sister have a yearbook we could borrow?" Janey asked.

"I'm sure she does. I can mail it to you this week."

Paul came to sit down across from Janey and Kyle. "I'm thinking we might need to take a drive up to Liberty."

Janey stared at him, not sure where he was going with this.

"Right now the connection to Liberty is our only lead. I'd actually like to talk to Kyle's sister ourselves. I'd like her to look at the ring in person and see if it jogs any memories."

"I'm sure she'll be happy to help, although that was eight years ago. I'm not sure how much she'll remember."

Janey stood and went to get herself a pop out of the cooler while Paul and Kyle continued to talk about the case.

Megan strolled up to her and got herself a water. "He's cute."

Janey smiled.

"I'm a little hurt you didn't tell me about him, though."

"Sorry. It's just that it's still so new. I wanted to feel things out first."

Megan twisted the cap off her water. "You sound like Paul."

Janey chuckled. "Maybe after all these years of being his partner he's rubbing off on me."

Paul got up and flipped the meat before returning to talk to Kyle. Janey stayed where she was, keeping Megan company. After last night, she really wasn't in the mood for shop talk.

"His sister wants me to spend Labor Day weekend in Liberty."

"That's great." Megan frowned. "Isn't it? I mean his sister must like you if she's inviting you to come visit them, right?"

"Ava's great. She's been very supportive of a relationship between Kyle and me from the beginning."

"But?" Megan asked.

"But nothing, I guess. I'm just nervous. I mean we live two hours apart. We both have dangerous jobs. What if—"

"You really are starting to sound like Paul." Megan placed a hand on Janey's shoulder. "Sometimes you have to live in the moment and go after what you want, even if on paper it doesn't make sense." She looked over at her husband, a smile pulling at the edges of her mouth. "Things have a way of working themselves out."

CHAPTER 15

"Hopefully you'll come back to see Janey soon and we can do this again."

Kyle grinned at Megan. "I would like that. Thank you."

He and Paul shook hands. "We'll give you a call and make arrangements to bring the ring up so your sister can take a look."

"Just let me know. I'm sure Noah would like to see it as well. He doesn't like a murderer roaming around in his backyard."

Paul nodded.

After saying their goodbyes, they drove back to Janey's condo. It was after four o'clock, which meant he would need to leave soon. As much as he'd loved to stay, he had to work tonight.

"What time do you have to leave?" Janey asked as she neared her place. She must have been reading his mind.

"I need to be on the road by five so I have enough time to swing by my house and change before I go to the station."

Janey pressed her lips together and nodded. She kept her eyes on the road, not saying anything.

"I wish I could stay longer. My bed's going to feel very lonely when I get home."

She glanced over at him. "I know what you mean."

Kyle reached over and took her hand, lacing their fingers together and bringing them to rest on his leg. "If you and Paul come to Liberty this week, then we'll see each other again sooner than we thought."

"True. But I doubt we'll be staying for more than a few hours."

He gave her hand a little squeeze and then released it so she could pull into the parking garage.

As they were exiting her vehicle, a feeling of melancholy surrounded them. He'd been there for such a short time and he was having to leave.

They held hands as they made their way into the building and climbed into the elevator that would take them to her floor. He waited until the doors closed before backing her up against the wall and capturing her mouth with his.

Janey responded immediately. She held him to her as if she wanted to ensure he wouldn't back away.

The elevator dinged and the doors opened. Someone cleared their throat.

They both looked up to find an older gentleman staring at them with a smirk on his face. "Hello, Detective Davis."

Janey dropped her arms and straightened her shoulders. "Hello, Mr. Ellison. How are you today?"

He stepped into the elevator as they exited, his smile even wider than it had been before. "Oh, I'm just fine. Not as good as you, apparently."

She didn't get a chance to respond before the doors closed again and Mr. Ellison disappeared.

A low groan escaped Janey's throat as she unlocked the door to her condo. "Of course the biggest gossip in our building has to be the one to catch me making out with my boyfriend in the elevator."

"Could have been worse," Kyle said, shrugging. As soon as they were inside her condo, he reached for her, pulling her flush against him once more. "We were only kissing."

Janey raised an eyebrow at him. "We were practically dry humping each other in a public place."

He chuckled. "I'm not sure I'd go that far. Although, if you'd like, we could try it again and you can show me what you mean."

She gave him a playful push on his shoulder, which only make him laugh harder. "Not funny. No more elevator make-out sessions."

"Now that I can't promise." He lowered his head and brushed his lips against hers. "I kept my hands to myself all afternoon. Once we were alone—" She opened her mouth to protest, so he altered his statement a bit. "Once there was no one else around, I took advantage of the situation."

"And we got caught. By my neighbor."

Kyle moved his lips to her neck and suckled right below her ear. He felt her pulse kick up a notch.

She tilted her head to the side to give him better access. "How do you always do this to me?"

"Do what?" he whispered against her skin.

Her only response was to cup the back of his head, encouraging him to keep going.

"Janey?"

"Hmm?"

"Tell me what I always do to you," he whispered in her ear.

Kyle felt her shiver.

She still didn't answer his question.

"Do you want me to stop?"

"No."

He smiled against her neck and went back to what he'd been doing. "Then tell me. I want to know what I do to you."

"You know what."

"No, I don't. Tell me." To add a little extra persuasion, he pulled her hips against him, letting her feel exactly what she did to him. Every. Damn. Time.

"Every time you touch me, you make me forget about everything but you."

He lifted his head to look at her. Janey's eyes were dark with arousal. She was feeling all the same things he was, and it wasn't only about sex. Yes, she could turn him on like no one else, but it was more than that. Knowing he had to leave her here in the city was near torture.

Without words, he lifted her up, wrapping her legs around his middle, and carried her into the bedroom. He knew they really didn't have time, but for the first time in his life he didn't much care if he was late. Kyle needed to connect with Janey on the most basic level. He needed to feel her surrounding him one more time before he went weeks without. Sure, they could fool around over the phone, but it wouldn't be the same as her fingers in his hair or her nails on his back.

He lowered her onto the mattress and began to remove her clothes.

"Don't you have to leave?" she asked, staring up at him.

"I need to be with you one more time before I go." He smiled down at her. "One more for the road."

Janey didn't even laugh at his corny joke. She reached up and pulled him down, her mouth dancing across his as she teased him with the most powerful drug. It was on the tip of his tongue to tell her how he felt, but he held back. As much as he wanted to put voice to his feelings, he knew she wasn't ready.

As they continued to kiss, their clothes slowly made their way to the floor. Neither of them spoke. Everything they needed to say was done with their bodies. When he came, it felt as if he were giving over part of his soul to her. And maybe he was. He'd never felt a connection like this with another person. Janey was special, and he was going to do everything in his power to make sure she knew that.

He just had to make sure he didn't scare her away in the process.

They lay tangled in each other's arms until time forced him to get dressed. The sleepy look of contentment as he leaned down to kiss her goodbye had his heart aching. He'd never had a long-distance relationship with anyone before, but he was beginning to understand how difficult they really were. Not because of the distance itself, but because it was so hard to leave once their short time together had ended.

Kyle knew he'd see her again. Knew it wouldn't be long. But in the moment, all he wanted to do was crawl back into the bed with her and forget about the outside world.

He brushed a strand of her hair away from her face. "I'll text you when I get home."

Janey covered his hand with hers, and then let it fall to the mattress when he backed away.

Stopping at the door to her bedroom, he took one last look at her in bed, rumpled from their lovemaking. Then he commanded he legs to move and headed back to his life in Liberty.

* * *

Janey and Paul spent most of Monday going through the list the jewelry store had sent over. There were forty names on it. By the time they called it a day, they'd narrowed it down to seven based on the symbols on the ring.

Paul had also called Sheriff Jenkins and made arrangements for them to drive up to Liberty Tuesday morning and go over what they'd found so far. He was anxious to hear any updates they had and was very curious about the ring.

At six o'clock Tuesday morning, Paul picked Janey up outside her condo. She thought maybe she'd be anxious about the trip to Liberty, but she was more excited than anything else, and it had nothing to do with the case.

She'd spoken to Kyle the night before and he'd told her he'd see her at the station. The sheriff wanted him to join them for their meeting. Then he was going to take them to Ava's so she could have a look at the ring.

"Nervous?" Paul asked about an hour into their trip.

"No. Why?" She'd been quiet for the most part, mainly because it was early. That, and she was gathering her thoughts. Janey had been doing that a lot lately. Thinking about her life. Her future. It was something she hadn't allowed herself to do in a long time. Her focus had been on living in the moment.

"You're awfully quiet this morning. That's not like you. Normally you're talking my head off."

Janey rolled her eyes. "I'm just thinking about some things."

"I see. And would those things happen to revolve around a certain deputy we'll be seeing this morning?"

"Some of them."

Paul chuckled but didn't go on.

"What?"

He shook his head. "Nothing. I'm happy for you. He seems like a good guy."

She nodded and went back to looking at the scenery.

"What is Liberty like?" Paul asked, apparently not done with the conversation. "I've never been there."

"It's your typical small town. The courthouse is in the center of town. There's a diner and a small hardware store."

"You said Kyle's sister owns a bed and breakfast?"

"Yeah. It's a few miles outside of town. Megan would love it." Janey grinned thinking about it. Paul's wife was taking art classes at the local community college. Ava's house was built in the early 1900s and was full of fun architecture. There were also a few paintings hanging around the house Janey thought would interest Megan. They might not be along the lines of Monet or Picasso, but Megan had developed a taste for the whimsical and Ava's place would be right up her alley.

"Maybe I'll have to bring her up here for a weekend or something. It's been a while since we've gotten away, just us."

Janey smiled. "I'm sure she'd like that."

It was a few minutes after eight when they turned onto Main Street. Nothing had changed since the last time she was there. In fact, as they passed the diner, she noticed the exact same specials sign in the window.

The courthouse was easy to locate, and on the back side was the sheriff's station. They found a place to park and went inside.

Janey couldn't stop herself from looking around as they climbed the steps. There were several patrol vehicles in the parking lot, and she wondered if one of them belonged to Kyle or if he was still out on the road. His shift was technically over at seven, but she remembered from her own patrol days that she rarely made it back to the station on time. A call always seemed to come in at the last minute.

They were buzzed in and escorted to Sheriff Jenkins's office. He stood when they entered. "Come in and have a seat."

Janey and Paul lowered themselves into the two chairs directly in front of Sheriff Jenkins's desk.

"It's good to see you again, Detective Davis." There was a sparkle in the sheriff's eye, and Janey knew that he was aware of her relationship with Kyle. Not that she figured they'd be able to keep it a secret. Small towns didn't work that way.

"Thank you, Sheriff. It's good to be back."

He turned his attention to Paul. "This your first time in Liberty, Detective Daniels?"

"Yes, although Davis was telling me about the bed and breakfast Kyle's sister owns. My wife and I might have to schedule a visit."

"I'm sure Ava would love to have you."

There was a knock on the door, and they all turned their attention to the new arrival.

Kyle stood in the doorway, still in his uniform. Her heart skipped a beat as he strolled into the room. His gaze lingered on her for a long moment before he addressed the room as a whole.

"Sorry, I'm late," he said. "I caught someone doing eighty in a fifty-five this morning."

Sheriff Jenkins waved him in. "That's all right. We were just getting started."

Kyle shut the door behind him and moved to take up a position a few feet from Janey. He leaned against the wall, crossing his arms in front of him. The material of his uniform stretched across his chest, and she felt her body warming. She had to make herself look away.

Needing a distraction, Janey removed the bag containing the ring from her pocket and handed it to Sheriff Jenkins.

He examined it closely before handing it back to Janey. "It does look like one of our class rings."

She took it and placed it back in her pocket. It was the best lead they had at the moment, and she was guarding it with her life.

"The ring came from a place called Kelly's. Apparently, they do most of the class rings around here," Paul said. "They provided us with a list of every ring that was purchased with that graduating year and the engravings selected. We've been able to narrow it down to seven individuals. Unfortunately, ring sizes aren't listed on the document, or we'd be able to narrow it down even more."

Paul handed the paper to Sheriff Jenkins and he looked it over. "Betsy Canfield died a few years ago. Cancer. So you can mark her name off your list. The others? I know most of them. Can't see them committing murder, let alone three murders."

"Sometimes it's the people you least suspect."

There was a tone in Paul's voice when he said it. Even the sheriff seemed to pick up on it. But Janey knew Paul wouldn't elaborate. He'd made the mistake of misjudging someone once and he was still blaming himself for it.

Janey knew she needed to move things along. "Maybe Ava can help us knock a few more names off that list."

"Yes," Sheriff Jenkins said. "Ava's eager to help if she can."

Kyle shifted. "We should probably get going."

Janey and Paul stood.

"Let me know if there's anything we can do to help. I want to catch this person as much as you do. Maybe more."

Paul extended his hand to Sheriff Jenkins. "We appreciate your help, Sheriff."

"Anytime."

It had started sprinkling by the time they made their way back outside, and Janey was mourning the sunshine that had provided a beautiful sunrise less than two hours ago. Kyle didn't seem to be bothered by the change in the weather. "I figured we could take my SUV over to Ava's, and then I can drop you both back here."

Paul already had his keys out and was moving away from them. "Why don't you two head over and I'll follow you?"

Janey opened her mouth to say something, but Kyle interrupted her. "Sounds good. We'll see you there."

Paul jogged the rest of the way down the steps toward his vehicle, leaving Janey and Kyle alone.

"Did you two have this planned or something?" Janey asked.

Kyle laughed. "Not at all." He motioned toward his truck. "Since Paul isn't riding with us, there's no need to take the SUV.

She followed him to his pickup truck. He unlocked the passenger door and held it open for her. "Thank you."

Once she was seated, he closed the door and made his way over to the driver's side. A minute later, they were heading out of town toward his sister's.

"You didn't have to do that, you know."

He looked over at her, and then back at the road. "Do what?"

"Open the door for me. We're here on official police business. I'm not your girlfriend right now."

Kyle frowned. "You breaking up with me?"

"What? No." Janey turned in her seat to look at him. Or she tried to, with the seat belt fighting her every step of the way. "Why would you think I'm breaking up with you?"

"You said you're not my girlfriend right now."

"What I meant was that Paul and I are here in an official capacity, so we should conduct ourselves in that manner." She paused and sat up a little straighter. "Would you hold the passenger door open for Hayden?"

Instead of confirming that he wouldn't, he asked a question of his own. "Why would I be driving Hayden to my sister's place?"

Janey sighed. "You're missing my point."

Kyle reached for her hand.

She jerked, but he held firm, bringing the back of her hand up to his lips. "Janey, no matter what's going on, you're still my girlfriend and I'm going to treat you that way. My feelings for you don't switch off once I'm on duty or you are."

"People will think we're unprofessional." She'd worked hard to get where she was in her professional life. Being one of the youngest detectives in the Indianapolis Police Department meant she'd had to deal with her share of challenges. She wanted people to have confidence in her as a detective, not disregard her or her opinions because she was Kyle's girlfriend.

He lowered their hands but didn't let go. "That might be the case in the city. Around here, everyone already knows we're seeing each other, so they'd be surprised if I didn't hold doors open for you."

"Everyone knows?" Her heart sank a little. She'd gotten the vibe from Sheriff Jenkins that he was aware of their relationship, but she knew he and Kyle were friends. Now she was wondering if some of the looks they got as they'd exited the building were less about having detectives from the city in Liberty and more about Kyle's girlfriend being there.

"Maybe not everyone, but I'd say more than half."

She groaned.

"What's wrong?" he asked as they turned into Ava's driveway.

"What if we have to interview suspects? It's going to completely diminish my authority. I need them to respect my position and take me seriously."

He put the truck in park and turned off the engine. "Things are different around here. If anything, people will be more likely to open up to you because we're dating. Not the other way around." The look on her face must have told him how much she questioned his way of looking at things because he continued. "Remember Mr. Mitchel? The first thing he did was ask who you were. People around here, they trust the people they know—the people they've known for years. It takes time to gain their trust and get them to open up. Being my girlfriend, you now have an inside ticket, so to speak."

"I don't know." What he said made sense. Sort of. But she was still doubtful.

"Trust me." Movement from the front of the house caught their attention. His sister was standing on the porch with Cole on her hip. "Come on. Let's go talk to my sister."

CHAPTER 16

Janey slid out of the truck and made her way up the steps to where Kyle's sister was standing, hair pulled back in a ponytail and wearing an apron that looked as if it had seen better days. No doubt she'd come from the kitchen. Janey even thought she saw a smudge of flour on her cheek.

Ava's smile grew wider the closer Janey came. She lowered Cole to the ground and embraced Janey. "It's good to see you again."

"Thanks for helping us out." Janey hugged Ava back, and then stepped away to introduce her partner who'd made his way up the steps. "Ava, this is my partner, Detective Paul Daniels."

"It's nice to meet you, Detective." She grabbed Cole's hand and tilted her head toward the house. "I made some coffee and banana bread if you're hungry." Ava didn't wait for anyone to respond. She turned on her heel and walked inside, leaving them all to follow.

"I can see what you mean," Paul said seconds after they entered the house. "Megan would love this place."

"Is Megan your wife?" Ava asked.

Paul nodded. "She's working toward her art degree, and while she appreciates the classical artists, she loves all types of art."

"Most of the pictures on the wall came with the house, as did a few pieces of furniture. The rest I found at antique shops." She removed four mugs from the kitchen cabinet and placed them on the counter next to the coffeepot. "Cream or sugar?"

"Black for me, thank you," Paul said.

Janey took a seat at the kitchen table next to Kyle. "Both, please."

Ava fixed them each coffee, made sure Cole was occupied in the corner with his toys, and joined them at the table with several slices of banana bread. "Did you bring the ring?"

Removing it from her pocket, Janey placed the bag with the ring on the table in front of Ava.

Kyle's sister picked up the bag and turned it over in her hand. "You think the person this ring belongs to is the one who killed those men?"

"We don't know. But it's a lead and we have to follow it."

Ava nodded and looked closer at the ring. "Looks almost identical to mine except for the stone in the middle."

Paul handed her the list of names. "We're hoping you can help us narrow down our list of suspects."

With a solemn expression, Ava looked over the list.

Kyle took a slice of the banana bread. "We already know about Betsy."

Ava took a deep breath but didn't say anything. Janey helped herself to some of the banana bread, and Paul followed suit.

Janey closed her eyes in pure enjoyment as she bit into the bread. It was moist and flavorful. The only thing that would have made it better was a smear of butter on top. Ava knew how to bake. There was no doubt about that.

When Janey opened her eyes again, she found Kyle staring at her. The look in his eyes said he wasn't thinking about the case or food.

She swallowed the banana bread she'd been chewing and swiftly turned her attention back to Ava. "Do any of these people jump out at you?"

Ava scrunched up her nose. "It's not Carrie. And I don't think it's Melissa either."

"What makes you say that?" Paul was still firmly in detective mode.

He either completely missed the vibe between Kyle and Janey, or he was ignoring it. Janey was hoping for the former, but it was more likely the latter. Paul was a good detective. And when he was paying attention, not much got past him.

"Carrie's . . ." Ava paused. "The ring would never fit Carrie. Not even in high school. It's too small."

"What about Melissa?" Paul asked.

"The same. She's lost quite a bit of weight since high school, but back then . . . there's no way this ring would have fit her."

Janey could still feel Kyle's gaze on her, but she tried to focus on what Ava was saying. She cleared her throat. "You're sure?"

Ava nodded. "It's smaller than my class ring. I'd say it's probably a size five or six. No way Melissa or Carrie would have worn that size back then."

That still left them with four names.

Paul took a sip of his coffee, appearing relaxed. Janey knew better. "Any of the other names stand out to you as possible owners of the ring?"

"No. I'm sorry. I mean, I know all of them, but I know that's not what you're asking."

"That's all right," Paul said. "You helped remove two more names from our list."

Ava gave the list of names back to Paul. "Can I get anyone some more coffee?"

Paul tucked the paper back into his jacket. "Thank you, but no. I'd like to see where your brother found the victim's body. I know Janey has already looked things over, but I'd like to get the lay of the land myself. See how it compares to the other locations."

"Of course," Kyle said. "You can follow me over. It's not too far from here."

They all stood, including Ava. She placed a hand on Janey's arm as she turned to leave. "Did Kyle say anything to you about coming for Labor Day weekend?" She shifted her weight. "It's kind of a big deal around here and I was hoping you could come."

"He mentioned something along those lines."

"Does that mean you'll come?" she asked. "I can keep a room open for you here if you want, but I kind of figured you'd want to stay at Kyle's."

"I'm on call most Saturday nights." Being that she was still one of the younger detectives, she got stuck being on call when the older detectives wanted time off to spend with their families. Since she was single, she didn't mind. She could go out on Friday night or Sunday night as easily as she could Saturday night.

"So come down Sunday morning. We have a festival that runs from Saturday through Monday." She leaned in as if confiding some big secret. "They're going to roast another hog."

Janey chuckled. "I'll keep that in mind."

When Janey exited the house, Paul and Kyle were talking beside Kyle's pickup truck. They both looked up at her approach, but their expressions were quite different. Paul quirked one eyebrow up in question, probably wondering what had kept her. In contrast, Kyle had an amused look on his face. No doubt he knew exactly what his sister was doing. They were both pushing her in their own ways, and she didn't know if she liked it.

"Ready to go?" Janey asked, already reaching for the passenger side door of Kyle's truck.

The two men exchanged a look before Paul strolled over to his vehicle.

Kyle eased himself behind the wheel. "Did you have a nice chat with Ava?"

Janey fastened her seat belt. "You knew she was going to waylay me and ask about Labor Day."

He shrugged and started the engine. "I had a pretty good feeling."

They drove for several miles down country roads, many of which didn't have dividing lines on them. There was nothing around except for fields full corn and soybeans.

Kyle turned right onto another road, and Janey realized they were almost there. Despite the fact that everything looked so similar—at least to her—she remembered the electrical lines in the distance.

Sure enough, a few seconds later Kyle pulled off the road.

The cornstalks rattled in the breeze as they left their vehicles and followed Kyle to where he'd found the body.

"Right here." Kyle pointed to the area where he'd discovered John Doe.

Paul looked up and down the roadway and then at both fields. "I see what you meant, Davis. This really is a great place to dump a body. No cameras. No lights. No houses."

"Over here is where we found the empty beer bottles." Janey crossed the ditch into the cornfield. The stalks that had been broken were still lying on the ground.

Kyle kicked at one of the fallen stalks. "Doesn't look as if they've been back since we were here last."

"I'm sure they heard about the dead body," Paul said.

Janey moved to the other side of the makeshift circle of destroyed cornstalks. "That wouldn't deter some kids."

A noise had all three of them freezing. They looked at each other, confirming they'd all heard something.

Kyle motioned he would go left. Paul slinked off to the right, leaving Janey to take the center position.

She moved with as much stealth as she could through the corn, hand on her firearm. It could have been a deer they'd heard, or a coyote. Or it could be a person. And if it was a person, what were they doing hanging out in a cornfield in the middle of the day?

"Let go of me!"

Janey rushed toward the sound, no longer caring if she made a noise. She guessed it was safe to say what they'd heard wasn't a coyote.

* * *

Kyle didn't loosen his hold until he saw Janey and Paul appear through the tall corn. Even then, he made sure the young man he'd caught wasn't going to take off at the first opportunity.

"Let me go. I didn't do anything." Johnny Vanhoose. A local boy.

Sixteen years old. Which meant he should have been in school at this time of day.

"Why are you sneaking around in a cornfield?" Kyle asked.

"None of your business." The young man struggled against Kyle's hold, but it was useless. Kyle had at least eighty pounds on the boy and a lot more muscle. That didn't stop him, though. Not until Paul took a step toward them. Johnny saw the movement and stopped fighting. He decided to change tactics. "Come on, Kyle. I ain't done nothing. Let me go."

Kyle didn't miss the use of his given name. Johnny's dad coached football at the high school, and Kyle helped run drills from time to time. The kid's attempt at manipulation didn't go unnoticed.

Steering them out of the cornfield, Kyle hauled Johnny toward his pickup truck. "No can do."

"Why not?" There was a hint of panic in the young man's voice as he continued to struggle. Kyle didn't know if that was because he'd got caught skipping school or because he knew something about the dead body that had been dumped there.

Once they emerged from the tall stalks, Kyle released Johnny with a warning. "If you try to run, I'll put you in cuffs. Understand?"

Johnny opened his mouth, no doubt to say something sarcastic, but then he seemed to catch himself. "Yeah. Okay."

"Good. I'm glad we have an understanding."

The young man snorted and stuffed his hands in his pockets.

Paul and Janey stood off to the side, neither saying anything. They both seemed to realize Kyle would have a better chance of getting information out of the kid than they would.

Kyle crossed his arms and leveled a hard stare at the kid. It helped that he was still in his uniform. Even though he wasn't officially on duty, Johnny didn't know that. "Now, let's try this again. Why aren't you in school?"

Nothing.

"Do we need to take this down to the station?"

"You can't do that!" The panic was back. That was good. Maybe the kid would think twice next time before he decided to wander around a cornfield in the middle of the day.

"I can and I will if we can't get this sorted out here."

Johnny kicked at a clump of dirt in front of him. "I decided to skip, okay?"

"Why'd you come here?" Kyle would deal with the young man ditching school later. Right now he needed to find out if he was there by chance or if he'd come to that area of the cornfield deliberately.

Again he was met with silence. Kyle was about to escort Johnny to his truck and follow through on his threat to bring him into the station when the boy finally answered. "A few of us come here to hang out sometimes."

"You mean you come here to party." Considering the amount of empty beer bottles they'd found, it was more than a few.

Johnny lifted one shoulder in a half shrug.

"You know there was a dead body discovered out here a few weeks ago, right?"

The young man nodded.

"Were you here partying the night before?" No sense in beating around the bush.

It was as if a light bulb went off in the kid's head. His eyes went wide. He brought his hands up in front of him and took a step back. "We didn't have anything to do with that, Kyle. I swear. You have to believe me. We didn't kill anyone."

"But you were here the night the body was dumped," Kyle said.

Johnny began shaking his head. "We didn't see anything. We just . . ."

"You just what?"

The young man's gaze darted around, looking for allies and finding none, before landing back on Kyle. "We heard a car, and we were afraid we'd get caught, so we ran."

"Did you see the car? Did you see who it was?"

He shook his head. "After we saw the lights and heard the car door open, we got outta there."

Now they were getting somewhere. "What time was this?"

His answer came quick. "Around midnight."

"You're sure?" Kyle asked.

"Yeah. I'm sure. I ran straight home, and when I climbed in my bedroom window the clock said it was twelve eleven." Johnny paused. "Am I in trouble?"

Kyle relaxed his stance a little. If nothing else, they had a time when the body was dumped. The road they were on didn't get much traffic, so the chances of another random car stopping the same night was slim. First things first, however. He met Johnny's gaze. "For skipping school? Yes."

"You can't just let me go? Come on, Kyle. My mom will kill me if she finds out." The panicked look was back. Kyle's mom was a teacher. He was right. She wouldn't be happy if her son got busted for truancy.

"Tell you what," Kyle said. "I want to talk to everyone who was here that night." Johnny started to say something, but Kyle cut him off. "If you can get them to meet me at the park near the statue today at three thirty—all of them"—Kyle made sure to stress that point—"I might be willing to forget about you not being in school today."

The young man still looked nervous, but he didn't hold his shoulders as stiff as before. He was probably considering the likelihood of being able to get all his friends to show up. "Thanks."

"But"—Kyle pointed a finger at him—"if I catch you skipping school again, not only will I be telling your parents, I'll also have to turn you over to the truancy officer."

Johnny nodded in quick agreement.

"I'm glad we understand each other." Kyle looked up and down the road, and then back at Johnny. "Do you need a ride home?"

"If I go home, Mom'll find out I skipped. Mrs. Epps is nosy."

Mrs. Epps was Johnny's neighbor. And he was right. She was nosy. In fact, she was one of the biggest gossips in the county. Kyle tried hard to hide his amusement. He'd been where Johnny was. Exactly where Johnny was, actually. Except he hadn't had the bargaining chip of possibly having overheard a murderer dumping a body. "You make a good point."

Johnny looked around him, taking in where Paul and Janey were standing. They'd been patiently watching the exchange, strategically placing themselves between Johnny and the cornfield. "Can I go now?"

Nodding, Kyle made sure to remind him of their appointment one last time. "Don't forget about this afternoon."

"Three thirty at the statue in the park. Got it." Johnny was already backing away. Once he was clear of the vehicles, he crossed the road and started toward the cornfield on the opposite side.

"Don't be late," Kyle yelled right before Johnny's figure was engulfed by the swaying corn.

Paul walked to stand beside Kyle. "I guess we're going to be sticking around here longer than we thought."

"Let's just hope they show up," Janey said, moving to stand beside her partner.

"They will," Paul and Kyle said in unison.

Janey sent them both a questioning look but let it go. "Well, it looks as if we've got a few hours to kill. Paul and I can hang out at the station if you want to get some sleep. We can meet you at the park at three."

Sleep? He had no idea how he was going to sleep knowing Janey was so close, but he knew he would have to try. There wouldn't be much time after the meeting for him to sleep before he had to be on patrol again. "Why don't you guys come back to my house and hang out for a while? I have an internet connection and a laptop. Maybe you can start looking into the four remaining women on your list."

Paul and Janey looked at each other, and Paul nodded. "Sounds like a good way to kill some time. Lead the way."

They climbed into their vehicles and made a U-turn back toward town. Kyle had to admit he had ulterior motives for getting Janey back to his place. Although they wouldn't be alone, he was hoping he might be able to steal her away for a few minutes. He hadn't been able to kiss her yet, and it was driving him crazy.

Janey sat in the seat next to him, looking out the window, deep in thought. Her hair, even though she had it pulled back, whipped in the wind and swirled around her face. She looked almost angelic.

He covered her hand with his and laced their fingers together as they drew closer to his house. She turned to look at him, a tiny smile pulling at her face. Was she thinking along the same lines he was? It had only been two days, but it felt as if it had been weeks since he'd felt her body next to his.

"I need to use your bathroom once we get to your house."

Not what he was expecting. "Okay."

Then he noticed a sparkle in her eyes. "I don't think I remember where it is. Think you can show me?"

"Yeah," he said, meeting her gaze. "I can definitely show you."

The ten-minute drive to his house felt like an eternity.

CHAPTER 17

KYLE UNLOCKED the door to his house and motioned for Paul and Janey to go inside. He turned on the lights and strolled over to the refrigerator. "Can I get you something to drink?"

"Some water would be great," Paul said.

Kyle grabbed a glass out of the cabinet. "Janey?"

"That sounds good."

He handed them both a glass of ice water and directed them into the living room. "Let me grab my laptop."

Without another word, he ascended the stairs two at a time, retrieved his laptop, and rejoined Paul and Janey in the living room. He handed the laptop to Paul.

"Thanks," Paul said, placing it on the coffee table in front of hm.

Janey set her glass down on a coaster and stood. "Can you show me where your bathroom is again?"

Anticipation curled low in his stomach. "Sure."

He turned, knowing she would follow. The only bathroom on the main floor was a half bath on the other side of the kitchen. It wasn't ideal, given Paul was only a room away in the living room, but it would be too obvious if they went upstairs. Then again, Paul was a smart guy. He probably knew what they were up to.

Not that Kyle cared. He doubted that if the roles were reversed Paul wouldn't be doing the same thing with Megan. Especially since he was pretty sure the two of them had done something similar on Sunday when he and Janey were there. It didn't take ten minutes to cut and serve cake, did it?

As soon as they reached the bathroom, Kyle tugged Janey inside and closed the door. His mouth was on hers a second later.

She molded her body to his, pressing her sweet curves into him. He was eternally grateful in that moment that he'd had the forethought to remove his gun belt while he was upstairs. It was impossible to keep his hands to himself, so he didn't even try.

Lifting her onto the counter, he stepped between her legs, letting her feel what she did to him. Janey responded by dipping her tongue into his mouth and deepening the kiss.

"Hmm. I've been wanting to do this all day," she whispered against his lips.

"Me, too."

"We can't stay in here long," Janey said. "He'll know what we're doing. He probably already knows what we're doing."

"Well then, we shouldn't waste any time, should we?" He quickly removed her sidearm from her waist and went to work on removing her pants.

She didn't comment until he had unzipped them. "What are you doing?"

He grinned up at her. "Having a snack before bed. Raise your hips."

A blush colored her cheeks, but she did as he requested. In less than twenty seconds, he had her naked from the waist down.

Kyle eased her bottom close to the edge of the counter and knelt between her legs. At the first lick, Janey's head tilted back. She tangled her fingers in his hair as he continued to worship her with his tongue.

It didn't take long for her breathing to become labored, and he enjoyed watching her chest rise and fall with each inhale and exhale. He inserted two fingers inside her, adding to her pleasure. "Come for me, baby."

"I . . . I . . ."

He redoubled his efforts, determined to send her over the edge.

Janey gasped, and then he felt her nails dig into his skull as she let go.

Removing his fingers, he placed a final kiss between her legs before getting to his feet again.

She rested her head on his chest, still trying to catch her breath. "Did I hurt you?"

He chuckled. "Totally worth it seeing you come apart like that. I'm going to have very sweet dreams."

A low moan vibrated through her chest and she pulled his mouth down to hers. She kissed him slow and deep. "I wish we had more time."

"Me, too. But if you don't get back out there soon, your partner is going to come looking for you." And as much as he hated to admit it, he did need to get some sleep. It was already after ten and he would need to be up by two if he was going to have to be at the park by three thirty.

She ran her hands down the front of his uniform. "I like seeing you in your uniform."

"Yeah?"

"Yeah. You're very sexy, Deputy Reed."

He groaned. "If you keep that up, I'm not going to care if your partner is in the other room or not."

Janey laughed and kissed him again. "Go on, then. I'll get myself cleaned up, and then Paul and I can spend the afternoon researching."

Kyle hated to leave her, especially when she made such a pretty picture sitting there half naked on his bathroom counter. He cupped his hand beside her neck and gave her another hard kiss. "I'll see you in a few hours."

The flirty grin she sent him did nothing to help the problem in his trousers. "Sweet dreams."

Before he could talk himself out of it, he opened the bathroom door and left her sitting with her legs spread, still wet from her orgasm. The image itself made his cock pulse. It knew what it wanted. Too bad it wasn't going to get it. At least, not anytime soon.

Kyle didn't miss Janey's giggle as he closed the door behind him and marched up the stairs to his bedroom. He needed to get to bed, but there was something he had to take care of first or he was never going to be able to fall asleep.

* * *

It took Janey a few minutes to clean up and get dressed. She tried to wipe the smile off her face, but it was impossible. Especially when her cheeks still had that postcoital flush.

As a last resort she splashed some cold water on her face, and rejoined Paul in the living room. He glanced up when she entered the room, and then went back to what he was doing. "Feel better?"

Heat crawled up her neck to her cheeks. He hadn't been fooled. He'd known exactly what they'd been doing in there. Okay, maybe not exactly what they'd been doing, but he knew they were fooling around.

Instead of responding to his question, she asked one of her own. "How's the search coming?"

"I'm looking through Cindy Fisher's social media. So far nothing out of the ordinary." He scrolled down through some more of her posts. "I called the captain to let him know what was going on and that we'd be here for the rest of day."

They spent the next few hours going through the social media accounts of each of the four remaining names. Two of the women still lived locally. One had moved to Indianapolis. And the fourth didn't have a location listed but appeared to travel a lot. Nothing they'd come across sent up any red flags.

She wouldn't call it a useless afternoon. They knew more about the women on their list, their lives, their hobbies. One never knew what small piece of information would lead to the next. It was always good to know as much as possible and then filter out what was helpful and what wasn't.

The sound of movement upstairs pulled their attention away from the screen. Kyle was awake.

Janey had been trying not to think about him so she could concentrate on her job. She'd be okay until she'd lean back against the couch and get a whiff of his scent. Then everything would come rushing back to her, his touch, the taste of him on her tongue. She'd had to get up more than once and refill her water.

Paul shut down the computer and closed the lid. "I'm gonna step outside and call Megan. I need to let her know I won't be home tonight in time for dinner."

Waiting until she heard the door open and shut, Janey headed for the stairs. It didn't take a genius to realize that Paul was giving her some time alone with her man. He really was a great partner.

Kyle wasn't in his room. She stopped to listen and heard the shower running.

Janey bit the inside of her cheek as she considered her options. She'd love to join him, but they didn't have time for that.

The shower shut off and her heart rate kicked up half a dozen notches. She could already feel her body softening, getting wetter, readying itself for him.

Glancing around the room for something to do, she settled on looking out the window. That wouldn't seem weird, right?

She heard the door open but kept her back to him. The sound of his footsteps echoed and then stopped. He'd seen her.

Silence filled her ears for what felt like forever before she heard him moving toward her. His chest brushed against her back, the heat from his body seeping into her pores and his presence making her a little dizzy. He leaned in, his breath teasing her ear. "I had some very pleasant dreams."

Janey released a shaky breath and turned.

He circled his arms around her, spreading his palms along her back. His heart beat a steady rhythm against her hand where it rested against his bare chest. He was naked except for the towel that was wrapped around his waist, and it wasn't doing a good job of hiding his pleasure at finding her in his bedroom.

She tried to swallow, but all the moisture in her body seemed to have gone south. "Daniels stepped outside to call Megan."

His eyes darkened and he lowered his head until his lips were an inch away from hers. "Good."

After that, all thought went out the window. His mouth covered hers and he pulled her in for a kiss that was bone deep. Her body didn't care if there was a murder to solve or even if her partner was downstairs waiting on them. All it knew was that it wanted Kyle.

She reached for his towel, but he covered her hand with his own. "Baby, we can't. As much as I want to, we can't."

He kissed her again, and then put some space between them.

It took her a few moments to calm herself down. No guy had ever got her motor running as quickly as Kyle did. She always needed a little warm-up, but with him all he had to do was touch her and she was ready to give herself to him in any way he wanted.

That was a scary thought, and one she wasn't willing to examine too closely. They were dating. That was all. It was a good thing that she wanted him. And that he wanted her. That's the way it was supposed to be.

Only it didn't feel like what she was feeling was normal. When she'd dated Ted, granted she was still a teenager at the time, but it was different. She'd been attracted to him and she liked him, or at least she had at first. But he'd never been able to get her heart racing with a single word or touch. There used to be a lot of foreplay first, and even then it sometimes wasn't enough for her. With Kyle, she didn't seem to have a problem. Ever. Even with the other men she'd dated over the years, it had taken work to get her there.

And it wasn't only the sex. She missed Kyle when he wasn't around. Their nightly phone conversations had become something she looked forward to.

"Penny for your thoughts?" While she mused about her feelings for Kyle, he'd gotten dressed in a clean uniform. He stood in front of his closet, buttoning his shirt.

No way was she going to let him in on the direction her mind had taken. Janey sauntered over to him, making sure to put a little extra sway in her hips. "I can't get over how sexy you look in your uniform.

It's a wonder the women around here can keep their hands to themselves."

Kyle chuckled and placed his hands on her hips. "Maybe you should stay here and fight them off for me."

"No can do. I have a killer to catch."

Sighing, he gave her a soft kiss. "I guess I'll have to do my best on my own, then."

Janey rolled her eyes. "We should get downstairs."

He picked up his belt, secured it around his waist, and checked his sidearm before holstering it. Seeing him do that shouldn't have made her hot, but it did.

She headed for the door and followed him out. They walked side by side down the stairs to find Paul waiting for them in the living room.

"Is Megan upset you're gonna be late?" Janey asked, trying to direct the conversation so it didn't end up on her and Kyle.

"She's a little disappointed, but she's used to my crazy hours." They all made their way into the kitchen. "Besides, she knows I'll make it up to her."

Janey shook her head, and Kyle laughed. "You guys hungry?" he asked, opening the refrigerator. "I think I have a pizza in the freezer I can heat up."

She liked pizza. Really, she did, but she avoided frozen pizza like the plague. "What about the diner? Would we have time to swing by there and grab something before we have to be at the park?"

Checking his watch, Kyle nodded. "We have about forty-five minutes. Should be plenty of time."

"Great." Janey smiled.

"Since we're going to be cutting it short on time," Kyle asked Paul, "do you think you could follow me to the station? I want to pick up my patrol vehicle. Figure it will make my questioning of the kids look more official."

Paul removed his keys from his pocket, ready to go. "Always a good idea, in my opinion."

The drive to the station was short. This time, however, Janey rode in Paul's vehicle. She sat beside him while Kyle ran inside the station.

"I don't know how you two do it," Paul said as they sat there waiting.

"Do what?" She had no idea what he was talking about since they currently weren't doing anything.

Her partner tilted his head at Kyle, who was striding toward the SUV he used on patrol. "The long-distance thing. I don't know how you do it. I'm not sure I could. I'd be driving to see Megan every chance I got."

She didn't want to lie. "I don't know. We just do, I guess. I mean, it's not like we have a choice. He has his job and I have mine."

"And how long is that going to work?" Paul asked.

"What do you mean?" Janey didn't know where he was going with this.

Paul maneuvered out of the parking lot, following Kyle to the diner. "It means I think I'll be breaking in a new partner in the not-too-distant future."

"You planning on requesting a transfer?" she asked, even though she knew that's not what he meant.

"I see the way you two look at each other." He glanced over at her, then back at the road. They were almost there. "Mark my words, sooner or later you'll be moving to Liberty to be with him."

His certainty irritated her a little. Even if he was probably right. "Maybe he'll move to Indy. Or maybe it won't work out. We haven't known each other that long."

Paul didn't comment. He parked along the curb, right behind Kyle's patrol vehicle.

She watched Kyle get out of his SUV and wave to someone on the other side of the street. Paul was right. If she and Kyle stayed together, he wouldn't be the one moving. She didn't know how she felt about that either. When it came to her relationship with Kyle, everything seemed to be all or nothing, and that scared her more than anything had in a long time.

Kyle met them at the front of Paul's vehicle, and they all went into the diner together. As they ate their food, Janey thought about what Paul had said. The more she thought about it, the more she knew he was right. Kyle fit here in Liberty. More than she had ever fit in Indianapolis. If they stayed together, she would be the one to move, and there was a part of her—the independent part—that fought against that idea. Why shouldn't he move in order for them to be together?

But even as the question crossed her mind, she realized how ridiculous she was being. They'd been dating for less than a month.

"You okay?" Kyle asked when Paul excused himself to use the restroom.

Janey needed to shake it off. They had an interrogation to do in less than thirty minutes. She needed to have her head on straight. "Yeah. Just have a lot of things on my mind, that's all."

"I know what you mean. I'm hoping one of Johnny's friends stuck around and saw something. Even if they got a glimpse of the car, that would be something."

He was wrong about the direction of her thoughts, but she went with it. "That would be helpful, but I'm not getting my hopes up. I still think the ring is our best chance of finding the person behind this."

Kyle checked to make sure Paul wasn't on his way back before leaning in closer to her. He lowered his voice to a whisper. "I'm kind of hoping the kids have some useful bit of information we have to track down and it'll keep you here another day."

"I can't stay here forever." Her voice sounded really breathy, but she couldn't help it. Not when he looked at her like that.

"A man can wish."

Paul slid into the booth across from them, and Kyle sat back in his seat. "You two ready to get going?" Her partner was trying to hide his amusement, but he was failing miserably.

Kyle signaled for the check. He insisted on paying, even though Paul tried to tell him they could expense it since they were on official business. It didn't matter, and eventually Paul relented.

Less than ten minutes later, they arrived at the park. It was three twenty-five and there were already a handful of kids hanging around the statue. They all stared at the two vehicles as they entered, looking nervous.

They'd talked about how this would go at the diner, and like before, it was decided that Kyle would lead the interrogation. He might not be a detective, but this was his turf. He knew these kids and they trusted him. At least, that was the hope. The fact that they showed up was a good start.

Kyle exited his SUV. Paul and Janey did the same. It was showtime.

CHAPTER 18

BY THE TIME they'd parked their vehicles, every one of the kids was staring in their direction. That was good. He wanted them to be paying attention.

Kyle exited his vehicle and strode toward them, taking in who was present. All the boys were members of the football team, most of them juniors or seniors, but there were a few underclassmen. Some of the girls he knew, but two were unfamiliar to him. Either they were new in town or from a school outside the county.

He stopped a few feet away from the group and addressed Johnny. "Is this everyone that was there that night?"

Johnny looked around. "Yeah."

Kyle nodded and spoke loud enough for everyone to hear. "I'm willing to bet that no one here is over twenty-one. I know most of you aren't. However, I'm willing to forget about the underage drinking if you all help me out with the case we're working on."

They looked from one to another. No one spoke aloud, but he knew they were deciding whether to help him or take their chances.

He could have hauled them all in and called their parents. Since he knew most of their mothers and fathers, he doubted he'd have a problem getting permission to fingerprint them. It would confirm the bottles of beer they found in the cornfield belonged to them.

Several moments passed before Jeremy Collins spoke up. "And you won't tell our parents?"

"I think we can keep this to ourselves." Kyle paused. "This time. However, if I catch you again . . ."

The threat was clear, and again they all looked at each other, deciding.

Jeremy was the one who answered. It was obvious he was the leader of the group. Kyle would have to remember that for future reference. "What do you want to know?"

He cut to the chase. "A few weeks ago, a vehicle interrupted your party. Did any of you see the vehicle?"

Everyone remained silent.

Kyle was about to move on when one of the girls he didn't know lifted her hand ever so slightly. "Yes?"

"I didn't . . ." She glanced around at the others again before returning to look at him. "I didn't see the car, but I heard a woman talking."

This was better than he could have hoped for. "Could you hear what she was saying?"

The young woman bit her bottom lip. "She said 'piece of shit.'"

He schooled his features, careful not to react. "Are you sure that's what she said?"

She nodded.

"What's your name?" Kyle asked.

"Becky." When he continued to wait, she realized he wanted her last name as well. "Becky Morris."

"I don't think I know your family, Becky. Are you new to the area?"

"Her family moved in this summer." Jeremy again. Kyle really was going to have to watch that young man.

Nodding, he looked over the group again. "Did anyone else hear or see anything?"

One by one they shook their head.

Well, it wasn't much, but it confirmed what they'd suspected. They were looking for a woman.

"You can go now. And lay off the partying. You want to have a few brain cells left for college."

Within seconds everyone had scattered, including Johnny, leaving Kyle, Paul, and Janey alone in the park. Paul and Janey joined him near the statue.

"What do you think?" Kyle asked, eager to hear their opinions.

Janey stood with her hands on her hips, all business. "Sounds personal. And if I had to go with my gut, I'd say this was revenge." Janey twisted her mouth. It shouldn't have been cute, but it was. "Although, either this woman offends easily, or she's had some really bad luck with men."

"So, what, you think it's more than one person doing this? A team?" Kyle asked. It was bad enough when they thought they were looking for one person.

"Maybe." Paul pulled out a notebook and jotted something down. "But serial killers have been known to have peculiar temperaments. It doesn't always take much to set them off."

This was true. Still, more than one person would explain the difference in location. Killers tended to stick to a pattern—and while the methods of all three murders were consistent, the where was not. "So what do we do now?"

"I still think the ring is our best lead at the moment. We need to find out who it belongs to," Janey said.

"Agreed." Paul pulled out his phone. "I need to call the captain and give him an update. The brass are chomping at his heels on this one."

Paul walked several yards away to make his call.

Kyle and Janey stood in awkward silence for several minutes before Kyle whispered, "You have no idea how much I want to kiss you right now."

Janey snorted. "You have a one-track mind."

"Only around you."

She rolled her eyes. "We're supposed to be focusing on the case."

"I can do both."

Janey didn't get a chance to respond. Paul walked toward them as he put his phone away. "The captain wants you to stay in Liberty for a few more days. He wants you to see if you can find out any more information and interview the women on our list who are local. I'm to head back to Indy and see if I can dig anything up on that end. I'll track down the woman on the list who's now in Indy and see if I can locate our traveler."

She narrowed her eyes at her partner. "You're the senior partner. Shouldn't you be the one staying here to follow the hotter lead while I go back home and start on a wild goose chase?"

Paul smiled. "I figured you might like to be the one to stay behind, so I recommended you for the job."

Images of Janey in his bed again filled his mind. It was difficult to concentrate on anything else, but somehow he managed.

"I didn't bring a change of clothes," Janey said.

"I'm sure Ava has some clothes you could borrow." The look Janey gave Kyle wasn't exactly what he'd hoped. Was she not happy about getting to spend a few extra days with him?

"I'll ride back to Indy with you tonight and drive back up tomorrow morning. There isn't much I can do tonight anyway."

Okay, so maybe her concerns were more of the practical variety. He'd been around his sister long enough to know that women tended to need things men just didn't care about.

Paul looked at his partner, seeming to consider his options. "That should work."

Janey's shoulders relaxed. "We should probably get on the road, then. I need to have time to pack tonight so I can hit the road first thing in the morning."

"I'll give you two a minute." Paul walked back to his vehicle and climbed inside, shutting the door behind him, giving them the illusion of privacy.

Kyle closed the distance between them but didn't touch her. "You'll stay with me while you're here?"

"I don't know." She bit the inside of her cheek. He noticed she did that when she was thinking really hard about something. "Maybe I should stay at Ava's. I don't know if I'd be able to concentrate on work if I stayed at your place."

"What if I promise to be on my best behavior while you're working on the case?"

She was tempted. He could see it in her eyes.

He lifted three fingers on his right hand. "Scout's honor."

"Were you a Scout?"

"Yep," he said with pride.

Janey hesitated, and then sighed. "Why can't I resist you?"

He chuckled and leaned in to give her a gentle kiss. "You shouldn't try."

Her eyes fluttered back open and she stared up at him for a long moment. "I should go."

Kyle ran the backs of his fingers along her cheek, reveling in the softness of her skin. She was so beautiful. "Text me when you get home?"

"I will."

Janey backed away from him, and he let his arm fall to his side. She stopped before getting in the vehicle and looked at him. A flirty smile played at her lips before she opened the passenger door and slid inside.

He couldn't help but chuckle. She'd be in his arms again in less than twenty-four hours and he couldn't wait.

* * *

It was after seven by the time Paul dropped Janey off at her condo. She'd sent Kyle a text as promised, and then went about packing for an indefinite amount of time.

Good thing she didn't have that pet they were talking about or else she'd have a whole other problem to deal with.

As it was, it took her until after eleven to get everything she needed washed, packed, and ready to go. By the time her head hit the pillow, she felt as if she'd run a marathon.

The next morning, Janey carried her suitcase to her car and set off toward Liberty. It was early. The first rays of the sun were peeking out from the horizon. She was hoping to get to Kyle's house before he got home from his shift so she could surprise him.

When Paul had told her she was staying behind the previous day, her first thought was to wonder what her captain had thought about Paul's recommendation. Captain Lane didn't know about her relationship with Kyle. If he did, Janey was sure he wouldn't have agreed to have her stay behind and work the case from Liberty.

Then there was Kyle. Her pulse kicked up every time she thought of him. His soft plea, asking her to stay with him, had pulled at her heart strings. She'd so badly wanted to say yes as soon as he'd asked, but her years of fighting for her place as a detective had made her reluctant to agree to his suggestion.

But she couldn't resist him. She never could. There was something about him that had her always wanting to say yes. It was dangerous. In her mind she knew that, but her heart wouldn't listen.

She pulled up in front of Kyle's house a little before seven thirty. His shift ended at seven, but she knew he'd have to stop at the station first before coming home.

Leaving her suitcase in her vehicle for now, she went to wait on the step for him. If she'd had a key, she would have gone inside and perhaps prepared a slightly different surprise.

About fifteen minutes later, Kyle turned into his driveway. Her heart pounded in her chest and anticipation curled in her belly.

He spotted her before he killed the engine. With a calm far removed from what she was feeling, he strolled toward her.

Janey stood and wiped her sweaty palms on the side of her pants. She opened her mouth to say hi, but before she could get the words out, he picked her up off her feet and planted a solid kiss on her lips.

"You're early," he said, not letting her go.

"I wanted to surprise you." She smiled. "Surprise."

He captured her mouth again in a searing kiss. "You can surprise me like this anytime you want."

She hummed as he went back in for another taste.

The sound of her phone ringing broke them apart. He set her feet back on the ground. "Luggage in your car?"

"Yeah. I—"

"I'll get it. Answer your phone."

Janey took out her cell and nearly had a heart attack when she saw the number on her screen. "Morning, Captain."

"Are you on your way to Liberty, Davis?" Paul must have told him that she'd come home to pack a few things.

"I just got here, sir."

"Good." There was some rumbling in the background. "I don't need to tell you how important this case is. We need a suspect and we need them yesterday."

"Yes, sir. I'm going to begin tracking down the women on the list the jeweler sent to us."

"Good, good. Keep me informed. And Davis?"

"Yes?" Kyle was walking back toward her, suitcases in hand, but she made herself look away. She couldn't afford to get distracted while talking to her boss.

"Watch your back. One of these women could be a cold-blooded killer. Don't do anything stupid."

"I won't, sir. And I'll call you with regular updates."

He huffed and then disconnected the call.

"Everything all right?" Kyle asked as he approached her.

His hair was a little wild from their kissing, and all she wanted to do was mess it up some more. Man, she could jump him right there. Unfortunately, she had work to do.

"Yeah. It was my captain. He wanted to remind me how important it is that we solve the case."

Kyle eased around her and unlocked the door to the house. He motioned for her to go inside. "Don't worry. We'll figure it out."

She set her purse down on the table and turned to face him. "We?"

"Noah wants me to tag along with you while you interview the local women on your list." He put her luggage along the wall and made a beeline for the coffee maker.

Janey wasn't sure how she felt about that. Not that she minded having Kyle's help, but did Sheriff Jenkins not trust in her abilities as a detective? Or was this a jurisdiction thing, like he didn't want her interviewing his citizens without one of his people present?

As if reading her thoughts, Kyle went on. "It's not that he doesn't think you can do it on your own, but he's taking this one personally. We don't get a lot of murders up here, and he wants this person caught as soon as possible."

How could she argue with that? Besides, if Sheriff Jenkins wanted, he could send her packing. The only reason the case hadn't been turned over to the state police was because her captain had gone to bat for her and Paul. They'd been on this case for more than two months and knew it inside and out.

Janey watched as Kyle made a fresh pot of coffee. "How are you going to help me and patrol?"

He looked over his shoulder at her and grinned. "I'm all yours for as long as you need me."

The way he said that made it sound like a lot more than him tagging along with her to conduct interviews. "So who's going to cover your shifts if you're with me?"

"Noah."

"Sheriff Jenkins is going to patrol for you?" she asked.

Kyle readied two mugs and got out the milk and sugar. "Yep."

She didn't say anything more while he finished making the coffee. Once it was ready, hers made exactly how she liked it, he brought it over and handed it to her. "Thanks."

He took a sip. "I'm not gonna lie. I'm kind of hoping this takes at least a week. That way you'll be here for the Labor Day weekend festivities."

"Did you and Paul concoct a plan so I'd be here for Labor Day?" She was trying to remember if the two of them had time to conspire.

Kyle chuckled. "No, but I like that you think we would. I kind of got the impression that Paul was a pretty straitlaced kind of guy, but it's good to know he has a devious streak in there somewhere."

Paul was a straitlaced kind of guy. Or at least he was most of the time. Megan had sort of rubbed off on him, though.

Deciding not to go down that rabbit hole, she moved the conversation in a more relevant direction. "Did you want to get a few hours' sleep before we head out to the first address?"

"Nah, I'm good. This cup of coffee will get me through till lunchtime at least."

She wasn't going to argue with him. "Okay. I was thinking we could try Cindy Fisher. She's the first one on my list. Any idea where she lives around here?"

"Not exactly," Kyle said. "But we can find out. Mary Fisher lives out on Mason Road, north of town. Cindy's her youngest."

"You think they'll tell us where we can find Cindy?" Janey was thinking more along the lines of looking Cindy up in the BMV records. She would have done that yesterday if they'd been at the station instead of using a laptop in Kyle's living room.

"I wouldn't see why not."

Janey looked at him over her mug. "We're conducting a murder investigation. It's been my experience that family members usually don't hand over information on their relatives' whereabouts all that often."

"This isn't the city. Things are a little different around here."

"So you've said."

Kyle downed the rest of his coffee and rinsed his mug out in the sink. "Besides, Mary likes me."

Janey raised an eyebrow in question.

"She was stranded on the side of the road a few months back and I stopped to help."

Instead of disagreeing with his assertion that Mary would gladly give up the whereabouts of her offspring, Janey finished her coffee. "So when can we head over there?"

He glanced at the clock. "Mary works the evening shift at the truck stop out near the highway, so she probably won't be up and about quite yet. Let's get your things upstairs and then we can head into the station. I think Noah wants to talk with us before we head out anyway."

"Maybe I should stay down here," Janey said when Kyle picked up her bags to take them to his room.

That seemed to amuse him. "Don't trust yourself to be alone with me, do you?"

"Something like that."

He shook his head and laughed. "Fine. I'll run these upstairs, freshen up a little, and then we can go. The remote is on the coffee table if you want to watch TV."

"Thanks."

His shoulders were still vibrating as he climbed the stairs.

Maybe she was being overly cautious, but she knew how she was around him—she lost all sense of logic and reason—and she needed her wits about her. She had a killer to catch. It was going to be hard enough to concentrate on interviewing potential suspects with him. The last thing she needed was to have fresh memories of sex lingering in her mind.

Deciding to take his suggestion, she sat on the couch and turned on the television. Janey flipped through the channels trying to find something to watch. She wasn't really paying attention—how could she when she knew Kyle was upstairs? He really was quite the distraction.

CHAPTER 19

AFTER KYLE SHOWERED and changed into a clean uniform, he drove Janey to the station. They walked inside and he caught sight of Mac. She'd been MIA every time he'd come into the station this week. He was beginning to think she was avoiding him. "Hey, Mac."

She stopped and turned to face them. Her gaze immediately went to Janey standing beside him. She clutched the folder against her chest and straightened her shoulders. "Are you just getting in from patrol?"

"No. My shift ended a couple of hours ago." He nodded in Janey's direction. "Noah wants me to tag along with Janey while she's here running down some leads."

Mac smiled, but he could tell it was forced. He hated that she was so uncomfortable around him these days. It made him feel as if he'd done something wrong by leading her on, but he hadn't.

"Good luck." She extracted some papers from her folder. "I was going to drop these off at your desk later. The lab reports came back. No DNA was found other than that of our victim. The only things under his nails were some dirt that matched the field where he was found and salt."

"Salt?" Janey asked.

"Yes. Common table salt." Mac shrugged. "Maybe he was eating not long before he was killed."

That meant they might be looking at a bar or restaurant as the last place their victim was seen alive. Again, it wasn't much, but he was hoping maybe all the little clues would add up to something big.

Janey accepted the lab reports from Mac and flipped through them. "The first victim didn't have any DNA evidence either. It would have been too much to hope that there'd be any on your John Doe."

"Any idea when the dental records will be back?" Kyle knew dental records took time, but they typically came in quicker or around the same time as DNA. It would be nice not to have to call the guy *John Doe* anymore.

"It should be any day now. I wasn't expecting the DNA results back this soon, but I'm guessing someone pulled a few strings and got it bumped up on the schedule." Mac made a point of looking at her watch. "I need to get going." A smile firmly in place, she said to Janey, "It was good seeing you again."

"You, too," Janey said as Mac disappeared into the stairwell.

Kyle guided Janey to the door that led to the offices and dispatch. The day shift was in full swing. He knew everyone there, but he rarely worked with them since they were typically coming on shift when he was going home.

Noah walked out of the break room and spotted them as he was taking a sip of his coffee. He lowered his mug and grinned. "I see you made it back to Liberty in one piece, Detective."

"Yes, sir."

The three of them weaved their way through the rows of desks to Noah's office.

"How was the drive? It's a beautiful morning. I'm betting the sunrise was quite stunning."

"It was beautiful watching the sun come up over the fields," Janey agreed.

Noah motioned for Kyle and Janey to take a seat. He shut the door behind them and sat down behind his desk. "I won't bore you with pleasantries, but I'm trying to keep the buzz in the office down to a minimum."

"I understand," Janey said. "I'd rather keep the details of the case isolated to the people who need to know for the time being."

"Agreed." Noah rested his forearms on his desk and leaned forward. "While you're here, I'd like you and Kyle to stop by my office every morning around this time for a briefing. I want to keep tabs on what's going on in my county."

"Understood, sir."

"So what are your plans for today?" Noah asked, leaning back in his chair.

Kyle glanced over at Janey before answering his boss. "We're heading out this morning to Mary Fisher's place. I figure she'll know where we can find Cindy. From there the plan is to work our way down the list of suspects."

Noah nodded. "Let me know if you need anything."

"We will," Janey said. "Thank you."

"Anytime." Noah stood, effectively dismissing them.

They exited Noah's office, and Kyle steered her toward his desk at the back of the room. He shared it with another patrol officer since the only time he used it was to fill out his reports.

Kyle grabbed a chair from a nearby empty desk and offered it to Janey. "I want to see if we have anything on Cindy in our database before we head over to see Mary."

Janey sat down and scooted closer. "Are you hoping to find anything specific?"

"Not really. I see Cindy around town from time to time, but we don't exactly hang out in the same circles." He typed her name into the search bar and waited for the results. "I just like to have all the information I can before going in."

"Always a good idea." Janey appeared pleased he was taking the initiative.

She scanned the large room, and he wondered how it all looked to her. They might be a small-town sheriff's office, but this wasn't

Mayberry. The office was bigger than most big city stations. The difference was the square miles they covered. A station in the city might be responsible for a five or ten square mile radius. They patrolled an entire county.

"So why don't you guys have a detective?" Janey asked, pulling him out of his thoughts.

It was a valid question. He was surprised she'd waited until now to ask. "We had one up until about three months ago. Jerry met a woman online and moved to Texas. Noah's interviewed a few people for the job, but he hasn't found a good fit yet."

They sat in silence for several minutes while the computer completed its search. Other than the basic information from her BMV record, which was three years old, only one hit came up. "Looks like Mike pulled her over for speeding last year. Other than that she's clean. I remember she got caught drinking a few times back in high school, but that was a long time ago and, of course, she was a minor so those records are sealed."

"What about Heather Sanders, Candy Wilson, Melissa James, Carrie Madison, and Angel Bryant?"

"I thought we'd ruled out Melissa and Carrie?" He vaguely remembered Melissa James. While he hadn't seen her in years, not since Ava was in school, he agreed with his sister. The ring that was found wouldn't have fit her. Not to mention he doubted her family would have been able to afford something as frivolous as a class ring. Carrie was another story. He wasn't sure he'd ever met her.

"I know they're both unlikely suspects, but I'm not ready to cross them off the list just yet."

Kyle nodded. He'd thought about all the women on the list last night while he'd been on patrol. "Let's see what we can find." Kyle typed Heather's name in first. "Heather is Hayden's sister, so I doubt there's anything in here on her. At least, nothing recent. She got picked up for a drunk and disorderly once, but that was at least three years ago."

Nothing new came up when he searched for Heather, so he moved on to Melissa. Her listed address was the same house where she'd grown up. Kyle wondered if that meant she'd never married.

He moved on to Candy. The address that came up for her placed her in a town about thirty minutes outside Indianapolis.

"Her social media was full of pictures from all over the world. Either she has a job where she travels a lot, or she's come into a considerable amount of wealth."

"She's a flight attendant."

They both turned toward the new arrival.

Patty Camp, one of the file clerks, was standing a foot or so behind them. "Sorry. I heard you mention Candy's name. She's my cousin."

Janey seemed to handle the intrusion better than he did. She smiled up at Patty. "Thanks. That helps."

Patty worried her bottom lip with her teeth. "Is Candy in some sort of trouble?"

Again, it was Janey who answered. But instead of responding to Patty's question, she asked one of her own. "Do you happen to know if she's still living in Greenville? There something on the case I'm working on that I think she could help with."

"Yeah," Patty said. "I mean she's usually home when she's not working."

"Thank you. We appreciate the help." Janey glanced over at him, raising her eyebrow.

He took the hint and stood. "Yes. We really appreciate it." He eased Patty away from his desk, asking her about a report he'd turned in the week before, leaving Janey to finish up the remaining searches on Angel Bryant and Carrie Madison.

When he returned from distracting Patty, Janey had already powered down his computer. "Anything?"

"Not so much as a parking ticket for either of them."

He knew it would be a long shot for them to find something on any of the women that would throw up a red flag, but it was better to check, especially if they were going to be interviewing them.

They began gathering their things. "Does Hayden typically work the night shift?" Janey asked.

Kyle returned the chair he'd borrowed for Janey to the desk beside his, and they headed out. "Yeah. She's a good kid."

Janey chuckled. "I wouldn't let her hear you calling her a kid. She has a crush on you, remember?"

"I'll try to keep that in mind."

The drive to Mary Fisher's house only took a few minutes. He parked beside a sedan that had to be at least ten years old. He knew it belonged to Mary since it was the car she'd been driving when he'd changed her tire. There was also a red pickup truck that was newer parked alongside. He'd lay odds it belonged to Mary's boyfriend, Clyde.

Kyle knocked on the door while Janey scanned the area. He hadn't been to the Fisher house in years. Not since Mary's husband died.

A minute or so later, the door opened and Clyde stood there looking half asleep in a pair of jeans. "Yeah?"

"Sorry to bother you so early, but we were hoping we could talk to Mary. Is she around?" Kyle asked.

Clyde ran a hand over the top of his head, sending what little hair he had pointing in all different directions. "Yeah. She's here." He looked behind him, and then back at them standing on the porch. "Come on in and I'll get her."

"Thanks."

The house was clean, although most of the furnishings were older. Clyde led them into the living room and indicated they should have a seat on the couch. "She'll need a few minutes to put herself together. Um, can I get you coffee or anything?"

Kyle lowered himself onto the couch. "Sure. That'd be great."

It ended up taking almost twenty minutes before Mary joined them in the living room. She was fully dressed with her hair and makeup in order. Clyde took up a post behind her.

"Sorry to disturb you this early, Mary, but we were hoping you could tell us where we could find Cindy," Kyle asked.

Mary released a loud breath. "Thank the Lord. I thought you were here to tell me something happened to one of my babies." She paused. "Is Cindy in trouble?"

"No, ma'am," Janey said. "We just wanted to ask her a few questions."

Mary really looked at Janey for the first time. "Are you Deputy Reed's girlfriend? The one from Indianapolis?"

He felt Janey stiffen beside him. "Yes. I'm also a detective with the Indianapolis PD."

"You're very pretty." Mary turned to look at Clyde. "Clyde, isn't she pretty?"

He nodded.

"Thank you, ma'am." Janey shifted. She was clearly uncomfortable with the direction the conversation had taken.

Kyle cleared his throat, hoping to get them back on topic. "Do you happen to know where we could find Cindy?"

Mary rattled off the address. "And if you can't find her there, she'll be at work in a few hours over at the feed store."

He and Janey stood. "Thank you. We're sorry again for dragging you out of bed so early."

She waved off his comment. "I needed to get up anyway. Always so much to do. You know how it goes."

The address Mary had given them was on the opposite side of town. Even still, it didn't take them long to get there.

They parked in front of a traditional ranch house. The shutters on the windows needed a fresh coat of paint, but the lawn was freshly cut and the flower beds well maintained.

Voices from inside greeted them as they approached the front door. A child squealed with delight somewhere inside, causing Kyle to smile automatically.

They knocked, and a somewhat frazzled woman came to the door. She had a smile on her face until she saw Kyle. "Can I help you?"

"Cindy Fisher?" Kyle asked.

"Yes."

"I'm Deputy Reed and this is Detective Davis. We were wondering if we could come in and ask you a few questions about a case we're working on."

A little girl about three years old threw herself around Cindy's leg. Her eyes got big when she saw Kyle. "You's a police officer."

"I am." Kyle knelt down to the little girl's level. "My name's Deputy Reed. What's your name?"

She pressed her face against Cindy's thigh, and then turned her head to look at Kyle again. "Sadie."

"It's nice to meet you, Sadie."

"We could talk out here if you'd prefer," Janey said.

Cindy looked past them, nervous, and then opened the door to let them in.

* * *

Janey was trying not to think about the interaction Kyle had with Sadie. When he'd knelt to talk to the little girl, it had done something to Janey's insides. She hadn't thought about having children in years . . . not since she'd given her daughter up for adoption.

"Sorry about the mess," Cindy said. Toys were scattered everywhere in the room they walked through. The kitchen, however, wasn't quite as chaotic.

"You've lived in Liberty all your life?" Janey asked Cindy as the three of them sat at the table. Sadie had stayed in the living room to play.

"Yep. Born and raised." Cindy brushed a strand of hair out of her face. "I always wanted to move to a big city, but things didn't work out that way."

"How old is Sadie?"

Kyle sat back and let Janey do the questioning. This was her rodeo. He was just along for the ride.

"She'll be four next month." Cindy played with a paper towel that was on the table. "Can I get you anything to drink? Water? Coffee?"

"No, thank you," Janey said. "We don't want to take up too much of your time. You graduated high school the same year as Kyle's sister, Ava, right?"

"Ava Reed. Yeah." Cindy rubbed the back of her neck. She was anxious, but Janey couldn't tell if it was because she had something to hide or solely because of who her visitors were. "Ava was one of the popular kids."

"Lots of guys asking her out?" Janey asked.

Kyle groaned. "Don't remind me."

Cindy chuckled.

"Such a big-brother response."

"Yeah," Cindy agreed.

"High school seems like another time, but it always seems to stick with you, doesn't it? No matter how many years pass."

A shy smile graced Cindy's lips even as she looked down at the table.

It was the type of opening Janey was looking for. "Did you get one of those class rings? Ava said they're really big around here. You wouldn't still have yours, would you?"

Cindy scrunched up her nose, slightly thrown by the question. "I think so."

Janey's tone was relaxed. She could have been asking Cindy about the weather. "Could I see it?" Figuring since everyone seemed to know she was Kyle's girlfriend, she asked, "Things are so different in these small-town high schools. I don't even recall if I got a class ring my senior year."

"Sure. I guess." Cindy stood. "I'll just . . . let me go see if I can find it."

"Thanks." Janey smiled. "That'd be great."

Cindy checked on Sadie and left them to go in search of the ring.

Janey caught the look in Kyle's eye. He was impressed, as he should be. She was a professional. She knew what she was doing.

Cindy returned five minutes later with the ring. It was in a small velvet pouch. Without pretense, Cindy removed it from the pouch and handed it to Janey. It looked exactly like the ring they had in their possession, with one exception. The stone didn't match. It confirmed what Ava had said. The ring they'd found was from Liberty-Bass High School.

"I haven't worn it in years. It just sits in my jewelry box."

"It's a nice ring," Janey said. "I like the dog on the side here."

"The Liberty-Bass High School Bulldogs."

They both looked at Kyle.

"What?" he asked.

Janey shook her head and grinned. Now that she was fairly sure Cindy wasn't the one they were looking for, she could relax a little. "I'm trying to picture you all decked out in your school colors, spreading school spirit."

"Oh, Kyle spread a lot of school spirit. Especially when he would come home on leave from the Army." Cindy's smile lit up her face. She was a completely different person from when they'd first sat down.

"Mommy, Mommy! Daddy's home! Daddy's home!" Sadie came running into the kitchen, excitement in her voice. She took off toward the front door.

Janey handed Cindy back her ring. "We'll get out of your hair."

"Sure." The nervous woman was back, and Janey realized instantly what was causing Cindy's unease.

Quickly, before the new arrival could interrupt them, Janey handed Cindy one of her business cards. "If you ever want to get together and chat, about high school or whatever, give me a call. I'll be in town for a few days."

At the sound of the front door opening, Cindy took the card from Janey and shoved it in the front pocket of her jeans.

"Cindy?" A loud booming voice vibrated through the house.

"In here," she called back, her voice sounding half as strong as it had five minutes ago.

A large man, close to six feet tall and with a chest as wide as Janey's torso was long, strolled into the room. He was at least fifty pounds overweight and swayed a little when he walked. He took one look at Janey and Kyle and narrowed his eyes. "What are you doing here?"

Kyle took the lead and Janey let him. If what she suspected was true, she knew that Kyle had a better chance of defusing the situation than she did. "Hey, Keith. How've you been?"

"Busy. Some of us work for a living. Unlike people like you who harass people for a living."

Ignoring the jibe, Kyle motioned to Janey. "Detective Davis is here from the Indianapolis PD working on a case. She wanted to ask Cindy some questions about her high school experience."

He looked Janey up and down. "What's so special about Cindy's high school experience?"

Janey knew for Cindy's sake she was going to have to give up some information she'd been hoping to keep under wraps. "We think someone Cindy went to high school with may be involved in a murder investigation I'm working on."

"Murder, huh?"

"Yes," Janey said, leaving it at that and hoping it was enough.

Apparently, it was. He turned his attention to Cindy. "You got my lunch ready?"

Cindy went to the oven, removed a dish, and set it on the stove. She scooped several large helpings onto a plate.

Kyle placed a hand on the small of Janey's back. "We'll leave you to your lunch. Have a good afternoon."

They made their way down the walkway to Kyle's SUV in silence, both no doubt hoping they were reading the situation wrong.

"You did good," Kyle said as he started the vehicle and pulled away from the curb.

She knew he wasn't talking about questioning Cindy regarding the ring. "It's not the first time I've been in that type of situation, unfortunately." The house faded away in the background. "Hopefully she'll call me."

He placed a comforting hand on her knee. "You did what you could. Now it's up to her."

Janey nodded. He was right, of course, but that didn't help the knot forming in her gut. This was a part of her job she hated. A part of her wished she had enough evidence to bring Cindy in for questioning. Not that she hoped she was the murderer, but to give the woman time to consider her options.

Then Janey remembered the little girl, Sadie. Leaving a situation like that was always harder when there was a child involved.

She took a deep breath. "Where to next?"

"It's still early. I figured we could grab some lunch at the diner and then head out to the Sanders farm."

Leaning back in her seat, Janey placed her hand over Kyle's where it still rested on her knee. Even though she wasn't really hungry, she needed some time to collect herself before they met with Heather Sanders. Hopefully, they wouldn't run into any more surprises.

CHAPTER 20

KYLE FINISHED his sandwich and pushed his plate away. "I wonder if Claire has any of her apple pie."

Janey was still eating. She'd picked at her lunch, taking small bites in between staring out the window.

He knew what was bothering her and he understood. Half his calls were domestic issues in one form or another. It was tough no matter how many times you encountered it. "I can make a few calls. See if anything's been reported."

She met his gaze. "I'm not sure it will do any good."

"You never know. Something could be sitting on someone's desk and they just haven't gotten to it yet."

"Can I get you two anything else?" Kennedy strolled up to the table.

"I'll take a slice of apple pie if you have any and a coffee." He winked at her.

"You big flirt," she said, giving him a playful push on the shoulder. "And in front of your girlfriend." She turned her attention to Janey. "What about you?"

Janey shook her head. "I'm good. Thanks."

"One slice of apple pie and a coffee coming right up." Kennedy hurried behind the counter, leaving them alone once more.

"You should finish eating." Kyle pointed to the half sandwich still on Janey's plate. "No telling how this afternoon will go."

She rolled her eyes at him, picked up her sandwich, and took a bite. "Happy?"

"Getting there." Especially since her response sounded more like the Janey he knew.

Kennedy returned with his slice of pie and his coffee. She also left the check. "Holler if you need anything else."

Janey pulled out her phone after Kennedy went to wait on another table. "I should give Paul a call. Check in."

Kyle dug into his pie while she made her call. From what he overheard, Paul had gotten an address for Angel Bryant, but he hadn't spoken to her yet. Janey had kept her update to him vague since they were in a public place but told him she'd text the information they'd found for Candy. Besides, it wasn't as if they had much else to share at this point. Nothing that had to do with the case anyway.

By the time Janey was finished with her call, he'd scarfed down his pie and polished off his coffee. He'd been in desperate need of a caffeine boost because he'd been up for almost twenty-four hours. "Ready to head out?"

They paid the cashier, and he swiped two lollipops from the bowl next to the counter. Once they were outside, he held both up in front of her. "Grape or cherry?"

"Those go straight to your hips, you know."

He grinned at her, determined to take her mind off how their morning had ended. "That's okay. I happen to like your hips."

Janey snorted and swiped the cherry one from his hand.

Kyle chuckled. He removed the wrapper from the grape candy and popped it in his mouth. It had been a while since he'd had a lollipop and the rush of sugar hit his tongue and filled his mouth. "I forgot how sweet these are."

Janey sucked on hers, pushing it to one side of her mouth. "I used to love these growing up."

He opened the door for her. "I preferred Tootsie Rolls."

"I never would have pegged you for a Tootsie Roll kind of guy," she said, climbing into the passenger seat.

"What can I say? I'm full of surprises."

The drive to the Sanders farm took about twenty minutes. Pete and Mae Sanders had lived there for close to forty years. They had four daughters: Hannah, Heather, Helen, and Hayden. Both Hannah and Helen were married, but Hayden, and as far as he knew, Heather, still lived at home with both their parents.

A dog barked inside, but other than that there were no signs of anyone around as they made their way up to the house.

"Let's check the barn," Kyle said.

Unfortunately, there was no one in the barn either.

Janey looked around, hands on her hips. He had to resist the urge to kiss her. "Any ideas?"

"I have a few."

She met his gaze, waiting. Then her mood shifted and she seemed to realize he wasn't talking about the case at all. Janey sucked in a breath and let it out slowly. "We're working."

"I know."

The energy in the barn began to change, and he knew if they stayed there much longer he was going to forget why he shouldn't drag her into an empty stall. For the life of him, though, he couldn't get his feet to move.

Luckily, there was a noise from the front of the barn. They both turned to see a horse being led into the stables. Hayden held the reins. She smiled when she saw him. "Kyle."

"Hey."

She shifted her weight and blushed. "Hey." Then she seemed to notice Janey standing beside him and she sobered a little.

He took the reprieve he'd been given. "Were you out riding?"

"Yeah. It helps to clear my head." She walked her horse over to the far wall and began removing his saddle. "Plus, it's fun."

He waited for a beat and asked, "Are your folks home?"

Hayden reached for the horse's bridle. "No. They'll be back

tomorrow, though. They went to visit Aunt Jenny and Uncle Bob in Terre Haute."

"Did Heather go with them?" He was hoping she wouldn't read too much into him asking about her sister since he'd asked about her parents first.

"Nah," Hayden said, removing a brush from the shelf. "I think she went shopping or something."

"Any idea when she'll be back? I was hoping to talk to her about something."

She frowned but continued to brush her horse.

"I could swing by later tonight if that works better."

Hayden stopped her movements. "Heather has a boyfriend."

Her assumption left him scrambling for a response. When he'd asked about her sister, it had never crossed his mind that she'd think he was interested in dating her. Especially since it was fairly common knowledge that he was dating Janey.

Stepping forward, Janey tried to salvage the conversation. "I didn't realize you had a sister. Is she older or younger?"

Hayden stared at Janey for several moments, then continued to brush her horse. "I have three sisters. They're all older."

"Do they all still live at home?" Of course, Janey already knew the answer, but Hayden didn't know that.

"No. Just me and Heather." The horse let out an impatient huff.

Janey walked closer. "You two must be pretty close, then."

Hayden shrugged.

"I always wanted a sister," Janey said. "One of the downsides of growing up an only child."

"It's okay. Most of the time." Hayden didn't sound all that thrilled about having siblings.

Janey ran a gentle hand along the horse. "I'd love to meet her. Maybe the two of you could meet us for dinner at the diner tonight. Do you think she'd be home by then?"

Hayden looked at Kyle before returning her gaze to Janey. "Sure. I guess. What time?"

"Let's say six thirty? Our treat."

Again, Hayden shifted her gaze to him. It lingered too long on a certain part of his anatomy before returning to his face. "All right."

"Great," Janey said. "We'll let you get back to your horse. He's beautiful, by the way."

The look of pride shone on Hayden's face. "Thanks."

Kyle and Janey took their time heading back to his vehicle. "Thanks for stepping in back there," he said, starting the engine.

Janey laughed. "I have a bit more experience with subterfuge than you do. Besides, it was fun seeing you squirm a little."

He turned the vehicle around and drove down the gravel driveway that led back to the road. "Do I need to be worried? About the subterfuge, I mean. Hayden I can handle."

"I've no doubt you can handle Hayden. She's a young girl with a crush. Eventually she'll get over it."

He nodded as he maneuvered the SUV back onto the main road.

"Got something to hide, Deputy?"

"What?" he asked, not understanding what she was asking.

"You were concerned with me being better at subterfuge than you are, so I asked if you had anything to hide. Do I need to do some digging on you? Do you have a secret past I should know about?"

Kyle chuckled. "I have plenty to hide, but for you I'm an open book. Ask me anything."

She contemplated that for a moment. "Would you ever consider moving to Indianapolis?"

That wasn't what he'd been expecting. "I don't know. I haven't really thought about it."

"But you love living here in Liberty." It wasn't a question.

"Yeah, I do. And Ava and Cole are here." Was she thinking about them? Their future? Was she trying to tell him that she'd never move away from the city? "What brought this up?"

Janey shrugged. "Something Paul said before he left."

Now he was really curious. "What did he say?"

"It's not important."

"Janey—"

She shook her head. "Let's just focus on the case. We have a few hours to kill before dinner."

He knew how they could kill a few hours.

As if reading his mind, she added, "We're not going back to your house."

Kyle laughed. "What did you have in mind, then?"

"Let's head back to the station. I want to talk to Mac again. Paul emailed me the file for the third victim. I'd like to see if she has any further insights."

Spending the afternoon with Mac wasn't exactly what he wanted to do. Then again, nothing was going to sound as appealing as spending a few hours in bed with Janey.

"I know what you're thinking," she said, a smirk on her face.

He raised an eyebrow. "Do you?"

"You're thinking you'd rather have me naked in your bed." She knew him too well.

"I'm a guy. That's pretty much a given."

She giggled. "Work first. There'll be time for fun later."

Kyle brushed his fingers down her arm. "Promise?"

He heard her suck in a breath.

When he glanced at her, Janey was staring at him. He waited for her response. "I promise."

* * *

Janey leaned against a file cabinet in Mac's office while she looked over the coroner's report on the third victim. The two of them were alone. Kyle had gone in search of coffee. He'd been awake for more than twenty-four hours and he was beginning to feel it.

Liberty's coroner chewed on the end of her thumb as she scrutinized the file.

"What do you think?" Janey asked.

Mac glanced up from her reading. "It looks very similar to our John Doe."

The look on Mac's face told Janey there was more. "But?"

"It may be nothing, but the Taser marks on this third victim, they're higher than on the other two."

Janey crossed over to the desk, and Mac pointed to the diagram in the file where it indicated the markings.

"On the first two victims, the Taser marks were down here, right above the pelvic bone. But on this victim, the marks are about six inches higher."

She was right. Although, there could have been several reasons for that. "Maybe the victim saw the attack coming and deflected it. Could also be the victims were different heights."

They flipped through all three files. Victim number one was five foot eleven inches. Victim number two was six foot. And their newest victim was six foot one. If anything, the marks should have been lower, not higher.

Janey leaned forward, resting her hands on the desk. "What do you think it means?"

"I don't know. But either the killer was standing on something when they tased the third victim—"

"Or we have more than one killer out there."

The two women were pondering that scenario when Kyle came back into the room nursing a cup of coffee. "What'd I miss?"

Janey and Mac shared a look but didn't say anything.

"What?" Kyle asked when he noticed the vibe in the room.

It was Janey who answered. "Mac thinks we might be looking at more than one killer."

He seemed to carefully consider the new possibility. "What makes you say that?"

The question was directed to Mac. "The Taser marks don't match on the third victim. They're a good six inches higher than on the other two."

"Maybe the third victim was on the ground when he was tased."

Mac was shaking her head before he finished his sentence. "I don't think so. If he'd been on the ground with the killer standing over him, the Taser marks would have come straight down. These were at an upward angle, exactly like the other two."

"Whoever tased the third victim was taller, standing on something, or wearing extremely high heels," Janey said. "I think we need to consider the possibility that we're looking for multiple suspects. They could be working together, and it just so happens that one of them tased the first two victims and the other took care of the third."

"Do we have any idea how the killer—or killers—are choosing their victims?" Kyle crossed the room and picked up one of the files that were on Mac's desk.

He stood so close Janey could feel the heat radiating off his body. It made it difficult to concentrate, but she forced herself to focus on the conversation and not her hormones. "Not yet. We should have the background check on the third victim, Luke Mayfield, any day now. Maybe we can find a common connection. That doesn't help us with your John Doe, however." She turned to Mac. "Any word on the dental records?"

"I was promised I'd have them tomorrow."

"Can you let me know as soon as they come in?" Janey asked. She hated waiting on lab results.

"You'll be the first to know."

Kyle closed the folder he'd been looking over and handed it back to Mac. "We should get going. I want to swing by the house and change before dinner. I think it might go a little better if I'm not in uniform. We don't want to give her any reason to be on guard."

Janey chose to stay outside in Kyle's pickup while he went in to change. She knew if she went inside with him, they'd most likely end up making out at the very least. They'd been working side by side all day, and other than a few intimate touches, they'd behaved themselves.

She filled the time by calling Paul again. Even though she enjoyed working with Kyle, it was weird not having her partner with her while she conducted interviews. Paul's experience meant he often picked up on subtle things she'd miss. "You got a minute?"

"Yeah. I'm on my way home. What's up?" Paul asked.

"I sent a copy of the file for the third victim to the local coroner here and had her take a look. She noticed something."

"She found evidence our coroner missed?" He didn't sound happy about that idea.

"Not exactly. She noticed that the Taser marks on the third victim were higher than on the other two victims. Given the third victim was the tallest of the three, it suggests the killer was also taller."

Paul immediately came to the same conclusion as Mac had. "There's more than one killer."

"That's what Mac thinks." Janey bit the inside of her lip as her gaze strayed toward the house. "I'm not sure what it means, though. I mean we have three victims, all with the same MO but with two different killers? Mac wondered if they were maybe working together."

"It's possible." She could tell he was thinking through the new information.

"Did you have any luck with Angel Bryant?" He'd mentioned he was going to try and track her down today.

"She wasn't home, but a neighbor said she works at a local bar. I was going to swing by there tonight after dinner."

"Just be careful, all right? I know you're a big tough guy, but you should have backup, too."

Paul chuckled. "I've got it covered. Reece is going to meet me there at seven."

Calvin Reece was another detective. He was close to retirement, but at least Paul wouldn't be going alone. "Call me if you find out anything."

"Always, partner."

Right as Janey disconnected the call, Kyle emerged from his house, dressed in dark jeans and a rust-colored T-shirt that hung loose. She should probably also have gone in to change, at least to move her sidearm to somewhere on her person that was less visible, but her current outfit would have to do.

When Kyle slid in beside her, he surprised her by reaching across the seat and pulling her closer. She let out a little squeal at the sudden movement, but it was quickly squashed when he covered her mouth with his.

"That's better," he whispered.

Her eyes fluttered open and she met his gaze. The way he was staring at her had her chest filling as if it were going to burst with emotion. She was falling in love with him. Giving her heart over to this man—any man—scared her, but she wasn't sure there was anything she could do about it. Sure, she could walk away, but even thinking about doing that hurt her deep in her soul.

Kyle rubbed his thumb along her jaw, making her feel as if she was precious to him. It was a feeling she hadn't experienced since she was little when she was with her grandmother.

Out of nowhere, the words came bursting out of her. "I had a baby. A little girl."

A look of confusion crossed his face.

Maybe it was seeing Sadie today and how he'd interacted with the little girl, but something made her want to tell him about her daughter. "You remember when I told you about Ted?"

He narrowed his eyes. "Yes."

Janey never talked about this, but the words kept coming anyway. "That's why he ended things with me. I got pregnant, and he didn't want to be a father."

Even though Kyle never stopped rubbing her jaw, she felt his muscles tighten and release. He was quiet for several long moments before he asked, "What happened to your daughter?"

"A nice couple adopted her." It was the one thing she hadn't regretted about the whole situation. A couple in their mid-thirties who couldn't have children of their own had adopted her baby. He was an accountant and she was a nurse. Janey knew, if nothing else, her little girl would have a good life. She'd be loved.

The muscles in his jaw clenched as silence filled the truck once more. She'd never told anyone about her baby or why Ted had left. No one knew except her grandmother and the social worker who'd helped with the adoption. "I want to punch him."

She didn't pretend not to know who he was referring to. And while his response was somewhat sweet, it was unnecessary. "He's not worth it."

"Maybe not, but you are." Kyle rested his forehead against hers. He opened his mouth to say something but stopped himself.

"We should get going. We don't want to be late."

Instead of releasing her, he placed a soft kiss on her lips. "Thank you for telling me."

The air around them changed again. She reached behind his head and brought their lips together once more.

Janey packed this kiss with everything she was feeling—even the things she wasn't ready to admit out loud. He took everything she gave and then some. By the time they separated, it took both of them a few minutes to get their breathing under control again.

He clenched the steering wheel several times before starting the engine. "Tell me about your grandma."

"What?" His question completely threw her.

Kyle kept his eyes on the road as he backed out of his driveway. "What was she like? Did she look like you?"

That was when Janey understood. He was trying to distract himself.

Janey glanced at his crotch, and sure enough he had a large bulge straining beneath his jeans. She pressed her lips together, trying not to laugh. From his point of view, she doubted it was funny. They had work to do, and it wouldn't look good if he showed up to the diner with a hard-on, so she tamped down her amusement and answered his question.

CHAPTER 21

HEATHER AND HAYDEN were already there waiting for them when Kyle and Janey walked into the diner. They were sitting in a booth about halfway back. He plastered a friendly smile on his face, hoping to give the impression to Heather that this was a casual get-together and not an interrogation.

Both women noticed them around the same time. Hayden focused solely on him, her eyes sparkling with excitement. She didn't seem as bothered about Janey's presence as she had been earlier. He was hoping that meant she was getting over her crush, but given the way she was looking at him, he was pretty sure that was wishful thinking on his part.

Heather, on the other hand, appeared to be a little more reserved. That could have been for a lot of reasons. Or that could have been her natural way of being. He didn't know her all that well.

Kyle let Janey into the booth first so she was opposite Heather, and he took the seat across from Hayden. Janey wasted no time. She extended her hand to Heather. "You must be Hayden's sister, Heather. I'm Janey."

Heather took the offered hand reluctantly. "Nice to meet you."

"Didn't I see you two earlier today?" Claire said with a smile as she brought menus over to the table.

Kyle took two of the menus and handed one to Janey. "We gotta eat, and I figured it would be better than poisoning Janey with my cooking."

Claire laughed and pulled out her notepad. "What can I get you all started on to drink?"

Once they placed their drink orders, Janey took control of the conversation again. He loved watching her work. She really was good at getting information from people without them realizing what she was doing. Before their food was on the table, she'd found out what Heather did for a living, where she'd gone to college, and that she'd recently broken up with her boyfriend.

"You and your sister both grew up around here, right?" Janey asked, even though she already knew the answer to that question.

Heather stabbed a piece of chicken onto her fork. "Yeah. We've lived here all our lives."

"Heather went to school with Kyle's sister," Hayden said in between bites. "They weren't really friends, though."

"You're the same age as Ava?" Janey asked.

Heather nodded.

"High school seems to be a big deal around here. Kyle was telling me how he helps out with the football team, and Ava was showing me her class ring." He liked how Janey segued to what she really wanted to ask. "Class rings weren't really a big thing in my high school."

Heather took another bite of her chicken, this one much larger. "Yeah."

"Do you still have yours? Ava said every student's was different depending on what extracurricular activities they were in."

Hayden was the one who answered. "Mine had a person playing the clarinet since I was in the marching band."

"Really? That's cool." Janey addressed Heather again. "What did yours have on it?"

Heather finished chewing, and then took a large drink of her pop. "I don't remember. It was a long time ago."

"Heather wasn't in the band like me. She was too cool for that." Hayden seemed to be oblivious to the tension radiating from her sister.

Kyle schooled his features so as not to give any indication he'd picked up on Heather's unease. Could she be their killer?

Heather shot her sister a look, but Hayden either didn't notice or ignored it. "She was a cheerleader. Always hanging out with the football team."

There was a cheerleader on the ring they had in their possession. Of course, they already knew the ring Heather purchased had a cheerleader on it. That was why she was on their list of suspects.

Janey didn't seem bothered by the sisters' exchange. "Well, I'd love to see it if you still have it. Seems like a big deal around here."

Silence fell over the table, and Kyle decided it was time for him to pull his weight in the conversation. "Hayden was out riding today when we stopped by. Do you do a lot of riding as well, Heather?"

The goal was to get her mind off the previous questioning and, apparently, he'd picked the right topic. Heather's eyes lit up, the first time he'd seen her perk up since they'd sat down. "I've been showing horses since I was eight."

"That's impressive," Janey said.

Heather blushed. "Thanks."

The topic transitioned from there to Heather's job, and then back to her college classes. In less than an hour, they'd found out several valuable pieces of information.

"Do you think she's one of our murderers?" Kyle asked once they were in his truck again.

Janey reached for her seat belt and secured it in place. "I'm not ruling her out."

"She seemed nervous. Both when we first sat down and when you were asking about the ring." He drove toward home, eager to get Janey back to his house.

"I agree. The big bite of chicken was a good cover, but it stood out, giving her away. She definitely seemed like she had something to hide. We just don't know what yet."

"I can't see her as a murderer," Kyle said. "Maybe it's because she's Hayden's sister, but it's hard to picture her bashing a guy's head in."

Janey didn't respond right away. "You'd be surprised what some people are capable of when given the right motivation."

He'd never been happier to see his house come into view. Pulling into his driveway, he parked his truck and hopped out. He was at Janey's door in two seconds, helping her down. As tired as he was, there was no way he was going to miss the opportunity to be with Janey. She was here. She was staying in his house, in his bed, and he was going to savor every moment of it.

After unlocking the door to his house, he went inside and turned on the lights. Janey closed the door behind them and flipped the lock. He raised an eyebrow in question. Not that he didn't normally lock his doors at night, but her action was rather abrupt. "We're interviewing murder suspects. I don't want any surprises."

He couldn't argue with that logic. Anyone who was capable of luring a man down an alley and hitting him over the head until he was dead was surely able to sneak into a house and try to harm the people who were attempting to bring them to justice.

Crossing the room, he pulled her into his arms and leaned down for a kiss. "I think we should call it an early night."

"Do you now?" She circled her arms around his neck, letting her fingers tangle in the hair above the collar of his shirt.

Kyle skimmed his nose along her neck before taking her earlobe between his teeth. "Uh-huh."

She tilted her head to the side to give him better access.

The sound of Janey's phone ringing caused Kyle to groan in frustration.

"I need to get that."

"I know," he mumbled against her throat.

Without losing contact, she retrieved her phone and put it to her ear. "Davis."

"I was expecting you to call me and give me an update." The sound of her captain's voice had her pulling away from Kyle's embrace. She couldn't be wrapped in her lover's arms while talking to her boss.

"I'm sorry, sir. I just called it a night. I was questioning one of our suspects."

"And?" Captain Lane wasn't in a talkative mood tonight. Then again, he rarely ever was.

"She seemed nervous and vague about her class ring. Her sister did confirm that her class ring had the image of a cheerleader on it, which matches the one we found. I told her I'd love to see hers but didn't really get a yes or a no out of her."

Kyle walked out of the room, leaving her alone in the kitchen.

"What are you planning to do now?"

"I might see if I can get any more information out of her younger sister. She has a crush on one of the deputies here. I might be able to use that to our advantage." Janey paused, gathering her thoughts. "I got the feeling Heather Sanders is hiding something. I just don't know what yet."

Before he could ask anything else, she filled him in on the rest of her discoveries. He was glad they were making progress, although it still wasn't fast enough, of course. He and the higher-ups wanted this case solved yesterday.

Janey disconnected the call and went in search of Kyle. He wasn't anywhere on the main floor, so she climbed the stairs to the second story.

As she neared his bedroom, she thought she heard a noise. It took her a moment to realize what it was, but her suspicions were confirmed once she reached his doorway.

Kyle lay on his bed, snoring away. He'd removed his shirt and his shoes, but that was it. Even his gun was still in its holster at his waist.

She stood there, taking in the scene. It almost looked as if he'd been sitting on the bed and just fell over on his side. One arm was draped over his head and the other hung off the side of the mattress. To be honest, the position didn't look all that comfortable.

Chuckling to herself, she creeped across the room as quietly as she could. Janey lifted his legs and placed them on the bed. Next, she removed his gun and holster, not wanting him to wake up with his gun grinding into his side. Moving down to his feet, she slipped off his shoes and put them in his closet. She considered attempting to remove his pants, but she didn't want to wake him.

After she was satisfied that she'd gotten him as comfortable as was possible, she went to her suitcase and extracted her toiletries. It didn't look as if her evening was going to end quite the way she thought it would, but that was surprisingly okay.

* * *

Kyle woke up the next morning with something digging into his stomach. He reached down to see what it was and discovered he was still wearing his belt. Peeling his eyes open one at a time, he glanced down to find that his pants and even his socks were still in place.

It only took a few moments for his sleep-addled brain to wake up enough to not only remember taking off his shirt and sitting down on the bed but to figure out that he must have fallen asleep and Janey had finished undressing him. He looked over to find her sleeping next to him in the bed. She was on her side, facing him, with the covers pulled up to her chin. Kyle's heart swelled as he took in her presence beside him. He knew he wanted to repeat this morning over and over. Although, hopefully without his belt buckle digging into his flesh.

Careful not to disturb her, Kyle padded into the bathroom to take care of business and grab a shower. His alarm clock said it was only six thirty in the morning and they didn't have to meet with Noah until nine, so he decided to let her sleep. There wasn't really any reason for her to be awake yet.

Okay, there was a reason. The erection he was sporting was hard to ignore, but she'd let him sleep last night when he'd needed it, and he was going to allow the same courtesy to her. He'd just have to deal with things himself for the time being.

Janey was still fast asleep when he strolled into the bedroom after his shower. He threw on a pair of jeans and a T-shirt, and snuck downstairs to begin making breakfast.

That was a bit of an exaggeration. He was going to pull out from the freezer some muffins his sister had made and unthaw them. It worked, right?

While the muffins were defrosting, he grabbed his laptop and checked his email. Yesterday when they'd stopped home before dinner so he could change, he'd sent an email to a friend of his in social services to see if Cindy or Sadie Fisher were on their radar. He'd been vague about why he was inquiring, wanting to see what she had first.

Karen's email was at the top of his in-box. He opened it and read through her response. The ER in the next county over had filed a report about a suspicious broken arm eleven months ago. Cindy had said it was from a fall, but the doctor had noticed some bruising that didn't match her story. The local police had come to talk to her, but no charges were filed.

That was all she had on record, which wasn't much. Either Clyde had only recently begun to get violent, or things were escalating over time. He was betting on the later. Abuse tended to get worse the longer it was allowed to go on. It rarely ever got better. And by rarely, he meant never. Kyle had never seen an abuser mend his ways. They tended to stick to a pattern, and it was never a good end for the person they chose to focus their energy on.

Kyle sent a quick email of thanks to Karen and asked her to let him know if she came across anything else. The sad part was that there wasn't much they could do at the moment. He only hoped Cindy would reach out to Janey for help. Then they could do something.

"Why didn't you wake me?"

Janey stood on the stairs in a gray nightshirt with a cat face across her chest. The material hung loose, but it gave hints at what lay underneath. He raked his gaze over her from head to toe before he answered. "I figured I'd let you sleep. We don't have to be at the station until nine."

He couldn't take his eyes off her as she came down the stairs. It was obvious she wasn't wearing a bra, and his brain immediately wanted to know if she had on panties. The possibility she was naked underneath that thin shirt of hers turned his brain to mush.

A knowing smirk from her told him she had a good idea what he was thinking. He should probably care that this woman had so completely enthralled him, but he didn't. As far as he was concerned, she could have him wrapped around her finger forever.

She strolled over to the couch and positioned herself between him and his computer. Instinctively, he sat back on the couch, and she took that as an invitation to straddle his lap. His hands gripped her thighs, staking their claim on her. It was as if they had a mind of their own. Then again, his brain was having difficulty forming a coherent thought at that moment.

He closed his eyes at the feel of her fingers threading through the hair at the base of his neck. She brushed her lips against his. "I thought you'd to wake me up this morning."

"We had a long day yesterday. I wanted to let you sleep."

Janey moaned as he moved his hands to cup her ass and bring her center in line with the bulge straining the front of his pants. He was right. She wasn't wearing panties.

"Sorry I fell asleep last night. I'm not sure what happened."

She kissed her way down his jaw to the curve of his neck. He tilted his head, enjoying the feel of her mouth on his skin. "You were tired."

He dug his fingers into her flesh as she scraped her teeth along his skin.

Before he could say anything, she went on. "So what have you been doing down here while I was sleeping in?"

It took a moment for her question to register. "I was checking my email."

"I see."

While he didn't want to ruin the moment, he also wanted Janey to know he hadn't been joking yesterday about doing a little digging on Cindy and her boyfriend. "I sent an email yesterday to a social worker friend of mine."

That brought Janey's head up as she abandoned her assault on his neck to focus on what he was saying. "And?"

"And there was an incident last year in the next county over. Cindy came in with a broken arm and some bruising that was inconsistent with her story."

The sexy vixen of a few minutes ago was gone, replaced by Janey the cop. The horny part of him wasn't thrilled with the new direction, but the more mature, rational part of his brain understood. What he'd found in no way dispelled their suspicions from the day before.

"She'll let us know if anything else comes across her desk about Cindy or Sadie."

Janey appeared to be deep in thought. She didn't move from his lap, which meant he was still very much aware of the scantily clad woman he had in his arms.

"What's going on in that head of yours?" he asked after several minutes had passed and she remained quiet.

"I'm trying to come up with a way to bring her in for questioning so I can talk to her and maybe convince her to press charges. But I don't want to put her or Sadie in any more danger."

"It's tough," he said. "I see it way too often around here. Murders may be uncommon, but domestic issues we encounter all the time. You'd probably be surprised at how many calls I get a month from neighbors complaining they hear fighting."

"It happens a lot at home, too, but I haven't had to deal with it as much since I've been a detective."

He nodded.

"I hate this," she said, sliding off his lap to sit next to him on the couch.

"I know. I'm not happy about it either. But all we can do is hope she calls you." Kyle reached for her hand and brought it up to his lips for a kiss. He knew he needed to get her mind off Cindy. "Are you hungry?"

Janey gave him a tentative smile. "What did you have in mind?"

He ignored the way his body responded and stood, offering her a hand up. "Muffins."

She blinked.

"My sister's muffins, to be exact."

"Well, why didn't you say so?" Janey began backing away from him toward the kitchen. "Your sister's muffins always trump sex."

The gleam in her eye told him she knew what she was doing.

He caught up with her in two seconds flat, picking her up and throwing her over his shoulder.

She squealed and started laughing. That was until he snaked his hand under her shirt.

His sister's muffins would have to wait.

CHAPTER 22

As it happened, Janey and Kyle barely made it to the station by nine o'clock. Janey wasn't complaining, though. No way was she going to complain about the three very intense orgasms Kyle had given her that morning. He'd seemed determined to make up for falling asleep the previous evening.

She'd rushed through a shower while he got dressed and got them coffee and muffins to go. It was crazy, but she felt a little like a teenager again. Not in the 'I don't have a clue what I'm doing' sort of way, but more that 'everything feels new and fresh and fun.'

Janey realized she was enjoying her time with Kyle. When she was with him, she could forget about the gruesome things she'd seen in her job, and all the baggage from her childhood didn't exist.

That was until she had time to think about it.

As she'd been getting dressed that morning, Janey realized again how comfortable she felt. She'd never lived with a guy before, but she'd always thought there would be a major learning curve. This was his space and she was invading it.

Granted, she wasn't actually living with him in the traditional sense. Even though he'd offered her a drawer for her stuff, she'd kept her things in her luggage. Janey didn't know how long she'd be there and there was no sense in getting too comfortable.

As much as it pained her to admit, she was scared. Kyle had the ability to hurt her. She didn't know when it had happened or how, but Janey knew if things didn't work out with him she'd be spending days, if not weeks, mending her broken heart in front of the television with a bucket of bonbons.

It wasn't a pleasant image. She hadn't cried over a boy since she was a teenager, and the prospect of sitting in her darkened living room, crying her eyes out over Kyle wasn't a pleasant one. There was a voice in her head that told her to run. To protect herself as much as she could —that maybe it wouldn't hurt as much if she was the one to leave him.

But even she knew that was a lie. Besides, she wasn't a teenager anymore. She didn't run away from her problems.

No matter how much they frightened her.

Sitting in Sheriff Jenkins's office later that morning, she tried to push her concerns out of her mind and focus on the case. On the agenda for the day was for them to go see Melissa James. She lived about thirty minutes away on the far edge of the county, almost to the small town of Bass. Even though, according to Ava, there was no way the ring would have fit Melissa, Janey thought she would feel better if she met the woman herself and was able to get a feel for her.

"You all right over there?" Kyle asked as they drove north toward Melissa's address.

"Yeah, I'm fine. Just thinking about the case." That wasn't a lie. She was thinking about the case . . . among other things. What Janey needed was to focus. "Take me through the call you got the morning you found John Doe again."

He glanced over at her but laid out the details once more. "It was around six forty-five when I got the call. I was already on my way back to the station when I got the call from dispatch. A passerby had spotted someone lying along the side of Butler Rd. I immediately turned around and headed in that direction."

"How far away were you?" Janey asked.

"Not far. Maybe five minutes." Kyle turned left onto a two-lane highway and almost immediately made a right onto another road with no center dividing line. "Dispatch had let me know it was between Monroe and Ada roads." He glanced over at her. "There's not much in the way of landmarks to reference on that stretch of Butler."

Janey nodded and waited for him to continue.

"It took me a few minutes of searching before I saw what looked like an arm poking up from the ditch. Once I got close enough, it became obvious the person wasn't alive. There was blood in his hair and on the collar of his shirt. I bent down to checked for a pulse, and the guy was already cold. I called it in and waited for the EMTs and then Mac to arrive."

"Did the person who reported it see anything else?

Kyle took a moment to answer. "I don't believe the caller gave their name. There wasn't one on the report that I recall."

She pondered that for a few minutes, and he let her have her thoughts while he concentrated on the road. The other two victims had been found next to a dumpster by employees taking out the trash. Janey had talked to each of them personally. They'd been eager to provide whatever information they could.

"So whoever called it in could potentially be our killer."

"What?" he asked, eyes wide, and he looked from her to the road.

"Sorry. I was just thinking out loud." She gave him a tight smile.

Instead of responding right away, he seemed to consider her assertion. "You may be right."

It was her turn to be shocked. "What do you mean?"

He shook his head. "When I pulled up to the scene, the only thing I could see was an arm, and I was looking. If I hadn't known it was there, I probably would've driven right past it."

"Maybe whoever called it in was just really observant," Janey said, playing devil's advocate.

"It was early. The sun was only beginning to rise above the horizon. Twenty minutes before that, it would have been too dark to see anything."

"Headlights?"

Again, he shook his head, understanding what she was asking. "I don't think so. As I said, it was difficult for me to see in the dim light, and I knew what I was looking for."

Janey pressed her lips together as she looked out the window. "I'd like to listen to the call when we get back to the station. Maybe there'll be something in there to give us a clue who it was."

"I'll call Noah when we get to Melissa's and have him retrieve the file so it'll be waiting for us when we get back."

As they pulled into Melissa's driveway, Janey got a text from Paul.

Paul: Talked to AB last night. Didn't have the ring on her, but I don't think she's our perp.

Kyle noticed her looking down at her phone. "Paul?"

"Yeah," she said, not taking her eyes off her phone. "He went to see Angel Bryant last night. He doesn't think she's the one we're looking for."

"Why's that?" Kyle turned the engine off and shifted in his seat to face her.

Janey shrugged. "Paul's pretty good at reading people. If he doesn't think she's involved, she's probably not."

Still, she was curious herself as to why he was willing to dismiss her so quickly as a suspect.

Janey: Why not?

His response was instant, which meant he was probably at the station.

Paul: She has an alibi for all three murders. She was working until close.

. . .

Solid reasoning, then.

Before she could come up with a reply, he sent another text.

Paul: I'm heading out to Greenville this afternoon. Will let you know how it goes.

Janey: We're at Melissa James's house. Will let you know how it goes.

He didn't respond, and Janey figured that was just as well. She and Kyle couldn't stay parked in Melissa's driveway all day.

She tucked her phone into her pocket and reached for the door handle. Kyle had gotten out of the SUV already to make a call to Sheriff Jenkins and to give her some privacy. Janey met him at the front of the vehicle. "Let's go see what Melissa can tell us."

* * *

Kyle hadn't seen Melissa James in years. He wasn't sure what he expected, but it wasn't the woman standing in front of him. She was at least thirty pounds thinner than the last time he'd seen her, and she wore enough makeup to stock an entire cosmetics store. Her clothes hugged her body and not in a good way. She wasn't unattractive, but the makeup caked on her face made her less appealing, at least from Kyle's perspective.

The cat must have had his tongue because after standing there for several long moments, Janey spoke up. "Are you Melissa James?"

"Yes." She was looking at Kyle, clearly wondering what a cop was doing on her doorstep.

Clearing his throat, he forced himself to get with the program. "I'm Deputy Reed and this is Detective Davis from the Indianapolis Police

Department. We were wondering if we could come in and ask you a few questions."

She thought about it for a moment. "Sure, I guess."

Kyle let Janey go first. It wasn't as if they were expecting trouble. Melissa wasn't a prime suspect.

One of the things he noticed right away when they entered the house was the knickknacks. The house appeared to be well taken care of, but there were little figurines everywhere he looked. He didn't think there was a horizonal surface in sight that wasn't covered.

They were led down a short hallway to the kitchen. It was much like the rest of the house, except the counters were empty of the clutter that seemed to plague the other rooms.

Melissa sat down at the table, and Janey and Kyle followed suit.

"How long have you lived here?" Janey asked.

The woman across from them glanced around the kitchen before answering. "It was my grandma's house. When she died, she left it to me."

"It's quite a ways from town."

Melissa nodded at Janey's observation. "I know. I don't mind. Actually, I love that I don't have neighbors on top of me."

Kyle knew that was a reference to her childhood. Melissa had lived in the poor part of town where not much more than a driveway separated one house from the next. That certainly wasn't a problem here. Melissa's nearest neighbor was separated from her by at least ten acres of soybean fields.

"You're lucky. I live in a condo. The only thing that separates me from my neighbors is a wall." Since Melissa seemed comfortable with Janey, Kyle sat back and let the two women talk. Hopefully Janey would be able to put her at ease enough that she would open up.

They went on discussing nothing in particular for the next few minutes until Janey decided Melissa was sufficiently relaxed. "We don't want to take up your entire morning, but we wanted to ask you a few questions about a case we're working on."

"All right." Melissa glanced over at Kyle as if she'd forgotten he was there, and then back to Janey.

"I know it's been a while since high school, but I'm told that around here it's a big deal to get a class ring your senior year."

"Yeah. It is." The woman sitting across from them frowned.

Janey cut to the chase. "Did you get one?"

Melissa's frown deepened. "Yes. We didn't have much money growing up. I mean we never went hungry, but there wasn't much extra for things beyond the necessities. I had to save up money from babysitting in order to afford it. Looking back, it was silly. I mean, it was just a ring, but back then it was a big deal. Or it seemed like it was at the time."

Janey reached into her pocket and removed the ring—still in the evidence bag—and laid it on the table in front of Melissa. "This was found at a crime scene. We're hoping whoever it belongs to saw something and can help us solve the case."

Kyle was stunned Janey had shown Melissa the ring. She hadn't done that with either of the other two women they'd spoken with. Then again, their talk with Cindy had been cut short, and Heather . . . well, he was still making up his mind about her. Yes, she was Hayden's sister, but that didn't mean she was innocent.

At first, Melissa just stared at the bag as if it might jump off the table and bite her. Then she leaned in to take a closer look.

"Does it look like it's from your high school?" Janey asked.

Melissa looked up from the ring, meeting Janey's gaze. "Yeah."

Janey let her look at the ring for a little longer before asking her next question. "Any idea who this one might belong to? Does it look familiar to you?"

She narrowed her eyes, looking closer. "Looks like it belonged to a cheerleader."

Given the little cheerleader with the pom-poms on the ring, this wasn't new information. Unfortunately, all of their suspects had been on the cheerleading squad at some point during high school. Including Melissa James. "Anything else?" Kyle asked.

"Not really." Melissa stood and walked over to the coffee maker. She retrieved a mug from the cabinet. "I haven't had nearly enough coffee this morning. Would you like some?"

Janey got to her feet, removed the evidence bag from the table, and returned it to her pocket. "We're good. Thank you."

Kyle followed Janey's lead and stood as well. "Is there anything else you noticed about the ring?"

After taking a long sip of her coffee, Melissa shook her head. "I'm sorry I couldn't be more help. High school was just such a long time ago."

"Well, we won't take up any more of your time." Janey began moving toward the door.

He placed one of his cards on the table. "Give us a call if you happen to think of anything else."

Melissa nodded.

Janey was already sitting in his patrol vehicle by the time he exited the house. She waited until they were on the road before saying anything. "She's hiding something."

"I got that impression as well." Kyle drove for another five minutes before he asked the question that had been on his mind since they left Melissa's house. "Do you think she knows who the ring belongs to?"

"Maybe. Or she thinks she might." Janey blew out a frustrated breath. "I knew this interview was a long shot, but instead of crossing Melissa off our list of suspects, she's worked her way to the top."

"We've eliminated two of the six so far. At least that's progress. Hopefully listening to the call will give us something else to go on." He turned onto the main road that led back to town. "Noah said he'd have it ready for us when we got back."

"I need to call Daniels. Let him know about Melissa."

Kyle listened to the one-sided conversation. Janey filled Paul in on the details of their meeting with Melissa James. It was interesting watching her work. She might have seemed completely relaxed during the interview, but she'd taken in bits of information he would have completely dismissed. Like the fact that Melissa kept glancing to her right. Kyle had chalked it up as nerves, but when Janey relayed the information to her partner, she pointed out that Melissa's cell phone had been sitting on the counter. Exactly where she'd been looking.

His girlfriend was good at her job and that was an incredible turn-on. He really wished they weren't on the hunt for a killer. He would have liked to take her home and keep her in his bed for a few days.

Unfortunately, that wasn't an option. They had a killer—or two—to catch.

She disconnected the call as they neared the edge of town. "Paul's on his way to Greenville now with Rollins. He did some more research on Candy Wilson this morning and confirmed she works for an airline, which is why she's constantly traveling."

"Do we know if she was out of town when the murders happened?" Kyle asked.

"Not yet. He's been trying to track her movements via social media since she likes to post pictures from her travels."

Kyle maneuvered into a parking spot in front of the station and turned off the engine. He covered Janey's hand with his and gave it a comforting squeeze. It wasn't what he really wanted to do, but that would require them being alone, preferably with a nice comfy bed nearby. Since that wasn't an option at the moment, he settled for touching her hand.

Janey met his gaze and smiled.

They were so lost in the moment they didn't see or hear Mac walk up to the SUV until she rapped on the glass.

Both Kyle and Janey jerked away from each other at the sound and turned toward the noise. Mac's face stared back at them.

He opened the door and climbed out of the vehicle. "What's up?"

Mac waited to answer until Janey joined them. "The DNA results came back on our John Doe this morning. His name's Martin Clawson. He was twenty-six years old and lived about forty-five minutes from here." She handed Janey a folder. "I figured you'd want the information as soon as possible."

"Thanks." Janey took the folder and immediately began scanning through it.

"Any progress?" Mac asked as they moved toward the building.

He opened his mouth to answer, but Janey cut him off. "Some. There are still quite a few pieces of the puzzle that aren't adding up yet."

Kyle held the door open for Janey and Mac while they went inside. "Well, let me know if there's anything else I can do."

"We will," Janey said. "And thanks again."

Mac grinned and crossed to the stairwell.

Once they were alone again, Kyle leaned in a little closer. He could smell the scent of her shampoo. "Seeing anything interesting in there that could help us solve the case?"

Janey took a step forward, putting some distance between them. "I don't know. I want to compare it to the other two files. See if there are any similarities."

She started to walk away, but he grabbed her arm and pulled her off to the side. It wasn't completely private, but it was better than standing out in the middle of the foyer. "What's wrong?"

"Nothing."

He held her gaze, waiting.

Janey sighed. "We shouldn't be . . . touching like that when we're working. It's unprofessional. Mac—"

"Mac knows you're my girlfriend."

"That's not the point." Janey looked around, surveying their surroundings. "I just . . . I can't think when you touch me like that, okay?"

A slow smile crossed his lips.

He didn't get to process his thought any further, though. Right as he opened his mouth to respond, Noah marched into the foyer toward them. "I need you two in my office. Now."

CHAPTER 23

Janey's heart raced. What had happened? Had there been another murder?

The sheriff ushered them into his office and closed the door firmly behind them. He didn't mince words. "I can't find any record of the call to dispatch."

He didn't need to explain what call he was talking about. They all knew what he was referring to.

"The record's missing?" Kyle leaned against one of the bookcases lining the wall, but he looked anything but relaxed. The muscle in his jaw flexed as he waited for his boss's answer.

Noah Jenkins walked over to the window. "I went to find it right after we hung up, but it wasn't there. I thought maybe in the craziness of that morning that somehow it hadn't been logged right, so I went through all the calls an hour before and an hour after you discovered the body." He looked at Kyle, deep lines creasing his forehead. "All the internal calls dispatching additional deputies were there, but nothing external. It's as if it didn't exist."

"That's impossible," Kyle said.

Janey took a step forward. "Could they have been moved somewhere else?"

"No." The sheriff shook his head. "All the files are recorded by the system and immediately archived. It's all automatic. As soon as the call comes in, it starts recording."

Janey knew this, of course. Incoming calls to dispatch could be used as evidence in court, so making sure they were not only recorded but kept secure was imperative.

None of them spoke for several moments, each mulling over what this could mean. Janey was the first to speak up. "Is it possible someone hacked into the system and deleted it?"

Sheriff Jenkins answered. "I suppose it's possible. It is a computer system, after all, but who around here has that kind of skill?" He paused for a moment. "And access."

"Brent?" Kyle asked.

Tension radiated from the sheriff as he considered that for a few seconds. "He could probably do it, but what would be his motive?"

"A woman?"

The sheriff seemed to consider the question for a moment. "I've never seen him with anyone or heard any rumors."

"Who's Brent?" Janey had met quite a few people since coming to Liberty, but she didn't recall being introduced to anyone named Brent.

"He works next door at the courthouse. You haven't met him, but he's a wiz at computers. If you ever need help finding something, he's your guy."

Kyle seemed to be as worried about the new development as Noah was, and Janey couldn't say she disagreed. It made her think that maybe she was correct. Maybe there was something on the recording that pointed to the killer. "Hayden was the one working dispatch that morning, right? Maybe we should talk to her. See if she remembers anything out of the ordinary."

"It's worth a shot." Kyle moved to stand beside Janey—a little too close considering they were in his boss's office talking about a case. But she was beginning to realize that no one here seemed bothered by her and Kyle's personal relationship. The more laid-back attitude of a small town was going to take some getting used to.

"Agreed." Noah crossed his arms over his chest. "I'll make a call to a buddy of mine who's good with computers. Maybe he can tell if the file's been tampered with."

Kyle placed his hand at the small of Janey's back. "Did Mac show you the DNA results on our victim?"

"Martin Clawson. I've got a call into the local sheriff to see if he has any information." Noah turned his attention to Janey. "I already put a call into your partner. He's running a background check as we speak. Hopefully we'll find a common denominator between the three victims."

Janey was a little shocked he'd called Paul, but it was his decision. "There's always something. We just have to find it."

Noah nodded and crossed to his desk. "How did the interview go with Melissa James?"

"She was nervous when we showed her the ring." It was hard to concentrate with Kyle touching her, but somehow she managed. "She said she didn't know who it belonged to, but I'm guessing she either knows who the rings owner is or she thinks she does."

"Do you think she's involved?" Noah asked.

Kyle and Janey shared a look before he answered. "We don't think so. While she was curious when we showed up on her doorstep, it wasn't until Janey pulled out the ring that she showed any signs of unease."

"Before you head over to see Hayden, why don't you swing by your sister's." Noah took a seat behind his desk. "See if she remembers who Melissa hung out with in high school. If she recognizes the ring, chances are it belongs to someone she was close to."

Nodding, Kyle began moving them both toward the door. Janey guessed they were done.

Kyle's hand was on the doorknob before Noah spoke again. "Watch your back. Both of you. We're ruffling some feathers here, and if whoever's involved in this is local, then they most likely own a firearm or have access to one. I don't want the next call I receive to be that one of my officers has been shot."

The drive to Ava's was quiet. Janey was mulling over the newest development and figured Kyle was doing the same. That and the possibility that somehow the audio files had been tampered with. And if those had been tampered with, had others? The implications were huge. Past cases could be called into question. Convictions could be appealed. The whole thing could snowball quickly.

They were each still deep in thought as they walked into Ava's house. A loud squeal greeted their ears, causing them both to grin for the first time since leaving the station. Cole's joy at whatever held his attention lifted their mood.

"Oh. Hey," Ava said as she came around the corner. Cole was in her arms, stuffing his face with a cookie.

Kyle extended his arms toward his nephew. The little boy didn't hesitate. He nearly leaped into his uncle's arms. "How're you doing, buddy?"

"Yummy cookie."

They all chuckled.

Securing Cole on his hip, Kyle addressed his sister. "We need your help with something. Do you remember who Melissa James used to hang around with in high school?"

Ava motioned for them to go into the living room. Kyle took a seat with Cole in the high-backed chair while Janey and Ava sat on the couch.

"Mommy, juice," Cole said.

Before Ava could get up, Kyle was already on his feet. "Is his sippy cup on the counter?"

She sent him a grateful smile. "Yes. Thank you."

Once the women were alone, Janey got back to why they were there in the first place. "We think Melissa may know who the ring belongs to. That makes us think it may be someone she's close to. Or was."

Ava walked over to a cabinet along the far wall. "Even though Melissa's family wasn't wealthy, she had a lot of friends."

"Any that stand out to you?"

She removed a book from the bottom shelf and brought it back with her. Ava set it on her lap and began flipping through the pages. It was a yearbook from Liberty-Bass High School. "Not really. I mean she hung out with a group of girls, but I don't recall her being closer to one more than the other."

Once Ava had found the page she wanted, she handed the book to Janey. It was group of five girls, all of them smiling. Three of them were in cheerleader uniforms.

"That's Melissa," Ava said, pointing to the girl on the far left. She was slightly heavier than the woman Janey had met earlier that morning and she wore a lot less makeup. "The other girls are Cali Mitchel, Riley Brennen, Heather Sanders, and Angel Bryant."

Janey had recognized Heather immediately. She hadn't changed much since high school. "What do you know about Heather and Angel? What were they like back then?"

Both were on her suspects list and both were wearing cheerleading outfits in the picture. Given Melissa's reaction, there was a good chance Melissa thought the ring belonged to one of them. Now all Janey had to do was figure out which one.

"I didn't really hang with either of them, but they seemed nice enough. Heather was really involved in showing horses. She would occasionally miss school to drive to shows and stuff. Angel was more of a bookworm. If she wasn't cheering or hanging out with her friends, she was reading. I think she missed out on being valedictorian by like a half percentage point or something."

"Either one of them show any violent tendencies?" Janey asked.

"Not that I remember."

Janey ran her fingers over the picture.

"I can tell by your frown I didn't help much, did I?"

"It's okay," Janey said, handing the yearbook back to Ava. "Every bit of information helps, even if it doesn't always appear to at first."

Ava bit her bottom lip and glanced over Janey's shoulder toward where Kyle had disappeared with Cole. "Can I be nosy and ask how it's going with my brother? You two seem to be getting along pretty well."

Much to her dismay, Janey felt her cheeks heat. She wasn't expecting quite such a personal turn in the conversation, but she guessed she shouldn't have been surprised. Of course Ava would want to know where Janey's relationship with Kyle was going. She was his sister after all, and Janey knew Kyle was the only family Ava had left. Still, it was awkward. "We're fine."

"Just fine?" Ava raised her eyebrows, eager for her to share.

Janey's gaze danced around the room before looking Kyle's sister in the eye. She didn't really know what to say. She wasn't used to sharing these things with anyone. "Things are . . . good."

The smirk on Ava's face said she wasn't fooled. "Well, I'm glad. I think you two make a cute couple. And Kyle seems really happy."

Not sure how to respond, Janey remained silent.

"Maybe we should go check on the boys." Ava stood and waited for Janey to join her.

Glad to be moving away from the discussion of her personal life, Janey let Ava lead her into the kitchen. They found Kyle and Cole sitting at the kitchen table. The sight of him with his nephew hit her harder than it had the first time she'd seen them together. He'd be a great father someday. And instinctively Janey knew he wouldn't shy away from his responsibilities.

Her breath caught in her throat as Kyle looked up and met her gaze. Their eyes were only locked for a moment, but it was enough to send her pulse racing. Every inch of her skin heated. She needed some air. Or maybe a cold shower.

"And what have we here?" Ava asked.

Kyle shifted his attention to his sister, a guilty expression crossing his face. It was then Janey noticed the cookie crumbs covering the table in front of Kyle and Cole . . . along with an empty plate.

Kyle swallowed and turned on that charming smile of his that always made her melt. "You ladies finished?"

Ava shook her head and sighed, not appearing to be affected by his smile in the least. "How many cookies did you let him have?"

"Just a couple."

"Uh-huh." Ava grabbed a cloth out of the drawer, ran it under some water, and began cleaning the mess from her son's face and hands. Then she moved on to the table itself.

In an effort to help with the cleanup, or maybe to make up for allowing Cole to eat an unknown number of cookies, Kyle carried the now empty plate to the sink and rinsed it off. "Did you need me to stop by later? We're heading out to the Sanders farm, but we could swing by on our way back if you need us to."

Ava finished wiping the table and dumped the crumbs in the trash. "You two have enough on your plate right now. Don't worry about me and Cole. We're just gonna hang around the house."

He pulled his sister in for a hug and placed a kiss on top of Cole's head. "Call me if you need anything."

Janey said goodbye to Ava and they headed out.

"Did my sister have any information that could help us?" Kyle asked as soon as they were outside.

She glanced down at the yearbook she held in her arms. "Maybe. There's a picture in here of Melissa with two of our other suspects. Both of them are wearing cheerleader uniforms."

"Let me guess," he said, opening the door to his SUV. "One of them is Heather Sanders."

"Yep."

He settled behind the wheel and put the key in the ignition. "And the other?"

"Angel Bryant."

Seeing as how Paul didn't think Angel was involved, that left Heather. Of course, that didn't mean she was actually involved. It did, however, mean she was now their prime suspect.

Kyle seemed to be thinking along the same lines as she was. "Maybe we'll get lucky and both Heather and Hayden will be home. Suddenly I feel the need to have another chat with Heather."

* * *

The minute they pulled up in front of the Sanderses' home, Kyle knew their visit was going to be a bust. The horse trailer was gone. Most likely the entire family had headed out of town for a show or rodeo.

"I don't think they're home."

Janey had already unbuckled her seat belt. "Why's that?"

He nodded toward the side of the barn where the trailer had been parked. "The horse trailer is gone and all the windows in the house are closed. So is the barn."

After several moments, Janey snapped her seat belt back in place. "Let's head back into town and grab some lunch. Maybe someone at the diner knows where they went."

Kyle grinned at his companion. "Now you're starting to talk like a local."

Janey ignored his comment. "Does the diner have WiFi?"

Her question caught him off guard. "Yeah."

"Good. Let's stop by your house on the way and pick up your laptop. I want to log into the files of the other two victims now that we know who John Doe is and see if we can spot any similarities."

He had to admit he was anxious to go over the files himself. Not that he had a clue what exactly they were looking for. Chasing bad guys he knew how to do. And interviewing suspects wasn't all that different from his usually job either. All too often he'd find himself talking someone down. Sifting through files, however, wasn't something he was used to. "Anything in particular we should be looking for in the files?"

She shrugged. "Anything that pops up for more than one of the victims."

"Not all three because it might have been missed."

"Exactly." Janey turned to look at him. Or she tried. The seat belt restricted her movement considerably. "After lunch, we should check in with Sheriff Jenkins and see if his tech guy was able to find anything. If not, maybe we should pay a visit to this computer wiz of yours. If he's not in on it, then maybe he can help us. If he is in on it, maybe we can get some idea of motive."

Kyle chuckled. "When are you going to start calling him by his name?"

"What? Who?"

"Noah. You always call him Sheriff Jenkins."

Janey shrugged. "I don't know. It doesn't feel right."

"You've got to lose that city way of thinking. We're a lot more laid back around here."

She didn't answer right away. "Does that mean this thing with us is just casual to you?"

Her question came from out of the blue. "No. Not at all. Why would you ask that?"

Again, she shrugged. "Just wondering, that's all."

He wasn't going to let her off the hook that easily, though. "Have I given you the impression that I'm not taking our relationship seriously?"

She pressed her lips together and stared straight ahead. "No."

"Then what brought this up?" When she didn't answer, he reached out and took her hand in his. "Talk to me."

"I'm just . . ." Her voice trailed off, leaving the thought unfinished.

He gave her hand a comforting squeeze and waited for her to continue.

Janey took a deep breath and released it. "I think I'm falling in love with you."

Kyle parked his vehicle in front of his house but left the motor running. "And you're afraid I don't feel the same way."

"Yeah." She gave him a sideways glance.

Given what she'd shared with him about her relationship history, he understood where her fear was coming from. He also knew he'd been holding back on telling her how he felt because he was afraid it would scare her away.

He removed his seat belt and cupped her cheek, bringing her gaze to meet his. Once he was positive he had her complete attention, he laid it all out for her in three simple words. "I've already fallen."

She stiffened and then her eyes opened wider. "Are you saying what I think you're saying?"

The look on her face was a cross between amazement and fear. He was hoping the fear was because she was hoping it was true and was afraid she was misinterpreting what he was saying and not that she didn't want him to have fallen in love with her.

"I love you, Janey Davis. Head over heels. Swept off my feet." He rubbed the pad of his thumb along her skin and watched her reaction. "You get the idea."

He was starting to get nervous when she didn't say anything. Or move. It was as if she were a deer in the headlights.

"You love me?" Her voice was barely above a whisper.

"I do." He didn't want her to doubt his sincerity. "Are you okay with that?"

It took her another handful of moments to answer. "Yeah. I'm okay with that."

"Good." He closed the distance between them and covered her mouth with his. The kiss was soft and gentle, reverent.

When they broke apart, he ran his thumb along her bottom lip, wondering if the kiss had felt half as wonderful for her as it had for him. "We should go inside and grab my laptop."

Janey released a shaky breath and leaned back in her seat. "I think it's better if you run in and get it. I'll wait here."

He couldn't help but smile. "Afraid you won't be able to control yourself if we're alone?"

She let out a sound somewhere between a laugh and a snort. "Something like that."

CHAPTER 24

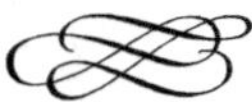

KYLE WAS STILL SMILING when they strolled into the restaurant fifteen minutes later. He'd decided to test his theory about Janey not being able to control herself before he'd gone in the house to grab his laptop. The cute half snort/half laugh she'd emitted had seemed like a challenge, and he'd accepted it with gusto.

Without warning, he'd cupped the back of her head and fused their mouths together in a heated kiss. He didn't hold back, letting her feel every ounce of passion coursing through his veins. She melted against him within seconds, tangling her fingers in his hair and trying to climb across the center console to get closer.

With the half a brain he had left, he'd broken the kiss. They were both breathing as if they'd run a marathon.

His point proven, he'd shot her a satisfied grin, announced he'd be right back, and hopped out of the truck. When he'd returned, she still looked a little flustered, although she was doing her best to cover it up.

"You all right?" He couldn't wipe the satisfied look off his face as they slid into a booth in the back corner of the diner.

"Fine. You?" Her tone was defiant.

"Peachy."

She rolled her eyes at him.

He picked up his menu and looked over the specials. "You know, you didn't have to kiss me back."

Claire came to take their order, so he let it go. They had work to do anyway.

"Been busy today?" Kyle asked Claire. It was late for lunch, so there were only two other tables with customers besides them.

"Breakfast was crazy as usual. Lunch was a little slow, though."

"Oh? Is there an event or something out of town this weekend? I noticed the Sanderses were away."

Claire paused for a moment. She knew what he was asking. "Yeah, they drove up to Huntington. Should be back before the parade on Monday, though."

He thanked her for the information with a nod and gave her his order. Janey did the same, and Claire hurried away to check on her other customers before putting their order in.

Once they were alone again, waiting on their food, Janey logged onto her department's website and pulled up the files she was looking for. Kyle switched to sit beside her so he could read over the files as well. Two sets of eyes were better than one, after all. Plus, it didn't suck sitting this close to her. The scent of her shampoo teased his senses, but he forced himself to focus. There'd be time for fun later.

Their food came and they ate while scanning over the pages of reports on each victim, including the coroner's reports and background checks, along with any other information they'd been able to find.

"There." They'd been scrolling through documents for over two hours when Janey's enthusiastic pronouncement caused him to jerk. He'd been staring at the screen so long he was going cross-eyed.

"What'd you find?"

She pointed at the screen.

He got a glimpse of the name of a college about an hour away from Liberty before she switched to another screen, bringing up the file of the second victim. The same college was listed.

"And here." Janey flipped to his email where Mac had sent him a copy of the third victim's file. Sure enough, all three victims attended the same college.

"Could be a coincidence," he said. "A lot of people go to college."

"True. But I've learned not to dismiss details like this. It's the first connection to all three we've found. The thing is I don't remember seeing a college listed for the first victim when I looked over his file the last time."

"Maybe Paul updated it. He's been working on the case, too."

As if they'd called Paul's name, Janey's phone rang and her partner's name came up on the caller ID. "Are your ears burning?"

He could hear Paul chuckle through the phone since he was still sitting right next to Janey. She filled him in on what they'd found, being as vague as possible given they were in a public place. As suspected, he'd been the one to enter the information after interviewing a friend of the first victim, Travis Merrick, earlier that morning.

"How'd it go in Greenville?" Janey held the phone so Kyle could hear his answer as well.

"She was home. I got the impression she doesn't like cops, though. She wouldn't let us in, and we were only able to ask her five questions before she told us she had to go. I'm not sure if she's hiding something or if she just has an aversion to law enforcement."

Janey frowned. "So we can't mark her off our list."

"The last question I asked her was if she'd been a cheerleader in high school. That was when she informed us she had better things to do and slammed the door in our face." Paul paused. "As frustrating as it was getting shut down, it isn't enough reason to haul her into the station for questioning."

"We need to see if any of our suspects went to the same college," Janey said.

"Heather did." It was the first time Kyle contributed to the conversation. "I think Candy and Angel did as well. Not sure about the others. We could probably find out, though." Janey raised her eyebrows in question. "It's a small town."

Janey shook her head. "We'll start looking into it."

"Meanwhile, I'll look into the college careers of our three victims. See if anything stands out. Maybe they have more in common than their choice of alma mater."

After the call ended with Paul, Kyle and Janey packed up their things and headed out. Their first stop was to Noah's. Kyle had texted him before they left the diner and found out he'd run home to grab some food and a nap after covering some of Kyle's shifts.

Noah met them at the door and ushered them inside. He was still in his uniform, so he couldn't have been home long.

They filled him in on what they'd found. "Do you know if Cindy or Melissa went to the school as well?"

"I don't recall Cindy going off to college. I do think she took a few courses at the community college a few years back, though." He stood deep in thought for a minute or two. "Melissa left for a year or so after high school, but then she came back. If she went to college, she didn't stay."

"Any idea who in town might know for sure?" Janey asked.

Kyle and Noah looked at each other for a long moment before they both answered. "Mrs. Wheatman."

"Who's Mrs. Wheatman?"

Kyle filled her in. "She's the high school guidance counselor. Or at least she was. She retired about three years ago."

"Okay. So we go see her. Does she live around here?"

Noah scribbled an address down on a piece of paper. "She lives about forty-five minutes from here in a retirement community."

Both Kyle and Janey looked at him, wondering how he knew where to find her without having to look it up.

He shrugged. "She was one of my favorite teachers. I visit her from time to time."

Kyle took the paper, glanced at it, and tucked it into his shirt pocket. "Any word from your contact about the missing recordings?"

"No." Noah placed his hands on his hips. "He's doing a little more digging, but according to him the file was never there."

"As in nothing was deleted because it never existed?" Janey voiced the question that had been swirling in his brain.

"That's what he says." Noah shook his head. "I'm not sure what this means. I mean, on the one hand, I'm happy Brent seems to be in the clear, but then how did it land in dispatch? I can't imagine someone walked into the station and left an anonymous note. That would have been in the file."

"Hayden was the one to send you out to the scene, right?" Janey asked Kyle.

The wheels started turning in his head and he didn't like where they were spinning. "You think Hayden was somehow involved? That she knew where the body was and directed me to it?"

"I don't know, but right now all arrows seem to be pointing toward Heather Sanders. There've been too many clues that keep leading back to her."

"But we know, or at least believe, there's more than one person involved. Heather had a boyfriend at the time of the murders." Kyle paused as another thought crossed his mind. "Or could Hayden be involved in the murders as well?"

"Let's not jump to conclusions," Noah said. "All we have is conjecture at this point. We need proof. If I'm going to accuse a member of the community of murder, I need to be one hundred percent confident we have the right person."

Janey checked her phone before slipping it back in her pocket. "Let's go talk to this Mrs. Wheatman."

"Call me if you need anything. I know the sheriff over there and can call in a favor if I need to."

"Do you need me to patrol tonight?" Kyle asked, knowing Noah had to be burning the candle at both ends. He kind of felt bad for his friend.

"No. I want you to focus on finding whoever did this. I can manage with a couple less hours' sleep for a few days."

* * *

"What are you thinking so hard about over there?" Kyle asked as they drove down the highway.

"The case. We're missing a motive. Based on what the teen overheard, this wasn't a random killing, and we have to assume the others weren't either. If it was Heather Sanders, what prompted her to commit three murders?"

"Good question."

The rest of the drive was spent bouncing ideas off each other as to what motivation the killer might have. It was something she and Paul did on a regular basis. It helped to put them in the head of the perp and could sometimes point them in a direction they hadn't considered before.

Mrs. Wheatman's neighborhood was quaint. The streets were lined with small white homes and all the lawns were manicured. Some had flowerbeds or tiny gardens along the front.

They located the address the sheriff had given them and parked along the curb.

"Think she'll remember you?" Janey asked as they headed up the walkway.

"I guess we'll soon find out."

Kyle rang the doorbell and they waited.

Less than a minute later, they heard shuffling inside. Not long after that, the door opened to reveal a woman almost as tall as Janey with salt and pepper hair. She took one look at Kyle, smiled, and opened the door wide, inviting them inside.

"Kyle Reed. It's been a few years since I've seen you, young man. What have you been up to?" She glanced over at Janey. "And who is this lovely young lady you've brought with you?"

He ignored the first question and answered the second. "This is Janey. She's a detective from Indianapolis."

"A detective." Mrs. Wheatman looked Janey over once more. "Vice?"

It was a popular misconception. When she'd first joined the force, she'd been encouraged to work vice because of her looks. Apparently they thought she would be a good stand-in for a prostitute. Janey, however, had avoided those duties whenever possible. And once she'd passed her detective's exam, she'd pushed for homicide, not vice. She wanted to catch killers, not case drug dealers or pimps. "No, ma'am. I work homicide."

"Murder." Mrs. Wheatman shook her head as if trying to clear it. "That's a gruesome business."

Janey found she liked Mrs. Wheatman. The woman was direct, but not obnoxious. "Yes, it is."

"My brother spent twenty-five years as a patrol officer in St. Louis. He used to tell me stories." She led them into the living room. "Can I get you anything? I have coffee, tea, water . . ."

They both declined her offer and got down to business. Since this was someone Kyle knew from his school days, Janey sat back and allowed him to ask the questions. She was learning he was a pretty good detective. If he wanted the job, she was sure he could step into the open position at the sheriff's department with no problem. "I wish I could say we were here to visit, but we need your help."

Her brow furrowed and she tilted her head to the side as if considering a question he had yet to ask. She looked at Janey. "If you're a homicide detective, then that must mean you're here about a murder."

Janey didn't feel there was any reason to keep the information from her. "Three, actually."

Mrs. Wheatman's eyes widened. "There've been three murders? In Warren County?"

"No," Kyle assured her. "One in Warren County and two in Indianapolis. Which is why Detective Davis is here."

"Oh my." Mrs. Wheatman placed a hand over her heart.

Kyle gave her a minute to digest that information before he went on. "We have reason to believe someone that graduated from Liberty-Bass High School might be involved."

"You think one of my students is a murderer?" Her voice went up slightly on the last word. Janey understood. It was hard to wrap your head around the thought you might know someone who had taken a human life.

"Or might know who the murderer is." Again, Janey was proud of

Kyle. He was trying to ease her fears without lying. They didn't know for certain if the ring belonged to the murderer.

She nodded.

"I know it's been a while, but we have reason to believe the person we're looking for was in the same graduating class as my sister, Ava, and went to Bailon College. Do you recall which students applied to that college?"

"Let me see." She listed off several names, including the ones they already knew. "I'm sorry, but that's all I can remember. They should have a complete list at the school, though."

"Records requests take time, especially on minors, which is why we came directly to you." Janey grinned at Kyle, then turned her attention back to Mrs. Wheatman. "Sheriff Jenkins spoke very highly of you."

A proud, almost motherly glow came over her. "He comes by to see me every once and a while. I'm so pleased to see him doing well. Now all he needs is to find a good woman to settle down with."

Kyle shifted beside her and stood. "We won't take up any more of your time."

"It was no problem, dear. You stop by anytime."

"Thanks."

Mrs. Wheatman held out her hand to Janey. "It was very nice to meet you, Detective."

"You, too. And thank you again for the information."

They were on their way back to the vehicle when Janey's phone rang. It was Paul. "Davis," she said as she climbed into the SUV.

"Kyle with you? I found out some information I think you both should hear."

Janey glanced at Kyle. "He's here." She put the phone on speaker and placed it in the center console. "You're on speaker. Go ahead."

"I called Bailon College and spoke with someone in the administration office. She wouldn't tell me anything other than the men went to the school and were all part of the same fraternity." Kyle and Janey looked at each other as they digested this new bit of information. "When I pressed her on whether or not there had been any incidents with the fraternity during the years the victims were there, she got really nervous and said I'd have to put in an official records request."

"Do we know anyone in the police department up there?" Janey asked.

Kyle piped in. "If you don't, Noah probably does."

"I didn't, but Rollins does. He used to go to high school with one of the local deputies." The sound of papers being shuffled filled the air for a few seconds before Paul continued. "The fraternity in question is known for hosting rather large parties. Lots of beer, music. Typical frat stuff." He paused. "There've also been some rumors that some girls have been drugged."

"How is this not public record? These guys would've been adults." Kyle asked the exact question that was on the tip of Janey's tongue.

"No charges were ever filed." She could almost see Paul rubbing the back of his head through the phone. "I'm driving up there this afternoon to see if I can find out any more information."

"We'll meet you there."

Kyle wasted no time getting on the road. "You thinking what I'm thinking?"

"That these guys did something to whoever our murderer or murderers are back in college and they're now seeking revenge?"

He met her gaze for a long moment before turning his attention back to the road. "Yeah."

"It would make sense. If they really were drugging women and doing who knows what else, that would explain the brutal nature of the deaths."

Kyle's hands tightened on the wheel. "Why didn't they file charges?"

Janey shrugged. "It's hard to say. Some women don't feel like they can come forward. Or maybe they tried and something or someone stopped them from filing a formal complaint."

"You're right. The woman Paul talked to at the college knew something had happened, which means it's most likely known to the locals." He blew out a frustrated breath. "Is it always like this?"

"What?" she asked, not sure what he meant.

He thought about it for a minute. "I feel . . . conflicted. The cop in me says murdering someone is wrong and the person who did it needs to be brought to justice, but the man in me understands the need to do violence against these guys if they really did hurt who knows how many women. If someone had hurt Ava . . ."

Janey understood exactly what he was saying, and she was right there with him. "No. They aren't always like this. In fact, I've only had one other case in the last seven years that has left me wondering if catching the perpetrator was the right thing to do." She let her thoughts drift to one of the first cases she'd handled as a detective. "I'd been a detective for less than two months when Daniels and I were assigned to investigate a shooting outside a bar. The guy had been about to get into his car when he was shot five times and killed."

Kyle kept his eyes on the road, but she knew he was listening.

"It didn't take us long to track down who the shooter was." Janey swallowed as the memory of the arrest hit her as clear as if she was still standing in the woman's living room. "The man had been beating his wife. He'd get drunk and then come home and take out whatever his frustrations were on her. She didn't see another way out, so she drove to the bar, knowing what time he usually left, waited in the shadows, and while he was fumbling with his keys she shot him in the back."

"He never saw it coming," Kyle said.

Janey shook her head. "No. And since it was premeditated, it wasn't considered an act of self-defense. At least, as far as the law was concerned." The case still got to her. Even after all these years. "It was one of the hardest arrests I've ever made."

Kyle let out a loud breath, reached for her hand, and didn't let go for the rest of the drive.

CHAPTER 25

KYLE DROVE around the campus until he found a place to park. They were meeting Paul in the common area. It was a small college—only about five thousand students—so someone had to know something. Five years wasn't that long ago.

As they made their way across campus, he couldn't stop thinking about what Janey had told him. He'd been in several domestic situations and they were never easy. Emotions ran high and could get out of hand fast.

After hearing Janey's experience, he understood her deep desire to help Cindy Fisher. Janey had gone on to explain to him that the woman who'd killed her husband had been too poor to hire an attorney and ended up with a public defender. He'd had no sympathy for her situation and had pretty much let the defense eat her for lunch. She'd gotten the book thrown at her and was now serving a life sentence for first degree murder.

He'd heard the emotion in her voice as she talked. Janey wouldn't want the same fate to befall Cindy. Especially given there was a child involved as well. A child who would have to grow up without a mother if she was convicted of murder.

Kyle didn't want to think about the parallels there with Janey's upbringing. Granted, her mother hadn't been convicted of murder—at least as far as he knew—but that didn't change the fact that she hadn't been part of Janey's life. Luckily, Janey's grandmother had stepped in and raised her, as Kyle was sure Cindy's mother would do as well, but a child needed its mother. He was an adult by the time he lost his parents, but it still stung. He couldn't imagine being Sadie's age and faced with never seeing his parents again.

Paul and another man were waiting for them when they arrived. He was wearing a uniform similar to Kyle's, so he was guessing this was the local friend Paul had told them about. If he was here officially, hopefully that meant the local department was on board as well.

"You got here fast," Janey said to Paul.

"I was already on my way when I called." He offered his hand to Kyle. "Good to see you again."

"You, too."

"Janey, Kyle, I'd like to you to meet Kevin Berkley. He's lived around here his entire life and knows a lot of the locals, including a lot of the staff here."

They all shook hands.

"It's nice to meet you," Kevin said.

Kyle looked around the area. It was almost three o'clock and most of the students had disappeared inside the various buildings. "So what's the game plan?"

"I figured we could split up into two groups. We have a lot of ground to cover. Kevin and I are going to head over to the fraternity house and see what we can find. Janey and Kyle, why don't you start in the cafeteria? Kevin said there are several ladies there who've worked for the school over twenty years. Maybe they've heard something."

"We're probably more likely to get them to open up than we would someone in the administration office," Janey said.

Paul nodded. "Exactly."

Once their game plan was in place with the agreement to meet back there in one hour, Kyle and Janey walked the short distance to the cafeteria. They tried the door, but it was locked.

"Let's go around back. Maybe one of them is out taking a smoke break or something." Janey didn't wait for him to comment before she turned on her heels and marched toward the rear of the large brick building.

As soon as they turned the corner, he could smell the stink of rotting garbage and the sound of women talking. It looked as if they were in luck.

Three women were perched on crates in a semicircle. They all stopped talking when Kyle and Janey came closer.

"Hello, ladies," Janey said.

All they did was nod. Not exactly the friendly greeting they were hoping for.

Their cool demeanor didn't seem to bother Janey. "We were wondering if you ladies could help us with something."

No response. Not even a twitch.

Janey went on. "We're trying to find out about a fraternity. Delta Theta?"

One of the women snorted. "Aren't you a little old to be chasing fraternity boys?"

Another woman, this one a little younger than the first, maybe in her forties, chuckled. "Never too old to be doing that."

Janey grinned and pushed on with her questioning, not allowing the women to get sidetracked. "I've heard they throw some pretty wild parties."

"You could say that again," the first woman said. "Some of those boys could drink me under the table, and that's saying something."

"Lots of alcohol is usually a given at frat parties. Any drugs?" Janey asked.

The women sobered a little, taking in Kyle's uniform. He was wondering if maybe he should have changed before they came. "What are you two looking for?"

Janey waved her hand dismissively. "Just some rumors we're trying to clear up. Do you know anything that may have happened at that fraternity roughly five or six years ago?"

They were all quiet for a few moments as if contemplating what they should say. Finally, the oldest of the three women spoke up. She'd stayed silent up until then, letting her younger counterparts do the talking. "There's always talk."

The younger woman flashed a shocked look in the other woman's direction.

"Any idea who was involved?" Janey asked.

The oldest woman stood, kicking the crate she'd been using to the side. "We're just cooks. If you want information on that kind of stuff, you'll need to be talking to the people up at the main office." She turned to the other women. "Come on, ladies. We have dinner to prepare."

As the three women walked back into the building, the youngest one, the one who'd said there'd been some talk about the Delta Theta fraternity and drugs, hesitated for a second before following the other two into the building.

Once they were gone, Janey turned to Kyle. "We need to talk to her alone. She has something to say but is afraid to in front of the others."

He completely agreed. "What do you suggest?"

"Let's see if we can talk to a few other people and then meet up with Paul and Kevin. I have a feeling we're going to be hanging out here until after dinner, and then maybe we can catch her on her way home. Preferably without her entourage."

They spent the next half hour roaming the campus asking random people they ran into about Delta Theta. For the most part it was a waste of time. However, one of the students they'd spoken with happened to be a member of the fraternity. He'd been reluctant to talk to them at first until Kyle decided to take a different approach. He started talking to the guy as if he were one of his Army buddies, asking about the parties and the girls.

After that, the guy couldn't stop talking. They'd learned there was a party at the house at least once a week and that they tended to include binge drinking and lots of sex. He'd added that the parties were way tamer than they used to be, but they were still the best parties on campus. Unfortunately, he didn't know the reason behind the change.

By the time they parted ways with the guy, they were confident they were headed in the right direction with their original assumption. The fraternity was the link they'd been looking for. Now all they had to do was find out what incident had driven someone to murder years later.

Paul and Kevin hadn't arrived yet when Kyle and Janey returned to the designated meeting area, so they sat on a nearby bench to wait and do a little people watching. He was watching a couple of guys throwing a Frisbee when Janey cleared her throat. "You seem to know quite a bit about frat parties. Been to a lot of them?"

He turned his body so she had his complete attention, somewhat amused by her question. Was she jealous or merely curious? "Not a single one."

"Then how—"

Kyle chuckled. "Get a bunch of college-aged guys together, add a significant amount of alcohol, and you'll end up with a similar result." He rested his arm on the back of the bench. The urge to touch her was strong when she was so close, but he resisted. "Also, I've watched movies like *Animal House*."

"So you just made it up?"

"I didn't say that." He leaned in as if imparting a secret. "I never said I was a saint during my time in the Army."

A sly grin spread across her face. "Anything I should know about?"

He skimmed his fingers along her shoulder, unable to stop himself. "That depends."

"On?"

A throat cleared behind them. Kyle knew who it was without looking. He sat up, putting some space between them once more, and faced the new arrivals.

* * *

"Are we interrupting?" Paul stood a few feet away with a knowing smirk on his face. Janey couldn't believe she hadn't heard him and

Kevin approach. She was off her game. That wasn't good considering they were investigating a case.

She did her best to cover up her embarrassment. "Just waiting on you. Did you get anywhere with the fraternity?"

"Nothing concrete. A couple of the guys mentioned there'd been a crackdown by the dean several years ago after some of the parties had gotten too out of control. They didn't know the details—or said they didn't," Kevin said.

"What about you? Have any luck?" Paul still had a knowing grin on his face that Janey wished she could wipe off. The only thing that made her feel better was that the shoe had been on the other foot a time or two. Still, she needed to stay focused.

Janey recounted their conversation with the three women. "Kyle and I are going to hang around here for a few more hours and see if we can catch her before she heads home."

Paul nodded. "I want to stop by the dean's office before I head back to Indy. I doubt he'll tell us anything, but you never know." He checked his phone, probably to see the time. "I'll call the captain and give him an update on the way back."

"We'll let you know if we get anywhere with the cook," Janey said.

Kevin had been standing off to the side during the exchange. He handed Kyle one of his cards. "I'll be around tonight if you need some backup."

Kyle tucked the card into his shirt pocket. "Thanks."

They watched as Paul and Kevin walked toward the admissions building. Janey was hoping the woman tonight would be able to give them a name. She knew it was a long shot considering how long ago the incident would have happened, but this was a small town. People talked. She'd learned that much from Kyle. Hopefully, that meant their memories were long as well.

"Hungry?"

"What?" His question pulled her back to the present.

"Food. We have a couple of hours to kill. Might as well get some grub."

He was right. It was only four o'clock and dinner on campus was from five to six. Other than wandering around the campus, there wasn't much they could do until they closed the mess hall. "Know any local restaurants?"

Kyle held up his phone. "That's what the internet is for."

They ended up at a pizza place a few blocks from campus. It was small—only eight tables in the entire place—but the food was good. She'd had a lot worse during stakeouts.

"You ever go to college?" he asked before taking a bite of pizza.

Janey nodded. "I have a bachelor's degree in criminal justice." She reached for another piece of pizza. "What about you?"

"Nope. The Army was my education. I took a few classes at the local community college after getting back, but it wasn't for me. I get too antsy sitting in a classroom for hours on end. I'm more of a hands-on kind of guy."

"Yes, you are." She flashed him a flirty grin.

Kyle chuckled. "You're lucky we're in a public place right now or I'd give you a demonstration of just how hands-on I am."

Some of the uncertainty that had been nagging at her eased. She liked being with Kyle. He was fun and genuine and good at his job. In some ways he reminded her of Paul, and that wasn't a bad thing. Her partner was the best guy she knew. Until him, she didn't think there were men like that still out there. Lucky for her, Kyle was one of them.

After finishing their dinner, they moved their vehicle so it was parked in the closest lot to the dining hall. The spaces were marked 'reserved for staff,' but given it was after five a lot of the spaces had been vacated. They positioned themselves along the tree line so they'd have a good view of anyone entering or exiting the back of the building.

"So what do you and Paul normally do when you're on a stakeout?" Kyle asked after a few minutes of staring at the back of the building.

Janey shrugged. "Not much. We just talk and watch our surroundings. It isn't that exciting. In fact, most of the time it's downright boring."

"What's the longest one you've ever done?"

She thought back. "I think it was about ten hours."

"That's a long time to sit in a car," he said.

"You're telling me. My butt went numb."

Kyle laughed.

"I'm serious. It wasn't a pleasant experience."

He cleared his throat, trying to stop himself from laughing. "Well, if your ass goes numb on this stakeout, I'll do all I can to help make it better."

Without her permission, her sex clenched at thoughts of all the ways he could make it better.

She opened her mouth to give him a snarky reply when movement caught her eye. Two women emerged from the back of the building. A few seconds later, the door opened again and the third woman walked out.

The three women chatted as they made their way toward the parking lot. Two of them walked toward where Kyle and Janey were parked. The other, the one they needed to talk to, went in the other direction.

They waited until the other two women were in their vehicles before pulling out. Janey wondered if it would have been better to take an unmarked car since Kyle's patrol SUV stood out like a sore thumb, but it was too late to do anything about it.

By the time they made it to the other woman, she was behind the wheel of her car, and she didn't look happy to see them.

"Do you remember us from earlier?"

The woman looked at Janey as if she'd lost her mind. "I'm not senile. Of course I remember you."

"We were hoping to ask you a few more questions."

She looked around, probably wondering where her friends were. "I don't want any trouble."

"Why would there be trouble?" Janey asked. When the woman didn't answer, Janey decided to try a different tactic. "Is there somewhere else you'd rather talk?"

With that, the woman relaxed a little. "Can you follow me home? I only live about ten minutes from here."

"Lead the way," Kyle said, not hesitating. By the way this woman was acting, she knew something. Janey just hoped it was something that could actually help them.

They ended up following the woman to a two-story house about five miles outside town. She invited them in and hurried down the hall, leaving them to follow.

She stopped when they reached the dining room and flipped on the light. "Have a seat."

The room was packed with furniture and random boxes. Either the woman was in the process of moving, or she was a bit of a hoarder.

Janey and Kyle each pulled out chairs and sat down. "Thank you for agreeing to talk to us." Janey paused. "I'm sorry. We didn't get your name before."

"Paula," the woman said. "My name's Paula."

"It's nice to meet you, Paula," Kyle said, turning on the charm. "You have a lovely home."

"Thanks."

"How long have you worked at the college?" Janey asked.

Paula thought about it for a minute. "It'll be fourteen years in January."

"That's a long time. You must enjoy your job." Even though she wasn't a suspect, it was always good to get the person you were questioning comfortable, in Janey's experience.

"It's a job and the pay's good."

Janey smiled again, trying to put her at ease. "We were wondering if you could tell us about something that happened roughly five years ago."

Paula frowned. "This is about the fraternity."

"Yes," Janey said. "Do you remember anything involving the fraternity?"

Standing, Paula walked over to hutch along the wall and knelt to dig through the bottom of the cabinet. After a minute or so, she pulled out a stack of papers and brought them to the table. Paula flipped through half the stack before she pulled out the page she'd been searching for. "Is this what you're looking for?"

Janey's eyes scanned over the page. It was a printout of the school newspaper dated nearly six years ago. The headline read *Members of Delta Theta Accused*. The article went on to say that three female students had claimed they'd been drugged and sexually assaulted after attending a party at the Delta Theta house. The article was very vague and didn't give many details. The female students weren't named and neither were the fraternity members involved.

"Are there any other mentions of the incident in future issues of the paper?" Kyle asked. He'd been reading the article over Janey's shoulder.

Paula shook her head. "No. There were rumors flying around campus for a month or so after, but then everything sort of went away."

"Do you mind if we take this with us?" Janey asked. Things were starting to fall into place, and she didn't like where it was going. They needed to find out who the accusers were, who the men involved were, and why there was no other mention of it after this.

CHAPTER 26

IT WAS a long drive back to Liberty. Janey called Paul and her captain to fill them in on the new information. Paul said he'd call Kevin in the morning and see if he could dig up anything more. Surely someone in law enforcement was contacted back then. Now that they had the timeframe pinpointed, they could narrow down who was involved and why it was apparently brushed under the rug.

Kyle unlocked the door to his house. He was glad to be home. More importantly, he was glad to be home with Janey at his side. While detective work wasn't really his thing, he was enjoying working with her. And he really liked having her in his bed at night.

"You hungry?" he asked.

Janey plopped down on the nearest chair. It had been a long day. "Starving."

"Pizza? Subs? Or I could pull something out of the freezer."

"I could do subs."

Not wasting time, he dialed Cap's Pizza and put their order in. "It'll be here in about forty minutes," he said after hanging up the phone.

She tilted her head to the side to stretch her neck muscles and rolled her shoulders. The latter move pulled her shirt tight against her breasts, causing his cock to pulse. It didn't matter that he was as tired as she was.

Moving to stand behind her, he placed his hands on her shoulders and began to massage her tight muscles. Her head fell forward and she hummed. "I could get used to this."

He knew her comment was in relation to being pampered, but he couldn't let it go. "I hope so."

Several seconds ticked by. He could feel the tension in her neck increase beneath his fingers. "What are you saying?"

This wasn't a time to mince words, so he didn't. "I think you should talk to Noah about the detective position here in Liberty." He paused, letting that sink in for a moment before he continued. "And I think you should move in here with me."

Janey stood and he let his arms fall to his sides. "You want us to move in together?"

No room for doubts. Not that he had any. "Yes, I do."

"We don't . . . I mean we haven't . . ." She stared at him as though he'd suggested she go join the circus.

He was prepared for this. She'd brought up the short time they'd known each other several times before. That didn't matter to him. When something was right, it was right. Time didn't change that. "You're concerned our relationship is too new."

"Yes." She said the word so fast he had to keep himself from laughing. "What if I give up my job, move my entire life up here, and you decide it isn't what you want?"

Kyle didn't miss that she'd said he would decide it wasn't what he wanted. He wished he could make her understand how he felt about her, but only time would do that. "Not gonna happen."

"How do you know that?" Before he could get a word in edgewise, she continued. "Things change. People change."

He closed the distance between them, placing his hands on her forearms. "I'm thirty-five years old, Janey. I'm not a teenager who doesn't know what he wants." Raising one hand, he traced his fingers along the line of her jaw. "I love you, Janey Davis. I know you're scared. I am, too, a little, but I know what I want—what I need in my life—and that's you."

The sound of her cell ringing broke through the intense emotions surrounding them. "I should get that."

As much as he hated it, she was right. He nodded and took a step back.

"Davis." Janey's voice wasn't quite as confident as it usually was.

A woman's voice came through the phone. He couldn't hear what she was saying, but he could hear the emotion and she sounded scared.

"Are you somewhere safe?" Janey asked.

That got his attention.

"Okay, where are you?"

Without being asked, he handed her a pen and paper he kept on the refrigerator.

Janey scribbled down the address. "I'll be there as soon as I can. You stay put, all right?"

There was a look of anger and determination in Janey's eyes when she hung up the phone. It only took a moment for him to put two and two together. "Cindy?"

She nodded. "This is the address she gave me." She handed him the paper. "Do you know where it is?"

"Yeah. Let's go."

They were halfway down the road before he remembered the subs. "Shit!"

Janey turned toward him. "What?"

Instead of answering her, he dialed Cap's. Luckily, he had the number in his phone. He was a frequent customer. "Hey, this is Kyle Reed."

"Hi, Kyle. Your subs are almost ready. Should be on their way soon."

"That's why I'm calling. I won't be there to get the delivery. I've been called out on police business." While it wasn't official, it still fell under police business. He was helping a woman being abused by her boyfriend.

"Did you want to cancel the order?"

"No." He shook his head even though he knew the man couldn't see him. "You've got my card on file. Go ahead and charge me for the subs, then you all enjoy them. I don't know how long I'll be."

"Are you sure?"

"Positive." He tossed his phone in one of the cup holders and continued driving toward the address Janey had written on the paper. It wasn't far, about twenty miles outside town.

"I'd completely forgotten about the food."

Kyle glanced over to Janey, who wore a grim expression. He knew she was worried about Cindy. She'd said her boyfriend had slapped her around. That could be anything from a few bruises to some broken bones. He knew all the scenarios were going through Janey's mind. They were going through his.

If she was ready to get out, though, they would help her. She needed somewhere safe to stay. Her mom's house wasn't an option. That would be the first place Keith would look.

They pulled up to the gas station ten minutes later. Cindy and Sadie were standing near the ice cooler, keeping to the shadows. When they exited his vehicle and moved closer, Kyle noticed Cindy's lip was busted and the area around her left eye was beginning to swell. She was going to have a black eye by morning.

Sadie was clinging to her mom's legs. Her eyes were wide as she huddled as close to her mother as possible. The fear on the little girl's face tore at his soul.

Cindy ran a comforting hand over her daughter's head. "Thank you. I didn't know who else to call."

"I'm glad you called me," Janey said, looking Cindy over and making her own assessment. "Are both of you all right?"

Cindy nodded even as tears began to form in her eyes.

Kyle made a split-second decision. He knelt so he was eye level with Sadie. "Do you like ice cream?"

Sadie nodded.

"Why don't you and me go inside and see if we can find some?"

He held out his hand, offering it to her, but she didn't budge.

"What's your favorite kind?" he asked, hoping if he got her thinking about it she'd be more willing to go with him.

"Strawberry." There was a slight tremble in her voice as she spoke.

Kyle rubbed his chin, pretending to be deep in thought. "Hmm. Strawberry's pretty good, but I'm not sure it beats out chocolate."

"Mommy likes chocolate." Sadie glanced up at her mom.

Cindy smiled at her daughter, the action pulling the skin around her busted lip. "That's right. I do."

Seeing his opening, he went for it. "Maybe we can find her some chocolate ice cream, too. I know when I'm having a bad day, ice cream always makes it better."

The little girl seemed torn. She wanted the ice cream, but she didn't want to leave her mom.

"It's okay," Cindy said. "Go get us some ice cream with Officer Reed. I'll wait for you right here."

Kyle stood and extended his hand again to Sadie.

This time she took it.

"We'll be back in a few minutes with the ice cream." As he strolled into the store with Sadie, he was already figuring out ways he could distract the little girl and keep her in the store as long as possible. Janey would need to get the whole story of what happened from Cindy, and he wanted to make sure she had plenty of time. Lucky for him, this convenience store had its own ice cream parlor with thirty flavors to choose from. He made it his mission to get Sadie to try each and every one.

* * *

Janey pushed all the emotions she was feeling to the back of her mind and went into detective mode. "Why don't we have a seat?"

There really wasn't a place to sit other than the curb, so they made do.

As soon as they were seated, Janey addressed the most pressing question. "Do you need medical attention?"

Cindy pressed her fingers to her lip. "No. I'll . . . I'll be okay."

Since Janey didn't see any other injuries besides the cut on Cindy's lip and her black eye, she let it go. They'd have to take photos for evidence later, but for now she wanted to get Cindy talking. "Can you tell me what happened?"

"Keith came home. He'd been over at one of his friends' houses and they'd been drinking." She paused. "He's not a bad guy, you know. I mean, when he's not drinking, he can be really sweet."

Janey had heard the story a million times. It didn't change anything. "What happened when he came home?"

"I was getting ready for bed. Sadie was asleep, and I was going to do a little reading." Cindy was quiet for a few moments. "I heard him come in the house. He was loud, and I was afraid he'd wake Sadie, so I whispered down the stairs that she was asleep so he'd know to be quiet."

The dread of what came next churned in the pit of Janey's stomach.

"When I saw his face, I knew I shouldn't have said anything. I tried to calm him down. Apologize. But . . ."

"But it didn't matter," Janey said.

Cindy shook her head.

Reaching out, Janey took hold of Cindy's hand. "What happened next?"

"He told me I needed to learn my place. That he worked hard to provide for me and Sadie." She gripped Janey's hand hard as she continued. "He slapped me across the face so hard I fell into the wall. He said that would teach me to talk back to him." Cindy sucked in a deep breath. "Then he dragged me into the bedroom, threw me down on the bed, and . . ."

Janey closed her eyes, steeling her own resolve before she asked her next question. "Did he rape you, Cindy?"

A muffled sob escaped her throat. "Yes. No. I mean, he's Sadie's father. My boyfriend. He—"

"That doesn't mean he can't rape you. If he forced you to have sex with him, then it was rape. It doesn't matter if you've willingly had sex with him in the past."

This time the tears flowed freely. Cindy hunched over and hugged her knees, and she let go.

All Janey could do was rub a hand along her back, trying to provide a little comfort. "We should get you to a hospital and have them do a rape kit."

Cindy shook her head. "No. I just . . . I feel like such a terrible mother." She wiped the tears from her cheeks.

"You're not a terrible mother."

Cindy didn't seem to believe her. "What am I going to do now?"

"Do you have a place to stay for a day or two?" Janey asked. "A friend or family?"

"Not really."

"What about your mom?" They'd met Cindy's mom a couple of days ago and she seemed nice enough.

"No. I don't want her to know. Not yet."

While Janey didn't completely agree with that, it wasn't her call. If Cindy didn't want to go to her mom's, maybe Kyle would have some ideas. He was always telling her how great small towns were.

The two women sat in silence for several minutes as the world went on around them. It was getting late, so there weren't that many people around, but every now and then someone would look their way. Janey ignored them. "Do you think they found the ice cream?"

Cindy glanced toward the entrance to the store and a tiny smile tugged at her lips. "I hope so. I could really use some chocolate ice cream right about now. Maybe an entire half gallon."

Janey chuckled. "You know, I worked in an ice cream shop in high school. My grandma told me I'd get sick of ice cream working around it all the time, but I still love it."

"I'm not sure it's possible to get sick of ice cream."

"Me either."

A few moments later, Kyle and Sadie came out of the store. Sadie was holding a round dish of ice cream with both hands, careful not to drop it. Kyle had a large container of what looked to be chocolate ice cream in one hand and a cone with two scoops of chocolate in the other. He handed the overflowing bowl to Cindy. "Two extra-large scoops of chocolate. Sadie insisted."

She stared down at the bowl for several moments before lifting the spoon to her mouth. "Thanks."

Kyle turned to Janey. "I figured we could share."

Janey raised her eyebrows in question. He just shrugged and held out the cone for her to take a bite. The whole thing felt out of place given why they were there.

She glanced over at Cindy and Sadie who were sitting on the curb, eating their ice cream. Sadie was filling her mom in on all the different flavors she and Kyle had tried.

"They need somewhere to go tonight," Janey said, taking the cone from Kyle.

He nodded. "Let me make a call."

Janey waited while he walked several feet away and took out his phone. She could hear him talking but didn't get more than bits and pieces of the conversation.

The ice cream was almost gone by the time he returned to her side. He bent down and took a large bite.

"Everything good?" she asked when he didn't say anything.

"Yeah. All's good." He took another bite of the cone. "Did you get what you needed from Cindy?"

"For the most part." Janey moved them farther away from Cindy and Sadie, not wanting the little girl to overhear. Once she was confident they were out of earshot, she filled him in on the details of her conversation with Cindy.

"I need to call Noah." Kyle looked over at the mother and daughter. "Do you think she's willing to press charges?"

"I think so. I didn't get the impression she wants to go back. Tonight scared her. Hopefully, it scared her enough for her to realize he's never going to change."

He popped the last of the cone into his mouth. "I'll get the paperwork rolling. Why don't you get them loaded up into the SUV so we can get going?"

It took a good ten minutes to get Cindy and Sadie, along with the stuff they'd brought with them, into Kyle's patrol vehicle. Kyle didn't want to bring Cindy's vehicle with them in case Clyde came looking for them. It was doubtful he would, at least tonight, but Janey agreed they didn't need to take any chances.

Shortly after they got back on the road, Sadie drifted off to sleep. She was still out when they pulled up in front of a log cabin in the woods.

"Wait here." Kyle got out and jogged up to the front door. After a few seconds, the door opened. A man stood in the entryway but Janey couldn't make out who he was from inside the vehicle. He and Kyle spoke briefly before Kyle returned to the SUV. "Let me help you get Sadie inside."

Cindy didn't argue. She was no doubt as exhausted as her daughter.

Kyle carried a sleeping Sadie into the cabin, and Janey and Cindy followed. The cabin was larger than it appeared on the outside. The main room was about the same size as her condo in Indianapolis.

Standing to the left of the large stone fireplace that dominated the living area was the man Janey had seen in the doorway. The first thing she noticed about him was the scar on one of his cheeks. It was about three inches long and curved, almost following the line of his jaw. The second thing she noticed was the look in his eyes. They were guarded as if he were gearing up to go into battle.

Kyle shifted the little girl in his arms, pulling her tighter against his chest. "Cindy, I'd like you to meet Austin Hughes. He and I served in the Army together."

Janey guessed that answered her question on how Kyle knew him. It most likely explained the scar as well. And the look in his eyes. She'd worked with officers who'd served in the military. Some brought the battle back home with them.

"The extra bedroom is all made up." Austin motioned toward the door behind him.

"I'll lay her down, and then we can go over everything." Kyle disappeared into the next room, leaving Janey, Cindy, and Austin standing in the living room.

Figuring this was as good a time as any, she motioned for Cindy to join her on the couch. "Are you sure you don't want to see a doctor?"

"I'm sure."

As if noticing Cindy's injuries for the first time, Austin jumped into action. He went to the freezer, pulled out a bag of frozen peas, and brought them wrapped in a dishtowel over to Cindy. "It'll help with the swelling."

"Thanks," she said, taking the bag and pressing it against the side of her face.

Janey waited until Kyle returned to the room, and then got down to business. "Cindy, we need to talk about pressing charges and what happens next."

Cindy winced as she touched her lip with the bag of peas. At least it wasn't bleeding anymore. "I don't want Sadie to grow up seeing her mom like this." She lifted her gaze to meet Janey's. "What do I need to do?"

CHAPTER 27

Janey could barely keep her eyes open. It was well after midnight by the time they left Austin's house. They'd taken pictures of all Cindy's injuries and got her official statement. Given the hour and that she and her daughter were safe for the night, Noah had decided to wait until morning to make the arrest.

"Didn't you need to turn back there?" Janey asked.

Kyle glanced over at her and then back to the road. "I don't know about you, but I'm starving, and the only places open at this time of night are out by the truck stop."

Her stomach voiced its agreement. The ice cream cone they'd shared hadn't filled her up for long. "What are our options?"

"We can go into the truck stop and get something, or there's Taco Bell."

She wasn't sure she could stay awake long enough to sit through an actual meal. "Taco Bell works."

Five minutes later, Kyle maneuvered them into the drive-through and placed their order. Once they had their food, he pulled into a parking space.

Neither said much as they scarfed down their dinners. She wasn't even sure how much of hers she tasted. It was all about a means to an end. She was hungry and so she ate. But the fuller she got, the more the need for sleep took over.

"I'm hoping I can make it up the stairs to bed. I might just pass out on the couch," Kyle said.

Janey was too tired to laugh. "I know what you mean. I feel like I need toothpicks to keep my eyes open."

"It's been a long day."

She sighed. "Yeah, it has. But a productive one. We confirmed something happened at the fraternity." Their visit to the college felt like days ago, even though it was mere hours.

"Noah knows a lot of the county sheriffs. I'm sure someone knows something about it."

Darkness surrounded them as they drove down the two-lane road toward Liberty. "I wonder what triggered it?"

"Triggered what?"

It was difficult to form her thoughts into words, but she tried. For some reason, her mind wouldn't shut off even though her body was more than ready. "It's been years. Why now?"

He seemed to think about it for a moment, and she wondered if he was having the same problem she was. "I don't know. People get triggered by different things."

As they came into town, Janey noticed a large banner suspended above the street. She leaned forward to get a better look.

"It's for the Labor Day festival."

She sat back in her seat and looked around for any more additions to the downtown décor but didn't see anything. It was dark apart from the few streetlamps. The moon was hiding behind a blanket of clouds.

"The banner's the first thing that goes up," he said, turning onto the street that led to his house. "Tomorrow they'll add banners to the light posts for the parade. Everything else takes place in the park."

He pulled into his driveway and turned off the engine. "I didn't think we'd be gone this long or I would have turned the porch light on before we left."

It took a lot more effort than it should have to climb out of the vehicle. She yawned as they made their way toward the side door that led to his kitchen. Kyle's bed was calling her name.

His hand was on the doorknob when Janey saw something out of the corner of her eye. If she hadn't been so tired, her reaction time would have been much faster.

Janey felt the sting of the Taser graze her arm, jolting her awake. She rolled in the opposite direction of the threat, needing to put some distance between her and whoever her attacker was.

As soon as she was on her feet again, she reached for her weapon. The only things she could see were shadows, but that was enough. Three petite figures stood less than four feet away from her. Two of them held what she assumed were Tasers.

The third figure held something long and slender over their head as they stood above Kyle, who was lying unmoving on the ground.

Janey's adrenaline kicked up as she pointed her gun at the most immediate threat. Understanding of the situation and who'd been waiting for them crystalized in her brain. "Drop the weapons. All of you."

They all froze, but none of them followed her command.

"Drop your weapons," Janey demanded again as she stood.

She needed backup, but there was no way she was dividing her attention with three armed suspects standing in front of her and the man she loved on the ground.

The two with the Tasers let them fall to the ground.

Two down. One to go.

Janey focused her attention on the suspect still holding their weapon, keeping the other two in her peripheral vision. "I won't tell you again. Drop the weapon."

Instead of following Janey's orders, the shadowy figure followed through with her original goal. With as much force as they could muster, they lowered the object toward Kyle's head.

Visions of the three victims' skulls being cracked open filled Janey's mind. She took aim at the suspect and moved her finger to the trigger, ready to take her shot.

* * *

Kyle had been aware of the scene going on above him from the moment he heard Janey yell her first command for their attackers to drop their weapons. His head was spinning a little, but he wasn't completely out of it. Not anymore anyway. The initial jolt had knocked him on his ass for a few seconds, but with each moment that passed he was feeling more like himself.

He tilted his head up so he could get a better look at the person above him. It was a woman. He could tell that much. And by the set of her shoulders and the way she was gripping the bat in her hands, she was thoroughly pissed off.

Yeah, well, he wasn't feeling all that happy-go-lucky himself.

When Janey gave her third order to the woman standing above him to drop her weapon, he knew he was going to have to act. He saw the bat come toward his head and took evasive action.

Swinging his legs out, he hit the side of the woman's knee with as much force as he could muster, knocking her off balance. She let out a squeal as she fell backward and landed on the ground with a muffled thump.

Kyle scrambled to his feet and lunged for the woman.

"You got her?" Janey yelled from several feet away.

"Yeah." It was then Kyle realized that the other two suspects had taken off. Janey raced after them.

"Get off me!" She was fighting him. Normally it wouldn't be an issue. She was no match for him physically. However, she hadn't just endured being tased.

It took a little more effort than it should, but he flipped her onto her stomach and reached for his handcuffs. "Stop resisting."

"Never, you pig."

Once he had her secured in cuffs, he reached for his radio. "This is Deputy Reed. I need all available units to my home. I have one in custody, and Detective Davis is in pursuit of two others on foot."

"Copy. Units are being dispatched to your location."

Kyle shook his head, trying to clear it, before rocking back on his heels and flipping the woman over. He kept one hand on her and reached for the flashlight on his belt. She turned her head away from the bright light, but it didn't matter. Even with her black clothing and her hair tucked under a baseball cap, there was no hiding it was Heather Sanders.

"Get up." He went to grab one of her arms and she tried to pull away from him. "It's over, Heather. Roll onto your side and let's get you on your feet."

He clipped his flashlight back to his belt as he helped her up. Even still, he could feel the daggers she was shooting his way. Her demeanor was a far cry from how she'd acted at the diner.

Once she was on her feet, Kyle stopped to listen for any signs that Janey was nearby, but he couldn't hear anything but sirens in the background. He knew Janey could handle herself, but that didn't make it any easier for him to stay with Heather while his girlfriend was out chasing two other suspects through his neighbors' backyards. The only thing that made him feel a little better was that the two Tasers they'd used were still lying on the ground where they'd dropped them. That didn't mean they didn't have other weapons on them, though, and that's what weighed on his mind as he waited for backup to arrive.

Kyle had just gotten Heather situated into the back of his patrol vehicle when another deputy pulled up in front of his house. Ethan had barely gotten out of his vehicle before Kyle ordered him to stay with Heather while he went in search of Janey and the two other suspects. He knew at least one more deputy was on their way, and most likely Noah, but he wasn't waiting for them to arrive. He jumped the fence behind his house and took off through his neighbor's backyard, keeping an eye out for any signs of Janey or the suspects.

* * *

Janey had no idea how far they'd come or whose yard they were in. She'd followed the two suspects through several backyards and across a road. She was pretty sure the sheriff's office had a K-9 unit and she was hoping they were on their way. It would make a search like this go faster.

And it would be a lot safer. The danger of tracking two suspects in the dark through a residential area was at the forefront of her mind. She had to be alert. Even though they'd left their Tasers behind, that didn't mean they didn't have any other weapons. Besides, she'd passed more than a few shovels that could easily bash someone's head in.

The sound of a dog barking in the next yard over drew her attention and she headed in that direction. Her heart was racing both from the adrenaline and the distance they'd traveled in a short amount of time. She needed to find her suspects.

"Shh." The female voice stood out in the quiet of the night.

Janey crept in that direction, her weapon drawn, making sure not to get tunnel vision. She needed to protect her back since there was no one else to do it at that moment.

As she drew closer, Janey could make out a small figure huddled under a wooden deck. She scanned the nearby bushes for the second suspect but didn't see any movement. The situation made her uneasy, but there wasn't anything she could do about it.

She pointed her firearm under the deck, straight at the person trying to make themselves as small as possible. "Come out and keep your hands where I can see them."

Silence.

"Now!"

A branch snapped under the deck as the suspect crawled out. "Please, don't shoot me."

It was a woman's voice. One she didn't recognize. As curious as Janey was, the person's identity wasn't important right now. "Lay face down on the ground and place your hands on your head."

The woman lowered herself onto her stomach and followed the instructions she'd been given. Janey wasted no time taking her into custody and reading the woman her rights. She helped her to stand and turned her around so Janey could get a look at her.

The woman looked to be in her mid-twenties. She wore no makeup and had her sandy blond hair tucked into a knitted cap. Her wide eyes looked innocent enough. No doubt they had gotten her out of a lot of trouble in the past. That was unlikely to happen this time around. Assaulting a police officer was a serious offence, and if the three turned out to be the ones who'd murdered those three men, it was likely they'd be looking at attempted murder as well.

Janey took one look around the immediate area and was about to walk her suspect out front to the street when she heard someone running toward them. She placed her hand on her sidearm and waited to see who emerged from the bushes.

It was Kyle. A rush of happiness flooded through her at seeing him. She'd taken off after the two suspects before she could be sure he was really okay.

As much as she wanted to run into his arms, she knew they had a job to do. There'd be time later to express her feelings for him. "I've got this one."

Kyle seemed as torn as she was, but eventually he nodded. "I'll keep searching. The K-9 unit is on its way."

He took off through the bushes into the next yard while Janey walked the woman she had in custody to the street in front of the house. "Sit down and cross your ankles in front of you."

The woman sat on the curb as instructed. Janey counted her blessings that the woman was cooperating.

Keeping an eye on her suspect, she pulled out her cell and dialed Sheriff Jenkins's number. It was the only local one besides Kyle's she had in her phone.

"Where are you?" He'd obviously been briefed on the situation, either by dispatch or by Kyle.

Luckily, the house the woman had chosen as a hiding place was near a crossroads. She rattled the names on the street signs to the sheriff. "I have one in custody. Deputy Reed is still in pursuit of the third suspect."

"I'll be there in two."

He disconnected and Janey had no choice but to stand in the middle of the street waiting for the cavalry.

* * *

Kyle was about to give up when he heard a mumbled "ouch" coming from a couple of houses over. It was almost two in the morning, so the odds were pretty good it was his suspect.

He rounded the corner to see a petite figure bent over, looking at their leg. Moving into position, he drew his weapon. "Put your hands where I can see them."

The suspect's head whipped around to stare at him for a split second before they took off. Even as tired as he was and after having been tased, he caught up to them easily. He closed in on them and pounced, tackling them to the ground.

"No."

He ignored the woman's muffled protest and swiftly got her cuffed. Rolling her over, he took his first good look at who he'd been chasing—who'd tried to kill him and Janey.

Nothing could have prepared him for who he saw staring back at him.

Hayden.

The young woman who'd smiled and flirted with him for the past year.

He wanted to tell himself that it was all Heather's fault. That she had to have put Hayden up to it, but it didn't matter. Even if it had been her sister's idea, Hayden had gone along with it. She'd willingly participated.

"Come on," he said, getting them both to their feet.

"Please. I didn't want to hurt you. Heather said we had to."

Knowing what he had to do, Kyle blocked out her pleas and read Hayden her rights as they made their way to the street.

Backup, including Breaker, one of the county's K-9's, arrived a few minutes later. Breaker's handler, Seth Russell, took possession of Hayden, patted her down, and placed her in the back of his vehicle until another unit showed up.

"You need a medic?" Seth asked. "You're looking a little pale."

Kyle shook his head. "Nothing a little sleep won't cure. It's been a long day."

"Missing patrol, are you?" Now that the danger was over, they could all relax a little.

"Something like that."

Two more patrol vehicles, Noah in his personal vehicle, and EMS pulled onto the street, their lights flashing. Lights had been turned on in some of the nearby houses, and a few people were gazing out their windows. With the additional vehicles, there was little doubt people would be venturing outside soon to get a closer look.

His boss and longtime friend marched toward him with a frown on his face. "You okay?"

"Yeah, I'm good." Kyle looked over Noah's shoulder. "Where's Janey?"

"She's at the crime scene with Ethan watching our other two suspects." The last word trailed off as he noticed who was sitting in the back of Seth's patrol vehicle.

Kyle knew what he was feeling. Or at least, he could relate to what he was feeling. "I'm guessing she knows why we couldn't find a phone record of the call she took." He paused. "If there ever was one."

"Nothing would surprise me at this point." Noah took in the entire scene. "Russell, you got this under control?"

"Yes, sir."

Noah nodded and turned his attention back to Kyle. "Let's get you back to your place. We need a statement from both you and Detective Davis."

Now that the surge of adrenaline was leaving him, all Kyle wanted to do was sleep. Correction: What he wanted to do was curl up in his bed with his arms wrapped around Janey.

He knew that wasn't going to happen, though, for at least another hour. Statements had to be taken while they were fresh, and the crime scene needed to be processed. They'd be lucky if they made it to sleep before sunrise.

CHAPTER 28

IT WAS WELL after sunrise before Janey and Kyle made it back home and into bed. After all the evidence was collected from the scene, they'd gone to the station, wanting to be there when Heather, Hayden, and the other suspect, who turned out to be a woman by the name of Christy Manning, were interrogated.

Heather had refused to answer any questions, demanding a lawyer almost immediately. Hayden, on the other hand, sang like a bird. She'd confirmed that there'd never been a call to dispatch the morning Kyle discovered the body along Butler Road. According to her, the whole thing had been orchestrated by Heather as a means of revenge. Hayden even showed Noah a text she'd received from her sister telling her where she'd dumped the body and to send a deputy out. Hayden swore, however, that tonight was the first time she'd helped her sister try to hurt anyone.

The woman neither of them had known before tonight, Christy Manning, spent most of the time crying. It had taken quite a while to get her to calm down enough to get anything out of her. When they did, though, the entire story unfolded.

She'd been Heather's roommate at college. They'd become best friends and did everything together. Everything except go to a party at the Delta Theta house the night Heather was gang raped by three guys.

Christy said she hadn't been feeling well that night, so she'd stayed in her dorm. She, or maybe it was Heather, convinced herself that if she had gone that night Heather wouldn't have been raped. The guilt was what had led her to participating in the murders of the three men Heather claimed had assaulted her.

Once all three women had been booked, Janey and Kyle had decided to tag along with Noah and Ethan as they went to arrest Keith. They wanted to be there early, hoping to catch him before he was fully awake and had come to the realization that Cindy and Sadie were gone.

By the time all that was finished and Janey had called both Paul and her captain to give them an update of the situation, Kyle had driven them back to his house and they'd crawled into bed utterly exhausted. Janey didn't even remember taking off her shoes, although when she woke up several hours later they weren't on her feet.

As she became aware of her surroundings, she heard movement in the hall and sat up. A second later, Kyle strolled into the bedroom wearing nothing but a pair of jeans slung low on his hips. Her sleep-addled brain warred with the ache in the pit of her stomach as she took in how sexy he was.

"I thought you might need some coffee." It was only then she noticed the two mugs in his hands and the tempting aroma coming out of them.

Janey hummed and reached for the steaming cup of liquid caffeine.

He took a seat next to her on the bed, the mattress dipping beneath his weight. "I called Noah. The judge denied bail."

Her brain was slowly waking up. "I'm not surprised given the seriousness of the crime and that they tried to murder two police officers."

They sat sipping their coffee for several minutes, letting the caffeine do its thing. She'd pulled a few all-nighters as a detective, but she'd never felt quite as drained as she did this morning. Or was it this afternoon?

Glancing at the clock beside his bed, the numbers read four twelve. Since the sun was still high in the sky, she had to assume that meant it was four o'clock in the afternoon. She'd slept longer than she'd thought.

"Paul called about an hour ago. I didn't want to wake you, so I answered it."

She was surprised to realize that his answering her phone didn't bother her. If any guy she'd dated in the past had done that, she wouldn't have been happy and would have made it clear that next time he should let it go to voice mail. "Did he need something?"

"Not really. He just wanted to let you know he, Megan, and Chloe were driving up tomorrow for the Labor Day festival."

Janey quirked an eyebrow at him. "They're coming up for the festival?"

He shrugged. "That, and I think he wants to get a look at Heather, Hayden, and Christy himself." Kyle took a slow sip of his coffee and met her gaze with a glint in his eye. "Is your partner a bit of a control freak?"

She nearly spat out her coffee. "Just a bit."

Kyle smiled. He took another drink of his coffee before focusing on some unknown object across the room. "I'd like for you to move in with me."

While she knew they'd visit this subject again, she'd hoped she'd have more time. She wasn't sure why. Maybe because it would be a huge change. But after what had happened last night, how she'd felt seeing him on the ground and knowing he was about to be hit over the head with a baseball bat, had made her realize how much she wanted him in her life. The question she really had to ask herself was if she was ready to leave her life, her job, in Indianapolis and move to Liberty.

She set her mug on the nightstand and placed a hand on his cheek.

He turned to face her. His eyes were guarded as if he was bracing himself for her rejection. Her heart squeezed in her chest as if there was a vise grip surrounding it. He was putting himself out there, leaving himself vulnerable. No man had ever done that for her. Not even close.

"I love you," she whispered.

He covered her hand with his, leaning into it. "But?"

Janey smiled and scooted closer. "No buts. You're right. If we want to try and make this relationship work, one of us has to move, and I doubt you'd be happy in a big city like Indianapolis."

Lowering their hands, he rested them on his leg, playing with her fingers. Little sparks of energy raced up her arm. She was awake now, which meant her libido was waking up as well. They'd been so busy the last couple of days that they hadn't been intimate. She missed that connection as they came together.

The direction of her thoughts almost made her miss what he said next. "I understand this would be a big step for you, and I don't want you to do it if you're not ready, but I didn't want there to be any misunderstanding. I want you with me. Whether that's here or in Indianapolis."

Closing the distance between them, Janey pressed her lips to his, giving him a soft kiss before meeting his gaze. "I'll talk to Sheriff Jenkins."

She didn't need to elaborate on what she meant. He knew.

A slow grin tugged at his lips until it was a full-blown smile. "He'll hire you in a heartbeat."

Although he was probably right, nothing was set in stone. She wasn't sure the fact she and Kyle had almost died the night before would be a glowing mark on her resume. "I'm sure my captain won't be happy. And even if I do get hired, I'll have to give notice, so it won't be right away."

He threaded his fingers in her hair. "I'll try to be patient."

Her chuckle was cut off by his kiss. She melted into it. Kyle dipped his tongue between her lips and tangled it with her own, tasting and teasing. She gripped his shoulders, pulling him closer, needing to feel more of him.

As their kiss grew more intense, he shifted, and she realized he was putting his coffee on the nightstand next to hers. A second later, his other hand was on her hip, lifting her higher on the bed.

He followed, his body covering hers as they continued to kiss. She ran her hands over the muscles in his back and shoulders, feeling them flex has he hovered over her.

Suddenly he stopped and held himself above her.

She blinked. "What is it?"

"Maybe you should call him now. Why wait?"

It took her lust-filled mind a moment to realize what he was talking about. "Because," she said as she pulled his mouth back down to hers, "I'm a little busy at the moment and I don't plan on us leaving this bed anytime soon."

As if to drive home her point, she slid her hand down to cup his erection. A low moan rumbled from deep in his chest. "You're right. It can wait."

* * *

They did make it out of bed later that evening. Noah stopped by to check on them and to give them an update. Heather and Hayden's father had almost gotten himself arrested when he'd stormed into the station earlier, demanding his daughters be released.

Now that they knew who had committed the murders, it was just a matter of filling in all the pieces of the puzzle. The judge had issued a search warrant for the Sanderses' home, barn, and the horse trailers, considering both Heather and Hayden's love of horses and the hours they spent around them. They'd also gotten a search warrant for Christy's residence in Indianapolis, even though they didn't really expect to find anything.

All the evidence pointed to Heather and it was only confirmed by what they'd found on her computer. From the looks of it, she'd stalked the three men for at least six months, tracking their movements, finding out the places they frequented. They were pulling her bank records to see if they could place her in proximity of the crimes on the dates in question, but Kyle had little doubt they'd find the evidence they needed. It was only a matter of time.

Janey sauntered into the living room and plopped herself onto the couch beside him. Kyle raised his arm and tucked her into his side. They'd taken a shower not long before Noah had shown up. Luckily, he'd called to give them a heads-up he was coming. Otherwise, Kyle wasn't sure what his friend would have interrupted.

It was a nice shower, too. For once, neither of them had anywhere they needed to be, and they took advantage of it. He still had the image fresh in his mind of the water sliding down her breasts and belly before it disappeared between her legs. Just thinking about it had him needing to adjust himself.

"You comfortable?"

He kissed the top of her head. "Nowhere else I'd rather be."

Janey laughed. "You're so cheesy sometimes."

"You like cheese," he said as he brushed his lips along her ear.

He heard her suck in a breath a moment before she turned her head and met his gaze. "Yeah, I do."

Accepting the invitation. Kyle pulled her lips to his, cradling the back of her head.

She wasted no time climbing onto his lap, straddling him. "I asked Noah about the job while he was here."

Kyle's heart rate increased as he waited to hear more. It almost felt as if his entire future hung in the balance. "And?"

Janey threaded her fingers through his hair, sending tingles down his spine and straight to his groin. They'd already made love twice since waking up, but that didn't matter. He wanted her again. He would always want her.

The look on her face was somber and serious. Had Noah told her he didn't think she'd be a good fit for the position?

He was already running through all the arguments in his head to try and convince his friend that hiring Janey to be their detective was a good idea. Great, even.

"Well . . ."

The suspense was killing him.

"He said he'd need to talk to my captain, but the job is mine if I want it."

"You little minx." Kyle reached for her sides and started tickling her.

She cracked up laughing, trying to get away from him.

"You enjoyed torturing me, didn't you?"

"Yes," she choked out between bouts of laughter. "You should . . . have seen . . . your face."

Flipping her over, he pinned her beneath him, her arms stretched overhead. The position lifted her breasts higher, drawing his attention.

Janey felt the shift in his mood and arched her back, tempting him more. He adjusted his grip so he could hold both her wrists in one of his hands. The sweetest sound left her lips as he rubbed his thumb over her nipple. His cock jumped in response.

"I'm going to make love to you now." He continued to run teasing circles over her nipple but made no move to take things further.

"Touch me."

A wicked grin crossed Kyle's face. "I am touching you."

She made a frustrated sound. "I need more. Touch me more."

"Like this?" He trailed his hand down her torso to her hip, and then ground his pelvis against her.

"Yes. More."

Kyle chuckled as he pushed her shirt up, exposing her stomach, and lowered his mouth to the skin right above her waistband. "You're so sexy."

She twisted in his hold, but he held firm. "I want to touch you."

He shook his head, letting the tips of his hair tickle and tease her belly. "Not yet."

Her frustrated sigh changed to one of longing when he popped the button on her shorts and slipped his hand inside. It was a sound he'd never get tired of hearing from her. He couldn't wait to have her here with him every day.

The way her breath hitched as she climbed higher toward her

climax had his cock straining for release. He ignored it, though, and concentrated on getting her there.

It didn't take long before Janey's eyes rolled back in her head a moment before she fell over the edge. Her face and neck were flushed and her chest was heaving as she tried to catch her breath. It was a beautiful sight to see.

She met his gaze and he couldn't keep the smug look off his face. "Is it your turn now?"

He released her hands and brought his face down to an inch above hers. She combed her fingers through his hair, holding him to her.

Kyle shook his head and brushed his lips against her mouth. "Tonight's about you, baby. I know moving here is going to be a big step for you, so I want you to have plenty of"—he dug his fingers into her ass and ground her against his erection—"*incentives* to remember when you go back to Indy."

She snaked an arm around his waist and lowered her hand to his backside. Without any pretense, Janey sunk her nails into his ass and pulled his lips down to hers. The mix of pain and pleasure went right to his cock. Then again, just about anything she did had that effect on him.

Her breath ghosted against his lips as she pressed her mouth to his in the barest of touches. A complete contrast to her nails digging into his flesh.

Janey held his gaze, a look of wicked promise in her eyes. "Something tells me I'm going to like Liberty just fine."

Kyle knew she would love Liberty. He'd make sure of it.

EPILOGUE

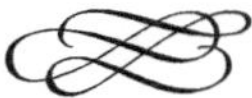

THREE MONTHS later

"That's the last one," Kyle said, walking into the house, carrying another box.

"I can't believe this is all mine." Janey had lived in her condo for a little over five years. She didn't think she'd accumulated a lot of stuff, but the stacks of boxes sitting in Kyle's living room said different. "It's gonna take me weeks to go through all this."

He came up behind her and wrapped his arms around her waist, pulling her flush against him. "It's a big house and we have plenty of time."

"True." She twisted in his embrace and circled her arms around his neck. The feel of his mouth against hers as their lips met in a slow kiss still sent tingles all the way down to her toes.

"Knock, knock." Ava's voice rang out, announcing her arrival. "Are you both decent?"

Kyle rolled his eyes at his sister.

Janey chuckled, gave him another peck on the lips, and dropped her arms. "We're in here."

Ava entered the room a moment later carrying a plate piled high with goodies. Cole trailed behind her with a toy truck in his hand. "I brought you some cookies. I figured you might like a little treat for when you're unpacking boxes. I remember how tedious that can be."

"Thanks, Ava." Janey took the offering and placed the plate of cookies on the coffee table next to a bowl she'd unpacked earlier.

"I wanted to make sure you were still coming to dinner tomorrow."

"Of course," Kyle said, lifting Cole into his arms. "There's no way I'd turn down one of your Thanksgiving dinners."

Janey's heart did a little flip every time she saw Kyle with his nephew. The longer they were together, the more she'd been thinking about them having a family one day. She knew it wouldn't be easy, not with both of them being law enforcement.

"I'm gonna see if we have some milk to go with those cookies," Kyle said before disappearing into the kitchen with Cole on his hip.

"You two thinking about having one of your own?" Ava asked once she and Janey were alone.

"Not really." Janey shot Ava a nervous grin. "I mean, maybe. Eventually."

Ava nodded. "He'll make a wonderful father."

Of that Janey had no doubt. "I know."

She cleared some space for her and Ava on the couch, and they sat and talked while Kyle and Cole were in the kitchen.

"Did you get everything finalized with your condo?"

Janey had spent almost every waking hour she wasn't working for the last month showing her condo to potential buyers. It was exhausting, but eventually the hard work had paid off. "Yep. All the paperwork's signed. Paul is going to meet them later today to hand over the keys."

"I'm glad it all worked out. I know you were worried you'd have trouble selling it."

It had caused her a few sleepless nights. "Everything worked out the way it was supposed to."

"Yes, it did." Ava smiled. "Oh, I ran into Cindy Fisher at the store the other day. She said she and her daughter are settling into their new apartment."

"Yeah, Kyle stopped by to check on her the other day. He said she seemed to be doing well."

Ava nodded. "I'm just glad the trial's over and her boyfriend's going to be spending some time behind bars."

Not enough, in Janey's opinion. He got three years—less with good behavior.

"She mentioned her mom was out of town visiting her sister, so I invited her and Sadie to join us for Thanksgiving dinner tomorrow."

"That was really nice of you." Janey wasn't surprised Ava had extended an invitation to Cindy. That was the type of person Ava was.

From there the conversation turned to Christmas. They were making plans to go shopping together when Kyle and Cole returned to the living room.

"Everything all right?" Ava asked when both of them remained unusually quiet.

"Yep." Kyle had a shit-eating grin on his face that told her he was up to something.

Cole giggled and climbed on his mom's lap.

"What are you two up to?" Ava asked.

"Remember what we talked about," Kyle said to Cole.

His nephew pressed his lips together and nodded.

Janey raised her eyebrows, but Kyle either didn't see or he ignored her silent question.

"You need us to bring anything for tomorrow, sis? I can swing by the store and pick up some pop or wine."

"Just yourselves. I've got everything prepped. The turkey will go into the oven tonight and I'll finish everything else off tomorrow."

Janey felt as if she should be doing more to help. Ava had done so much to help with her transition to Liberty, including driving down to Indianapolis with Kyle to help them clean her condo from top to bottom before she put it up for sale. "Did you need us to come early to help with anything? I may not be a great cook, but I can chop and mix with the best of 'em."

Ava chuckled. "It's fine. Really. I made all the casseroles and pies this morning. All that's left to do is pop the casseroles in the oven to bake and add the dressing to the salads."

"You're so organized. I don't know how you do it," Janey said.

"Baking's easy." Ava shifted Cole so he was standing on her legs in front of her. He was getting restless. "I don't know how you two do what you do."

They sat and talked for several more minutes until Ava decided she'd better go before Cole had a meltdown.

Ava hugged her brother goodbye before turning to Janey. "I'm so glad you're finally here. Officially." Then she pulled Janey in as well. Kyle's sister was a hugger and it was taking Janey some time to get used to it.

Alone once more, Kyle and Janey began working through the mountain of boxes she'd brought with her. The sad part was she'd slowly been bringing items to his house over the last few months and she still had at least thirty boxes worth of stuff to find homes for. It was going to take a while.

* * *

The next morning, Janey woke up to Kyle kissing his way up her spine. It tickled a little, but more than that, it had all her female parts sitting up and taking notice.

"Good morning," he mumbled against her skin.

"Hmm. Morning." She stretched her arms out in front of her, not wanting to do anything to divert his current trajectory. "What time do we have to be at your sister's?"

"Not for a few hours yet."

Janey yawned, making sure to exaggerate it for effect. "Good. That means I can catch up on my beauty sleep."

He slid his arm around her waist and inched his hand up her torso until he zeroed in on her breast. "I had something else besides sleep in mind."

She couldn't stop the moan that escaped her throat when his fingers began massaging her flesh in the most delicious way. He'd gotten to know her body well and knew what she liked. It didn't help, of course, that neither one of them was wearing a stitch of clothing.

Still, she wasn't going to make this easy on him. "I suppose we could cuddle."

Kyle responded by pinching her nipple at the same time as he grazed his teeth along the sensitive skin of her neck.

Her eyes rolled back in her head and she felt the space between her legs warm.

"This is our last day off before we both head back to work. I plan on making the most of it." Kyle rolled her onto her back and hovered over her. "Any objections, Detective?"

Without any conscious thought on her part, Janey's legs parted, making room for him between them. She pulled his face down to hers. "Not a single one."

* * *

Somehow, they managed to make it to his sister's on time. Kyle was ridiculously happy. He was sporting a goofy grin and he didn't even care.

That smile slipped a little when they walked into Ava's kitchen to find Noah seated at the table, playing with Cole. He hadn't noticed his friend's vehicle out front.

"Hey," Noah said when he noticed them. "I came over to see if your sister needed any help with dinner, but she insists she's got it taken care of, so I offered to keep Cole out of her hair."

Kyle glanced over at his sister but didn't say anything.

Janey must have picked up on his discomfort. She gave his hand a squeeze before going to take a seat across from Noah and Cole. "We offered to help, too, but she insisted she had it all under control."

"*She's* right here," Ava said, sending a glare in their direction over her shoulder as she continued chopping carrots.

In an effort to change the subject and to get his mind off the reasons why Noah was there more than an hour before dinner was supposed to be on the table, he ambled over to stand next to his sister and plucked a carrot from her pile.

She batted his hand away.

He popped the carrot in his mouth and gave her a kiss on the cheek. "Are you sure we can't do anything to help?"

"I'm sure." She glanced over again at her son. "Cole wanted to go out and see the chickens earlier, but I haven't had time."

"Say no more." Kyle pushed himself away from the counter. "Want to go check on the chickens?"

Cole practically jumped off Noah's lap. "Chickens!"

They call chuckled.

Janey joined Kyle and Cole as they headed out to the chicken coop. The basic structure was there when his sister had bought the place, but she'd made quite a few improvements. While Janey and Cole watched the chickens, Kyle did a quick inspection of the rainwater collection system his sister had designed. It was quite impressive and seemed to be working well.

They hung out at the chicken coop for a while, and then walked over to the barn where Ava kept all her gardening supplies. Janey had never been out there, and she was fascinated by his sister's extensive collection of all things gardening related. He honestly wasn't sure there was a tool she didn't own.

Eventually, though, it was time to go back inside. "You ready to go in?" he asked Cole. "Your mom will have dinner on the table soon. Are you ready to eat some turkey?"

After getting detoured by a wildflower that caught his nephew's attention halfway to the house, they made their way inside. The smells that greeted them had his mouth watering. His mom had been a good cook, but he was pretty sure his sister was better.

"Oh, good. You guys are back," she said upon their arrival. "Could you help bring everything to the table?"

They were setting the last of the food out when there was a knock on the door. "I'll get it."

Kyle jogged to open it.

On the other side stood Cindy and Sadie.

He smiled. "You're right on time."

Dinner went off without a hitch. It took a while for Cindy to relax, but eventually she joined in on the conversation.

Throughout the meal, Janey kept putting a hand on his thigh. It was distracting, but then he realized why she was doing it and it wasn't to get his libido going. Noah was sitting next to Ava, and every now and then his friend and his sister would share a look that made Kyle distinctly uncomfortable. He kept trying to tell himself there wasn't anything beyond friendship between Noah and Ava, but if he was honest with himself, he wasn't so sure of that. Still, he wasn't ready to think about it.

Apparently, he wasn't as good at keeping his feelings to himself as he thought because Janey leaned over and whispered in his ear. "Your sister could do worse."

She was right. Ava could do worse. A lot worse.

Kyle took her hand under the table and laced their fingers together. He brought her hand up to his mouth and placed a kiss along her knuckles. She really was the best thing that had ever happened to him.

They finished eating and Ava brought out the pies. Even though he was stuffed, there was no way he was passing up some of his sister's pie.

"You ready to get back to work tomorrow?" Noah asked Janey as he tucked into a slice of pumpkin pie piled high with whipped cream.

"More than ready."

Noah grinned around his mouthful of pie.

As they were finishing up, Kyle got his nephew's attention. He whispered a reminder to Cole, and then sat back and waited.

The little boy ran out of the room. Less than a minute later, he returned carrying Janey's purse.

He took it to Janey, handing it to her.

"Thank you," she said, confused as to why Cole brought her purse to her.

"Look. Inside." His little voice was confident.

Janey glanced around the table at all the adults. Kyle was doing his best to keep a straight face. Ava shrugged.

Cole stood there waiting while she opened her purse, and then took off to go play again as if nothing had happened.

As soon as she slid the zipper open, he heard her suck in a breath. "What's this?"

Inside her purse was a note and a small box. She removed the note first.

"What is it?" his sister asked.

"A note."

Everyone was paying attention. Even Cindy. "What's it say?"

Janey cleared her throat and began reading the note.

Janey,

The first time I saw you, I knew you were someone special, but even I didn't know how special. You've changed my life for the better and now I can't imagine it without you.

You moved your entire life here to be with me and I want you to know how much that means to me. I want to share everything with you. My life. My love. My future.

Kyle

She met his gaze, moisture glistening in her eyes.

"Open the box," he whispered.

Janey removed the small box from her purse and flipped the lid open. She sucked in a breath as she stared at the ring.

His chair scraped against the floor as he got down on one knee and took her hand. "Janey Davis, will you marry me?"

She blinked several times before her lips pulled up into a smile and she nodded.

Kyle released a shaky breath. "You had me worried for a minute there."

Janey chuckled. "Had to make you work for it."

He snorted and then crushed his mouth to hers for a hard kiss. "I love you."

"I love you, too."

Removing the ring from the box, he slipped it onto her finger.

Janey looked at it for a moment, and then back to him. "This is what you and Cole were conspiring about yesterday?"

He just smiled.

"Sneaky."

Ava rushed over to hug Janey and get a closer look the ring. He'd kept it simple, wanting her to be able to wear it when she was working.

It didn't matter, though. His sister oohed and aahed over it while Noah came over to pat him on the back. "I was wondering how long it would be until you popped the question."

Cindy joined Ava and Janey, commenting on how lovely the ring was. Every now and then Janey would glance his way, a huge smile on her face. His chest felt as if it might explode with the joy he felt seeing her so happy. They had forever in front of them and he couldn't wait to see what came next.

***

Haven't read Paul and Megan's story yet? **Get Crossing the Line and start reading today!** Turn the page to read Chapter 1 of *Crossing the Line.*

Sign up HERE or at www.sherrihayesauthor.com to make sure you don't miss any of Sherri Hayes' new releases.

CAN'T WAIT FOR SHERRI'S NEXT BOOK?

☆☆☆☆☆

Let her know by leaving a review and telling her what you
SEDUCING JANEY (LIBERTY CROSSROADS #1)

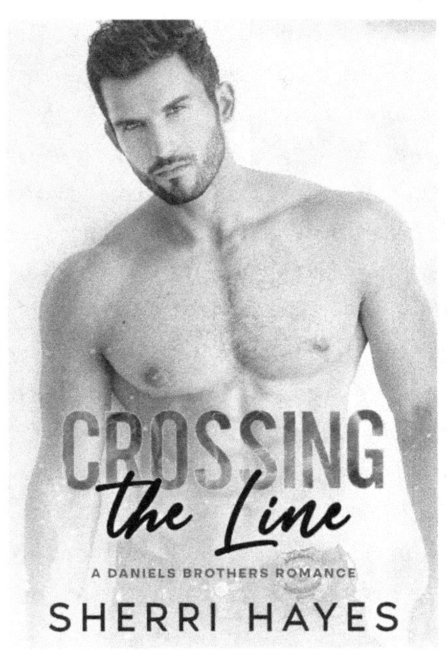

Crossing the Line (Daniels Brothers #3)

Chapter 1

"Did you see me, Daddy? Did you see me?"

Paul Daniels bent down and lifted his five-year-old daughter, Chloe, into his arms. "I did."

He gave her his best smile, not that she noticed. Chloe was too excited to pay much attention to anything for long. Paul thought nothing could top the excess of energy his little girl displayed the day Chris and Elizabeth called to ask her if she'd be their flower girl. He'd been wrong. Three months ago, Chloe had been full of questions about the unknown—she'd never been to a wedding before. Today, she was bouncing off the walls, and her smile matched his new sister-in-law's in pure joy.

It was as if he hadn't commented at all.

"And Eliz'beth's dress is sooo pretty. Isn't it pretty, Daddy?" Chloe didn't wait for his response this time either, before she continued. "Now she's my aunt." She concentrated to make sure she got it right. Megan had been working diligently to help Chloe improve her speech before she started school in the fall.

Paul searched the crowd of people bustling into the reception hall for the woman in question, as Chloe squirmed wordlessly making her desire to be put down known. He lowered her feet to the floor, and watched as she slipped in between two wedding guests while he continued to scan for Megan.

Megan was the younger sister of his baby brother Gage's wife. Paul had met her when she'd come to Thanksgiving with her sister. Little had he known what a savior she'd turn out to be. She'd brought life back into his house. Life that he hadn't realized was missing.

She'd rescued him when he'd been in desperate need of someone to watch Chloe. Hours before he'd loaded Chloe into the car to set off for the holiday with his parents, his in-laws had announced they were moving almost two hours away. For four years, they'd lived nearby and were able to take Chloe whenever he was called in to work. His job as a homicide detective meant that he could be called out at all hours, and he couldn't leave his young daughter alone. Megan had fit the bill by offering to move to Indianapolis and into his house as a live-in nanny. She'd saved Paul from having to spend countless hours searching for an alternative.

As if knowing the direction of his thoughts, Chloe weaved through the people in her path until she was beside her nanny. Megan smiled when she caught sight of the little girl, and she circled her arms around Chloe's shoulders, lifting her off the ground, and twirling. They were both laughing—happy. The two of them had clicked from the beginning, and his chest clenched almost painfully watching the two of them together. It should have been Melissa standing there twirling Chloe, but he couldn't be upset that it was Megan. She'd put her life on hold for them—helped them out when they'd needed it most. Paul wished he could be as carefree.

His brother, Chris, wanted to give his fiancée, Elizabeth, the wedding of her dreams, right down to the ceremony being held in a quaint little church not far from where they lived in Springfield, Ohio —and it was. Elizabeth had walked down the aisle in a long white gown, his brother in a tux. Everyone who meant something in either of their lives was present. It was . . . perfect.

Unfortunately, it brought back too many memories for Paul. Memories that were raw and painful. Almost fifteen years ago, he'd been where his brother was—marrying the love of his life. He didn't begrudge Chris and Elizabeth their happiness. No, he was grateful. His brother had had a rough time of it after his first marriage fell apart. For Paul, it was a sharp reminder that he no longer had his wife at his side. She'd been taken from him by a drunk driver.

Starting to get choked up, Paul cleared his throat, and made a beeline for the bar. He didn't drink often, and never when he had to drive afterward, but tonight he didn't have to go anywhere but upstairs to his hotel room. Chloe was here, of course, so he couldn't go overboard. He just wanted to numb some of the pain.

Paul leaned his elbows on the bar as he waited for the petite blond bartender to finish with the drink she was making for another guest. He thought the guy standing patiently waiting for his drink was one of Chris' employees. Paul was also fairly certain that the guy was single by the way he was openly eyeing the young woman from head to toe. She was pretty—Paul wasn't blind, after all. Unfortunately, there was no spark. There never was. Not since his wife, Melissa.

Six months after Melissa's accident, he'd tried. He'd left Chloe with Melissa's parents and gone out to a club. It had been loud and he'd felt out of place, but he'd met a woman he found attractive and went for it. They'd ended up at her place an hour later, clothes on the floor, with him hovering over her.

He hadn't been able to go through with it, though. As he reached for a condom, he'd seen Melissa smiling up at him, her chest vibrating as she attempted to suppress her mirth while he fumbled trying to roll the rubber down his erection. It was an old memory, from when they were teenagers, but it had stung all the same. He'd gathered his clothes, dressed, and apologized, leaving the woman, whom he only knew as Karen, lying naked on her bed staring after him.

The bartender handed over the drink she'd made, and then turned to Paul without giving the other man a second glance. Looked like he wouldn't be getting that after-closing booty call.

She turned to Paul and smiled. "What can I get ya?"

"Scotch. Neat."

Her smile got wider. "Coming right up, handsome."

Paul glanced over his shoulder, and caught sight of his mom and dad. They appeared to be engrossed in a conversation with two people he didn't know. His dad looked in Paul's direction, and Paul quickly turned back around. The last thing he needed was his dad zeroing in on his less-than-festive attitude.

The bartender placed the half-full glass of scotch down in front of him. She made sure to lean in a little closer than normal. "Here you go."

"Thanks." Paul picked up the glass and took a drink. It burned as it went down his throat, which was good. Anything was better than the knife twisting in his gut.

"So how do you know the bride and groom?"

Not wanting to be rude, Paul answered her. "I'm the groom's brother."

"Older or younger?"

Paul laughed, before backing away. "Thanks again for the drink."

He made it halfway to the corner he'd scoped out as a decent hiding place, before he was waylaid by his brother, Trent. "Hey, man." Trent looked down at the drink Paul had in his hand, and raised his eyebrow.

"Something wrong?"

"I was going to ask you the same question. Since when do you drink anything but beer?"

"I like to mix it up sometimes." Paul didn't add that those "sometimes" usually involved his wedding anniversary and the anniversary of his wife's death. Chris' wedding didn't fall on either of those occasions, but Paul was making an exception.

"Since when?"

After taking another sip of his scotch, Paul narrowed his eyes at his younger brother. "Did you have a reason for coming over here other than to give me a hard time?"

Trent frowned, but let it go. For now, at least. "Megan and Chloe were looking for you. Chloe wants some pictures of you, Megan, and her together. Chris and Elizabeth don't have a problem with it, but they wanted to make sure it was okay with you before they agreed to anything."

The last thing Paul wanted to do was pose for more pictures, but there were very few things he'd deny his daughter. Pictures of the woman she'd grown extremely close to over the last four months weren't one of them. "It's fine."

Again, he saw that look of doubt cross his brother's face. "Okay…"

Paul ignored Trent's curiosity. "Where?"

"Out in the lobby. The photographer has been taking some pictures in front of the fountain."

Not waiting to see if Trent would come up with more questions regarding his odd behavior, Paul took off toward the fountain.

Before entering the lobby, he took one last gulp of his scotch, feeling the heat. He could do this. For his daughter, he could do this.

Setting his now empty glass down on a nearby table, he plastered a smile on his face, and went to find Megan and Chloe.

***

Megan Carson held tight to Chloe's hand as she continued to flutter about without a care in the world. They were in the lobby waiting on Paul. At least, Megan hoped they were waiting on Paul. It hadn't escaped her notice that he'd been tense all throughout Chris and Elizabeth's vows. And a couple of times she noticed him getting a look on his face. She couldn't help but wonder if he was thinking about his wife.

He'd smiled and laughed along with everyone else, but she could tell his heart wasn't in it. She now knew him well enough to know the difference. And she'd guess his family did, too. Although, technically, Megan was his family now as well—ever since her sister married his brother.

Chloe squealed, and pulled harder on Megan's arm. "Daddy!"

Releasing the little girl's hand, Megan stood back and watched Paul scoop up his daughter. Seeing them like this gave her a warm feeling. He smiled at Chloe, and this time it didn't look fake or forced. Then again, whenever it came to Chloe, Megan didn't question Paul's love or willingness to do anything for her. Chloe was the apple of his eye—a tangible reminder of his dead wife.

"I was told there's a picture that needs to be taken out here." Paul tickled his daughter's sides.

She giggled. "Yes, Daddy. I want a picture with yous, and mes, and Megan."

Paul glanced down at Megan, and she took in his warm brown eyes. She loved when they sparkled with joy, as they did in that moment. No one could do that to him but Chloe. Not his mom or his brothers. Not even her. No matter how much she wished otherwise.

The photographer approached them with his camera hanging from a strap around his neck. "Ah, good. Everyone's here, yes?"

He quickly corralled them into the correct position, with Megan and Paul flanking Chloe as the three of them sat on the edge of the fountain. To an outside observer, they'd look like a normal family. Appearances could be deceiving, though, and in this case they were way off. Megan was Chloe's nanny, nothing more. She took care of Chloe when Paul was working, making sure she had everything she needed, and that the house wasn't a disaster when he came home.

That was where it ended. Occasionally, Paul would allow Megan to cook dinner for them, but it was rare, and usually only on days when he knew he wouldn't be home until after six. Paul took taking care of his one and only child seriously. She was his responsibility, and while he allowed Megan to take over when he had to leave, he didn't take advantage of her presence in their life—although sometimes she wished that he would.

With the pictures over, Chloe ran back into the reception with an announcement that she was going to find her grandmother—Paul's mom—leaving Paul and Megan behind.

"Thank you."

She looked up at Paul. He towered over her, at just over six feet to her much shorter five foot five. "You know I'd do anything for Chloe."

He was ultra-serious again. "I know, but you don't have to. You're not working tonight."

Megan frowned. He had that melancholy look she noticed crossed his features all too frequently. "Are you all right?"

It was Paul's turn to frown. "Of course. Why wouldn't I be? It's my brother's wedding."

His answer didn't ease her concern. Paul was a good guy—the best guy she'd ever met in her twenty-three years. He put every other man who'd crossed her path to shame, with the exception of Gage and the rest of his brothers and father. The Daniels men had certainly upped her standards in the opposite sex.

"I don't know. You just don't seem like yourself tonight."

Paul waved off her observation. "It's been a long day, that's all."

Yes, it had been a long day. Megan and all the other Daniels women, including Chloe, had met at the spa a little after eight that morning. They'd all gotten their hair and nails done while the guys did whatever guys did to get ready for a wedding. Since then, they'd all been going strong. Megan didn't think that was the problem, but she let it go. For now. "It *has* been a long day."

In what seemed like an effort to steer her away from any further questioning, Paul held out his arm, and motioned toward the reception. She took a deep breath, and smiled, allowing him to deflect. Whatever was going on with him today, she figured it had to do with his wife. One thing she'd learned about Paul in the four months she'd known him was that he was still very much in love with Melissa. It didn't matter that she'd been dead for over four years. She was still alive in his heart.

Once back inside, Megan was hijacked by her brother-in-law, Gage. "Would you please talk to your sister?"

Megan laughed. "What's up, Becca?"

Her sister, Rebecca, gave her husband a disapproving headshake. "Nothing, except Mr. Overprotective here doesn't think I can do anything on my own."

"I'm trying to be a gentleman." Gage huffed his response, but at the same time, he wrapped his arms around Rebecca's middle, pulling her up against him. It still amused Megan to see how Gage had changed since falling in love with her sister. He'd gone from the cocky playboy to the overprotective husband and daddy-to-be.

Rebecca leaned in to him. "I do *not* need for you to walk me to the bathroom. I'm not a child." She paused. "And before you say it, I'm not going to get sick. I haven't had a bout of morning sickness in over a week."

Gage kissed her temple and inhaled. "I'm sorry, beautiful, but you know how much I worry about you."

Megan watched her sister—her sister who could take down a man three times her size with her bare hands—melt in her husband's arms. "I guess you two don't need me anymore, then?"

They both chuckled, and Rebecca stood to her full height. "Of course I do. You, I don't mind accompanying me to the ladies' room."

Before she knew it, Rebecca was pushing her toward the bathroom. "Hey, slow down."

Rebecca stopped and released Megan's arm. "Sorry. It's just . . ."

"He's driving you nuts?" Megan laughed.

"It's not funny. You'd think I was terminally ill or something, instead of pregnant."

Although she knew Gage's attentiveness was probably getting to her overly independent sister, she also knew that Rebecca loved the attention. It was something Megan and Rebecca had lacked growing up—Rebecca especially. "You know you love it." Megan paused. "And him."

It took a few seconds, but then a soft smile brightened Rebecca's features. "It's sad, but I do. I know I shouldn't, but to know that he'd drop everything for me and the baby, no matter what, is a pretty amazing feeling."

"Yeah, I bet. I mean, we didn't have that growing up. He's going to be a great dad."

Rebecca glanced back to where Gage was now talking to his father and Trent. "He really is."

The talk of dads sent Megan's mind drifting back to Paul, and she immediately began searching the crowd for him.

"Looking for someone?"

Megan turned back to face her sister. "Huh? What?"

"I asked if you were looking for someone." Rebecca had a strange look on her face, and Megan knew Rebecca was going into big sister mode. It was the last thing she wanted.

"Not really."

Her sister frowned. "Is something going on I should know about?"

Now Megan was confused. "Like?"

"I don't know. I mean you've gone four months without chasing after a guy. That's a record for you."

Megan rolled her eyes. "Thanks."

"I didn't . . . I didn't mean it like that. I worry about you. I want you to find a nice guy—someone who will treat you well. I don't want to see you hurt again."

"I know. And when I find him, you'll be the first to know."

Rebecca reached up to brush a strand of hair away from Megan's face. It was something she'd done since Megan was little—a motherly gesture from the only real female authority figure Megan had ever known. "Come on. Let's get to the bathroom before I burst. I think I drank way too much water earlier."

Following her sister, Megan took one last look around trying to spot Paul, but she didn't see him anywhere.

GRAB YOUR COPY OF CROSSING THE LINE

ALSO BY SHERRI HAYES

Finding Anna

Slave (Finding Anna, Book 1)

Need (Finding Anna, Book 2)

Truth (Finding Anna, Book 3)

Trust (Finding Anna, Book 4)

Finding Anna Boxed Set (Books 1-4)

Indulge: A Finding Anna Novelette

Change (Finding Anna, Book 5)

The Daniels Brothers

Behind Closed Doors

Red Zone

Crossing the Line

What Might Have Been

Daniels Brothers Box Set (Books 1-4)

Serpent's Kiss

Welcome to Serpent's Kiss

Burning for Her Kiss

One Forbidden Night

Longing for His Kiss

Claiming His Kiss

Tangled In His Embrace

Liberty Crossroads

Seducing Janey

Strictly Professional

Strictly Professional

A Christmas Proposal

ABOUT THE AUTHOR

Sherri picked up her first romance novel when she was twelve and immediately she was hooked. She would stay up reading long after everyone else in her house had gone to bed, needing to see the hero and heroine get their happily ever after. But Sherri never imagined becoming an author.

At the age of thirty, all that changed. After getting frustrated with the direction a television show was taking two of its characters, Sherri decided to try her hand at writing an alternative ending to give the characters the happy ending they deserved.

Since then, writing has become a creative outlet that allows her to explore a wide range of emotions, while having fun taking her characters through all the twists and turns she can create.

patreon.com/SherriHayes
facebook.com/SherriHayesAuthor
bookbub.com/authors/sherri-hayes